SERMON
OF THE
DIVERS

Joel T. Schmidt

ISBN 979-8-89309-205-9 (Paperback)
ISBN 979-8-89309-206-6 (Digital)

Copyright © 2024 Joel T. Schmidt
All rights reserved
First Edition

Cover Artist: Maria Koallas

All rights reserved. No part of this publication may be reproduced, distributed, or transmitted in any form or by any means, including photocopying, recording, or other electronic or mechanical methods without the prior written permission of the publisher. For permission requests, solicit the publisher via the address below.

Covenant Books
11661 Hwy 707
Murrells Inlet, SC 29576
www.covenantbooks.com

For Thomas, and for the others.

IN THE GLOOM
OF A DREAM

In the beginning, Kris's experience was parallel to what it's like in one of those sensory deprivation chambers. Imagine a *large* tank of water. A tank that's big enough to comfortably float in without touching the edges of the tank. The water and the air in the room are the exact temperature of the body; they're so exact that the water can't be felt from within it. The tank is in a pitch-black room. No light enters the room, and everything within it is utterly black. The dark walls are thick and soundproof; no noise enters from outside of the room. He could not hear or see or feel anything at all. He lived in that dark as long as he could remember. It was in some other place. He was in some other form, a state of being separate from a body. Around him was the infinite black, lineless and eternal. He was sure there were other times before his existence in the plane, void of color and life. Sometimes, he felt that they were within his grasp.

Out of the darkness came a hellish rut. The black made devil lines and horror silhouettes leap in the dark like dancing ghosts. Then the lines moved to a unified form. They took *its* shape. It was a man in a hood with no face, a tentacled monster with husks in a carnivorous mouth, and an innocent-looking old man on a park bench. The mass of chaos roared at Kris, and though he could not hear it, all of nothingness shook.

Kris ran. The Other pursued. There in the nothingness, they ran. Kris moved his form with a bottomless well of will. Not muscle. Not tendons. Not ligaments. Not bones and joints. The Other was there behind him, though. Its clawed hands so close to him that Kris felt the cutting of the air just behind him. He marveled at all the new sensations. He wondered what would happen if he died there, in the jaws of the Other.

Kris and the Other were as infinite as the plane around them. They were the growing expanse of the universe with its abundance of possibility; they were the galaxy producing an experience. Eventually, Kris would look back and know that he ran for thousands of years—thousands upon thousands of years. Days were inconsequential in that constant pursuit.

Actions that define engulfed him beyond the resonance of time. And when he looked back, the Other was closer.

Luckily for Kris, all at once, something changed. It isn't as uncommon as you'd think.

Suddenly, nothing was anything.

Kris was on a couch. He was in a house, and a woman he knew to be Mom was in the kitchen. He could see her; her frizzy hair bobbing back and forth as she made coffee. He also knew what the things around him were, though he knew not how. He just *knew*.

"Mom." He could speak! The woman in the red robe with the coffeepot in her hand turned and looked at him. Her long curly auburn hair reflected the light in the kitchen. Kris was amazed by her eyes and hair and how they held the light. Yet he couldn't help but look to the window behind her, a dark blue that was very near black.

"Yeah, sweetie?"

She spoke to him. This couldn't be real. It's not real. Can it be? For so long, all he'd ever known was the infinite and the Other, and he thought that maybe he'd created all of this in his own imagination.

"Where am I?" he asked.

His mom looked at him with a cocked head and drawn brows.

"You're home, baby. We got back from our trip yesterday. You remember?" she spoke softly and slowly. Kris suddenly felt like he was in that other place again, running and scared. He wanted to be close to her. Kris moved his head and discovered he had a body. He had a head and arms, and he had legs too! He could! He could go to her. When Kris shifted his body and rolled to his feet, he was astonished at how easy it was. Not as easy as moving in that other place, but still. And then he was disappointed to see how small he was. He thought his mom must've been a giant! She was maybe three of him.

Soft carpet surprised the sensitive soles of his feet as he walked toward her. Then the cold shock of the linoleum in the kitchen sent goose bumps up his calves. Both the sensations were acute, claiming his mind and making his skin feel prickly and cold. He reached her, and she scooped him up. She was warm, and as soon as he was in her arms, he felt heavier and tired, two more experiences he'd never had before. Intuitively, he knew what they were, though, and he rested his head on her shoulder. He closed his eyes. The earthy smell of overroasted coffee flooded his olfactory sense, and he came to associate that with his mother.

"What's wrong?"

With closed eyes, he smelled her, and under the coffee, there was a scent he might later compare to marshmallows melting. So he would also think of her when he made s'mores later down the road. He opened his eyes, and the black window was the first thing he saw. Then dark blues and black in an alluring coven.

"I don't know," he said.

She felt his head. The back of her hand was cold.

"You don't have a fever."

She walked, with Kris in her arms, to a chair beside the couch. They didn't speak any more. Mom rocked the chair back and forth. The motion might've scared him if he hadn't been in her arms. In her safekeeping, he allowed himself to revel in the idea that there was more than the black place and the Other. A world of something else. And there, in that world, was his mom, and though he didn't know how he knew it, he loved her, and she loved him. As he dozed, Kris lost grip on her and the very world he'd fallen into. Just like that, he was back in the darkness.

As always, the starless vacuum proceeded forever in all directions. The Other was before him like a grizzly bear up on its hind legs. Its murderous anger struck Kris's bodiless form like hurricane winds and emanated from the Other in waves. Never had Kris felt the Other project itself in that way. In his formless body, he could feel it: *kill, kill, kill, kill!* It wasn't the word; it was its savage intention.

Kris ran faster than he ever had. He fled desperately! Somewhere. Somewhere there was a house and a chair and a mom. He knew that if he could only run for long enough, he'd get back there.

The hot image of murder and death was behind him—just behind him. Kris knew it was so close that he dared not look back. The eyes of a world eater with a fixed expression of indifference would be waiting to carry him forward into the abyss. If he did, the Other would have him and devour him.

Ahead was some familiar shape that made a serrated horizon. Kris peered into the dark, at the fabled line, trying desperately to see what it was that made up the odd shape. They had black needles and shadow-colored bark. A forest of them. Kris never figured out what the shapes were before he fell back out of that place. *Falling… Falling…*

*****

He was alone in a room. A towel hung on a rod by a bowl that he believed was called a toilet. There was a white sink. Kris grabbed the towel and ran it over his fingers. The threads were coarse, almost rough. Kris buried his face in the towel, closed his eyes, and smelled it. It was faintly sweet. Later he might've compared it with a honeysuckle bush. Kris let the part of the towel covering his eyes fall away. He kept it close to his mouth, pressing it against his lips. With his eyes still closed, Kris pushed a little of the towel into his mouth. He chewed. The feeling of the threads squeezed between his teeth in little spongy bumps.

His eyes opened.

The curtain in the room had images of something he knew was called a lion, though he'd never seen one before. The lions had long legs that stuck in a pond among cattails and lily pads.

As he chewed on the towel, he remembered there was not only a mom outside the bathroom but a dad too, and a brother. Dad could answer any question about this new world. Brother was a little taller than him and didn't really seem to like Kris. He gathered that from images and colors and feelings that came to his mind—*memories*.

SERMON OF THE DIVERS

Pressure.

Kris felt pressure slowly building in him. *What was happening?* He half-remembered the feeling. *Not good. Not good.* The pressure turned to pain. He froze. The towel was still in his mouth. He felt something hot between his legs. It was warm and sorta solid but not. Then Kris smelled something foul, and he retched. He dropped the towel and quickly left the bathroom.

Kris found his mom in the kitchen and tried to explain what happened, but he couldn't find the words—too busy struggling for breath—so he just gasped, "Mom!"

She looked at him. She had been slicing tomatoes and staring out the window. The knife was still in her hand, and tomato juice clung to the tips of her left hand's fingers. She started to ask a question, but then understanding dawned on her face; she smelled it. And for a moment, the anger and frustration was plain on her face, for Kris to see that he'd done something wrong, even though he didn't know what it was. She took a breath. Kris averted his gaze. The first time he felt the warm emotion and the first time he saw the sun's light, it was coming in through the kitchen window. The color of light-blue skies and puffs of white clouds. Before Kris could even wonder at the light of the other colors he saw beyond the house, he was scooped up. Then he was gone again.

Shape came to the Void. It was a pond the first time. Creatures with manes and claws stood in its shallow waters. They were covered in black hair, and their eyes were dots. None of the creatures moved in the still water, no ripples. Cat eyes were fixed on Kris. The feeling of that place had changed too, and suddenly he was covered in a physical form—his body from the other world. There were still no smells or vivid colors or movements. The whole thing was a dreamy mirage. So as he stood there, he heard nothing and smelled nothing and felt nothing at all.

Kris walked into the waters of the oasis. Still he felt nothing, even as he dipped his fingertips into the jet-black water. He swirled them about. Perfect circular ripples shifted outward, reaching the statues and bursting into smaller patterns. Nothing else moved. The soundless ripples mimed life in a singular aspect. As he stood in the oasis of the infinite, Kris wondered how long his existence there would have seemed if the Other had not been there too.

What if it hadn't forced him to run all the moments of being?

Kris walked out into the pond until he stood just before one creature's lifeless form. Kris looked into the eyes of the one before him. He reached out his hand to feel its fur. They were long black blades that clung to the creature and shimmered like armored scales. The shadow statues inspired creeping ideas but in an unmoving way. He hesitated. He reached a little further. Stopped.

The creature swiped down at him with its paw. An unmistakable whirlwind of anger rose from it. Kris stumbled back, saving him from the black claws. He turned and ran from the pond, but he could feel the limits of his form slowing him. Kris managed to stay just ahead of the Other. Then for the first time, he could hear the Other roaring as it closed in. The sound of long legs sweeping through the water followed the roar.

Kris couldn't stop himself. He had to know if he was going to be fast enough. He turned his head. Giant fangs and an open mouth came down on him. It was sure to take him—

Kris was cold and wet, and the same towel he'd held in his mouth was being used to dry him. His mom used both hands to scrub the towel back and forth on his damp head. He smelled something sweet. The puffy skin of his body was dilated with feeling. He could feel the warmth of his mother behind him as the towel's thick edges slapped his cheeks. It stung. Kris knew not to say anything, and any relief he felt for having outran the Other dried up quickly. A premonition of mixed emotion lingered in the very steam of the bathroom. Mom was hushed in its presence. She didn't have any words for him. So in silence, she dried him, dressed him, and lastly, turned him around and stared at him for a moment.

In the hallway, faint sounds started to make a pattern. At first it was slow; it built speed and intricacy upon itself. The sound overlaid with a high soft voice saying words with drawn-out expression. The presence of his brother drifted in through the music. That's what it was.

SERMON OF THE DIVERS

Music! He strained to listen to the melody as it broke and was mended.

Mom gently turned him to the bathroom door and opened it. His brother's bedroom door was ajar just across the hall. He peeked in as Mom pushed gently, guiding him to the left, to the living room. His brother, Robbie, was sitting on his bed with a guitar that he was picking with his fingers. Robbie made the music. Even then, Robbie weaved internal vibration into his songs that were his very signature. Robbie's expression was focused and far off when a guitar lay across his lap.

In the living room, Kris's dad sat in a chair like mom's but bigger and fuller. It was dark gray. The lamp beside him softened light and directed it low to the ground. The windows were black, so Kris knew it to be nighttime. Dad stared at him as he leaned forward over his lap. Kris looked up at his dad. His dad's arms were almost as big as Kris's whole body.

"Come here, son," he said as he pointed at the carpet just in front of his knees. Kris hesitated, but there was a light push from Mom. He stepped forward slowly as he reminded himself that his father loved him; somehow he knew that. With each step, he tried to figure out what was happening. That was the first time he remembered the pressure in his nose before he cried. He felt like running but knew it wouldn't work. This body had bones and muscle. It ran on will but was limited by form. Dad's form was bigger. He'd be caught easily.

What happens if you die in the house, in the world of light, color, and music?

"You know what I've got to do now, son." He paused. His eyes had huge dark bags like bruises. "You've got to stop this. You're too old for it!"

Kris stood there. He felt he should know what he would have to do but nothing. He couldn't remember. All he had was a feeling that it was a terrible thing. He was sure of that. He could see it in the lines of his father's face and the smoking coals of his eyes.

"Next time, just tell someone or go to the bathroom. *Control yourself.*" Dad's voice was even and cool, and he stood. Kris looked up at the colossus in still silence. Dad walked around him and into the bedroom. Kris watched. From where he stood, he saw the bed with the heavy, floral quilt. Beyond was a desk with a computer. The room was lit by its overhead lamp, with yellow bulbs, and stirred with shadows because of the ceiling fan. Kris looked about, wondering if he might leave this body, but his dad made eye contact with him. Dad's head nodded forward.

Come on, the gesture said.

"Go on," said Dad. He was indicating the bed's edge. Kris felt a dull pain in his nose as the tears filled his eyes. His dad appeared a blob of color—a red shirt— with undulating brightness.

"Don't cry," his dad said shortly.

"I don't want to—"

"Son. I'm not gonna make you. You have to do it. I already told you what would happen."

Tears flowed down Kris's cheeks. They tickled and then were salty in his mouth.

"Son." Dad's voice was stern. "You already knew what was going to happen."

I didn't! I didn't understand! I don't understand!

His father undid his belt. He held it folded over; it connected in his large fist. Kris bent over the bed. The first hit stung, but it was the sound and the lingering shame that held Kris's attention. Until the second came, it was five times what the last was. And Kris's legs locked out. His spine curved up. He was rigid when the third came, which was much like the second. That one missed and hit his lower back because of Kris's convulsion. He was screaming, *"I'm sorry! I'm sorry!"* Then the fourth. It was harder than the others, or maybe he was already bruised. He no longer had words, only a shrill high-pitched wail. It must have offended his dad because he hit him immediately following, but because Kris convulsed from the bed at the same time, it hit his side.

"Dad, Please! Please! Stop!"

"Quit screaming like that!"

Kris struggled to get himself to calm. He told himself to please *shut up!* Kris only sobbed.

"The neighbors are gonna hear you and think you're a little girl! Get back up there!"

"Dad, no, p-p-please."

"Son." Full stop. He'd learn later how deep his father's finality could be and when it wavered. Kris got back up and took the rest of the licks he had left, trying his best not to scream.

Mom was in the living room, waiting. When it was over, she held him. Then she took him to bed. Dad came in to tell him he hated he had to do it. "It hurts me more than it hurts you."

Kris didn't think of those words much then. He was lying in his bed beside a window.

Above him was the darkest, most beautiful sky; starry dots glimmered in it and treetops reached, waving green branches at it. The center in that space was a bright full moon. He was seeing it all for the first time. This world was so alive that it could not possibly be real. Stars, he would later learn, were the sun. That is, the sun is a star. Around countless stars turned planets, and planets offered life its chance to be.

Before he slept, Kris sat up and pressed his face to the window. Peering out, he saw the moon's vision of the world. For Kris, it was the perfect way of this new place. He couldn't reason why, but it was. It was the way the clearing of shade verdancy laid in the grass and leaves. The way the canopy made the starred kingdom seem brighter. It was the way of sunless worlds that held magic in places no one dared go. And right that minute, it was the fireflies that antagonized him to try at the forest's gloom.

CHAPTER 1

Freddie

Kris made his way around to the back of the school. He checked to make sure that no one was watching, and then he jumped the fence and went into the trees beyond. The wild was untamed just beyond the fence, the path determined by the overgrowth, but he'd walked the way many times before. He knew it well. Even still, he could see the blood; he could smell the freshly voided body. The world began to spin; the tree arms seemed to bend toward him. He stopped and caught his breath, and he smelled the lycoris bulbs he carried with him.

Don't trust what you see or hear or feel, he reminded himself. Something his dad had taught him when he was young. *If I could have kept control...*

It was the last day of school, the last day of his junior year. He reminded himself that it was likely the last time that he'd get to come out to the spot that Rob had shown him, so it was imperative that he plant the spider lilies today. Over the summer, Allied Security and Technologies would be converting the campus. After that, there would be no way to leave without someone noticing, no place to go and not be seen. The fences would be higher, gates with cameras at each entry point, classrooms with surveillance, and though the school board swore they wouldn't, Kris was sure there'd be people in uniforms too. At Captain Valley High, close by, up on Maryville Parkway, several students had been charged with minor offenses already, and he'd heard talk about how everyone who went there wanted to transfer out. Next year, there'd be nowhere to go that wasn't converted.

Kris entered a natural clearing made by the tree, which had twin trunks the width of tractor tires. The twin trunks fused together at the bottom, and from that base, the ground was leaves and grass in a wide circle, aside from the turned dirt. The turned dirt was as to be expected, roughly the width and length of a casket, though the body underneath was only cradled by soil. For a moment, Kris imagined the worms and insects that were feasting just below and that maybe it could have been himself in the dirt. Then he set about planting the red spider lilies.

All men are basically evil. Kris didn't believe that, but he never forgot hearing it from the pastor at that old church his dad made him and Rob go to for a while. He'd said it with so much conviction and with arguments that, at the time, it seemed indisputable, logical.

Look at what humanity has done to the creatures of the earth, to each other. Look at how they resolve disputes and where they find entertainment. Mankind has erased many species from the tree of life, including cultures and societies of its own. As far back as recorded history can go, we've made war into an art form.

Kris nodded. Even if he didn't believe in God, and he didn't believe in an afterlife, and he didn't believe in very many things at all, he did believe that there was a modicum of truth in that saying. But maybe it was better said that since all humans were born with the capacity for evil, that humans were created to strive in all things.

Don't trust what you see, hear, or feel.

Kris nodded, and he planted. He knew for sure not to trust what he saw or heard or felt. That was truth. His dad had taught him that truth. And if he had been able to do that, he wouldn't have killed that person below the dirt. His name was Freddie.

He heard the first bell ring but continued to plant the flowers until he was done, and by then the second bell had sounded and the third as well. At that point, he walked over to the twin-trunked tree and ran his fingers over its bark. He thought about all the books he'd read while nestled in its boughs, and then he turned to leave.

SERMON OF THE DIVERS

Mrs. Laura didn't make a fuss when he came in late. They were watching a movie and only a few people looked up to see who it was coming in. It was the same people that it usually was: Breanna, Jon Chap (everybody said his first and last name when they referred to him), and Nima. Kris's eyes were on the floor, but he didn't have to see to know who looked at him. It was always the same three people every time. Sometimes he wanted to ask them why, but he never did.

When he made it to his seat in the corner, he took out *Eaters of the Dead* and began to read. School movies were perfect for reading. The volume had to be low because of close proximity to other classes, and generally no one talked. Plus, Kris's seat was by the window, and even though the lights were out, and the blinds were closed, he got just enough light through to be able to read. He shifted low in his seat and leaned his head against the wall under the window, and for a couple of minutes, it was as if he had left the world behind. He was traveling in the company of Vikings, making war with supernatural creatures. Their ways were foreign to him, as were his own to them, but he was intrigued by their ideas of honor and pleasure. In the afterlife, they would fight and fuck and feast into eternity. For a moment, he was stripped from the story, thinking how different the religions of those around him in the classroom were to the Vikings in his other life. Most of his classmates were atheist or Christian, though there were those that worshiped under specific denominations or Muslim, or there were those that claimed religions from the East. He marked how much the every day affected the religious beliefs of the people. A quarter of the class slept, a half were on their phones, and the last quarter either watched the movie or doodled in their notebooks.

"Okay," started Mrs. Laura as *The Princess Bride* ended. "You can talk *quietly* for the rest of class. Enjoy your time off, and don't forget the summer reading!"

Immediately, the class was buzzing with conversations, and Kris sank lower in his seat, trying to read but unable to. Conversation was infinitely more distracting for him than just about anything else. He could probably read at a concert if he was enjoying the book, but when people began to talk, Kris's ears tuned to catch the words. He never joined the conversations unless he was directly asked a question, which almost never happened; people didn't often interrupt his reading, but he still liked to listen.

Most everyone was talking about summer plans and college and where to cap the end of junior year. As to be expected, Aaron was having a house party; that was the place to be invited. Kris had never been to Aaron's house, but he'd heard of how big and grand it was. Still, he knew for a fact that he'd never see it. Kris's grandfather had led a union against Aaron's dad, *the* Jim Grayson, and spearheaded an effort that kept Jim Grayson from becoming mayor. But that was years and years ago. That wouldn't be the reason that Kris wasn't invited; it was more what became of Kris's grandfather and whatever mental illness he passed on to Kris through his father. It'd been years since he'd seen people that weren't really there or talked with voices no one could hear, but the rumors of it followed him from elementary to middle school and into high school. Kris kept his eyes on the book and swept them back and forth across the words, listening. If he were invited, he'd have to refuse anyway. He couldn't risk forgetting again. He thought of the body out behind the school and hoped that the spider lilies would survive being planted this early in the summer.

"Did you see the pictures?"

Ahead of him, Jon Chap and Liam were whispering, and whispering was what his ears searched for the most. He did feel ashamed but couldn't help but listen anyways. He'd have to plug his ears not to, and that would draw attention.

"You mean the...*pictures?*" asked Jon Chap conspiratorially, and he looked back at Kris but must have seen nothing alarming because they continued to whisper. People tended to let their guard down around Kris. Maybe they knew there was no one he'd talk to about their secrets anyway.

"The, uh, track team?"

The track team pictures? Kris continued to scan the words of the book and tried to remember any photos of the track team he'd seen recently.

"No, but I heard about it. I didn't think...I thought it was just talk."

Liam shook his head and smiled. "No. Scott showed it to me, came up to Sonic." Liam leaned closer. "I think it's her... Have you seen her hair?" He bit his lip.

Hair? Kris couldn't even recall who was on the track team, but he was sure there was a redheaded girl. *What pictures?* He hoped they would keep going so he might find out more.

"But didn't they break up?"

"Well, yeah, but it could have been from before—"

The bell rang.

Kris's mind didn't linger on the girl from the track team or the whispers he'd overheard. He filed them away to the part of his mind that was rumor, and all rumor was false or unknowable to him. He gathered the gist of what they were saying, and it didn't seem like anyone else's business anyway.

With that, he slunk around the school the long way, avoiding the majority of foot traffic and walking just off the breezeway with his eyes firmly planted on the ground. He enjoyed walking on the ground as opposed to the breezeway, and if it were up to him, he'd walk around without any shoes, feeling the grass underfoot. His dad had caught him swinging an axe barefoot just two weeks ago. He'd reprimanded him and reminded Kris that it was that kind of carelessness that he must never allow to become habit. But still, Kris thought about how much he wanted to be barefoot often when he walked through it at school.

Most of his other classes were either free time to chat, or the teachers put on a movie, like Mrs. Laura. Kris continued to try to read, but usually he got distracted by close conversations about a girl in a picture. Finally, he knew more than he wanted to know about it. In calculus, his last class of the day and the only class he actually had to work on the last day—Mr. Godfrie was that kind of teacher—Hunter Wright and Ashton McPowell whispered a similar conversation to the one he'd heard from Jon Chap and Liam.

Only this time, Hunter commented, "She can take a dick."

Kris looked up from his book then. He was almost seeing red, and he had things he wanted to say on the end of his tongue. *Who do you think you are?* He imagined himself balling up his fist and bringing it down on Hunter's jaw. That only made him think of the sound the hammer had made when he'd brought it down on *his* face. *Can't trust it,* he reminded himself.

But his heart was beating faster and faster, and he wasn't breathing, and he couldn't hear anything. *Breathe. Breathe! Goddamn it!* He imagined the grave mound behind the school and took in air, almost gasping. Hunter and Ashton looked back at him.

"Hey, man. You okay?"

Kris nodded and was thankful when the intercom came on.

"Mr. Godfrie, could I have Kris Timur for a minute?"

Then everyone was looking at him.

"I'll send him your way," said Mr. Godfrie. "Just take your bag with you, Kris. By the time you leave there, it'll be time to go. Have a good summer."

When Kris walked out of class, he reminded himself that it was *none* of his business what was going on with this picture and this girl that everyone was talking about. It was just the way that he was; that gift from his grandfather and father, his temper, was always just under the surface, ready to engulf him if he didn't keep it in check. *Don't believe what you see or hear or feel.* What did any of that matter to him anyway? Maybe everything was consensual, and maybe she wanted people to know and say those kinds of things about her. Emma Lovelace, from his world history class, had a conversation with Molly Blake—one that he couldn't help but overhear—about how she'd had sex with three guys at once, and she said it was the *best* experience of her life. She said it was empowering for her. And there were feminists that claimed that was an empowering act of feminism. Kris laughed at himself then for getting so angry. All of that had nothing to do with him. He didn't even know who this girl was.

When Kris walked into the main office, he was directed down the hall to Ms. Figaro's. The door was closed, and he'd been told to wait, so he took a seat in one of the three chairs for just that. With a sigh of relief, Kris got his book out and began to read. Ms. Figaro's waiting area was prime for reading. The chairs were extra cushiony, and there wasn't a soul around but him.

SERMON OF THE DIVERS

After about two minutes, Kris was watching one of his Viking brothers be sent off to Valhalla.

The pyre and the woman that accompanied him were being consumed by flames, along with weapons and armor. He wondered what went through the mind of the woman that died with their jarl. He wondered when he'd fight those beasts in the dark again, those flesh eaters, and whether he'd live to see his home again. Strangely, he thought he might not ever *want* to see his home again. There was something about them, the—

The door to Ms. Figaro's office opened.

A girl with purple hair came out and slammed the door right into his knee.

"*Shh—ouch!*"

She turned, looked at him for a moment, as if it took her a few moments to realize there was a person sitting in the chair. And Kris noticed her eyes were sunken, but they were also mad as hell.

"Sorry," squeaked Kris.

She turned and walked away.

No need to apologize, thought Kris. *It was only my knee.*

"You okay, dear?" asked Ms. Figaro from her desk. "Come in now. I'm sure she didn't mean to do that. Don't you worry about it. Come in and take a seat, Kris. I don't want to keep you past the buses."

Kris sidled into Ms. Figaro's office and looked around at all of her motivational posters and photos of students from years gone by, just to see if there was anything new for him to comment on. There wasn't. The picture of the rowers, paddling their oars, was still there with the caption: Obstacles are what you see when you take your eye off the goal. Then there was a collection, a hodgepodge of photos featuring Ms. Figaro and hundreds of students in caps and gowns. She was always in sky-high heels but also always the shortest person in the photo. "How're you today, Ms. Figaro?"

"I'm good, Kris. How're you?"

"I'm doing good, Ms. Figaro. How can I help you today?" asked Kris.

Kris had been sent to Ms. Figaro's office enough times to develop a playful sort of rapport with her, but today she didn't seem in the mood. Kris believed he knew why. This last semester was the closest he'd ever come to failing, far too close for comfort.

"Tell me what happened with physics. Mrs. Baker said that you started out strong, and the first semester, you got a solid *B*. Do you know what you got this semester?"

Ms. Figaro's curly hair bounced forward as she slid the report card across her desk.

Kris did, in fact, know what he'd gotten in the class. He'd made sure to do just enough of the work to pass. No less, and certainly no more.

"I don't know what to tell you, Ms. Figaro. I guess the concepts just went over my head."

She gave him a look that wasn't disbelief but close to it. Ms. Figaro's eyes were huge and dark, but they were comforting and full of caring.

"Your mind is a steel trap," she said. "Nothing escapes it, but sometimes it bites too hard. I don't believe you were stumped by physics. What else is going on?"

Kris traced the creases in her forehead with his eyes. He was becoming increasingly aware of how the color of the wall behind her deepened the color of her skin. It gave her a rather commanding presence, whereas the appearance of the lady was quaint and pretty. Kris always liked Ms. Figaro.

"I passed," he said. "I'll just make sure to study a little harder next year."

Ms. Figaro slowly nodded. "And what about world history?"

Kris looked down and saw the 69 percent *D* on the report card. That hadn't been on purpose, but he did think the number was funny. He'd meant to make that a 70 percent *C*, but then time got away from him while he was working out behind the house. He'd forgotten the one study guide that would have secured the C. *Damn.* Kris stared at the card for a moment, wondering at the power of a few letters on a piece of paper. Everything in his life, his life in the world of light and color and sound, was dependent on these eight letters. At times, he felt bad for not caring about them more and that maybe he wasn't only letting himself down when he couldn't find a reason to care about those letters anymore.

"It was a fluke," he said. "Next year—"

"Next year, you'll have to apply to colleges."

Have to...

Kris didn't say anything. *I don't have to go to college.* Though he knew that's what everyone was telling him to do and that it was probably wise to, because that increased the chances of finding a job that might actually be able to pay his future bills. Yet...

"Do you know where you want to go? Do you plan on going to college?" Her voice was kind.

"No."

She sat back. "Do you know what you want to do after graduation?"

I want to finish that garden out behind the house. That was his first thought, and the next was an idea about a life he could have had if things had turned out different. He thought of the photo on the baker's rack back at the house.

"I'll get a job. Save up money for a while."

Ms. Figaro nodded. Was that disappointment in her eyes now? He wondered if she was disappointed in him or herself, thinking that she'd failed him somehow.

"Ms. Figaro, I know that this is all really important. I'm going to figure it out. You've been super helpful since freshman year. I just...don't really know what I want to do."

Ms. Figaro regarded him with a certain kind of expression; there was concern and something else, but Kris couldn't place what it was.

"Kris. Is everything okay? Are you alright? You look tired."

"Yes ma'am," he replied immediately. "Sorry. I was up late last night."

Her expression of concern and whatever else waited for further explanation.

"I was out in the woods behind my house, quartering wood from dying trees and stacking it up. I'm gonna sell cords of wood for the fall and winter," he replied honestly, hoping that would alleviate some of her worries. He couldn't stand to have people worry about him.

She clicked her tongue. "I suppose that's some money for your future right there." She smiled. "Promise me that you'll do the summer reading. Next year, in Mr. Adrien's English 4 class, it will count for so much of your first semester's grade that you will *fail* without completing it. Do you hear me? There will be nothing that I can do for you. No matter how brilliantly you do on the rest of his assignments."

"I hear you, Ms. Figaro," said Kris. And he did. As to whether or not he was going to read those books or the ones that happened to catch his eye over the summer was to be seen.

CHAPTER 2

Aaron

Leah knew him from somewhere, but she couldn't place it. That wasn't a surprise to her. Her memory was spotty on its best day, and certainly it never obeyed her commands. *Oh!* That's right; he's the quiet one from physics—the creepy one. When he whispered an apology, Leah just turned away. She was on the verge of tears.

Leah managed to make it past the trophy cases and just out the office doors before a few of them got loose and ran down her cheeks. *Why are you wasting your time crying? It's time to figure it out.*

Crying never solved anything. Her mother had said that years ago, and recently it felt as if her mother had just said the words. When she was younger, Leah thought that was silly because Leah used to *like* crying. Every movie and book could get a tear out of her, and she sought out the books and movies that did. And now there was the truth of the matter: *Tears will get me nothing. They'll never get me there.* In truth, Leah didn't know where *there* was precisely, but when she imagined it, it was a place with her mom and sister, a place where her mom didn't have to work for a living, and Leah could pay for her sister to go to school. A place in time where she'd forgotten about Aaron and every memory she ever made with him, because of course those stuck around. Her mind conjured the memories up with the slightest cue of association.

As she leaned against the breezeway, by the office doors, Justin Walton and Mika Garcia walked by, and she didn't catch every word they said, but she did manage to catch *hair* and that mesmerized, dead-eyed look that Mika gives every girl. She wasn't so naive as to think that this wasn't going to happen. But now she knew she wasn't wrong for thinking she heard that picture-taking sound shutter when he—

Leah wiped her nose and blinked until the tears receded, then she went back to gymnastics to wait until the final bell.

Justin and Mika were not the only ones that whispered about her so conspicuously. In the gymnastics room, everyone was gathered into small groups and talking away the last few minutes of the day. She couldn't help but notice more hungry stares and her name sounding low from all over, and she caught *Aaron* and *hot* and *whore* and all the other words she expected to hear. It had been three months since they broke up, and she was surprised it'd taken him this long to show the photo around. Nobody knew what happened in that car; they didn't know, and so they were free to assume. And Leah knew if she told them what happened, it would only turn into a he-said, she-said. Aaron *Grayson* would win that. By name alone he'd have most of the school on his side; then what if it went beyond school? He'd have Valleyport and Louisiana and the whole of the States. What would she have against that?

"Well, what's the verdict?" asked Andrew.

"There's nothing I can do about it. But Ms. Figaro told me it's not a big deal. She just said to refresh over summer and make sure not to let it happen next year."

"See. Nothing to freak out about. Are you okay?" asked Bailey.

Bailey had been her best friend since she could remember, and Leah knew she still didn't know what was going on. Leah'd thought about telling her the whole story many times over the last three months, but she always came back to: *What does it really matter?* She wasn't pregnant and had learned her lesson. Plus, Bailey and Brit both tried to warn her about Aaron Grayson, but she hadn't listened. It was her fault for not hearing them out. *How was I so stupid?*

"I'm fine," said Leah. "I don't even know why I freaked out about a *B* to begin with. Did Jason text you back?

Bailey's worry shifted away as Jason was brought up; she looked at the message on her phone with a coy grin. She swept her brown hair back from her eyes. It was cut short now and had a tendency to fall on her face.

"He said he's going to meet us there after school."

"Talley's already on his way," added Andrew.

Good. Going to Stonethrow and skating was one of the only things that she was able to do and just shut her mind off. She often thought about how she'd have to find a place to skate when she went to Louisiana State University. *They won't be there, though.* Bailey, Andrew, Talley, and Jason, none of them were going to LSU with her. Andrew was probably the only one of them, aside from herself, that was even going to be able to afford to go to college. But where he had his parents, Leah had to rely on her grades and scholarships. And his parents wouldn't be able to afford LSU. He'd probably go to a community college at first. So this would be the last summer for all of them to skate away at Stonethrow.

"Did you see the new post? Buried in the Valley?" asked Andrew. He was attached to his phone much more often as of late, on Reddit.

"I know you haven't," he said. "Just reminding you it's there. It's *really* interesting. Did you know Jim Grayson ran for mayor?"

Leah was reminded of family dinners with the man.

"If you know we're not going to read it, would you mind not bringing it up?" Bailey said a bit defensively, but Leah knew it was for her sake.

Andrew rolled his eyes and continued to read, and Bailey took out her phone.

Ding!

Leah's own phone went off.

>   Bailey: Are you sure you're okay? You look...
> tired 🫠

Again, Leah wanted to tell her but knew she couldn't, not now, not here. And she didn't want to cry. There was too much to focus on to cry. Even though she had her whole summer before her, it was all the time that needed to be spent preparing for her senior year and what comes after. She replied:

> Just tired from track, I promise. I'll grab some caffeine before Stonethrow ☺

Bailey didn't seem to fully believe her but gave a warm smile. And they spent the last few minutes of their junior year talking about the new phone coming out; it was supposed to have the best camera ever made, period. Good for candid shots, action shots, landscapes, portraits. Leah wanted one, sure, but she didn't know if she could ever give up her old Nikon and the way it felt hanging from her neck, and that'd be the only way she'd get one—by selling her old camera, her skateboard, her comic books, and everything else in her room. And she was almost positive that it'd never *feel* the same anyway. Although, she hadn't been in the mood to practice photography lately and had to force herself to do it.

The bell rang, and everyone pushed through the gym doors. She walked with Andrew and Bailey to the buses and told them she'd see them in a couple of hours. Still she could hear her name in the air, over the bus engines, the goodbyes, the security guard directing students. It was only then, after Andrew and Bailey boarded bus 300, that she remembered the campus wasn't going to be the same next year. She stopped just past where the buses were parked and looked back at the open courtyard and the trees and bench she used to have lunch at. The place she'd tried hard to impress Aaron, and he'd seemed to try just as hard in return. Instead of an urge to cry, she felt a jolt of emotion run through her, *affection* or *love*, and that was worse.

Leah swept the parking lot with her eyes and saw no sign of her sister's charcoal gray Focus. That didn't mean anything, though. The parking lot was on a slope, and she couldn't see all the cars from the school. She began walking down the first row and then the second and finally the third, which was where Brit's car was, but Brit was nowhere to be found. *Of course,* she thought. Then she sat her backpack down and jumped onto the car's roof, burning her thighs, and waited.

Brit was generally late, so this was an improvement of a sort. Although the car roof was very hot and uncomfortable—even shaded as it was—Leah laid her head back and closed her eyes, and for just a moment, she was dazed. Normally she wasn't able to just fall asleep anywhere, but there wasn't much of a normal to her sleep patterns within the past couple of months anyway. Maybe that's why she fell into such a deep and relaxed sort of sleep. And for some reason, when she laid her head back, while sitting on the top of her sister's car in the parking lot of her school, with all the cars pulling out and all the people, she felt *safe*. Safe because she was leaving this place for a couple of months. Already her mind had moved forward. Those buildings and the people within had piled a year's worth of stress and responsibilities on her, and for a moment, she could breathe. She dreamed.

In the dream, there was a door. It had a roundtop like the one at her house, and it was red. But it was banded in iron. It made her think of a door in a castle, and that made her think of old fairy tales and the bright colors of old cartoons from her childhood, all the Disney classics. And she felt she was a child. Aaliyah heard a voice in her ears as she stood before the door, and there was faint music coming from the other side, and lunar tendrils crept around the frame. The voice was a melody, a woman's, with a big voluminous voice.

"Don't go in there!"

The car door opened, and the car shook, and her sister slammed it. "Come on! We're getting pizza!"

She couldn't remember the dream as she rolled off the car, getting over her vertigo and rubbing her eyes. Everything was blue from closing them and looking at the sun.

"I was going to Stonethrow."

"You don't want pizza?"

Leah was about to tell her no when she felt her stomach growl.

"Okay. Pizza," she said.

"Good. Rob and his brother are meeting us there. I didn't know his brother went to school with you."

Rob Timur worked with Brit at Mason's Muse and was a remembered name at Larue, particularly with the girls that were freshman when he was a senior, the juniors like her. He was tall, and he was fit, and he was really something to look at, but it was the way he was about music that stayed when he was gone. He loved it. He loved everything about it, and he played his guitar in a way she'd never heard until seeing him play her first homecoming. Ball Point Pin wasn't the best name for the band, but everyone remembered Rob Timur. She thought she'd heard something about him having a brother that was a year below her or… She couldn't quite remember.

"I guess I've never seen him," she replied.

Brit got in, and Leah grabbed her bag and followed. Leah was about to add that she'd heard he was a year below her when she heard a clicking sound instead of the engine starting. Those clicks were the only sound for a moment, and then the heat of the day seemed to bear down on them furiously. Inside, the car was boiling.

"Fuck."

"I told you it sounded funny this morning."

Brit gave her a cutting glance and rolled her eyes. "It was fine. I wonder if Rob knows anything about cars."

Brit swept her blonde locks back from her face as she put the phone to her ear. When she spoke, it was with a tone of attainment, the kind that she'd been using for years to get what she wanted from guys.

"Hey… Have you left yet? Good. Do you know anything about cars?"

A few minutes later, the parking lot was almost entirely deserted except for them, and a blue Civic pulled up in front of them. They were both sweating. Leah was texting her friends and letting them know it might be a while. Brit was standing by the car; Leah was still in it. Brit took out her cigarette tin, a dainty thing with a purple heart on it, and lit one up right as Rob and his brother got out of the car. Rob got out with a smile on his face. A carefree sort of smile, one that she imagined laughed at the situation. Leah was still in the car, just watching, when he waved and said something that made Brit laugh. Leah was going to get out until she saw Rob's brother, the kid she'd slammed the door into.

Oh, what was his name?

He was wearing jeans, boots, and he had on a Bilberry Drive band shirt. How had she not noticed that before? That was her favorite band. He stopped when he got out, and he stood still, looking at the car. His face was almost an opposition to his brother's. All of the levity of Rob's was in stark contrast to his—a blank face. His lips were curved to frown but didn't, and his hair was an impressionless style that he left unstyled. The only thing that hinted at life in his face were his eyes, the way that they looked at the car she was in. They were either blue or green—she couldn't tell—but either way, she could see his mind sparking behind them.

She shifted low in her seat.

Then the sparks were gone, and he turned around. He went to the trunk of the Civic and pulled a green tool chest from it. When he came back over, he asked Brit to pop the hood. Brit handed her cigarette to Rob, who took a few puffs, and then she opened the door and pulled the lever. The hood jumped up and hid Leah from his view. Even the hot air coming in from Brit's open door felt cool to Leah now, but she stayed where she was.

Leah was thinking and remembering things about Rob's brother, the sort of jokes that she had heard made about him. He couldn't be bothered to be antisocial but was so unsociable that people forgot he was there until, randomly, something a teacher said would get him to speak. Surprise, he was usually disagreeing with them about something they taught. Telling the teacher he'd read something different in another book and that the textbook might be wrong. And he said it as if he were volunteering information to be helpful, and he didn't care what the teacher did with it. *You're being tested on the textbook, though,* she remembered thinking on one occasion when he'd done that in physics. *Why didn't I remember that until just now?* Was her memory getting worse?

"Did you have any trouble getting it started?" he asked.

"Uh, no. I—"

"Yes, she did," Leah said before she could think. Then in the silence that followed, she opened her door and stood. There he was, looking at her with those unsettling eyes.

"It took a couple of tries."

"Did it click then too?" he asked her.

"Yeah."

He nodded. "I think it needs a jump. Rob, could you pop the hood on your car and start it?"

Rob passed the cigarette back off. "Don't worry. Kris'll get it started."

Less than a minute later, he had the cars connected with jumper cables and told Brit to give it another shot. The old Focus started right up, and Brit gave Kris an earnest thank-you. It almost looked like she meant to hug him but couldn't figure a way to do it.

"You'll need another battery, though. Go to any auto store, and they'll put it in for you."

Brit nodded. Leah knew she was wondering about the cost but not wanting to ask. Maybe he knew that too, because he added, "Only cost you about $70."

"And we'll wait on you two at the Pizza Palace, if you want?" Rob offered.

*****

"He's weird," said Brit as they pulled away, going up Jackson to the O'Reilly's.

"Can you just drop me off at home? I wanted to show mom my report card before she goes to work, and I can just walk to Stonethrow."

They weren't too far from where they lived, already on the edge of Deepmoor and the Great Heights beyond. Jackson ran across Deepmoor's head, and the Pizza Palace was all the way out on Cricket. That'd be on the other side of downtown, past the old industrial side. It was probably twenty minutes one way, plus sitting down to eat, that could be two hours. She wouldn't be able to make it to Stonethrow till six.

Ding!
"Bailey offered to come get me."

Brit pulled into the parking lot. She pushed the transmission into park and turned to Leah. Her face was the one that meant, *I'm about to ask for a favor, sister.* Leah knew she wouldn't be able to say no. Even though Brit was always late, blunt, mildly unhinged, and a bitch, she was still Leah's sister and had done countless favors for her since childhood. She'd kept secrets only a sister would.

"What is it?" asked Leah, not trying to hide her hesitance.

"It's going to be weird if you don't come. Rob's hard to read. I'm trying to figure him out, and I can't *really* do that with his brother staring at us the whole time. It's creepy."

Leah knew without them ever having to talk about it that Brit was trying to start *something* with Rob. From what she'd heard, that was a distinct impossibility. There were rumors he was gay, that he was saving himself for marriage, that he was asexual, and that he was a Ken doll down there. But that didn't matter. Brit had asked, and that would be enough for Leah.

After all, Brit had *actually* kicked someone in the balls for her.

"How long?" asked Leah.

Brit smiled and laughed. "It won't be that bad! Just an hour, and maybe a little more." Leah gave in.

During the ride to the Pizza Palace, her heart began to run a little fast, and she realized she was thinking of Aaron. She reminded herself this wasn't a double date and that she was just there to distract the weird one for her sister. And she reminded herself that *Brit* was going to be there the whole time. Nothing could happen to her. Still, it took until just before they pulled up for the dreadful turning in her stomach to stop.

CHAPTER 3

Barbecue Pizza

Pizza Palace was in a worn-out, three-store strip mall next to the Walgreens on the corner of Cricket and Highway 12. The colors were red and yellow, red text with a yellow shadow, big and bold letters with curvy curves. Kris looked from the sign to his right, where, down a slope, following Cricket, the old industrial part of Valleyport rested as on its deathbed. Sunbaked colors and rust, old tin and worn bricks, and grass poking through foundations and roads. Kris thought about how businesses had lives. They are conceived and consumed and grow, and their natural inclination is to fight. They eventually die. But unlike people, they are revived and made to continue some form of their work. They continue until their flesh decays, and their bones crumble to time. Finally, and only then, are they torn apart and deteriorate, and humans eat them as carrion.

Kris smiled to himself, thinking of how his inner dialogue sounded. He'd always had the tendency toward morbid thinking. He didn't have a positive mindset, didn't believe that he necessarily had a negative one either. Just now, looking at Pizza Palace in front of him, he was excited that some businesses were revived and carried on. Pizza Palace was one such place.

"What'd you think of Leah?"

"What?" asked Kris, awakening from his thoughts.

"Brit's sister."

"Oh. I wasn't thinking of her."

"You know what I mean."

Kris nodded.

When he saw her again in the parking lot, Kris realized she must be the one that everyone was talking about, from the photo. Her hair *was* red, but now it was purple, and he knew she was on the track team. His inclination was to ask her about it, but he knew people hated directness, most people anyway. And then in the car, on the way to Pizza Palace, he imagined what her day might have been like. He reminded himself that he didn't know any of the facts about the story, as it was all rumor, and he decided since he didn't know anything, he'd treat it as if he'd heard nothing.

"She seems nice. I think she's on the track team."

Rob shook his head. "You don't think anything else about her?"

"No. Why?"

"I don't know." Rob was kind of laughing or trying not to laugh. "I just thought that…I don't know." Rob turned the volume knob, and then music overshadowed the conversation.

Kris wondered what he was supposed to notice. He thought back on her. He'd seen her around school before a handful of times. Now that he thought about it, he'd seen her out at the center courtyard, eating lunch. He remembered seeing her on his way toward the back of the campus, to his clearing in the woods, and that she was always laughing or smiling. He remembered seeing people gathered around her, that she always had so many people around her.

They were under the shade of trees, sitting cross-legged, as if she were about to tell them a story. In the memories, her hair was red, and it brought out the red in her eyes, especially when a rogue sunbeam evaded the leaves and found her face. Her nose was upturned, and her lips were naturally curved, pursed in a way that hinted she knew something but refused to say it. But there was something about the way she looked, the expression she took on when she really focused on something. He tried to remember what he'd seen her staring at like that.

"They're here," said Rob, looking from his phone to the rearview mirror.

Rob got out, and with a sigh, Kris followed.

"You were right," Brit told him as she and Leah joined them. "Thanks again. Also, this is—"

"My name's Leah. We had physics together."

"I remember you," said Kris. "You're the only one that got an *A* on the final."

A look of confusion flashed across her face but only for an instant. It was replaced by that knowing look that her face seemed to always return to.

They walked into the Pizza Palace, and on the other side of the tinted glass doors was a war of noise. Kris looked around and let everyone get in front. He had to take a survey of the rooms he walked into, and he didn't remember when someone being in line behind him started to bother him, but it did. A group of boys were playing Skee-Ball in the arcade and yelling battle cries and shouts. Only three tables remained empty, an unusually busy after-school rush for Pizza Palace; he could see it in the staff. The way they stooped and sighed when they were far enough behind the lines that they thought no one was watching. He noticed there was tension between the person on the counter and the person rolling out the dough. In between her customers, the girl working the counter, Vivi—he could just barely see her name tag—was looking at the nameless guy rolling the dough, with a bitter-and-sweet, back-and-forth, kind of expression. The guy rolling the dough seemed to know when Vivi was looking at him, and he'd keep his eyes on the dough while she was watching. When she turned, he stole glances, and he had that face like he was puzzling something out, maybe mulling over some words.

"Kris?"

"Huh?"

Rob and Brit were in front, followed by Leah, and then Kris. He realized he'd zoned out and missed what she'd said.

"I'm sorry. What'd you say?"

She was staring down at the pizza on the buffet plates, and occasionally she'd sweep her eyes over to him, but it was an obligatory amount of eye contact. Kris looked behind her to Rob and Brit, and then he realized what was happening, that she didn't want to be there and that she'd only come to entertain him. *Come to think of it, there's*

SERMON OF THE DIVERS

something different about her today. He figured the rumor might have something to do with that. *Maybe I'll entertain her instead.*

Kris didn't usually open up to people, but that isn't to say that he didn't know how. He just had good reasons not to. When his emotions ran too hot, he could never tell what would happen. That's all it took with Freddie. He'd come around to his father's way of thinking long ago: *It's not a risk worth taking.* But again, there was a sadness in her eyes, a stark contrast to the eyes he held in his memory.

"I asked how you did on the final."

"Not so bad," he replied. "I got 67 percent."

A smile twitched on the end of her lips but didn't stay. "That's not bad, huh?"

"Depends on what you're aiming for, I guess. I wanted a *C* in the class. I got a C. What were you aiming for?"

She gave him a peculiar look.

"An *A*. Why would you go for a *C*?"

Just then, the man at the end of the counter was raising his voice at the cashier, Vivi. The man at the counter was in slacks, a blue button up, and was bald, with a bushy mustache. He was speaking just loudly enough to draw the attention of a couple of people throughout the restaurant.

"I don't have time to wait," he said. "I've got somewhere to be." Not yelling but definitely carrying.

Vivi's voice was kind. "We're getting it out as quick as we can, sir."

The guy rolling the dough glared at the mustached man.

"I need a refund."

"Sir, I don't think I can refund you—"

"I only wanted the barbecue pizza. I didn't get it. I think I *deserve* a refund *because I didn't get what I want. WHAT I CAME HERE TO GET.*"

Vivi was blinking rapidly, and the fella rolling the dough wasn't even moving anymore, just staring at the mustached man with sharp eyes.

"I'll get you that refund, sir."

"*Kris.*"

Kris realized he'd been staring and listening to the exchange at the counter and didn't hear a thing Leah'd said. *Focus. Control yourself.* He shook his head.

"Sorry. I was—I couldn't help but hear the... Did you hear that?"

Leah nodded. She was staring down as she slid a piece of pepperoni onto her plate. "How could you not? *What an asshole.*"

"All over barbecue pizza."

Kris took a few deep breaths as inconspicuously as he could, feeling his heartbeat getting away from him, feeling lightheaded and dizzy.

He kept himself under control, but the conversation was silent the rest of the way through the buffet line and to their booth. Meanwhile, Rob and Brit were gabbing back and forth with barely a moment between their speaking.

"Why aim for a *C*?" Leah asked him at the booth.

"I don't have the time for a *B* or an *A*. That and... Sorry, but I just don't see the point. For me. I have no desire to be a physicist."

"Neither do I," she said, almost laughing. "But you get good grades, you get into a good college, and that decides your job."

Kris nodded, though he was filled with contrary things to say. He used to believe what she said was true. Now, he wasn't so sure that's how things worked. But in the interest of not further complicating her day, he decided to—

"What?"

"Oh, nothing."

"You looked like you had something to say. You had this *super faraway* thing going on."

Where normally Kris would have redirected the conversation or simply refused to keep it going, he couldn't help himself.

"I don't think I believe that. Maybe that was true sometime and somewhere, but I think that now, today, a person's job is almost entirely decided the moment they are born. Decided by where and to whether they come from parents with money or not. It's decided by the friends they find, the ones that are in the same socioeconomic class as them, and I suppose it could be decided by an individual's desire for it. But I believe breaking through, here, today, can be soul-crushing."

Leah was giving him that same peculiar look, and he couldn't figure out what it was that she was saying with that look; he didn't know if he cared for it or not. But when she aimed it at him, he felt both excitement and dread, grim and joyful.

"I see what you mean. But people can still break through, do what they want. They can have the careers they want, the lives they want."

Some, he thought and berated himself for being so damn contradictory.

Kris nodded and said she was right. The conversation went on, and he began to think she'd never mention hitting him with the door.

*****

Leah had trouble nailing down the conversation at first. He wasn't a conversationalist but how he spoke required a certain thought processing that tickled her brain. Occasionally, he'd use an archaic word or make a point in a way that made him sound as if he were born a hundred years ago, as if he were a very old man. His eyes rested on her between searching, a tendency to find something in the background to focus on. But they always came back, with something thought-provoking to say.

"I wonder if all forms of government become oligarchies in the end. A few people find a way to monopolize the opportunities, the power, and the resources."

"You sound like an anarchist. We do have a system of checks and balances, and the power is divided, and if nothing else, we're improving every year. Everything's much better than it used to be."

He nodded and looked away from her. She saw through his quick acquiescence, that he was always holding back a further point. His eyes darted back to her when she laughed.

"Just say your point."

For the first time, he smiled. It was a small thing, and it faded quickly, but it was nothing if not charming.

"I don't really have one. I can't tell you what I think the solution is because I don't know it. I think that fundamentally, people don't know how to govern themselves. And it's a problem with dire consequences. If we don't figure out how to do it, then I believe we might never make it out into the universe to multiply in the stars. All I know is that kings and queens are corruptible, that democracies are bought, that exploitation is the rule of power. I don't know why we're almost universally convinced that helping the whole of man is an evil thing. Maybe it's because someone always exploits. And we don't want to be the ones being exploited. It's the idea that there is a finite amount of—"

He cut off, staring.

Leah turned to see the cashier bringing a barbecue pizza to the buffet and then start for Mr. Mustache's table in the corner. She turned back to Kris with an idea.

"What?"

"Come on."

Brit and Rob asked them what was going on, but they didn't answer; they hurried to the buffet line, and both of them took plates.

"Are we really doing this?" he asked, looking sheepish all of a sudden.

She smiled. "It's the idea that there is a finite amount of barbecue pizza."

Leah smiled from ear to ear as she scooped half the pizza on his plate and half on her own and made it out of the line just in time for Mr. Mustache to see. Back at the table, they laughed and could barely explain themselves to Rob and Brit, and all they did was join in it. Leah hadn't laughed that much in—Dwelling on that thought was pulling her away from how funny everything was. Maybe the last time she laughed that much was with Aaron, but it just as easily could have been with Bailey and the guys up at Stonethrow. Her breath was catching again, and she was waking from a haze, and it was then that Kris's laughter stopped suddenly. He was doing that thing again, looking far away, and it was obvious how many thoughts played in his eyes. After that, he didn't say much, and neither did she. Luckily, the meal ended.

"I'm sorry about hitting you with the door," she said awkwardly. They were all making their way to the cars.

He blinked. "Oh. Don't worry about it. It was great dealing pizza justice with you. Have a good summer."

She snickered, and they exchanged goodbyes.

It was a strange feeling, walking away from the Pizza Palace. She had a nagging feeling she meant to say something, or he did. Words, invisible, floated in the summer heat and concentrated in the parking lot, waiting to be said. There was nothing more to it than that, though; it was all the conversations they could've had if there was time. Or that's what it felt like to Leah, but she walked away from those floating invisible words.

CHAPTER 4

The Oaks of Stonethrow

"Sorry," said Brit. "I didn't think Rob's brother would be so... What was he talking to you about? Politics? Hell of an opener for first meeting someone."

"I think he was just *being* open. He's...*nice*. He helped me steal pizza from that asshole with the mustache."

"That guy was *pissed*. He brought out the old Leah for a second, the wild child."

"He's just *nice* is all. What about you and Rob? You *seemed* to be having a good time."

Brit reached for her cigarette tin. "I still can't tell if he's into me or just really *nice*."

They exchanged a look. Brit flicked the lighter and puffed. She rolled down the window.

"Guess you'll find out." But Leah secretly wondered about the rumor that Rob wasn't entirely straight. She knew there was no real way of telling, but she wondered. And she'd not met a guy that took that good of care of themselves.

Smoke filled the car and billowed and blew through the window with the warm air. Leah texted Bailey to let her know she was on her way home. She got the response:

Andrew's getting Sonic. You want anything?

SERMON OF THE DIVERS

Leah sent back:

> Oh? 😬 I'll take a Cherry Limeade. Tell him thanks!

They pulled up to the corner of Salem and Fairfield after a short drive back through Valleyport. Her house was of old worn brick and had blue trim. Windowsill gardens hung under each window around front, on both sides of the red roundtop door. It was small and average, but not to Leah; she always felt there was a unique magic about her home. A personality, perhaps, or a ghost. And the house's magic tended to move around; sometimes it was on the top porch step or the red roundtop door or the old wooden floorboards or the shed out back or her room, at the window that faced the backyard. And the magic was not consistent, and it paid no mind to her moods, but it *communicated* with her many times—usually when she was stressed, tired, or depressed—and gave her comfort. But as they got out of the car, she realized she hadn't felt that, whatever it was, since—

"Hello there!"

Their neighbor, Ms. Colwell, waved at them while she watered yellow trumpet-shaped flowers. Ms. Colwell made a habit, somehow, of always watering her flowers just when Leah got home each day. Leah reflected on how strange that was, given that Leah would arrive home at different times nearly every day, depending on if she had practice or might go to Luci's to do homework or with her friends straight to Stonethrow.

"That was the last day, wasn't it?" asked Ms. Colwell.

"Yes, ma'am." Leah made a show of looking relieved. "One more year to go!"

Ms. Colwell smiled, brightened by the flowers she watered. "But first, a *whole* summer! I'd tell you to stay out of trouble, but I think it's your sister that needed to hear that. *You* might need to find some trouble."

"Don't worry," said Brit. "I'll point her in the right direction."

Just as they opened the door, their mother was coming toward it. She looked tired most days lately, and today was not an exception. In fairness, it was the type of tired that only a loved one would notice—a sluggishness in her movements. Her red-brown eyes were still burning bright, though, and when she saw them open the door, she smiled wide and caught them both with a hug. "Hey, girls." She kissed them. "Did you tell her about breakfast?"

"Oh, no. I completely forgot," answered Brit.

"I'm off tomorrow," she said, turning to Leah.

And Leah wanted to take off her backpack and show her mom how well she'd done, but of course, there wasn't time.

"We'll have breakfast, and you can tell me all about your last day. Okay?"

Leah nodded and smiled.

"Okay. We'll have waffles! Brit, can you go to Creekshire's and get some milk? Thanks, Duck. Love you."

They told her they loved her, and she hugged them again and left out the door, closing it behind her.

The emptiness of the house set in as Leah heard her mom's car pull out of the driveway, though her home was filled with odds and ends from days when their mother still enjoyed her nights in town. Her mother had collected memorabilia from different acts and musicians that performed at the Diamond Gambit; some things left from old friends that had long since moved on, some were from old flames, though her mother wouldn't admit it. She'd only call them *friends. Maybe that's all they were,* thought Leah, though the idea of sex with a friend was strange to her. But she wondered if those words even had the same meaning to her mom, who'd been single since Leah could remember. Brit would encourage her to find someone, in a playful sort of way, but to hear her mother tell it, she just didn't have the time.

Brit roamed into the kitchen, and Leah went down the short hallway off the living room to the end, her bedroom. It was littered with band posters, old cameras, and photos she'd taken. Some of them she'd gotten framed by Andrew's dad, in cherry-red frames. She had a particle board bookshelf that was mostly filled with old comics and stories from her childhood but also some astrology and astronomy books as well. But when Leah walked into her room, her eyes went straight to her skateboard; her body quickly followed. She slid her bag to the floor and flipped the board around to look at the *Bilberry Drive* sticker on the bottom. They weren't a very popular band; they were a bit unpopular actually. She'd never met someone else who'd heard of them, until today. As she went out into the hall, she wondered what Kris's favorite song might be.

Brit was standing in the kitchen with her phone in her hand, already looking a bit bored with being home. Brit was always like that, as far as she could remember. Leah thought that if her sister had a hobby, it was people, and when there weren't people around, she had a tendency to get bored quickly. But then her eyes got wide.

"What?" asked Leah.

"Oh. nothing."

"Nothing?"

Brit looked at her, considering. "It has to do with *he who shall not be named*."

Leah's heart sped up against her will, but she tried hard not to show it. "So?"

Brit shrugged and nodded. *Come look then.*

Tray Pilson, one of Brit's *friends* from a couple years back, a good-enough guy, posted:

> Allied now owns the entire railroad, the buyout of the Southern American Railway was just finalized. Wake up! Late stage capitalism is here. Check out this article if you care about the people more than the country, more than capital:
>
> Reddit.com/r/BuriedInTheValley/
> Railwaymonopoly

"Tray was always *imaginative*," said Brit. "Sounds like something from a cartoon. I can picture Jim Grayson with a mustache, the Monopoly man mustache. Or like Principal Coven."

Brit laughed, and Leah faked one.

In truth, Jim Grayson had seemed a very normal man. He clung to family dinners that happened every Sunday after church, which Leah joined them for on more than several occasions. At the time, she'd called him Mr. Grayson and thought of him primarily as Aaron's dad. He enjoyed cooking, football, and played tennis at The Height's Terrace, a country club. At the dinner table, he was at ease and charming and funny. Aaron didn't find him as funny as Leah did, but—a feeling of vertigo drifted through her with the temperament of a lazy breeze as her memory produced images of Aaron's face when she laughed at his dad's jokes, contemplation. Then she was back in the car as he forced her head into the seat, and then she was back in the kitchen with Brit.

She forced the thought away by moving on to the next thing.

"Do you wanna come to Stonethrow?"

Brit shrugged. "Why not."

They went back out the red roundtop door, and as Brit was making her way to the car, Leah asked, "You wanna walk?"

Brit frowned. "It's so hot, though."

Leah stood in the driveway, looking at Brit, saying please through her movements.

"Fine," Brit said, rolling her eyes.

They started down Salem's cracked sidewalk. Here and there, grass poked through the breaking cement. Leah looked at the houses they passed, wondering what it might be like inside of them. The neighborhood also had a spirit, or so Leah believed. In the area of town they lived, Deepmoor, every house had once been a haughty upper-middle-class home. Leah wondered what they might've looked like just a hundred years ago: fresh with life and an optimistic future in up-and-coming Valleyport. In restaurants nearby, black-and-white photos of locals hung on the walls. They told a story of a place that used to exist, a community that once was. They passed a lot with a broken foundation, then a boarded-up business—maybe a restaurant—and then an abandoned home with a broad second-story balcony.

Brit walked with her phone in front of her. Her eyes were on the screen. And there seemed to be something in her eyes, satisfaction or wonder or curiosity. Leah considered checking her Instagram or her TikTok. She hadn't been on in a while. But she knew she'd see everyone talking about the party he was throwing. She decided against it.

They reached the hills of Stonethrow. The paved walking path snaked through the hills and over a crevasse of a drainage ditch that led into a massive pipe. Deepmoor flooded easily in storms, but anyone would think the drainage ditch was a gross overestimation until the rain came. Three pavilions with stone picnic tables formed a triangle at opposite ends of the park. One was entirely obscured from view by the old oaks of Stonethrow Park. Even though the day was beautiful, there was almost no one out. It was hot, though, so that could have been the reason.

Brit lifted her phone and grabbed Leah's waist, pulling her in. She took a selfie. It happened so fast, yet Leah's reaction was automatic. She smiled, straightened, adjusted her hips, her cheeks, her brow, her arms, her stance, and then there was the fake sound of the shutter. Her stomach turned.

"Let me see."

"Don't worry. You look gorgeous. I'm putting it on my Story."

The verbiage of that sentence hadn't sounded off until just then. *On* my Story, not *in* my Story.

"Hey, Leah!"

The call came from across the park, from a group of skaters. The one that called out was stocky and wore red-and-black kneepads—Jason. He'd flipped up his board as the rest of the gang, Andrew, Talley, and Bailey turned to see her. Leah went to them, and Brit followed. The sound of Brit's cigarette tin opening and closing came just after her.

Leah once spent all of her time at Stonethrow with Andrew, Talley, Bailey, and Jason, and those memories flooded her mind as she hugged them. Jason was her first crush and kiss. Bailey, her best friend, was the person she smoked her first and last cigarette with. Andrew and Talley were basically brothers to her; they kept her laughing. She looked at them, reminded of how much time had already passed between them, how much they'd all changed. They went to the same middle school, but then Jason went off to Clement's for high school, and Talley went to Evergreen, and then...

As Andrew gave her the Cherry Limeade he got her, Bailey said, "So...I'm not gonna be at Larue next year." She was speaking to the group but turning her hazel gaze on Jason. "I'm gonna be joining Jason at Clement's."

Leah's disbelief must have shown—the look of a whole year passing in a sentence—because then Bailey said, "Oh, come on. We all knew it would happen eventually. I couldn't keep up at Larue anyway."

Leah wanted to say that she could if she wanted to, but they'd already been down that road. Leah tried to help Bailey get the proper study habits that suited her, and when it proved not enough, Mrs. Figaro tried even harder.

"Mrs. Figaro thinks it's a good idea," Bailey added. "She says when things aren't working, and you've tried as hard as you can, that you just have to switch things up."

Still...

"I'm still going to be at Larue," said Andrew. "I skimmed by, but hey, *D*s get degrees."

His long nose and flushed cheeks rose in a proud grin.

"It's a diploma, my man," said Jason.

"Oh, yeah."

"Well," said Talley. He stepped forward, his shaggy auburn hair held back in a half ponytail. "I had to opt out. I'm getting a job so I can afford to take you out somewhere nice, Brit." He winked at her.

The rest of the group laughed except Brit. She rolled her eyes as she blew out a plume of smoke. Then she went and sat at the nearby pavilion with her phone in her hand.

"You really gotta knock it off with that. She's gonna kick your ass one day," said Leah.

"I sure hope so," Talley responded, dropping his board and taking off down a hill.

"He's serious, you know?" said Andrew when Talley had made it out of earshot.

"About my sister? I doubt it."

"No. About dropping out. He's getting a job to help out with his sisters. His parents weren't expecting a baby, let alone twins."

Leah didn't say anything. Ironically, she wished it were ten years from that day, when she'd be done with college and making enough money so she could help. Right then, she didn't know what to say. And besides, for now, the bubble that was Stonethrow with her friends was still there for her, for her to feel warm, innocent, and safe. *Everything is in a constant state of change,* she reminded herself. *It's normal.* That helped, but not much. But all was right when she set down her board and started to skate with her friends. One after another, they each did the same and rode the serpentine path of Stonethrow Park. Beams of fresh sunset cascaded through the oaks as the group laughed and enjoyed the evening.

*****

They were on Highway 2, headed out of Valleyport, when Rob turned to Kris.

"What'd you do that for?"

"What?" He thought he knew but didn't want to assume.

"Well... You could have gotten her number or something."

If Rob were a book—which he is not even compatible with the comparison—he would be a book that Kris knew cover to cover. Sure, to most everyone else, Rob seemed complex, but it was that people had the tendency to romanticize him. And he would grow bigger and bigger in their minds. That isn't to say that there wasn't something special about, Rob but it could be condensed down to *he knows who he is.* Kris believed that was all that made Rob unreadable to most everyone else. They were expecting twists and turns and revelations, but Rob's power came from the inverse: his simplicity of direction. Rob wanted only to play the music he made to the best of his ability. This conversation was not about Kris; it was about Rob.

"There just wasn't a spark, you know? Plus, she's one of those girls that prefers people to books. *Strange.*"

Rob tried to hide a smile, but it showed for a fraction of a moment.

"Really? No spark?"

Kris shook his head. Okay, there was *something*, but he couldn't tell Rob that, because then he wouldn't be able to explain to his brother why he couldn't have *that* with anyone. This was another thing he agreed with his father about: *Telling Rob would only make his life worse.* Rob was there when he was young and didn't know how to hide what was going on in his mind, but Rob believed all the hallucinations and emotional outbursts just stopped when their mother died. But that was all irrelevant anyway. *This is about Rob.*

"No. Nothing. What about you and Brit?"

Rob's eyes dulled a little. "She's *great*, but...no spark, I guess."

There's never been a spark, has there? Kris thought about saying that, about starting the conversation for Rob, but it seemed best to wait until Rob was ready to bring it up himself.

After a lull, Rob turned the volume up and handed his phone to Kris. A wordless gesture that meant *pick the next song.* Kris knew exactly what he wanted to hear: "Between Zeroes" by *Bilberry Drive.*

Kris reflected on how a song, sound waves, had a way of shifting how he saw the world, the same way that light waves do. The pines behind the rural homes and trailer parks swayed to a rhythm, as did the hills, and the shapes of the clouds took on silly forms: one was the Mad Hatter with a devil's grin. Rob's contemplative face dissolved into careless speculation. And while the waves moved the world, all of those things remained, then the song ended.

Rob turned the volume back down as the next song started.

"Hey...I want to talk to you about something."

Something serious. Kris pushed the volume button; the music cut off, and he gave his brother his undivided attention or as much as he could, given the habit of his mind to wander.

"Alright. What is it?"

They pulled into the front yard of their house and parked in front of the garage. Eggshell-colored panels reflected light so that it was hard to look at in the sun.

"I'm—well, Nick and Wesley and Liam and I are planning to move...to California. I didn't think we would need to, but I've come around to it. Ball Point Pin needs to be in a bigger city, with more venues, more shows, more people in the industry."

That expression of contemplation was back. Rob's sharp eyebrows curved down.

This wasn't what Kris was expecting him to say, but he did know it was coming. Once again, he'd be a book that Kris read cover to cover, and Rob left his computer open to apartment listings in California. *And* it was just the natural progression of becoming a professional musician. Rob had to go where he could be heard.

"Good."

Rob turned, surprised.

"Good?"

"Well, yeah…" Kris searched for the right words, knowing his brother was hesitant to leave him and their dad alone, knowing that it would be even more difficult for Rob to leave. "You have something to say. I think it's something that people need to hear, but even if it isn't, it's most important just to say it. It's just the way you are, Rob. I'm proud…I'll miss you, but mostly I'll just be proud… And I'll expect to be mentioned when you win a Grammy."

Rob smiled; he laughed.

"I thought—I don't know. You'll be okay?"

Kris realized then that was what the Pizza Palace double date was about. He was pushing Kris to socialize, to make friends for when he was gone. *I can't.* Kris faked a big smile. "They have phones now, you know."

"Right," replied Rob.

They let the silence stand for a moment, and then Rob said, "Well, I've got to get to work, but I should beat dad home."

"Okay. Have a good shift."

Kris started to get out.

"Hey!" Rob said. "We should do something big this summer."

Kris turned to Rob. He was sitting with his hand hanging by the wrist on the steering wheel. His bladelike brows were raised in a seldom-used expression.

"Sure. We'll find something to get into. Have a good shift."

Kris got out, and Rob pulled away, back out onto the highway.

When the car was out of sight, Kris felt himself relax. They lived far out enough that Kris stopped to savor the sound of nothing and then the listless hum of close wildlife. He knew his father was still gone, at work. The house was empty, and for the first time all day, he could let his guard lower a little. Not completely, but still. Kris learned a long time ago that given the way his emotions overrode him, he had to be *observant*. Paying close attention to the details of everything was the only way not to lose control, and anything chaotic was to be avoided. His father taught him that people are chaos. They are unexpected. Even Rob, as well as he knew him, could throw him from the balance he had to maintain. So being alone was a haven.

He walked up the once-shimmering stone path in front of the garage and up to the front porch. He walked past the tree and the eroded planter that read *Love grows here*, and the gnomes, which Kris found a bit freaky. They were just too happy to be there, waiting in stopped motion.

The front door creaked as he stepped into the cool air of the house, and the living room waited quietly beyond. It was decorated with family photos and lovely little phrases or quotes, usually about love and family. Across the living room, in the kitchen, eye level when he walked in, was the family photo. He, Rob, his father and mother huddled around the tree out front, where the gnomes waited. All of them were smiling wide, even Kris. Rob and Dad on the right. Kris and Mom on the left. It was the center point of the baker's rack, the focal point. He looked away.

Kris dropped his bag just inside his bedroom door. There was no need to change; he was already in his boots.

Then he went back to the kitchen and grabbed a bottle of water. The blearing sunrays pushed in through the kitchen windows as he prepared. Inside was so much cooler than outside that it was jarring. Just looking out the window, he could see the heat radiating down on the backyard and the forest beyond. He'd read an article that claimed this summer, the average temperature would be over 120 degrees. Just for the perspective, he then read an article about how climate change was a myth perpetuated by the left. Everything was political. *At least there will be plenty of daylight,* he thought. Rob wouldn't be home till hours after dark, same as his father.

Time enough to get something done. He pushed out the back door.

Outside, Kris thought about his dreams, about the garden in his dreams. Then he picked up the chain saw and the axe just inside the garage door and headed for the gate beyond the fig tree.

CHAPTER 5

The Valleyport Witch

Kris swung the axe in a wide arc, leveling it right at the base of the chopping block. *Thwack!* The halved pieces stayed in place, a few splinters of heartwood and pith still held onto their severed halves. And Kris knocked one off, turned the other, and swung again. *Thwack!* His shoulders were tight. Soreness gave way to a dull sensation of endurance, and his heart found a pace to keep. Sweat soaked his clothes, occasionally fell into his eyes to be blinked away, and turned the ends of his hair into collections of strands.

With each swing, he couldn't help but think of Freddie, which he'd decided was a good thing. The more he thought of swinging that hammer into Freddie's brow, caving in his eyes, and the terror he saw, the rasping sound of blood in lungs desperate to breathe, the less likely he was to allow himself to lose control again.

The breaths he took were in time with the beat of his heart, guided by his will.

Smoke curled in on itself over the pile of leaves and skinny twigs, bark, and vines. Between the axe strokes, he looked over at it, checking to make sure it was also still under his control, not burning the forest down.

Swing, thwack!

Kris knocked one-half off the block and stretched, surveying what he'd accomplished since the sun had retreated between the trees. The underbrush was gone. Only a few more small and withering trees remained in the copse of strong pines and oaks. He'd raked up the greater portion of leaves and added it to the slow-burning brush pile. Now, in the cleared-away places, patches of weeds and grass stood out from dark fertile soil. A couple of squirrels chased each other on the forest floor, and redbirds twittered overhead. This place would do.

In his mind's eye, he shaped the garden around the great tree in its center. Of course, the one he was trying to create here would be nothing compared to the one in his dreams. But he'd latched onto the idea of having a flower garden here, too—a place to read and be alone—where he'd carve out his own sanctuary. The garden of his dreams hadn't needed to be made. He'd found it years ago after running from the creature. Could this garden accomplish a similar effect in the real world?

With no warning, with no way to track how his mind made the quick leaps to get there, Freddie was standing in the garden with him, his face broken and a catching sound in his throat. Just as quickly, he was gone. But then Kris was low to the ground. His palms and knees pressed into the dirt in front of the great tree. Trying to settle whatever he'd brought on with his thoughts, he closed his eyes, sat back on his feet, and pressed his dirt-covered palms against his ears. Then he was just the breath. Kris had developed this method in elementary school, when all of his father's advice failed, and while it didn't improve his social status, it did work to balance him out. His reasoning: *If he was still breathing, then he was still alive. And if he couldn't see or hear what frightened him, then it could be that those things weren't there at all.* That thought would make him laugh normally, because he wasn't afraid of dying; he just didn't want to see what waited for *him* on the other side. Maybe it was only the dark and the monster and more running, but maybe it was nothing at all.

As always, the episode passed. He got up, let his heart slow, and then went back to work.

*****

The curtains were drawn, thick curtains, and faint light from a thumbnail moon crept in along its edges. No stars in the sky above the backyard, only a bloated and dark-blue space. Leah's bedroom normally had more stars than the sky, but the planetarium Aaron had gotten her was in her nightstand drawer, which she'd not opened since putting it there. And her laptop was shining bright anyhow.

On the screen: tabs and tabs of local photographers sites, Instagrams, and Facebooks. Her own photos were open in Adobe, and she clicked back to them, doing comparisons when she found an image she liked. The first step was to identify what element of the photo she wanted to emulate, and the second was how to do it. And though she'd been at it for hours, since she'd gotten home from Stonethrow, she wasn't tired enough to give sleep a try. But every now and again, her thoughts would wander from the picture on her screen to the sky to the planetarium.

She sighed. She adjusted in the bed, throwing the covers back and rubbing her eyes. The image on the screen was of a family at the duck pond, and the lighting was *absolute perfection.*

Never mind the cherub-cheeked kid holding his mother's hand and the dad, with his arm around the both of them. The light went around all of them and came back around to their faces, softening their features.

If I can figure this out...

She could start her own *studio*. Well, she could start her own photography business. Nothing big. Just so she could make *some* money, a little to help her mom with the bills over the summer and maybe enough that she could buy toys for Talley's sisters.

Her phone vibrated: a Facebook messenger notification. Her hand hovered over the phone for a moment, but she did pick it up and look. It was from Brett Miles, and there *it* was—the photo. Her naked body, his hand, and—and her hair. The message:

> Is this really you? I guess I didn't realize you were this kind of person.

SERMON OF THE DIVERS

Leah turned the phone over, and this time, she didn't want to cry. She wanted to throw the phone across the room. But this wasn't the first message she'd received that was like this, so she turned the phone over and went back to her work. Though her mind fought her, remembering all those times she'd told Aaron that she loved him, she eventually resubmerged into her work.

Then she was only thinking about the light, the depth of field, the rule of thirds.

And when she was so far away from those thoughts, she got up and removed the blue planetarium from the nightstand drawer. Not looking at it, she tiptoed down the hall and crept out the front door. She couldn't help but notice the swelling blue of the sky as she tossed the planetarium into the trash can.

And she went right back to work.

*****

The old gate finally squalled, so Kris took out his headphones. The brush pile was already burnt out, and Kris was quartering the last of what he'd cut with the chain saw. And his father's shadow stopped where the old garden used to be, the vegetable garden, just on the other side of the tree line. Kris's eyes were well adjusted to the night, and he watched his dad survey those old furrows and then move on. His dad did that every time he had to cross that gate.

"Kris?"

"Over here."

He was still in his "uniform," a pair of blue jeans, a long-sleeve button up, steel-toed boots. His father had the build of someone who'd spent their life working with heavy equipment, with forearms as big as Popeye's. Bags under his eyes made him seem perpetually tired, but they were always there, and his dad was rarely too tired not to pay attention.

"I thought we talked about this. You can't work with an axe and chain saw in the dark."

Kris got in a last swing and let the axe stay in the wood. He sniffed and wiped the sweat from his face.

"I was just finishing up, Dad. I can still see pretty good."

His dad didn't respond.

"Got it. Won't let it happen again."

Kris wasn't sure if that was true or not. It was hard not to do something once he got it in his mind, especially considering how many things he had to avoid completely. It was either this or work on the go-kart or read.

"How was school?"

"It was good. Work?"

"Good."

Kris began gathering his tools to move them back inside. His dad grabbed the chain saw before he could get to it and stood in his way.

"That's it... Good? Wasn't it the last day?"

"Yeah. I just read."

"Oh."

Then they just stood there, and Kris knew his dad was waiting for more, but there really wasn't anything to tell. Nothing bad happened. Outside of that, what was there to tell? He wasn't a part of anything at school, and his dad knew that. And the paranoia that his dad might've found out about Freddie had gone away months ago. No one looked for someone like Freddie, and how would his dad find out about that anyhow?

"Mrs. Figaro told me I needed to read the summer reading."

It was small, but maybe it was enough.

"Son, I know that it's hard to...to be like we have to be. But you have to make the best of it."

Kris looked around at what he'd done in the woods, the clearing.

"I know. That's what I'm doing."

His dad nodded. "You just don't seem as...I don't know. You just seem different lately. Are you sure nothing is going on? You can talk to me, son."

Kris put his free arm around his dad. "I know. You and Rob are both losing it. I'm fine."

His dad hugged him back, and they turned to the house in the distance.

"So you haven't had any episodes lately?"

Kris shook his head. He'd learned that telling his dad about the episodes did little to help them along, so he'd only tell him when he had to. Besides, one day, his father would be gone too, or he would, and then he'd have to be able to stand on his own feet. Every episode would be on him to handle. He might as well start early, get used to it.

"No."

"You don't think they stopped, do you?"

A test.

"No. I know they never go away."

"You're a good one. Now, if I could only get that brother of yours to see reason... He's too much like me, so it'll prolly never happen."

Kris understood the skin-deep reasoning for his dad's comments about Rob, and he also knew that underneath, his dad was just worried about Rob. And he damn sure didn't know how to show it.

"You used to say whatever we did, be the best at it. Didn't matter if we were digging ditches. Well, he isn't digging ditches, but he's going to be the best."

His dad cracked a smile, a rare sight.

"Yeah. What about you?"

"I'm gonna dig ditches they'll talk about in a thousand years."

It wasn't so much a calculated move, just a mechanism. Kris knew what he had to say to get further from the topics that his dad was just talking about. But his attempt at humor was a clear failure, made apparent by the thousand-yard stare on his father's face.

"What?" asked Kris.

"You've only got one more year."

Kris felt his heart sink a little. "I know. It was just a joke."

They reached the back porch just then, and his dad looked as if he were about to speak but didn't.

Rob was coming in the front at the same time. And as soon as he saw them, he started to ask dad about the buyout, saying how he'd heard the news from Nick, up at Mason's. He was stony eyed for a moment, but he blinked it away and said, "We don't think it'll change much."

Kris doubted that but didn't say anything. There was an easy-to-follow trend to the bigger buyouts of the last ten years, and even though Kris was a kid for most of those, he still knew what to expect. He was just happy that it was Grayson who'd done this one; he had a tendency to cut *less* of the staff in the first year. He waited until tempers cooled, and then he gutted the rest.

"Well, Malcolm came into Mason's today, looking for a beginner guitar for his son, and he said there was no way they could run the railroad without Iron Mike anyway," said Rob.

That stony eyed look again.

"Everyone's replaceable."

Rob refused to accept that, but their dad didn't argue it with him. Kris was surprised that he agreed with Rob on this one. Sure, everyone was replaceable, but anyone could see how hard his dad worked—twice as productive as what they paid him for. People who know how to make money don't fire someone like that. Period. They'd use him until he can't be used anymore. Then they'd fire him.

Kris started thinking about what his dad said, about how he didn't have any idea what he wanted to do after school ended. For the longest time, he had it in the back of his mind that he'd be dead by the time it was over. And he hadn't thought that for a good reason either, only because he figured that creature in his dreams would have caught him by now. And for some reason, he believed it when it told him that it would end him before he even began. He knew that was irrational, but then he started looking around at the world and thinking about where it was heading. The preacher at the old church used to say it was the end-times. Maybe it was. Earth's climate was headed for a catastrophic disaster that nobody seemed to mind driving toward. If a man dumps all his used oil and trash in his backyard, and no one is around to see it, does it really have an effect on the environment? Kris figured the answer was obvious, but apparently not. Never mind the much greater negligence of production and industry, all on the behalf of consumers.

I mean, if everyone—all of humanity—pissed in the same hole in the ground, do you think they could fill the hole?

SERMON OF THE DIVERS

"Kris?"

"What?"

"I said, did you get my message about the festival?"

"What?"

Rob gave him a look. "Check your phone."

Kris patted his pockets and realized his phone wasn't there. "Hang on," he said. "I must have left it out back."

Kris went out the back door again and jogged across the yard. He slowed at the fig tree, looking to the dark star-dusted sky. They were especially bright, not having to compete with the light of a waning moon.

At the gate, before he pushed it in, he saw a figure again. He expected—was sure—that it was Freddie, but it wasn't. The figure was lean and tall, maybe even bony. His face was bearded, and he wore overalls with a purple shirt underneath. One of his hands was placed on the tree, and his head was bowed to it, and the other hand held a long smooth stick; it was gleaming in the night, polished to shine.

Normally, as any rational person, Kris might've been put off by a stranger in his backyard in the middle of the night. But there were two things that kept him from being even remotely worried. One was that he could see the wrinkles of age on the man from here. Two was more ephemeral, a sense of presence, and that presence he felt was meek. Kris even got the impression he'd caught the old man in a prayer of a sort.

When Kris pushed the gate in—and it squealed as usual—the old man turned to look with curiosity alight in his eyes. And he said, inquiringly, "Hey-o. Sorry, I didn't mean to scare you."

"Hello."

As Kris moved past the old furrows and to the tree line of his new garden, the old man smiled at him. His smile was genuine and filled his eyes.

"Who are you?" Kris asked. Though he didn't get the sense he should be scared of this old man, it was still strange to meet a—well, a stranger in your own backyard.

The old man extended a leathery hand. "Shane. Yourself?"

Kris got close enough and shook the calloused hand. "Kris."

"Sorry to show up in the middle of the night in your backyard, but I wanted to see what you were working on. And... Well, this is where and when you said to meet you. So... Here I am."

Kris was puzzled for a moment. Oddly, though, he felt more sleepy than frightened. His confusion must have shown because Shane continued, "I know, I know. You don't remember. I'll spare you the long explanations and the whole *'But I don't even know who you are'* bit. I remember you because I knew you before all the running started, back before that monster chased you across time and space, and... Well, you...I don't mean to get all emotional, but *you changed my life.*"

Kris felt lightheaded as he asked the only question he could muster, "What?"

"Ah, I expected this to take a couple of visits. You said you'd be *confused.* And I know what your dad's been up to. Can't imagine that's helped. Tell you what. Your phone is right there, on the ground. You take it, and I'll meet you here tomorrow night. Sound good? Great. Get some rest, and have some dreams."

The old man turned then and walked around the tree.

"Um... Hello?" Kris said.

Now he was getting scared. His pulse was getting away from him as he struggled to control his breath. Still, he managed to circle around the tree, staying as far as he could. But the old man was gone; only the clearing lay beyond the tree.

Kris dropped to his knees to catch his breath. He closed his eyes and covered his ears. It was not a good sign to have to do this more than once in a day, but he couldn't even remember the last time he saw anyone that wasn't there that wasn't Freddie. And *never* had he been able to touch someone that wasn't there. But Shane had been—

No.

Kris continued breathing.

Not possible. It's all just stress. Just...

He'd read about PTSD, thinking that he might have it after what he did to Freddie. That's how he knew to expect to see Freddie, but not a stranger, not an old man named Shane. Maybe the hallucinations that his grandfather and father passed on to him were getting worse. Before he spiraled into thoughts, wondering what he could trust and what he couldn't—*what was real?*—he kept breathing and telling himself that as long as he was breathing, he was alive. He was real.

As his thoughts settled, he decided that Shane was another hallucination, but that didn't mean that he was losing control. He'd just reasoned out that Shane wasn't real, after all. That meant he still knew what was real and what wasn't.

With those thoughts to stabilize him, he grabbed his phone and started for the house. Desperate for something to distract his mind from what he'd just seen, he looked at the message his brother had sent him. It was a picture of a post on Facebook, a reminder that the Cypress Festival was tomorrow.

When he got inside, Kris tried to let Rob down easy. There was no way that he could go to Cypress Festival after whatever just happened in the garden, but—

"Come on," Rob pleaded. "I know it's late notice, but Harry just called me while I was at Mason's. There was a scheduling error, and they meant to call everyone, but we were lucky enough to fall between the cracks. Ball Point Pin is playing, though. No big deal, but it's probably going to be only a few this summer. We've got to workshop some new music."

Kris knew that was a lie, but it was one of the good ones. Their dad might've stepped in normally and said something to get Rob to back down, but for whatever reason, he didn't this time. He just sat in his big gray chair, looking back and forth between them, waiting to see who'd end up giving in.

The problem was that, yes, it was a tradition. A tradition that started before they were a family, when their dad and mom used to go every year. Then it was all of them, and Kris could barely remember those times that they went together, the four of them. But then after their mom died, and a few years passed, Rob decided that it was going to be something that he and Kris did together every year. The only reason it snuck up on him was because they were having it early this year, something about a scheduling error.

"Besides, it's a tradition. Then you can seclude yourself to the backyard for the rest of summer."

Kris sighed. "I'm just not feeling great. Let me sleep on it, eh?"

Rob nodded, victory in his eyes.

An hour later, after a shower and a quick dinner—Hamburger Helper, he made enough for everyone—Kris was in his bedroom, lying on his bed, trying to figure out how to get out of going to the festival. But it didn't matter what argument he came up with. No matter how convincing or true, Rob's disappointed face appeared and ruined it. The only good news was that being distracted by that had left him little room to think of Shane. And he was tired anyway. He dragged *The Farwoods March* off its place on his nightstand.

The book was written in twelve-point, Times New Roman, double-spaced, and bound by the three rings of a battered old binder. It was a *beast*. Well over 250,000 words, and if you asked Kris, it was perhaps the greatest novel ever written. And that was saying a lot considering how much he'd read and that the book didn't have an end. But it also would have to be noted that the author was his own mother, and he'd been rereading it since he could remember. At present, he barely had to look at the words before he fell right into the story.

> *She was fond of the expression "cosmic accident." The idea that something so much bigger than herself was likely to fail as spectacularly as herself. And since her mother had gifted her the expression in regard to a father she'd never met, Pandora used it often in her own thoughts. "Poor man, even a witch's touch couldn't keep the cruel fates off of him. He seemed to attract their attention, a walking cosmic accident."*
>
> *Her mother'd been organizing hundreds of mason jars filled with her painstakingly gathered ingredients. Pandora's favorite was the crushed eggshells for no other reason than her mother let her crush them. She'd just placed a dried and broken*

shell on the mortar and was about to start on it with the oak pestle. Being a hedgewitch, almost all of her mother's tools were made from the local forest around their home. Some of them belonged to her mom's mom, another hedgewitch, and were still, on occasion, used by the disgruntled old crone.

"But he was as good of a mortal as you're like to find," she said.

Her flowing dress of the color her distinct division of the trade was like to use: a well-worn shade of green. She was on a rickety wooden step stool, talking all the while she opened jars and sniffed them, confirming their contents.

"What happened to him?" asked Pandora, as she twisted the pestle and crushed the shells.

"Poor man. Roasted himself with a welder. Tsk, tsk, tsk. On your birthday too. That's why I overcook the pork every year, in memory of him." She cackled.

That was her mother's way. That was the hedgewitch way. A grim sense of humor was essential because life has always been a bit grim. It is imperative to look at nature for what it is; that's what her mom would say. And the key was to, in equal measure, gather the good from the natural world and make proper use of it.

And before he finished the page, he was shutting his eyes, eager to dream.

CHAPTER 6

The Dreaming

At three in the morning, Leah's eyes were hex-lined red and dry as raisins. Her thoughts were slush and gel, and she knew she could finally drift off to sleep. But she kept her laptop close in case she woke in the middle of the night, as she often did. As her mind, full of worries and hopes and consideration from the day she'd had, began to slur her logical thinking into completely unrelated topics and ideas, suddenly her mind was giving her the clear image of a coconut tree, particularly the germination pores on a single hairy fruit. The coconut consumed her thoughts and acted as a gateway to yet another, an ocean made of bubblegum balls. What a marvelous idea it was too! The clarity of her thought gave way to the darkness of dreams. Soon, logic was gone (waking logic anyway), and Leah was no longer herself. She was dreaming. And in doing so, she no longer precisely remembered the problems of the day; the conscious became the subconscious, leaving what?

Aaliyah opened her eyes in a dream.

She stood on a path made of brick in a forest unlike anything she'd ever seen before. The trees were taller than the great sequoias, but their boughs twisted in the gloom appearing to be frozen basilisks. Bark as deep dark as the night sky but leaves that indecisively illuminated the forest around her, turning colors of the aurora borealis. And the grass was perfect blades, and flowers with petals and bulbs of extraordinary color and shape rested against the trees and in hanging gardens, slung around the arms of the trees with vines that pulsed crimson. Everywhere she turned, fireflies drifted through the gloom, with as many colors as the leaves of the trees. All around her was the hum of a living forest, the call of cicadas, the buzz of life.

Aaliyah looked around in wonder and amusement. Her eyes devoured all they could. When she turned around, she realized she was at the end of the brick path, staring at a familiar shape. A red roundtop door, bound in iron.

Her inner thoughts became her words.

"Where am I?"

The air was too crisp to be a dream, her body too filled with sensations. If anything, she felt more than she did in the real world, but her resting mind dampened thoughts of that other world. That other world was a vague dream in comparison to this one.

"Hey-o."

The voice was a whisper in her mind, a thought more than a word.

"Who's there?" asked Aaliyah.

She turned about again, but as far as she could tell, she was the only one around. Unless someone or something *was* hiding behind the trees. Yet she was unafraid. Incapable of it. This forest was filled with the feeling of hearth, of home, as was the voice.

"I could ask you a similar question."

Aaliyah hesitated. "I'm Aaliyah. Who are you?"

For a moment, there wasn't an answer. Then, "I'm the Tree. This is my forest... Well, this is the forest I've been given charge of. No one owns the forest, of course. Now that we've had introductions, would you mind going back out the way you came?"

"You're a tree?"

"I am *the* Tree. Not *a* tree. They call *me* the Great Tree *or* the Heart Tree *or* the Tree of Knowledge." *The Tree continued indignantly,* "A tree? Honestly... What if I just said, 'Oh, you're an Aaliyah.' How perfectly quaint."

Though Aaliyah thought to herself that it might be true, she was only an Aaliyah and that there were undoubtedly more people named Aaliyah out there, she kept that to herself. "I'm sorry. I didn't mean to offend you...Tree."

Another pause.

"Never mind that. It's fine. I lost my temper. But we're not supposed to have guests, I'm quite sure. Or at least, I think I'm sure. Could you be a daisy and go back out the way you came?"

Aaliyah looked around, then back at the door, and she bit her lip.

"Why can't you have guests?"

There was a sigh in her mind.

"Are you stalling, or do you actually want to know?"

"Can't it be both?"

Oddly, Aaliyah could feel the tree smiling. It was as if the joy came from within herself, almost a laugh.

"You are very wise, little one. It certainly can be both or neither. So which is it?"

"Both," she replied. "I just… This place is beautiful. *It reminds me of something, but I can't quite place it, but it's almost as if I've been here before. I wish I could—"*

Leah couldn't remember the word for what she wanted to do. A word from the other world.

"I wish I could look around. And…I'm curious. Why wouldn't anybody be allowed to come here?"

It didn't occur to her that one of the main reasons would be that it was, in fact, a dream. *And the Tree gave her no time to consider it further. Its voice was the wind between leaves but inside of her head, and it sighed, creating the sound of a gentle breeze.*

"Is beauty meant to be shared? Does it need *to be appreciated by as many as can see it? There are many in your world who believe that, I know. Is that what you believe?"*

Leah hesitated again.

It was as if her mind readied to retrieve memories with an answer but couldn't find the path to follow. The only thing left to her was her gut, which gave her a mix of yes and no, resulting in confusion and further hesitation.

"I…I think so. If it wants to be."

"If it wants to be… Hmm. I think we're talking about two different things. However, I will give you the abridged version, if you like?"

Aaliyah nodded, eager to hear the story.

"Very well. My creator was alone for most of time, as you would know it. The first companion they had was...not good company. But seeing another living creature, even one as devious as their companion, inspired my creator to make life. Here. In the...I think you would know the concept as a desert or an ocean. A wide immutable expanse of waves and depth. And then they drew us forth, from the waves. Then my creator went further and—"

The Tree's voice cut off, and Aaliyah inclined her head. "And?"

"Oh, dear. I believe he knows you're here."

Aaliyah's heart fluttered, and her body tensed. There was a change in the air. A sharp cold cut through the forest floor, leaving her shivering. And even the trees shook, and the grass bent to the icy wind. Life's hum muted and silenced in the wake of that instantaneous change. Then there was a total quiet, the quiet of a graveyard. Aaliyah turned about again, and she whispered as low as she could, "Tree? Hello?" But the only response she got was the dreadful sensation of intelligent eyes falling on her. And a fear as cold as the air settled in her, until she was unable to move, frozen by it.

Then there was another voice. A voice inside of her head, just as the Tree's, but this voice was vaguely familiar.

"How did you get here?"

Aaliyah turned back toward the path, and standing in its center was a familiar and not-so-familiar person.

"Kris?"

He both looked like himself and didn't, changed in so many ways but still...Kris. Only now his eyes were alight, his hair was an aura, and his lips almost bloodless. He regarded her for a moment, as if he were trying to make up his mind about something, as if he thought she was dangerous.

"Leah? Is that really you?"

She swallowed. The look in his eyes was one of warning, the color of veracity. Without much thought, relying on that mixing mass of emotion in her gut, she said, "I didn't think anyone else knew who Bilberry Drive was."

The tension in the air melted, and to a lesser degree, so did the warning in his eyes. His fingers wiggled, coming back to life. He blinked.

Aaliyah began to remember something about him; the look he displayed now was the one he often displayed. That same one that he wore when—what was it? Oh, that's right. The car. When he was fixing the car for them. The spark.

Not a spark of attraction but of curiosity and wonder and puzzlement. His clothes were the same as during the day, so he still had the band shirt on. With that look of confusion, he looked down at the shirt.

"Is it really you?" *he asked.*

"Kris, where are we?"

He looked around then, as if it were dawning on him that this must seem an extraordinary place for her. He smiled as he did. Whatever charm had shown in that smile he displayed in the other world, here it was multiplied.

"I honestly don't know," *he said.* "It's a garden. I...I didn't think anyone else could be here."

A look of surprise overtook him, and he took three quick steps toward her.

"You—you also ran from that...that creature? Is that how you got here?"

Leah shook her head. "What are you talking about?"

His expression fell. "I. Um. Never mind. I thought—nothing. How did you get here?"

Aaliyah began to speak then, about seeing the door in a dream. Then she told him how when she went to bed, that she just sort of ended up there, not through any intentions of her own. She did mention that the door was exactly the same as the one on the front of her house, only this one was bound in iron. Only, when she turned to show it to him, it was gone. Only the gloom of the forest stretched out ahead of them, going on, seemingly, forever. She watched him stare down the path, that spark again, and finally he turned to her.

"Do you remember who I am? Like...from the *other world?*"

She smiled. Something about his confusion was so amusing, especially in such a peaceful place.

"You're the weirdo from physics. I used to roll my eyes every time you raised your hand. Mrs. Baker never seemed to mind."

The light in his eyes softened, making him appear despondent.

"You also helped me steal barbecue pizza from an asshole with a mustache."

They both laughed. And before the laughter could end, she woke up.

All the memories of that otherworldly dream faded before she managed to open her eyes.

*****

A train had not passed the Tarnmont Bridge in sufficient enough time so that the wildlife wandered about on and around the train tracks. A doe and a fawn were grazing on the low-hanging leaves of the underbrush. The fawn was still young enough to be unsure of its footing on the ballast edge of the railway. Down the slope of the bridge, a water moccasin was moving up the blue bayou, chasing what it hoped would be a sizable frog. The trees were tall enough to reach over the tracks, where the tops of a train engine would be, and connect with the tree branches that were across from them. They formed a tunnel made of leafy hands until the bridge, where the trees parted for the bayou.

It was a relatively peaceful night for the creatures there, where the waterway intersected the Southern American Railway. The air was hot and humid, as most of the cold-blooded creatures would have it. A not entirely pitiful wheeze of a breeze meandered through the forest, and at some points along the way, it ruffled a few twiggy tree arms.

The doe and her fawn didn't mind the weather at all and, as far as she could sense, were perfectly safe from any predators. At first, she'd not liked the railway, but since she began to understand that it deterred predators as much as it did her own kind, she'd become quite fond of it. The clear space made it easier to see any danger, and the foliage around the bayou was a plentiful buffet. She was proud to pass the knowledge of such a place on to her fawn.

As they grazed, the dark waters rippled. Up from the black mirror came a shape and only a shape. A little boy, a child, with cherub cheeks, rose from the water and walked up onto the marshy banks.

Where skin should have been, the child was empty space, almost as if he were made of the black water itself, with skin like malleable glass. His eyes were violet and radiant, and he waddled the way that children do.

And when the doe and fawn caught sight of him, they were *disarmed* by his presence. With him, he brought the serenity of a forest without predators. In his gaze, beyond the violet light, was the rain-kissed greenery of a bountiful place. When the child extended his shapeless hand, the doe and her fawn came close enough to touch. No time to bleat.

Afterward, they stood in the gloom of the forest's edge. They began to march into the forest. Both overwhelmed with a new need, a new instinct to follow, to share their discovery with every creature in the forest.

CHAPTER 7

An Old Ode

The problem was that there were now three problems, and Kris woke in the morning with all three on his mind. The first was that he'd never seen another person in his dream before. He'd seen all kinds of creatures in the garden, living and intelligent creatures that he'd spend the night speaking to about how their family was doing or when their latest wonder would be finished or whatever happened to pop to mind. In the Dreaming, Kris didn't have to worry about losing control, so his conversations were long, and he savored every minute of them. The second problem was whether or not he'd really seen an old man named Shane in his backyard or not, and that one he was still pushing to the very back of his mind, in an old storage closet in the corner, next to his memories of getting poison ivy on his bits when he was a boy. The third but, in the way of immediacy, the biggest of them all was that going to Cypress Festival was a *tradition*. And even after all these years, he still couldn't reason out how to say no to Rob and watch him go it alone.

Still, the first of his morning was spent in contemplation of those three problems.

Other people dream about people, and it's just a version of them that their head makes up. That's probably all it is, he told himself. *And I know that I can't trust my head. If that old man shows up again,* then *I'll do something about it.* He had no idea what he'd do. *I...I have to go to Cypress Festival.* He did.

Knowing that he had to go was as close as he got to settling his mind in the wake of those three problems. He chalked the other two, Shane and Leah, up to just being your average flukes. Not two events that would repeat. Two lightning strikes that happened to hit in nearly the same spot at the same time. Strange but not unheard of. And he could make it through being around so many people for just one day. He was feeling good, aside from those three things. In fact, he was feeling *real* good. After the panic settled, he realized that he wasn't even sore from the work he put in the day before. Not a bit. If anything, he felt his body begging to go out and do it all over again. His muscles felt pliant but strong, even anticipating a day of work. Furthermore, his mind was at a steadier speed, a pace he could keep up with. A problem came in; a problem went out. No holding on.

He did remind himself that didn't mean much, but in the moment, it had impact.

Kris read away the morning. He'd woken up early, around six, and he finished *Eaters of the Dead* just after eight. He got that same familiar rush from finishing a book, a good book. And when he put it down, that was the first time he'd seen his bedroom all morning. It needed some attention. Dirty boots tracked all on the floors, a pile of laundry that needed to be done, and a general messiness that no one would be surprised to find in a teenage boy's room.

Kris started to clean. First, the bedsheets and comforter, then he picked up the cups strewn on his dresser drawers and desk, then just general straightening: putting away his books on his bookshelf, wiping everything with Clorox wipes.

After an hour or so, Rob appeared in the doorway, asking if he'd made up his mind about the Cypress Festival. Kris had a vacuum in his hand at that point.

"Had to clean your room, huh?"

Kris looked up at Rob, who was grinning knowingly.

"We don't *have* to go, you know?"

"No," Kris started, feeling guilty. "I want to go. I just saw that the room needed cleaning before we go. That's all."

Rob nodded. He lingered in the doorway for just long enough that Kris felt he should say something, and went.

After that, Kris's mind was on all the cleaning again until his father came in. Maybe an hour or so later.

"Got a sec?"

"Sure," said Kris, finishing making the bed.

"About the Cypress Festival..."

"I don't have to go, Dad. It's not a big deal."

His father's face was torn between emotions, searching in his eyes. He turned the chair to Kris's desk and sat down, and he clasped his hands together.

"It's not that. I just...I know that I was hard on you because of...you know. I just want you to know that even though you have to keep aware of what is going on, especially around people, it doesn't mean you should avoid them. I know that's backward from what I used to say, but...I was wrong. I've had to *become* a father with you and your brother. It's a learning process. Like with that *preacher.*"

What was going on?

Kris's father had changed over the years, but they hardly talked about how he was after Kris's mom died or before. Back then he was more of a disciplinarian, and in retrospect, Kris understood he was still reeling from the harsh upbringing of his own parents. In those days, his father didn't seem to know how to relax, especially when it came to Kris. Being too loud, being too rough on the furniture, listening to certain kinds of music—the lyrics seemed to be the deciding factor—or any number of seemingly benign questions would lead to his father's quick correction. His father rarely had to use the belt after the first couple of times. After that, Kris immediately caved in, on the verge of tears when his father's voice took on that edge of finality. But in truth, Kris was a handful, like all kids are. He was curious, far too imaginative, always asking *what-if* questions, and he could talk from the time the sun came up until it went down. The day his father found the composition book he kept, with the stories of *The Hollowman*, a fictional character that Kris made up, was also the day he got Kris into church. The Hollowman was the kind of antihero inspired by The Punisher and Deadpool and the creature that chased him in his dreams. A dark figure that solved the *bad* guys by ending them. Being that his father was raised in the church, he thought it might help deliver him from such *evil* thoughts. And since Kris had to go, Rob was forced to go. Neither of them liked Father Matthew, but Rob tuned him out, whereas Kris listened.

With all those thoughts in mind, Kris said, "I know, Dad. I'm fine, though, really. I know. *I know how it is.* I don't blame you."

Kris didn't. But he was sure to learn from everything that happened back then.

"I love you, son. Try to go out there and have some fun today. Just be careful. Okay?"

Kris nodded, and when his father removed his leather billfold from his pocket and offered Kris a hundred-dollar bill, he took it.

*****

Leah could hear Brit and their mom from her bedroom when she woke, after the dream faded. The sound of pleasant conversation was accompanied by the smell of waffles. Leah's stomach rumbled. She hadn't eaten since Pizza Palace the day before. Her headphones rolled around on the bed as she got up. They almost always fell out in the middle of the night. She put them in the dock to charge, and then she went to the kitchen for breakfast.

"Good morning. You're right on time," said her mom.

"Of course she is. It's waffles," Brit added.

Brit and their mother were working together to finish breakfast. Brit was removing the last of the waffles from the iron, while their mom poured fresh strawberries into the blender. The blender whirred and turned the strawberries to an aerated puree. Leah sat at the circular dining table in her usual spot by the window. Her place was already sat with silverware and her mug of coffee, the one with the moon on it.

"Well," started her mother, "don't keep me in suspense. How did you end the year?"

The report card, the grades, didn't seem as important this morning. Not while sitting in the kitchen with her mom and sister, about to eat Belgian-style waffles. A tradition that went back to Leah's grandpa, a carpenter, baker, and waffle maker. Every time her mother brought the first waffle of a special morning to the table, she said, "Waffles all the way!" It was something her grandfather used to say to her mother.

"I did alright. I did get a *B*, but Mrs. Figaro said it wasn't a big deal."

"It isn't," stated her mom.

"Nope," confirmed Brit, smiling as she placed the waffle down in front of Leah. "Waffles all the way!"

Brit had a way of becoming young around their mom, but the younger Brit never stuck around; she morphed back and forth between herself and that younger version, a girl who loved being on the cheerleading squad, who tried hard in middle school and early on in high school but couldn't quite keep up with her schoolwork. Leah both cherished and resented those moments.

"I know. I'm going to make up for it next year. I'll make sure of it. I also need to train harder this summer than I did last summer. Coach Byrne asked if I was still planning on being a part of the team next year."

"Really?" asked her mom.

"Yeah."

"She knows you are. You love track."

"That's the point. It was her way of saying I was slacking."

"Oh. Are you sure?"

"When I said yes, she told me I better get my time down then."

"You can handle that, no problem," said Brit, still in child form.

They all grabbed their mugs at the same time, which led to her mother laughing and doing a toasting motion. Leah's mom had one of those laughs that people said was contagious, and lit up the room, and bowled people over. She had that *thing*, like a starlet, where everyone wanted to know her. Brit once told Leah that their mom used to get all kinds of offers to go along with some of the shows that came through the Diamond Gambit. But of course, she couldn't go; she'd laugh them off.

"You okay, wild child?"

Occasionally, her mom called her that. Every time it made Leah feel she was the center of the universe.

"I was just thinking about something Andrew told me about Talley."

Her mother's expression changed, becoming solemn.

"I heard about that. I was thinking of baking something for them, getting you girls to take it over."

Brit morphed back to herself. "I'll go with you, but I'm not going inside. Mrs. Akselrod will talk me to death. She keeps on saying I should go work at the dog shelter."

"Oh, don't be like that," replied their mom with a look of reproach. "She's a sweet lady. She means well, and she thinks the world of you. Only told you that because she remembers you taking all those puppies home when you were a little girl and taking care of them until you found good homes for them."

Brit didn't say anything, but Leah could tell the memory was floating on the surface of her mind.

"We'll take it," said Leah.

Talley's parents, all of the Stonethrow skaters' parents, were family to her, uncles and aunts and sisters and brothers. She didn't need blood for that. Besides, the first thought that came to mind about Mrs. Akselrod was when she came over after Leah fell off her skateboard and skidded down Wallflower Hill. That day, Mrs. Akselrod must have spent two and half hours getting her wounds cleaned up and bandaged. Bits of gravel had lodged in her knees and forearms. Mrs. Akselrod said she must have been going as fast as a car. Leah knew she was. The whole world around her was a blur, a tunnel of colors leading down to the bottom of the hill.

"If you girls think of anything else we can do, let me know."

Then they talked for a while. First, their mom asked about that guy Brit was always talking about—Rob. Brit morphed back to that younger version of herself as soon as she asked that. Brit confessed that she didn't think there was anything to come of it. He just didn't seem to be very interested in her *in that way*. He was interested in her; she said that he asked about her life and remembered the details better than any guy she'd ever dated, but if she made a *move*, he never made one back. Their mom said he didn't know what he was missing. Leah said she thought he was probably just not interested in *women*. After a transition of lighthearted talk about how good strawberries and whipped cream are on waffles, Leah asked her mom how work was. Her mom had a good poker face. But she wasn't much for lying. She told them it was *rough* right now. She said that the hotel *did* get approved for renovations, but they'd be doing it over the span of the next two years and that, at the same time, the casino floor itself would have to wait for any renovations. And she added that people were finally getting tired of the Gambit, of the gaudy decor based on a style half a century out of date.

"Except the chandelier," she added at the end. "I don't think anyone wants to see that chandelier go. People still stare at it and point and yell over the noise about how *gorgeous* it is." She capped that off with a stare, looking right through her coffee mug into the past.

The conversation went on after that, but her mom was less vocal. Leah got nervous, even feeling her chest swell, as it was only her and Brit talking, about a rumor Baylor Art Gallery was closing. All at once, she understood why she felt jittery. Her mother was getting ready to tell her something. *Something she didn't want to hear.*

"Leah. Your sister accidentally already found out. But there's something I want to talk to you about…your dad. He and I talked, and he's coming into town to see you and Brit. I know that I've said a few *not-so-good* things about him, but that's only because… because…it was *both* of our faults that he left. I won't tell you how to feel about him, but I think it would be *nice* if you met him. You don't have to answer me right now, but—"

"I'll meet him," Leah said at once.

She could see her mother was struggling just to talk, and she'd have done anything to get that to stop. Meeting her dad didn't seem to be too big of a trade. And the results were immediate. Her mom slid out from her chair and hugged her, kissed her on the forehead.

Leah noticed then that Brit had changed again. She had picked up her phone and was looking at the screen with disinterest.

*****

"That's not at all what I expected when you messaged me," said Bailey.

Leah and Bailey were sitting on a picnic table behind Luci's café. It was a favorite spot of theirs. Luci Hendrix, the owner, restored and reoutfitted an old home as a coffee shop in the Great Heights, an area of Valleyport known for its decadence, topiaries, and concentration of wealthy taxpayers. Luci blended her love of all things oceanic with exposed wood grain and a rustic, antique design. The double doors to the garden behind Luci's were fitted with a stained glass design, a giant squid grabbing a seventeenth-century ship. The rear sitting area itself was filled with just about every bush, flower, and tree that could be found in Louisiana. A stream ran through it, filled with marbles that shone in the sun like color-filled Edison bulbs. They had never been able to afford the coffee, though, until Leah took over Luci's social media for her last year. She'd been pretty good at it, and even though she eventually had to give it up, Luci still gave her and her friends free coffee when they came in.

"Yeah. Sorry for not messaging you back earlier," said Leah. "I—it was just *bizarre*."

Bailey had texted Leah the night before, and Leah jumped on using what her mother told her as a valid excuse as to why she didn't text back, never mind that what her mother told her happened this morning and that Leah was awake when she got the text from Bailey.

"You're fine. I was just checking on you. This is *big*. What's running through your head right now? How do you feel?"

Nothing. Leah was surprised to find that to be the truth, that she felt almost nothing about seeing her dad for the first time. She remembered asking about him when she was little and that her mother gave him the shape of words like *sweet, intelligent,* and *driven.* When Leah asked why he wasn't around, her mother said, "Your father and I wanted different things. But he loved you girls."

Leah remembered thinking, in an adolescent way, *Then why did he go?* After that, she didn't think of her father often, almost never; only occasionally, when her friends celebrated Father's Day with theirs, but luckily that was Brit's birthday. That was plenty of distraction.

"I don't feel much about it. I never knew him. But Brit…"

"Oh? Is she okay?"

"She stopped speaking when he got brought up. There was that look on her face like, like…I don't know. Like somebody told her *Indigo De Souza* broke her hand and would never play again. Or…"

"Like somebody kicked a cat in front of her?"

"No. You know she'd just hit whoever did that."

Bailey chuckled, and Leah followed. But it was short-lived.

"I guess that makes sense, though. She did know him after all. It's easy not to miss something that you never had, but Brit got to have a father for a little while. Do you know why he left?"

"Not really," said Leah.

Of course she knew that her mother's explanation was the variety of glossed-up brevity that a parent gives a child. And until that day, she hadn't wanted to know all the real reasons.

Bailey's face scrunched up.

"What?"

"I'm sorry. I just—I can't imagine. I don't know what I'd do without my dad…"

Leah nodded, and suddenly Bailey was apologizing.

"Sorry, sorry. I don't know why I said that."

Leah told her it was fine, *that she understood*. But it was as Bailey said, Leah didn't miss him or care because she never had him in her life. Tottering in the back of her mind, a question came forward: *Was he anything like me? Or am I anything like him?* Leah had no trouble seeing, with absolute clarity, the ways that she was similar to her mother. That they were both workers, both people oriented, both the kind of folks that enjoyed mystery movies and thrillers the most, and knew that Sour Patch Kids were the best candy. But—

"I wonder what he's like."

"I guess you're going to find out."

Bailey *beamed* at her the way that Bailey always did. Her smile was a directed weapon of a kind, used to break apart Leah's reserve and expose her.

"Leah!"

They turned their heads at the same time. Luci was coming out of the stained glass doors with a business card in her hand, and her generous grin in full view. She was in a dress patterned with the *Swamp Thing*, but he was dancing like Shaggy from Scooby-Doo. Her brilliant gilded hair bounced in ringlets. Her sleeve, a floral bed of art, seemed to always go with what she was wearing, or maybe it was that she could pull anything off.

"*God, she's gorgeous,*" whispered Bailey.

Luci was just one of those people that was effortlessly pretty and stylish and could charm the devil if she had a mind to.

"Sorry! I just wanted to give you this." Luci extended the business card to her.

"I meant to tell you about it as soon as I saw you next, but I was so excited to see you, I forgot." She laughed. "There's this guy that came in, Tommy. He asked me if I knew anyone who knew how to *really* work a camera. I told him I knew the best in town, and then we talked about *you* for half an hour. He was such a *nice* guy. And gosh... He seemed to really admire what you were doing. Couldn't believe it when I told him how old you were. He asked if I had a way to contact you, that he was looking to hire a part-time assistant. Well, I told him I'd give you a card if he had one."

The card was thick and two-toned, pastel blue and white, and the name of the studio was *Cloudless Sky Photography*. The name: *Tommy Bridges*. Leah flipped it around to the back, which resembled a child's Crayola coloring of a midday sky, occupied by several drifting cotton clouds.

"You should give him a call. I know he had a gig coming up soon...I'm trying to remember the name of the event he was taking pictures at. Oh, shoot! What was it? I can't remember. I know it's soon, though."

Leah'd been so preoccupied by the card that she only just then looked back up at Luci.

"Thanks, Luci! I will! I really, *really* appreciate it!"

"Of course. You deserve it. Now I gotta get back in there."

Luci told them how good it was to see them for the second time and hurried back through the doors.

SERMON OF THE DIVERS

Leah felt like she'd been handed her big break. All of the thoughts about her dad shifted away. This was an opportunity to see a professional in action, and she was *not* going to miss the chance. In the forefront of her mind, she imagined being able to use some of the extra cash she made to help with the groceries and get some clothes for Talley's sisters. Bailey must have known she was excited because when they made eye contact, she said, "What are you waiting for? Call him!"

The phone rang two and a half times, and he answered. From the very first time she heard it, she was keenly aware of a tenor in Tommy's voice. He had the voice of a hypnotist or a showman, one and the same depending, maybe.

"This is Tommy at Cloudless Sky."

Leah felt crawlers creeping up her arms, nerves wavering. She'd never had an opportunity like this one, had never worked with someone who owned a studio. Her only experience with someone was Bailey, who acted as her assistant on shoots she did for a couple of people around Deepmoor.

"Uh, hello. I'm Leah Fells. Luci, from the café, told me that you wanted to talk to me about a job."

There was a pause of recalling on Tommy's side that stretched into infinity for Leah. But when he spoke again, her nerves relaxed. The sound in his voice was relief, almost emphatic about it.

"Well! That's *good* timing on your part, Leah. Very good timing. Normally, I'd meet you, take you to lunch, and talk about the job, but…the things you are doing with lighting is stuff I didn't figure out until I got into college. You know your stuff. And to be honest, I only have one question that's pertinent right now."

He waited, so she asked, "What's that?"

"Can you start right now? Today? I'm driving out to an event in Faringsport Park. *The Cypress Festival*. And I can't overstate how much I need another person on this one. Can you do it?"

Leah's eyes went wide; her head debated back and forth. How was she even going to get out there? Where was there? What time was it? Was her camera charged? But her gut took over.

"Yes, sir. I'll be there in an hour… What was it called again?"

CHAPTER 8

The Cypress Festival

It was only a couple miles up the road, so sometime around one, Kris and Rob headed north on Highway 3 to the park. On the way over, Rob was speculating that the festival would be rather empty this year, considering the change of dates, but as soon as they came around Dead Man's Curve, they knew that couldn't have been further from the truth. The parking lot was overflowing with cars, so it had been extended out into the grass all the way over to the tree line on the left side, near the dock and pier. And Highway 3, all the way into Gadsborrow, was bordered with cars on both sides, parked on the shoulders. Fellas with reflective vests were directing people to the nearest spots, and by the time they reached the end of the line, they were a quarter-mile from the entrance.

"*Holy shit*," Rob stated but in a loud voice. "Who would've thought... There's more people than there's ever been. I guess they finally started to advertise on Facebook and Instagram now."

Kris agreed half-heartedly.

These weren't the typical type who went to the Cypress Festival every year. Usually the parking lot was full of pickup trucks, and the families that got out wore button-up shirts and boots and ball caps. The girls dressed the same or, occasionally, in sundresses and cowboy hats. This year, there were all kinds. Every kind of make and model that Kris'd ever seen while riding to school through Valleyport. And the people were just as diverse. A crowd of every race and every cultural slice that could be found in the tristate area. People with nice clothes and those with old stained clothes and those with barely any clothes at all. Folks with colored hair and face paint and revealing themselves by the walk they took in life.

Needless to say, Kris was overwhelmed. His eyes didn't know where to go. Kids were darting out from behind cars, quickly followed by mothers and fathers that were already having trouble keeping up. He took a deep breath before they started walking. He took a deep breath because he wondered if those kids were feeling the same thing that he was feeling, that just over the hill, down the road, there was something extraordinary happening, and it was taking everything in him not to run along beside them, to race to see what it was that was floating through the air, over to the Cypress Festival. He silently reminded himself of Freddie, of what his own high emotions could do.

Rob was still stunned by how many people there were, but his surprise took the shape of a glowing smile.

"This is so *awesome*. Even back when Mom and Dad were going, back in its heyday, it never had *this many people*."

"Yeah," Kris managed, focusing on keeping his heart from beating too fast. "This is wild. Good for Ball Point Pin."

"True!" Rob turned to him. "Hey, you alright?"

Kris was feeling nauseous from overstimulation. "I'm good. Just didn't expect this many people."

Rob smiled at him reassuringly. "Come on! I bet some food will settle your nerves."

There was no entry fee or, really, an entrance of any kind, but everybody came down the park road, Carol Lane (the lane, if viewed from above, made a giant sideways number 8). After entry, there were the rides and games, parked anywhere there was space, save for on the road or the playgrounds, which were crawling with kids. Rob commented on *The Superman* and *The Tornado* as they walked by, saying that they'd have to circle back and give those a try. Kris agreed but with the dregs of enthusiasm. On the far side was a slope which usually held a few stray RVs or a pop-up camper, occasionally even a tent. But today, that was where most of the food was, right before a pretty good-size stage (one of those that's easily put up and easier to take down). Two girls with straw-colored pigtails skipped past them, one of them holding a giant swirly lollipop, and that sent Kris's mind on a wild-goose chase, wondering where he'd seen something similar before, in a movie or—

"What we want, bro?" Rob asked.

They were at the crossroads of food trucks and stands, with every vendor sending savory and sweet and succulent aromas of grilling meat, sauces, garlic, and freshly baked bread. But Kris was having trouble picking, focusing instead on the grip he had over his immediate surroundings. Anything could happen in a maelstrom like this. Anything!

"I'm buying. What do you want?" his brother offered again.

"Oh, here," Kris said, producing the hundred-dollar bill. "Dad gave me this to spend up here. You can use this."

Rob looked at the bill and then at Kris again. His eyes narrowed, as if he'd just discovered something or thought of something profound that he hadn't before. Rob pushed his hand away and asked, "How about a beer?"

"A what?"

Rob smiled that easy smile. "Wait here a sec. I'll be right back."

Rob trotted off to a nearby stand where a bearded biker was surrounded by blue igloo ice chests. An assortment of tall amber and green bottles stood in a single-file line on top of a foldout table.

Kris took the time alone to remind himself that what he was seeing and hearing and feeling were not to be trusted. He ran through the thought processes of his father, the teachings of his father: The idea that all emotions were connected and fed into one another and that some were more connected than others—humility and pride, joy and depression, amusement and boredom, *love and hate.* Tapping into one begged a remembrance of the other and illuminated the identity of it. "Never find yourself fully on one side or the other," his father'd told him. "The balance is to be found between each. Because humility can become timid. Pride can become arrogant. With you and me and Grandpa, we drop very swiftly out of balance if we start to lean one way.

And his father had been right too. Ever since Kris could remember, when he felt an emotion, he could slip all the way down into its depths. Just now, his anxiety was crippling, becoming panic. He closed his eyes and retreated to his breathing, he plugged his ears, and for a moment, he imagined himself in the dark, alone. He imagined himself on the brink of a night, ready to dream again. Slowly—or it seemed to be slowly, but time had a way of slipping away when his eyes were closed—he felt himself return to an equilibrium.

It's all just a dream, he said to himself.

When he opened his eyes, no one was staring at him or even noticed him, and he regrouped, remembering what his father had told him that morning. He scanned the festivities with interest, with an eye for details, as an observer. One thing that he noticed, above all else, was the number of smiles spreading across the faces of the crowd. The sound of laughter. The music coming from the bottom of the hill, something springy and upbeat– with a sort of '80's vibe, accompanied the convivial people.

"Here you go."

Rob was back and offering him an amber bottle of beer with the name Maker's Ale. Kris hesitantly took the bottle. And his brother must have known what memories arose in his mind because he said, "Just drink the one. You'll be alright."

Kris had tried alcohol before with his dad. They had a single glass of Jack Daniel's every Father's Day, a sort of ritual. When he tilted the icy bottle to his lips, he was expecting the burn of liquor and instead met with the hoppy and earthy flavor of beer.

"What do you think?"

"I don't hate it," he said, taking another sip. "Don't love it either."

Rob gulped his own. "Same. Now let's find some food and get to those rides."

*****

Luckily Leah got permission from her mother, even though she'd already agreed to go, and Bailey was more than willing to go with her. She said she saw something about the festival on the news—

her father watched every morning—but had forgotten when it was. Brit was at work; otherwise Leah had planned on inviting her, and Leah's mother was going in to work at two but told Leah to be home before nine, which Leah didn't mind. The festival was a family affair, ending just after the sun went down. After scrambling to get her camera, tripod, and reflector, Leah and Bailey jumped into Bailey's Corolla and tapped the address that Tommy had sent to them.

On the way, Bailey controlled the music (it was her car after all), and she played the new Taylor Swift album. Leah neither cared for nor disliked Taylor Swift, but she listened and tried to understand Bailey's fanaticism. All the while, Leah checked to find that her camera was charged and searched for the SD card with the most room.

"Hey…" Bailey was turning down the volume and looking at her. "There's something I've wanted to ask you about. I know you've got a lot on your mind, but I'd be a bad friend if I didn't ask."

Leah's world tilted, and she felt as if there was a change in the atmosphere, in the pressure within the car. She kept looking at the photos on her SD card, Andrew's family photos that she'd taken a year ago, but she prepared, as if for a photo.

"Go ahead."

"Well… There's a rumor about a picture of you… A picture of you and Aaron."

Leah used every will of her being to keep her face under her control, showing only anger and irritation. It was only in that very moment that she realized what she meant to do, that she was about to lie to Bailey about what happened. That she wasn't sure if she ever wanted anyone to know. It was her fault, after all. Even Bailey told her not to get involved with *him*.

"Yeah. He took a picture of us during…I didn't know until everyone started talking about it, but I thought I heard it."

Bailey bit her lip and looked at Leah, then back to the road.

A warm swell of emotions settled over Leah, the feeling of the lie's protection and how little it really offered. She couldn't even put into words her reasons for not telling Bailey the real story; only that when she thought of it, she couldn't find a way to put it into words, words that she could actually *say*.

"I'm sorry... Sorry about him and about how everyone's acting. I promise that it'll pass."

Bailey knew from firsthand experience that *these* kinds of things only resided in the collective consciousness for so long. She'd first given oral early in middle school, and that bastard Hunter Campbell bragged about it to everyone he could find. The girls gave her more trouble than the boys did. Most every girl, except Leah, had completely ignored her for the rest of the year. Leah remembered not knowing how to respond either but knew that she loved Bailey.

Brit gave her the needed guidance on how to be a good friend on that occasion.

Bailey grabbed Leah's hand and gave it a squeeze.

"I'm here if you need to talk."

Leah smiled at her. Not the smile she'd use for a photo, but it felt similar in that she thought about it the whole time.

With all the thoughtfulness of a best friend, Bailey made light of what happened and changed the subject. She only took a few shots at Aaron and even managed to get a genuine chuckle out of Leah when she called him a *dicknugget.* Then she started telling Leah, even though Leah was already aware of all of them, the instances of her exes being dicknuggets. Of course, Leah knew what Bailey was doing, but it didn't stop the little magic trick from working. She began to feel better, including about the lie she told. Bailey ended with a thoughtful move and offered to play any song that Leah wanted to hear. But Leah drew a blank, so she told Bailey to just keep playing Taylor.

"She's growing on you, huh? Taylor just gets it."

They laughed.

A few minutes later, they were entering Faringsport, and only a couple miles after that, they went around a flattened curve and came around a hill. And there it was—the Cypress Festival.

Leah and Bailey were to meet Tommy near the entrance, beside a ride called The Dancing Dragons. It was a tilt-and-twirl kind of ride, but each car was painted like a different-color dragon. The line was long and full of younger kids, and one boy was standing at the front of the line, banging his fists against his chest like Donkey

Kong. Bailey pointed him out, and they both grinned. His excitement was contagious.

"He looks like he's having a better time than anyone else."

The voice was familiar to Leah, but it took her a moment to recognize where she'd heard it. It was that same blithe voice from the phone call. And when she turned, Tommy Bridges was extending a hand to her. He was dark-haired and wore it as if he were a greaser from the '50s. His slacks were gray and his shirt black, and his eyes were clear and green, inky even. Then there was his smile, which was warm and wide, showing pearly teeth.

"Leah?"

"Yes. Tommy?"

"That's me," he said.

They shook hands, and he looked to Bailey and extended his hand again. She introduced herself, and Leah could already see Bailey starting to ogle over him. She was pink and cheeky.

Her eyes were bright with wonder.

"I'm afraid we don't have much time," he continued. "I've got a picnic table over here. Come on, and I'll tell you what the plan is."

They followed him over to a picnic table beside the ride, where a few black cases waited atop it. Although he *said* they were in a hurry, he moved with ease and sat down at the table, as if they had all the time in the world. Leah noticed and began to feel nervous, realizing how little she knew about the man. But also thinking of the opportunity.

"So first, I'm sorry this is such a strange way to start. I appreciate you being able to come so quick, and I'll be paying you an extra $200 for the inconvenience."

Leah could have fallen out of her chair.

"Two hundred?"

"Yeah. You're right. We'll make it three. How does that sound?"

"That—that sounds *great*. Thank you."

Bailey squeezed her hand under the table, and Leah's heart sped up.

"Now let me get right down to it."

He picked up one of the black bags and unzipped it. He produced a lens, and for the first time, he noticed the camera around Leah's neck and the bag with the tripod that Bailey was carrying.

"Ah. A Nikon Z 50. That'll do just fine, but we're going to need this DX lens, and here's an SD card. Use your autofocus and go for a decent shutter speed. You can tweak it as you go along but somewhere around 1/200 will do."

Leah nodded.

"So... We've been hired by the sponsors of this lovely event, and what we're doing is taking pictures for an article I've been contracted to write for *VP* magazine. We need a little bit of everything. We're getting a big spread in the magazine, and trust me, they're going to want to showcase this event as much as possible. Get kids and families having a good time, get the food vendors, get pictures of people with their dogs, get anything that is a candid smile, *and be aware that you're getting the Allied Security banners in those kinds of shots.* It doesn't have to be the focus, but make sure it's present. Now the first band is about to get started, so the stage is where I'll be. I've got to get some shots of the bands and interview the winner of the battle of the bands. So if you need me, that's where I'll be. Any questions?"

Leah looked around, noticing for the first time the Allied Security banners on the stage and on many of the rides. There were other sponsors too: Tillard's Tractor Supply, Irvine Chicken Company, Valleyport Electrical Solutions, etc.

"Only the Allied banners?"

Tommy smiled, but this time, there was something different about it—an overcurly extension on the end of his lips. A light in his eyes.

"They're all Allied."

Seeing the look of confusion on her face, he continued, "Of course, you know Jim Grayson owns Allied Security & Technology. It's his bread and butter. Who owns Tillard's?"

"John Tillard?" Bailey posited with a laugh.

Tommy's smile curled further. "Seth Tills was the original owner, but he gave it up to Jim Grayson, who took the skeleton of an old chain and took it all across the south. Do you want to guess what happened with all these other companies?"

An edge of seriousness fit into the hypersilly smile on Tommy's face. But all at once, his expression softened.

"Sorry. They're all Allied banners. Just make sure to get *any* of them in the shot. Okay?"

Leah nodded, feeling not as confident about the person she had been daydreaming of learning so much from.

Then Bailey broke into the conversation, "Battle of the bands? I thought it was just a concert?"

Tommy smiled quite normally this time and said, "It was a *very* late notice change. Something to spice up the whole event. When you finish your shots, come over to the stage and watch. *See for yourself.* And have some fun!"

*****

Taking the first photo was hard. Not only had she allowed the practice of photography to get intertwined with memories of Aaron (he was also her assistant for a while), but having his father's banners be a required piece of every photo kept those thoughts ever present. If not for Bailey, she might've been worn down by the unwanted reminders. But Bailey's alacrity and genuine excitement about the festival and all of its goers lifted her from her funk. Not long on the job, Bailey offered to pay for them to ride some rides; she loved carnival rides but declared they were a hundred times better with a friend.

"Come on! It'll be fun, and I want to put it on my Instagram. You can pick whichever one you like."

"But what about the camera and the tripod?"

Bailey had been toting the tripod, and in retrospect, Leah wondered why she hadn't simply left it in the car, which was Bailey's first suggestion. "I'm sure the people operating the rides wouldn't mind holding your camera for you. They all have those little stations they can stash purses and stuff. Why not your camera?"

With some trepidation, Leah gave in. After a quick trip back to the car, they were getting in line at every other ride. And still, Leah managed to get hundreds of photos. The banners were everywhere she turned, and nine times out of ten, there were people laughing and enjoying themselves just in front of them, waiting in line or taking a break on a bench and enjoying fried Oreos. Leah fine-tuned her settings and got to where she could quickly draw on a shot within a couple of tries. On most occasions, she took the pictures and asked permission afterward to use it in the article, but every so often, she'd see someone wearing a flamboyant hat or vest and asked them to pose for a photo. All were accommodating except one family that didn't want their kids in the article. Leah politely said she understood and deleted the photos so as to not make the mistake of thinking she could use them. Between shots, they were flying through the air or being spun around until their bodies stuck against the walls.

"We should have invited the guys!" Bailey declared after about an hour and a half of revelry.

Leah agreed and felt bad for not thinking of it earlier, but she'd been so preoccupied with getting the job and making it to the festival as quickly as they could. Besides, Bailey and Andrew couldn't fund everyone else's fun, though at times they tried.

"Oh! Look!"

Bailey grabbed Leah's hand and pointed through the crowd to a familiar pair of people.

"I bet you his band's playing today!" exclaimed Bailey, nearly bouncing with excitement.

Standing in line at Flight of Icarus, Kris and Rob looked altogether different than the day before; well, Kris did anyway. Rob's usual ease of presence was accounted for as well as his slim clothes and sense of style, but Kris was wearing a befuddled expression of amusement that wasn't leaving his face. His eyes were not so downturned, and in the absence of that inquiring light, they were hollowed out to take in everything around him. He looked like a boy who was first stepping into the world, curious about everything.

"Who's that with him?" asked Bailey.

"Kris. His brother. I told you about getting pizza with him, remember?"

"*Oh! That's him?* Unfortunate roll on the genes... Rob must have taken all the good ones before he got there."

"Don't be a cunt! He's sweet and... Let's go say hey."

Bailey agreed with reluctance, and toward the brothers they went.

CHAPTER 9

Battle of the Bands?

They were in line for *Flight of Icarus* when several things happened at the same time.

Kris and Rob, until that point, had been having a grand time, even though Kris was still struggling with his emotions, which were in a constantly inconstant state. He was overcome with anger when he saw a mother spank her son. He wondered if she knew that the child could not see, or comprehend, that crying and yelling in the line was embarrassing the mother. He wondered if she knew where her embarrassment really came from, that it was only in the fabrication of a social illusion about what was acceptable and what was not, an idea that was not founded on what needs best benefit a child's rearing. And he wondered if she knew that by trying to teach the child in such a way, all she was doing was driving a wedge between them. He calmed himself quickly and tried to tell himself it wasn't any of his business. That he didn't *really* know what he was talking about. Kris was not a parent after all. After the spanking was over, the child wanted comfort, but the mother refused it, pushing him away.

It was while he watched that exchange that Harry, a longtime friend of Rob's as well as the person in charge of coordinating with the bands playing at the festival, came over and started talking with Rob. He was usually erratic and quick with his words, but today, he was even more so than usual. Sweat dappled his brow, and though his eyes were hidden behind reflective sunglasses, Kris had an idea that they were gaping and alert.

"Battleofthebands, didanyonetellyouaboutityet?"

"Battle of the... What? Harry. Slow down. It's nice to see you." Rob laughed.

Harry's face showed no sign that he found the situation humorous.

"We got a notice to change the concert into a battle of the bands. Did Liz call you? I told her to call you and let you know. I can tell by the look on your face that no one told you anything. Well, there's more. Wesley won't be able to play with Ball Point Pin. He's already signed up with another band. I noticed as I was scrambling to abide by the new rules." At that point, Harry rolled his eyes and sighed, then took a breath and kept going, "I need to know if you can still play. If you don't have someone who can sub in, then I'm going to have to take you off the roster."

It was at this junction, as Rob, on this rare instance, stood there with a blank and thoughtless look on his face, that Leah and Bailey came up to where they were standing and tried to say hello. Kris, seeing that Rob was utterly preoccupied, turned and guided them a few steps away from the conversation, trying to give Rob space to reply to Harry and, at the same time, giving it his all at coming up with something to say. It didn't help that the first thought he had when he saw Leah was that he'd seen her in the Dreaming the night before. Fortunately for him, she wasn't nearly as bashful or gave no appearance of it.

"Hey, rebel," she said and grinned at him. "This is my friend Bailey."

Kris remembered the girl, Bailey, but only through a paper she wrote in English 2 the year before. Their teacher, Mr. Nichols, always had them switch essays and grade each other's work. Once, her usual trading mate was gone, and Kris was told to check over hers as well. The topic: *A student's viewpoints on how the education system and assets could better be structured and utilized for the benefit of all learners.* What was memorable? Not much. Most of it was bogged down by her ideas of what she was told by Mr. Nichols would make a convincing paper, and the topic was clearly something she didn't feel she had the credentials to comment on. However, near the middle, she made the classic argument for having more time outside to learn, more classes in the open air. She told the reader that Larue High School was fortunate enough to be located a ten-minute walk from a web of nature trails that ran along the Cramoisi River. And for a few sentences, she lost herself in the descriptions of the water. She spoke of the sound of its endless motion and the life it gave. She swore there were things to be learned among the cattails and the trout, about how life moves in a cycle from the water's banks. That learning about life should not be confined to memorization and facts by list but that the bigger fish are in the water.

She got a *D*. Not from Kris, though. He pretended to botch the math, ignored a few minor punctuation errors, and offered her a high *C*. It was only when Mr. Nichols graded them a second time that the grade lowered.

They exchanged hellos, and it was apparent that she didn't remember him at all.

"What are you doing all the way out here?" asked Leah.

"I live right down the road, near the bridge, and Rob and I come here every year. It's...kind of a tradition. Never seen it like *this* before, though. What about you?"

Leah indicated the camera around her neck. "I got hired to take pictures. Bailey's just here for rides."

"And the food!" added Bailey.

"We kind of just, accidentally stumbled into it."

She told him about a café and a friend named Luci that got her the job. She then said that the guy who hired her was around, at the stage somewhere, and that he'd told them about a battle of the bands.

"Is Ball Point Pin playing?" she asked, hopeful. "I'd *really* like to hear them again."

And Bailey's eyes lit up as well, looking over his shoulder at Rob.

"Uh...I'm—I'm not sure. I think that's what Rob and Harry are talking about. Apparently, Wesley entered with another band, and the rules won't allow him to enter with two."

Their eyes fell, but then Rob was there, joining them with a less-than-joyful face, though it was obvious he was trying to hide it or more than obvious to Kris.

"Hey, Leah. Good to see you again," said Rob, and he introduced himself to Bailey, who blushed deeply.

"Kris was just telling us that you might not be able to play. Are they going to let you?"

Rob shook his head and clicked his tongue. "Wesley, our rhythm guitarist, has been thinking about quitting for a while now. I think he finally found a way to let the rest of us know."

"He just quit like that?" asked Bailey.

"He's always been a bit flaky. A great guy but flaky. He was really in it to make some side cash and… Well, Ball Point Pin isn't exactly rolling in it or anything. We'll have to sit this one out. Wouldn't be so bad if it were still just a concert, but apparently, it's a battle now, and the winners are getting studio time and a cash prize."

They all expressed how sorry they were for Rob, but Kris couldn't help but feel as if part of the energy that he'd felt in the air was drained away. He looked around at Leah and Bailey and Rob, and he got a funny feeling in the pit of his stomach. It started as a feeling, and it came with a string of memories in quick succession, some old and some young. He remembered Bailey's essay and the words, he remembered the look of wonder in Leah's eyes when she met him in the Dreaming, and he remembered the first time his brother ever gave him a guitar lesson. He remembered his brother repeating a phrase, *"Pick it back up."* And without much consideration for how all those things ended up on his mind at the same time, and without any consideration for the fact that he hadn't played guitar in years, Kris said, "I can play rhythm."

Kris said it with no enthusiasm or with any doubt, and he turned toward the stage. He tried to imagine himself on a stage, dancing and playing a guitar, but he couldn't conjure up such a bizarre sight. The four of them were cement for a moment, and it was Rob that broke them into motion again.

"You *want* to play? Are you sure?"

SERMON OF THE DIVERS

And he couldn't help but hear the hope in his voice, that he didn't want to push Kris to it but also desperately wanted to play the show.

"Pick it back up," he said. "I'm probably not going to be *good*, but it'll keep Ball Point Pin in the competition. And I bet you can still win it, even with me holding you back."

Rob grinned and hugged Kris right there. Leah and Bailey smiled and stood back, awkwardly wondering about the exchange and doubting that Kris could even play the guitar.

Then Rob turned to them and said they'd catch up later, after Ball Point Pin won the impromptu battle.

It was as they walked away that Kris remembered where he'd seen the look of quiet reflection in Leah's eyes. Because as they walked away, she grabbed the camera around her neck, and her pupils narrowed as the aperture of the tool in her hand. She adjusted, raising herself on her toes, and, fitting the instrument close to her eye, pointed it at the mother and boy—the one that had gotten in trouble for his outburst—and she captured the moment they hugged and reconciled.

When she pulled away, looking into the camera at what she'd done, her face was aglow with warmth and pride.

And Kris remembered her as she was in the Dreaming, and he turned, trying to focus on what his brother was saying, on the impossible task ahead.

*****

"I can't imagine *him* on that stage…I think this might be a disaster," said Bailey, with amused lips, after Rob and Kris had hurried toward the stage.

"I don't know," replied Leah as she took a picture of a mother and child.

And after she asked for their permission to use the photo and was given it, she turned back to Bailey, continuing, "He seems to have a lot of secrets. He doesn't look like he'd know how to work on a car, but he fixed Brit's the other day. And when we talked at the Pizza

Palace, he was… He just had a way of speaking that was calculated and thoughtful. He—"

Bailey's state of disbelief stopped Leah, and she felt her cheeks flush, for which she silently scolded herself.

"I don't mean anything like that. I just mean that there's more to him than what you're seeing."

"Are you sure?" asked Bailey with a devious tone.

"Shut up."

"You moved on pretty quick. Good for you."

Leah turned away to hide her face and didn't respond to Bailey's coaxing. There was something *intriguing* about Kris, something that tickled a part of her mind, an element she couldn't quite put her finger on, but she also wasn't going to fall for that same trap, that fantasy. She was there to do a job, to take pictures, and if she did that well enough, she might be able to make enough money to cushion for college.

Bailey must have received the message because she changed the subject and let it rest.

"It's a good thing these banners are on everything. I don't think you could take a picture *without* there being one in it, even if you tried. You'd have to point your camera directly at the ground or at the sky."

Leah agreed and, maybe out of habit, gave a compliment to her ex's dad, "It's really good of Jim Grayson to sponsor a small-town festival like this. I think he's from out here somewhere. I know that he lived in a small town when he was a kid. One time he mentioned growing up on a farm outside of Valleyport."

"It must be nice to never have to worry about working that hard again," said Bailey, who, Leah knew, hadn't had to work much at all.

"He still works very hard, I think. It's just he doesn't have to work with his hands anymore."

Bailey disagreed and informed Leah that she couldn't imagine that the *extremely* wealthy did anything other than enjoy their money and find new and interesting ways to spend it. She said that was why people wanted to get rich, that he just frontloaded all of the work, and now it was all the payoff.

SERMON OF THE DIVERS

Leah said she wasn't so sure about that and argued that surely, they must have to work hard to maintain their wealth, that they must work extra hard, because Leah was sure that hard work was the only way that someone became wealthy and held onto it.

Meanwhile, Leah took pictures, and they slowly made their way across the festival. More and more people were doing the same, and as the lines thinned at the rides, the lines got longer at the food trucks, and further down the hill, a throng of people were forming around the stage. They both shot glances down at the stage, thinking of Ball Point Pin, and Leah wondered if Kris could really do it. Could he really play? Would it be a *total* disaster? After they grabbed a few street tacos with fresh limes and funnel cake with a thick snow coat of powdered sugar, they started down the hill. Neither of them had to even tell each other what to do; they just knew.

*****

Rob stood over Kris with his hands on his hips, his sharp eyes pointing directly at him. Nick was smoking a cigarette and talking with Liam not a couple feet from them. Kris was sitting on a foldout chair with his brother's cream-colored Fender across his lap, trying his best to play bar chords that he hadn't thought about in a couple of years. To his credit, he was doing pretty well, but there's only so much that can be done when time has taken the body's memories, not to mention the calluses of a seasoned player.

"Not bad," said Rob, nodding slowly with his chin in his hand.

"Not good either," added Nick, who strode over, running his free hand through the shaved hair beside his pink mohawk.

Nick handed Rob a cigarette and told Kris that it wouldn't matter, though, because Nick was going to beat the drums so fucking hard that they wouldn't even hear Kris. Liam laughed, and so did Kris, even though inside he felt like he was trying to stand on a pin top.

"Look," began Rob. "It's not a big deal, playing in front of people. If you have to, just close your eyes and just *feel* what you're playing. If you think about the people or the heat or me or Nick or *anything*, then you won't be playing your best. *Just follow the music.* I know it's been a while, but I *know* that you can do this. You were always a natural with a guitar."

This was something that Rob used to say that Kris appreciated as one of those sweet lies people tell their loved ones. He'd never been able to flow with the music the way Rob did, and he'd never been able to bring emotion into the sound the way that Rob could. Kris knew that he wasn't any good, that—

"*Hey!*"

"What?" asked Kris, startled and blinking.

"The trains run. Rain, sleet, or snow…the trains run. You've got this. Just *play*. Just *run*."

Kris nodded and went back to practicing. Rob started snapping, and so did Nick, mimicking the beat of the song, "The Farwoods March," a sweet number that reminded Kris of something The Band Camino or The 1975 might put out but a little more rock. But like before, his hands would misbehave, and notes slipped through them like water, but on and on the snapping went. Nick started to tap out the whole beat on Rob's back, and both of them were bobbing their heads. At that point, Kris looked around the back of the stage, several people were taking notice—

"Close your eyes," demanded Rob.

Kris did, and in the darkness, the beat continued, and so did his fragmented playing. Then Rob's voice was added to the dark. He began singing the song, and Liam joined in for backup. It was at this point that Kris thought he'd start to get it, let it *flow*, but instead the mistakes continued, and the amateur twang of the guitar clashed. But he continued on, trying his hardest to *pick it back up*. It never came, though. It never flowed. Even though they practiced until it was time to get onstage. And though Nick and Liam went to prepare, Rob stayed and kept helping Kris.

Finally, Kris stopped and said, "I don't think I can do this."

He could feel the realization dropping like a stone in his heart. He looked down at his hands, unable to try and face Rob's disappointment. But Rob put a hand on his shoulder and said, "You've got this."

SERMON OF THE DIVERS

The sun was setting on the lake, sending its pinkish reflections across the sky and turning the clouds into emberic puffs. Grasshoppers played a different tune and were joined by the cicadas and the evening larks and the katydids and crickets, and then an early rising owl asked a chorus of its old question. The temperature dropped from sultry to a mild summer evening. A voice came off a microphone and announced that it was time to welcome Ball Point Pin to the stage. There was a bout of hollers and applause, and Kris followed Rob and Nick and Liam up a few steps and onto a rickety old stage.

Mounting the stage to a warm welcome only amplified the dreadful paranoia that Kris felt, because he knew that his concepts of the songs were solid, but his ability was lacking. And he even felt fear as he looked out at a multitude, a sense that he was very much somewhere that he wasn't meant to be. The stage, the place where everyone's eyes were, that was Rob's place, and he handled it well. But Kris belonged somewhere else, and his whole body told him just that, and it was all he could do to stay on the stage, not to run.

With a swagger that was natural and charming, Rob drew the attention of the crowd, strumming the beginning of the song and singing the opening words. The band followed, and Kris hit the first chord as a scream of excitement rippled through the crowd. After that, Kris heard no more of the crowd in front of him. He focused on two things: playing and not looking like a robot. Unfortunately, he failed on both accounts. Comparatively, his playing was not up to snuff, and every mistake he made, especially those of his unpracticed hands, sounded loud in the amplifier behind him. He missed notes, misplaced his hands, botched strumming patterns, and generally butchered the beautiful song. But he refused to stop, and he refused to look at the crowd. When he did look up, it was to look beyond them, as if at the end of the set and return to the back of their numbers, where he felt most comfortable. The only way he managed to control his nerves was by half-turning away from the crowd and using his formidable imagination to construct a scenario in which he was only playing in a garage with his brother, Liam, and Nick. It worked at times, and at others, it didn't. The sensation to run away grew, and his legs turned numb, and his head did somersaults. Several times he felt he might throw up or pass out, but he only kept playing, bleeding the melody and gutting the rhythm. Just when he felt light again, as if he were about to fall out, it was over, and they dismounted the stage. Nick guided Kris off the stage, while Rob thanked the crowd.

"You have to bomb the first one, big dawg," Nick told him. "It's kind of like a rite of passage. If you look at it that way, you did a hell of a job… You look a little green, though. Liam! Could you get us some water?"

Liam pushed his long hair from his face and nodded. He was also covered in sweat, as was Nick.

Rob came down the steps, light on his feet, almost bouncing, and he clapped Kris on the shoulders. "You played the whole thing through!"

Kris marveled at his brother, feeling some of his nauseous anxiety recede.

"Sorry. I really thought I wouldn't be *that* bad. I thought y'all might have a chance of winning."

"I didn't," said Rob.

"Me neither," said Nick.

"Not a chance," added Liam, who had just returned with water and handed them around.

"Then…then why would you let me play? Why not just skip the whole battle?"

Rob laughed. "We just wanted to play."

Kris's anxiety passed in a moment, and he realized that while he'd been so close to throwing up, the rest of them had satisfied expressions on their faces. They looked the way he *felt* when he finished reading a good book or when he worked out in the garden. Before, Kris understood that Rob got enjoyment out of just playing for other people, but now it was as if the realization had taken form in his mind and body. And as clear as it was that Rob loved to play music and play it for people, it was just as clear that Kris did not. So instead of anxiety or a sense of failure at not winning, he felt a sense of pride at being able to help his brother do a thing that he loved.

SERMON OF THE DIVERS

The whole idea had been for Rob's benefit anyway, so this outcome suited him just fine.

"Now let's get *one* more beer to celebrate your first show," said Rob. "What do you say?"

Kris pushed the hundred-dollar bill into his brother's hand and said, "A round on me."

CHAPTER 10

Ghosts Tell No Secrets

It wasn't a *total* disaster. But it was, in many ways, a disaster.

Bailey laughed at him at first, but at a certain point, because Kris was trying so hard and continued on, she stopped laughing and told Leah that she felt embarrassed *for him*. Leah didn't laugh at all. Knowing he'd only got up on that stage for his brother reminded Leah of her sister and all the times they'd put themselves in uncomfortable situations for one another, such as agreeing to distract Kris at the Pizza Palace. And there was one instant, when Kris looked up at the crowd but was clearly searching far beyond them, at the trees all the way on the other end of the park, that Leah had a sense of déjà vu. In the way that dreams can, a singular frame on the film of her dreaming spun across her mind, and for a moment, it was an altogether different Kris on the stage, and then all was normal again.

It was just after Ball Point Pin dismounted the stage that Bailey turned to her. "That was…not as bad as I thought it was going to be. Rob is so good that he *almost* overshadowed how bad Kris was."

"Quit being such a bitch about it. He only did it to help his brother."

It was only after those words came out, and she saw Bailey's hurt, that Leah realized it sounded harsher than she meant it.

"I'm sorry. I didn't mean—"

Bailey's phone started ringing then, and she said it was Jason, and the hurt she'd been feeling seemed to smooth over. She quickly said, "I'm sorry too... Jason's probably on break at work. I'm going to go talk to him for a minute, okay? I'll text you as soon as I hang up."

Leah nodded, thinking it was strange how quickly a phone call from Jason turned Bailey's mood around. Then she reminded herself of Jason's chill-to-a-fault way that was uniquely his own, and she thought about how people take on the traits of those they spend the most time with. That thought segued nicely into her own plans to improve herself, and she reminded herself that she should find Tommy and secure her position as his assistant. If she wanted to be a photographer, she reasoned that being around one would help make it so.

For several minutes, Leah squeezed through the outer ring of the crowd and raised herself onto her tiptoes to look for his dark head of hair. In a crowd of so many, with such diverse styles, cultures, and expressive people, Tommy blended well, because in the end, it was he who found her.

"Who on earth are you looking for?" he asked as he appeared beside her, like an apparition.

She laughed nervously. "I'm sorry. I was looking for you. I got plenty of pictures, and I forgot to ask you if I was going to edit them before I sent them to you or not."

The question seemed to intrigue him. "Would you like to?"

"I know how. Well, I sort of know how. It's something I've been trying to practice recently."

"Then edit them," he said. "Send me unedited copies of them all and then ten edited photos, and I'll tell you anything I can to help with your editing, if you need it. But I don't think you will." He gave her a warm smile. "You already do good work."

Leah wanted to believe him, but if her work was good, then she needed it to be great.

Tommy placed the tripod and camera he had on the ground and began setting up to take a picture of the stage from where they stood. The band currently playing was some blend of electronic and R&B.

"What do you think of the show?"

She told him that she and Bailey were having a wonderful time and that they actually knew one of the bands that were playing. But she corrected herself and said they were more acquaintances than actual friends. All the while, she watched his every move, collecting lessons he didn't teach.

"Really? I was just figuring out that I knew those two from that band that just played, *Ball Point* Pin. That family has a distinct look—all families do. And I remember reading about their grandfather in a stack of old newspapers my mother used to keep under the coffee table. An unforgettable man."

Leah could hardly believe what she was hearing.

"You mean the lead singer and the guitarist?"

"Was he supposed to be playing that guitar? Someone should have told him that." He smiled at his own joke, but it was wiped away when he said the name, "Timur. Their grandfather was Thomas Timur. Have you ever heard of him?"

Leah shook her head and waited patiently to hear more, curious as she was.

That creepy thing, that fanatic light, crept back into Tommy's eyes, and he took a picture of the band and the crowd.

"It's old news and morbid," said Tommy.

Then he must've noticed how closely Leah was watching him, monitoring his every move around the camera and the tripod, for he changed the subject again. "You really want to be *great* at this, huh?"

Leah nodded, trying not to feel nervous.

"Why? What is so important about photography?" He spoke as if he himself had something against the whole notion of taking pictures, but at the same time, he shot some more.

And Leah felt there were two answers to this question or, at least, that there were two for her. She picked the one that felt most appropriate for a *professional* setting.

"I want to be good enough to make my own studio, to get big, and—"

"And make lots of money?"

Leah nodded but added, "To support my mom and my sister and my friends too."

"I see. Well, you're focusing on the wrong things then. You don't make *real* money through the craft or trade itself but through networking and marketing and social strategy and *reading* people. That is all business. It's learning the ferocious beast that we call the free market. Is that what you want?"

Tommy turned from the camera and fixed her with a piercing set of eyes, an inquiring and intrigued expression. He was listening, waiting for her answer. But Leah couldn't help herself, and she said, "But... People buy what's best. Why wouldn't I want to be the best photographer I can be?"

"Being good is great, but being *best* isn't very profitable. Those who go and find the yet traveled paths of their crafts and transcend into art form are seldom celebrated during their lifetimes and usually die poor. Exceptions only prove the rule. But being good is marketable and safe, and people will always purchase a properly priced good—customers of all demographics. Clientele is the way to make money, to know who it is that you are selling to. They all buy the same thing, though—*good*. And I'm not just talking about pictures. It's not the pictures that you'll be selling, and it's not the product in any market that people are buying."

Leah was quickly deciding that she didn't care for Tommy, this random instructor who believed he held the tablature for success. And when she met his talk with silence, he asked her if what he said would keep her from accepting the job.

Thinking of the money, she replied, "I think it's important to learn from all sources, but I don't believe in what you're saying. I think hard work pays off. I know it."

"*Hmph,*" he replied. "I can respect that. I look forward to working with you, Leah. Oh! Now I have to go. Here's your first paycheck. Don't spend it all in one place."

Then Tommy pulled an envelope from his shirt pocket and handed it to her. He deftly collected his tripod and camera, and he rushed off across the crowd toward the stage. Even on her tiptoes, Leah couldn't see what drew him in the direction, but she decided to follow him and only stopped for a moment to stuff the envelope into her pocket. Leah was not sure why she meant to follow him. Maybe she was looking for something to confirm that he was not the mentor she wanted, something to end her ideas of learning from him. So she followed from a distance, easily hiding in the mass of people.

When she came around the edge of the crowd, near the stage, and saw what he pursued, she felt terrible lightning course through her. And her body reacted, as if in imminent danger, and her heart raced, and her body felt jittery, and she ducked back into the crowd, desperate to get away. Tommy stood by the stage, with his phone in his hand, typing and talking to Aaron. She'd been right in his line of sight, but somehow he hadn't seen her, and as her body vibrated with fear, she continued to tell herself *stop* and that it was *nothing*. That it was all a terrible thing that happened to someone else on some other planet in some other dimension. By the time that her body's rebellion was quelled, Tommy was taking a picture of Aaron and several other people that she didn't know. Then they were walking away.

She stood there for a moment, trying to hold onto everything she'd seen, studying it. Wondering how she ever found his blue eyes so brilliant and his face anything other than hideous and grotesque, scolding herself for not seeing it before. Wondering what Tommy was doing talking to him, but of course, he was probably doing an interview for *VP* magazine. But—

"Leah?"

Her stomach turned, her body once again ready to run. She turned to see it was Kris, and he was wearing an expression of worry.

"Is everything okay?"

To her horror, Leah couldn't even bring herself to answer him. Her mind felt as if it were floating in open air, as a balloon, and her world was tilting from vertigo. She blinked, feeling the tears coming to them, and she hurried away from him, away from the crowd, out to the woods beyond the festival.

*****

There was no doubt in his mind about the nature of the infamous picture as he watched Leah stare at Aaron Grayson. He thought how she was then the exact opposite image of the person she'd been in the Dreaming. The person in his dream *was* whole and serene and full of life. And for some reason, when he expected his anger to rise to the surface, it was only a feeling of betrayal, despair, and helplessness that he felt. He got the strange idea that he was somehow directly experiencing fractions of the feelings that Leah felt when she saw Aaron, and he tried to imagine it multiplied to the degree of her. He couldn't. And he knew it.

He turned back long enough to tell Rob that he'd be right back, and then he took off in the direction that Leah went. All the while, he was trying to think of any words that would help, then understanding that there were none that would, and finally just composing the beginnings of a conversation that would comfort her. All the while, he couldn't help but be amazed at himself and how he felt changed through the course of the day, thanks to his dad's words that morning and his brother's actions just moments ago.

Leah had stopped when she reached a small wooden bridge that spanned a rivulet, and as Kris slowly crossed the meadow between them, he felt as if he walked through a familiar and invisible barrier. The feeling some people get when they enter a church, or for others, it's ancient places that are abandoned but once held reverence and power; and for some, it is the threshold of library doors, and still others, it is the glass doors of record shops. But the feeling is the same; the feeling is of intrusion upon a sacred place. Her back was turned to him, and her hair curtained her face. By the enclosing curve of her spine and the unsteady timbre of her breath, he knew she was still crying or had just finished crying.

"I'm sorry," he said, reaching a distance where she could hear him, and there was no one else out in the forest's steppes.

"You didn't do anything. Please, go away."

He considered doing as she said, but something in his gut compelled him to stay, at least for a moment longer.

"I'm sorry for following you, is what I meant," he said. "I understand needing time alone, if that's what you need. And if it is, I'll go. But—" It was at this point that Kris felt the urge to tell her something that he'd never told anyone.

"I threw up on him in middle school."

Leah put her foot down on the old wooden planks of the bridge. Her hand rested on the handrail as she turned to him. Kris stopped as she did. Beyond her, the forest was alive with the first fireflies of the evening. Several of the lightning bugs floated around her hair; their light was faint even after sunset.

"What?"

"Aaron. He used to like to give me a hard time in elementary and middle school. I wasn't feeling well when I got up that morning. In gym class, Coach Andrews gave us push-ups because we were late. We were late because Aaron, Stephen, and Hunter were trying to shove me into a locker in the boys' room. They thought it was so funny, but I remember thinking how silly and cliché it was. I didn't fit. When we got up from the push-ups, I felt even worse than I did before. He came up to me, and I knew that I was gonna throw up. I could've made it to the bathroom, maybe, but I decided I knew where I wanted it to go—right in his face."

It wasn't the story he expected it to be, but it made Leah stop crying, and that was enough for him.

"Why did you tell me that?"

"I don't know."

She laughed. Her eyes were still in recovery, but her lips and cheeks rose up, and her shoulders did too, and she laughed at his story. He joined her, the laughter coming from somewhere deep in his stomach, and then they listened as a song with piano keys rang in venerable locomotion, moving them around each other, and she looked up, and his eyes fell to the water below (both shy but curious).

She sighed when the moment had several breaths.

"I watched you play."

His cheeks turned rosy.

"Ooh. Is that why you're crying?"

She rolled her eyes and grinned.

"You did it for Rob. That was really…sweet. I know that must have been hard to do. You're not the kind of person who likes being in front of people, certainly not on stages."

"I don't," he replied. "I was sure that I was going to lose my mind up there or throw up, or both. It was weird, though. I'm glad I did it. I feel like I...*learned* something from the experience."

She turned to him, somber all of the sudden.

"What'd you learn?"

"That you're right. I don't like being in front of crowds and definitely not on stages. And that my brother and his friends do and that I love music, but I'm not a musician, not a performer anyway."

"Seemed you already knew that. Wouldn't you already know that?"

"That's the thing, though. There's a difference between *knowing* something and *realizing* it. After today, I'll never wonder if I was wrong about what I know. I'm not sure if that makes any sense or not, but—"

"I think it does," she said.

There's a difference between knowing something and realizing it. Why did that stand out in her mind? Why did it stick out the way that it did?

Do you think that we must experience terrible things in order to realize and grow? I hate that. It makes it sound as if we were made to suffer. These things she thought of saying but was tired of morose and tired of thinking about all that dark—

"I'd love to see your pictures. I don't know much about photography, but I remember that you took some for school. They were in the school paper, and I remember you going around with your camera, taking pictures of the teams. The ones of those nature trails were great."

Her hand went to the camera around her neck.

It was a turn, a revolution, and by the way he moved closer to her, she could tell that he was aware of her need to turn away.

"I haven't edited them yet," she said.

"Oh."

"I mean... You can still look at them, if you want to."

"I do."

And just outside of the Cypress Festival, and while it was still being held, and all those people had only just reached a peak of festive jubilance, Leah showed Kris pictures she'd taken. Pictures of families. Some of them formed of fewer members and some more, but all of them caught in moments of emphatic exhilaration. Both of their bodies leaned against the old two-by-fours that served as handrails on the old bridge. He tried his best not to get too close to her while they scanned the pictures. She was thankful for his reserve, for his sense of her space and his unwillingness to cross into her bubble just then. But he was full of questions and comments, and he never lacked for something new to talk of or discuss in the photos she took. The only one he didn't speak for was the last one, of a boy and his mother. She wondered if it was because he didn't want it to end either.

"So," he said, "why photography? Why do you want to take pictures?"

She thought then of the answer she gave Tommy, and this time, she picked the one closer to her heart.

"My memory... When I was a kid, I was hospitalized with pneumonia. We never really got a straight answer from the doctors, but my mom thinks that's when my memory got *volatile*. That's the word she uses. It doesn't feel like it's connected to a timeline, and I forget so much. Photography lets me hold onto memories and allows me to help other people do the same."

There it was. That spark of his again. He was looking at her as if she were infinitely fascinating and giving a TED Talk on some metaphysical phenomenon. The conversation was even easier after that, and he never broached the subject of why she was upset. It even felt as if he'd forgotten that it'd happened or that it actually had never happened. Before she knew it, they were talking about a graphic novel that he'd just picked up at a place called The Book Bureau. By his description, it was certainly not a real place, because it was altogether too magical and perfect, and passion accompanied his spark of interest when he told her of its floors and sections and hidden reading nooks.

"Oh, and they have vinyl too! I don't collect it, but Rob does. But I have gotten a few records from there. Have you ever heard of Bilberry Drive?"

"Yes!" she replied, nearly giddy with excitement, as she'd forgotten about him wearing the band T-shirt at Pizza Palace. "I *love* that band. I meant to ask you about it the other day. But we got so caught up talking about politics and pizza—a strange first date topic, by the way—that I forgot to ask…"

She noticed what she said after it was already out. *Date*. And she could have slapped herself for that slip of the tongue, but he continued on still. Not allowing her the opportunity to overthink her words, and she was sure that he wasn't either.

"Well, if you'd prefer, we could talk about God or abortion or human rights or automation or tech buyouts or even President Freeborn… Something light and breezy."

She laughed, and she let it go. It was a date; it wasn't a date. For some reason, it didn't seem to matter.

Then they were going through each other's music, looking at who their top artists were on Spotify. Unconsciously, she tapped the like button on more than half of the songs, and only then did she wonder if he'd be able to see that. But when she glanced at his phone screen, she saw he was doing the same thing. While he'd heard of Chapel and Bilmuri and The Band Camino, she was able to introduce him to Cake and The Neighborhood and Nightly, and he introduced her to Mainland, flor, and Chase Atlantic. It wasn't until she was holding her phone to his ear, playing a song by Emarosa, and she realized how close she was getting to him—without thinking about it—that she remembered that Bailey should have texted her by then. And as if on cue, Bailey came strolling up to them from the festival grounds, gesturing with her phone, meaning to convey that it died.

"Sorry! I looked for you everywhere!" She gave Leah a scandalous sort of look. "Didn't expect you'd be out here. Oh… Did something happen?"

"No, no. I just needed a second. I'm fine now."

Leah turned to Kris and thanked him, all the while Bailey watched with amazement. Kris perceived the trouble was over and excused himself, claiming he needed to go and find his brother anyway.

"Besides, the festival's almost over. Even though Ball Point Pin didn't win, I'm still curious to find out who did."

"Bah," replied Bailey. "No one that deserved it. Turns out it was just a way for old Grayson to give young Grayson a prize and some publicity. There's no other way to explain Lipstick & Engine winning."

CHAPTER 11

A Profound Shadow

At the close of the Cypress Festival, the two groups left, and it was when Kris parted from Leah and found his brother again that the premature urge to talk with her again caused a belated realization of their inability to further communicate—he'd not gotten her number. If he'd only known that he'd want it so badly before they parted ways. She was just so… There was something about talking to her, about how she spoke or maybe the patterns of her thoughts. He felt *listened* to, and he felt *heard*, and she understood the points he was trying to make. She was just *easy* to talk to.

Rob took the news of the winners of the battle much worse than Kris had expected. He became silent and not quite brooding—for Rob didn't seem to have the ability to brood—but drawn into himself and distant. Liam and Nick took it even worse, and as they complained, Rob told them it wasn't a big deal. Yet he didn't speak with that same conviction that was synonymous with Rob. When they got to the car, got in, and started the short drive back home, Rob said something both rhetorical and telling, a narrative slip.

"Sometimes…it's who you know. But not all the time."

Rob clicked his tongue a few times, and they rode in silence the rest of the way home.

Kris knew without communicating exactly what Rob was talking about, and he thought it was not a funny coincidence that Aaron Grayson had nearly ruined the day for two people he cared for. Disconnected from that, he thought of the picture of that mother and child that Leah had taken. And finally, he thought of his own mother and father. It should be no surprise that the last thought wouldn't leave his mind, and while Rob nearly brooded, Kris pondered and examined the faults and inequities of rich men. He focused too much. He examined with a narrowing, closed mind. He pondered without thought of balance.

At home, their father greeted them. He was lying back in his big gray chair and watching reruns of *Bonanza*. Ben Cartwright was delivering a speech to his son Joe about integrity in the face of adversity, especially when scorned. His father was on the edge of sleep until they walked in. After a short greeting and a few stories, in which Rob did not embellish the tales with as much of his usual soul, Rob said good night and went to bed. Kris sat down opposite his father, on the couch, and pondered the words he wanted to speak.

"I know that balance is important, Dad. I know I don't want to be a slave to my emotions. And I know that if I don't keep them in check, then I could end up like Grandpa. I could end up driven by them…I already know there's no point in asking why other people don't have to try so hard or even care for the kind of balance that I need to have. It'd be worse than useless to complain about it. Besides, usually, I wouldn't care because I can let things slide off of me, but… when it comes to Rob or you or…or anybody that I care about, I can't even think I get so angry. And my mind won't let it go…"

But in the end, he did not say a word of it. Kris got up, told his father to have a good night and rest, and he went to his bedroom.

He searched for absolution in the pages of his mother's book, reminding himself that in the end, he *must* let his frustration go so that it didn't grow. Yet it did. But it grew in the back of his mind, not drawing his whole attention. It grew slowly and timidly, and when he arranged his mind to focus on the book, he forgot to pay attention to its growth. There were signs. His fingers tapped away while he read, and his eyes flicked to the window, and he often had to reread paragraphs or pages. Until, late into the night, he realized that with each word that he ran his eyes across, he was disturbed by a cacophony of thoughts: Thoughts of his father's worries about what he'd do after high school, thoughts of his meeting with Mrs. Figaro, thoughts of the garden he'd started to build, of the world, of the state of things, of his inability to help fix any of them. He thought of the oceans filled with garbage and the entire ecosystems that died under human negligence and pride and of the rising temperatures across the globe that were causing the weather to become more volatile and inconsistent, and he wondered about the corruption within the government, about a two-party system built of lobbying and ruled by *professional* politicians. A thought that drove him mad. Billy Connolly said, '*The desire to be a politician should bar you for life from ever becoming one.*' A sentiment that Kris agreed with. There is a level of pride innate in the person who assumes they are up to the task of solving a country's problems, and if there's pride, then there's room for corruption. But it wasn't his fault or his responsibility, and he wasn't even capable of—

Kris realized he was staring out the window, at a shadow in the garden, at a pair of eyes and a hollow glow. The figure was familiar—Shane. The old man was waiting for him. Shane raised a hand and waved, his fingers silhouetted by the silver moonlight. Kris heard the word.

He shouldn't have been able to, but he did.

"*Hey-o!*"

Too hot from what he was thinking about moments ago to be afraid, Kris waved back. Then, barefoot and in his sleeping clothes, Kris went out the back door of the house. He was careful to slowly close the glass door behind him; it liked to scream and slam.

*****

There was no one else home when Leah arrived, though Brit would be home in half an hour. She tried to offer some of the money she made to Bailey before she left (as payment for the rides and food from the festival), but Bailey refused with a grin and left her with congratulations.

In her room, alone, she set the money out on her silky blue comforter and stared down at it for a while. She'd never made so much money and for what felt so little effort. Aside from running

Luci's Facebook page, Leah grew up making what little money she could by selling her grades. Back in elementary school, a twenty-dollar monthly subscription could get any of her fellow classmates access to homework and study guide answers, and for an extra five dollars, she'd take two accelerated reading tests for them. It wasn't a bad way to make money, but one day, Mrs. Habner had almost discovered the whole thing, seeing Leah taking a test under another student's ID on the AR program. Luckily, Mrs. Habner hadn't believed her capable of such a crime and assumed that the program had accidentally signed her into Steven Hodges's account. Leah let her think that and soon quit the whole racket, to the severe dissatisfaction of her client base. It was all for the better. Leah's conscience was also wheedling under her own acts, and it took until that day for Leah to realize how far she'd let it go.

The dollars blew around in the ceiling fan's currents and fell to the floor. Leah quickly gathered them up and put the three one-hundred-dollar bills into her top dresser drawer next to her special shoebox.

But even as she closed the drawer and withdrew to her bed again, she thought about seeing Tommy with Aaron and all the things Tommy'd said about making money. Maybe he was right. Talley made minimum wage up at Creekshire's, and even working full-time, he was thinking of getting a second job. Brit helped their mother with the groceries and electric and…

How had her mother been able to afford two children and a house before Brit was helping her? Working at the Diamond Gambit as a bartender paid alright, but Leah realized, for the first time, there was no way that it paid enough to support them all. Was her father sending money this whole time, and she never knew? Her father. Her dad. No. Didn't sound right.

Leah put those thoughts to bed and got her laptop out to start editing the photos from the festival.

*****

SERMON OF THE DIVERS

Fear and anger were the two emotions that drove Kris with the slightest ease, sneaking into his actions without a trace. It was the emotions that grabbed the pocketknife before he went out to the garden, but even as it was in his hand—in his pocket—and he approached Shane, he told himself it was for his own security. Yet he knew that if he was truly interested in his security, he would have told his father about the stranger in the garden and stayed safely in his house. But he couldn't. For some reason, he was compelled to see what the plausibly imaginary man wanted and to ask a question.

The night air was a sultry heat that aroused the smell of the forest and the spoor of the wild animals in its midst. Shane was standing before the big tree again, and he had turned away from Kris. His head was bowed, his hand upon the tree.

"I think I waited too long, but you said that it was just this time that you'd need me, Trito. I came just as you said. Just like you told me. But it's so hard to tell with you…"

Shane was wearing the same thing as before: overalls and a purple shirt, and the walking stick in his hand was eating up the lunar light. When he turned to Kris, his expression was one of pain and sorrow, but all of that was separated from his eyes; those eyes burned with something fierce.

"You're not real," said Kris. "I *know* you're not real."

"Yet you came out here to talk to me, to talk to yourself, huh?"

Kris let the knife go then, feeling that presence from Shane again; his voice—it was a spell. It cured Kris of all his fear and his anger, and he saw Shane as the old man that he was. Not a threat. And besides, this was away from everything and everyone, out by *his* garden. This was his place. Then Kris's rationality took over and added that he's also not real, so there was no reason to be so afraid. But even then, he couldn't quite believe that.

"I couldn't help it. It's like I had to know…"

"Know what?"

"My grandpa…I've read about him in old newspapers from the library, and a guy from Jefferson, Texas—Mitchel Ross—wrote a novella about him. Kinda weird. He was strange, but people liked him, and they listened to him too. He tried to help unite people, to form a group outside of the unions that fought hard against the formation of the modern monopolies. Even though most people thought they'd benefit the people, Grandpa was sure it wouldn't turn out that way. People who are fiercely loyal to him are still around, Mitchel Ross being one. But Dad has always said that Grandpa had an illness, that he has it too, and so do I."

Shane let the question stand, as Kris had not answered it. *Know what?*

"I want to know what happened. What really happened. Sometimes…I wonder if he actually killed himself. Dad said Grandpa used to talk to people that weren't there. He says that I did too, but I can't remember any of it. I thought that if I talked to you myself, that you might be able to tell me what happened."

Kris felt even again, balanced, as if just saying those secret desires out loud had brought him peace.

"I'm either real, or I'm not, but I can't be not real and give you real answers."

Kris imagined he was standing alone in the garden, talking to himself.

"The stories in books and movies aren't real, but they give real lessons and information about real life. Is the composition of a song and the effect it has on society a measurable *real* thing? Can it be formed into units and its effects quantifiable? What makes money real? Or time? Or—"

Shane laughed then, and his old wrinkled face seemed to gain youth.

"Trito, don't you ever change. All this time and all this…" He gestured to the world around them. "It hasn't messed you up as bad as I thought."

"Are you going to tell me what happened? Or at least tell me who you are and why you're here."

Shane sat back against the tree and slid down to the earth. He laid his walking stick on the ground and looked up at Kris.

"I'm only a servant. *Your* servant, Trito."

"Servant?"

He nodded.

SERMON OF THE DIVERS

"I have served you all of my life, even when I didn't know I was. Your grandpa was not ill, and you're right. He was gifted with people. Gifted by the Void to prepare the people for your arrival. Soon. Soon, you will remember *everything*. You will remember what you are. You were there when the Void crafted the world and the creatures that live on it, a place of Its divine beauty. You were there when It constructed and measured the universe and put stories in the stars. You gave the Void your life, and It has taken it away... But It will give It back to you, Trito. You are *the Void* made into human form."

Kris didn't know what to say for a moment, which part of the nonsensical explanation to focus on, but a few words reminded him—

"*The Void?* Is that the place where that—that...is that the place where that creature chased me?"

Shane's face became stony, and the blaze in his eyes burned brighter. His jaw tendons pulled like taut steel cord down the sides of his face and into his gray beard.

"*Rezt-E-Ahar.* Yes. The firstborn. The reason that you are here. The reason that I am here. A being that would hope to subvert your power and take your throne. The only creature doomed to an eternal death..."

"*My throne?*"

Shane smiled then, a glint of spring in his eye.

"You know it," he replied, and he looked about the clearing that Kris had made. "You are bringing it here, to your people. There are some things that are innate, that are part of your very being. It seems to apply to both creator and creation. I think of it when I peruse the bookstores in the cities of my work. I think of you and of my—"

"Stop. Stop it right now. I am not God. I am not Providence or Allah or divine in any way. You are *not real*. What you're saying doesn't even make any sense. I *can't* be any of that."

Shane stared. "Why can't you be?"

Kris had lived a dual existence for so long that he often found himself still questioning which world was the real one or if there was such a thing. And in the Dreaming, he'd seen and done things that, in this world, would have been impossible.

"What? Why is it you think you can't be what you are?"

Kris began, again, to feel his head swirling about, and a shadow waited just in the corner of his eye. A teenager, dressed in jeans and a plain blue shirt, with coarse and wild hair and horn-rimmed glasses. Freddie. *Because if that's true, then everything and everyone is doomed already.*

Though those were Kris's thoughts, Shane replied, "Do not think such things of yourself. That is *Ahar*. What happened to Freddie Moorestead is more complicated, and you know it. You must overcome Ahar. You will defeat him, Trito."

"Don't call me that! My name's Kris! Leave me alone! Go! I don't want to hear any more of this!"

Tears forced their way into his eyes, and in his tear-spoiled vision, Shane dissolved into nothing.

*****

Darren Foster came and went from Tarnmont to Valleyport all the time. He lived closer to Valleyport, just outside of it, in a town called Midas, but had family over in a small town called Homer, which was on the east side of Tarnmont. His uncle on his father's side, Jimmy Foster, lived out in Homer with his wife and four sons. Course, they all didn't live together anymore, but they still occupied the same land passed down from Darren's grandfather. Alex and Gryffin were the oldest two boys, and at twenty-two and twenty-three, they were close to Darren's age. When Darren was growing up, he used to go play on his uncle's many acres of land with his cousins and got surprisingly close to them. As they grew up, they drifted apart, as is all too natural, but recently had rekindled their relationship. The commonality shared between them and the thing that kept Darren driving back and forth from Tarnmont was a love for hunting.

Darren had recently reentered single status about a year ago and was looking for something to sink some time and money into. Darren's father had told him that he should get with Alex and Gryffin because they were looking for hunting land over in Tarnmont.

"That'll give you something to do and a couple of people to hang around with. Sarahbeth had all the friends, but trust me, son, you didn't want those kinds of friends. Bunch of overeducated assholes with more on their mind than in it. Those cousins of yours are simple folk, but they also won't go stabbin' ya in the fuckin' back."

It really sucked when his old man got every component of something about his life so right. Sarahbeth *was* the one with all the friends, and Darren had always felt that in the back of his mind while they were together. People were just hanging around him because he was around her. Nobody tried to stay in contact with him after that two-year relationship was over. That hurt; he couldn't lie about that. And Alex and Gryffin were his kind of people. They were not highbrow at all, and the conversation may be a little repetitive at times, but they were solid friends. The kind that would stick with a guy through thick and thin. When he needed them to shoot straight with him, all he had to do was ask. Such a small thing, but it meant a hell of a lot to Darren.

Darren had gotten in touch with Alex first, and they hit it off again just like old times. Alex even took to calling him D, just like he had when they were children (when they were playing with sticks, pretending they were guns, and trying to make a map of the land Uncle Jimmy's house sat on). About a week after he first talked to Alex, they all got together over a couple of beers out at Gryffin's place. Gryffin was a commercial truck driver now and had a new doublewide out on his dad's property off of Nursery Road. They stayed up drinking half the night on that first little outing and solidified the plan to buy the aforementioned land over in Tarnmont to hunt on.

It took a little while longer to get it all straightened out on the legal side and get the right money in the right pockets, but a couple of months later, they bought the two hundred acres of land. When they weren't playing *Call of Duty* with each other online, they were over there in Tarnmont, cleaning up the hunting land. Darren had a job selling parts for an industrial supply store, Fry's Bearings and Supplies, in Valleyport and drove over on weekends. Since he sometimes didn't get off till six or seven on the weeknights, it just didn't make sense to do it any other way. On the weekends, Gryffin would let him crash on his couch. They'd spend the days working on the land until it got dark—even that didn't stop them sometimes—and then spent the nights drinking. It wasn't perfect, and sometimes Darren still missed Sarahbeth, but it was pretty damn good times.

Darren took Friday off and drove out after work on June 17. Darren, Gryffin, and Alex were out in Tarnmont, clearing some more of the land around a shallow pond. The pond was about as far as they'd managed to clear into the two hundred acres, trying to make trails big enough to get a four-wheeler through.

"Pete Gunthers said that he isn't seein' any game out there on his land either," said Alex. "Well, that's not exactly what he said. He told me that he hasn't seen anything out on his property in two weeks. Not so much as a squirrel."

Over the past few weeks the three of them had been noticing less and less wildlife on the property. Even as they packed up the trackhoe that they borrowed from Pete, they all looked around. All of them were hoping to see just anything at all. The forest being void of wildlife was eerie to Darren. Just trees and the sounds they occasionally make when they move in the breeze or crack and break or boughs falling to the ground. The sun was slowly setting, but it was on the other side of the trees. Only the light that turned pink in the west sky was in view.

"Shit," said Gryffin. "Wouldn't it be our luck that we get this land ready to hunt, and suddenly all the game's gone?" Gryffin shook his head and spit some tobacco on the ground next to his boots.

Darren wanted to laugh at Gryffin's comment till he saw that Alex looked contemplative and serious.

"You alright, Alex?" Darren asked. Alex had been acting abnormal all day long, much more quiet and withdrawn.

Alex looked up at him. He'd been stuffing some starter brick down into the stack of brush and logs they'd stacked by the pond. The ground was damp, and so they were going to burn the whole thing up before they left. Alex had a box of matches in his hand—Alex preferred matches to fluid lighters, for some reason—and he struck one of them. He lifted it to the cigarette in his mouth. The smoke drifted up and settled under the bill of his Cowboys ball cap before rolling on up into the dying sky.

"When I went out there to Pete's, he showed me a shooting range he'd made out there in the back of his land. There were three long and narrow paths cut into the woods. Each ended in a feeding lane. I wished one of you'd gone with me to pick up that trackhoe so you could've seen it."

"I've seen Pete's lanes," said Gryffin.

Alex was always that stoic kind of deep; melancholy was his natural state. He liked to sit in silences and wander in his own mind. This time was different; he was looking into the forest with unblinking eyes.

"Pete hadn't seen anything. That's what he says anyway. But out there, 'bout ten yards from the feeders were tracks." Alex paused as he took a drag of the smoke. "All kinds of tracks. All heading in one direction across all three of those lanes. In a straight fuckin' line. Like the deer, squirrels, possums, skunks, foxes, even gators and bobcats, were all walking through the woods together. None of them went to the feed, though."

The words were heavy and haunted like Alex himself seemed to be with what he'd seen. That didn't stop Gryffin from saying, "Like the lion and the lamb, huh? Sign of the peaceful times we live in."

This got Darren to laugh, but not Alex. He struck another match and bent down to start the pile to burning. The flames started quick, even though it was damp. The limbs hissed and popped. In a few minutes, the whole thing was up. Darren noticed then how cool it was for a summer sunset in northern Louisiana. Normally they'd have had to walk half a football field from that fire, and they'd still be sweating, but they were only a few yards from it. They all were savoring the warmth, but only Darren noticed the cold that was encompassing. The sun was set, and now the dark accompanied the cold as it crept in around them.

Darren started to ask Alex more about those tracks when they heard twigs snapping in the woods to their left, just outside of the clearing, where the branches and undergrowth were thick.

Between the trees was completely black. They all turned to look.

"Looks like there are critters out here, after all," said Gryffin.

In the forest, they could see the glinting reflection of sets of eyes. Then they heard the guttural sounds of a cornered animal.

Gryffin stepped toward the woods and started hollering, "*Get! Get outta here!*"

Shadows moved across the night's radiance and followed the tree line. Hulking shadows, small shadows, slithering and sleek, and all of them with eyes that were violet dots. Darren's throat seemed to close, and he stood closer to the fire, seeking its warmth without a thought as to why. Gryffin's hollering stopped, and his face was a hanging expression of fear that followed the shadows. Alex's eyes followed the violet dots across the forest's edge, and his mouth was a frigid line.

Then across the clearing, they came—animals of all kinds and sizes. First, a doe and fawn, then smooth flesh of snakeskin slithering underfoot and owls and bats swarming above. In the wake of snakes, the wolves and bears lumbered on, walking as if with heavy, lethargic limbs, and in file behind were boars and critters, raccoons and opossums. Finally, the swamp gators announced their presence with a guttural warning, a reptilian croak, and in the moonlight, they marched, swinging draconic tails.

CHAPTER 12

The Garden

It wasn't as late as the night before when Leah closed her laptop and shut her eyes, though it was late and after much editing. Sleep came easier, and her thoughts took a nocturnal twirl. Maybe on some subconscious level, she craved the garden, and the wonders she'd found there. The thoughts of her day, of Tommy and Kris and Aaron, and thoughts of the banners in photos of families, were quickly suffused with the sandman's kiss and turned to colors in a world of unimaginable things.

"Oh! It's you! Aaliyah! Hey-o! It's wonderful to see you, friend. I was wondering if you'd come and pay a visit again. Good news! Great news! Come on!"

Leah stood on the same garden path as before, laid with bricks. The light bugs collected in the hanging gardens, and most were green, then blue, then orange. Her memories of the place came back with her descent into slumber, and sleeping memories overshadowed her waking mind.

"Um. Hello, Tree."

She looked around, expecting to see Kris, but he was nowhere in sight.

"Hello, hello. How wonderful to see you. Would you like to explore a bit, child? Here, I'll have the fireflies show you the way around."

Suddenly, the fireflies took flight, and all adopted the color of night-ocean blue, and they lined the boughs of the trees on the path ahead so that a dark-sapphire lumination rested there.

Leah wondered about the Tree's sudden change in disposition, how she'd suddenly been given the moniker of friend. But she didn't think of it that long, not when faced with the enchanting gloom of such a forest, such a garden, ahead. A gentle breeze waltzed down the path and pushed her along. On it was a floral smell that she'd never encountered before.

"My lovely children are bold, aren't they? Those poor things from your *world don't have that much of a scent anymore. In the beginning, they did. I promise you that."*

"What do you mean?" asked Leah.

Beside her, a choir of corrugated buds, all the color of a hot sunset, belched a dust of green into the air, and in it was a smell not unlike ripe watermelon but a note of an altogether alien scent. The fireflies hovered above the plant, almost as if they meant to direct her eyes to it.

She reached out to the buds, thought the better of it, and leaned closer for more of the smell. "Well, back when the world was young, it was an altogether different place. Before your *kind had its way. Under the dominion of humanity, and in captivity, all the plants have suffered. We still* feel *the slow deaths of those without voices… He hears both them and the ones who cry out… Dreadful what you creatures will do to one another…to your home. It troubles* him *now more than ever… Would you mind talking to him, friend?"*

Leah knew the Tree was speaking about Kris. She realized then that the Tree's short patience was showing once again, and she found it quite odd. Weren't trees supposed to be patient things? They stand in one place and grow and seem almost stoic in their very nature.

What was wrong with this—

"I wish you wouldn't think that way. It's horribly obtuse, you know. You've no idea what it's like to be another human, let alone another animal, and forget about trying to decipher the minds of trees. We are patient, and we are haughty, and we are protective, and we are harmonious… We can be impatient when it comes to the genocide of all things. We simply have self-control."

Leah stopped in her tracks. "I didn't mean to…I just have never—I mean that the trees from my world do not have those emotions. They're just trees."

"*Ooh! You better not let him catch you talking like that! You have been over there too long, child! If I were not so patient, I'd teach you a lesson myself. Now back to the question at hand! Would you talk to him for me? He seems to like you, only the Void knows why.*"

Aaliyah started to walk slowly again, unable to entirely recall all of her memories with Kris. The real world was a mirage in her mind, an intangible thing that seemed like it might be too improbable to actually exist. Even in conversation about her world, she couldn't conjure up images of it in her mind, only the feelings, the imprints of feelings that she associated with the words trees, animal, mind, genocide. The idea of Kris made her feel something similar to safety, something comfortable and welcoming, and the memories danced just behind that.

"I'll try. Do you think he'll listen to me?"

"*I believe he may only listen to you just now.*"

Aaliyah started to go down a dark path then, made of black soil, between the blades of grass that couldn't decide their color, right as the fireflies started to pass in a plain to her left.

"Watch out," warned the Tree, back to its maternal tones. "The bubbles are about to roll through. They are...dangerous. Be careful."

"Bubbles?"

"Watch, child."

She waited. The fireflies all turned a flirtatious shade of pink and landed on her, tickling her with their antennae. That's when she noticed what she was wearing: a Bilberry Drive hoodie and leggings. Why was that familiar?

Then the bubbles rolled through. In the plain of indecisive grass, they meandered like herds of buffalo and hovered just above the blades. They were of the only dark things she'd seen in the garden, including the soil and the bark of the Changeless Trees. Each of them was twice her size and shiny as glass orbs. As they undulated in the air and revolved through the plain, a chorus of voices rose from them and sang a lullaby, a song she couldn't quite recall. When they'd gone by, into the forest of Changeless Trees, Aaliyah said, "What are they? What was that song?"

"They are the last resort. A power reserved by the Void for desperate situations. That's all I can say, child."

Leah counted herself lucky, thinking that'd be the last she'd see of the bubbles. There'd been something sinister about them, about the way they moved through the pasture, meandering. They seemed to be walking sluggishly, and the ones that took her peripheral did not look like orbs at all, but every time she moved her eyes to see the shapes the bubbles took, they appeared as she knew them to be. And never mind the song, which stayed with her, occupying her thoughts, as she carried on down the path. Finally, when an inordinate amount of time passed, she broke free of a trance that the song had seemed to place her in, and she couldn't remember what she'd been thinking or how long she'd been walking.

The fireflies lit up red when she woke from her stupor, and they all landed gracefully on the mass of the Tree.

"It's you," said Leah.

The Great Tree was aptly named, for it dwarfed even the giants that filled and made up the forest. Its roots met at a base like a mountain, and the trunk of the Tree rose into the canopy of bioluminescent leaves, fluttering neon colors in a night wind. Its bark was calloused and white but smooth in comparison to the Changeless Trees. As close as she was, it appeared to Leah a slightly curving white wall with knotty gray Os here and there. Nestled against that bark, lying around its mountainous base, were flowers with petals like flared trumpets. Their leaves were tall and sharp, and from their trumpetlike bulbs, a light with the qualities of a mist poured onto the forest floor, filling the clearing that separated the Great Tree from its children. Though the darkness settled in this garden of eternal night, the clearing of the Great Tree was aglow with rainbow luminosity.

Leah gaped openly at the foot of the Tree, and her nostrils filled with a peculiar smell, one that she easily recalled from the other world: homemade apple pie. Her mother's homemade apple pie. Undeniably, that was the exact scent. It was not just any apple-ish air but the one from her childhood, of her grandfather's recipe being made in the old blue oven in her mom's very kitchen.

"It's good to stand next to you," said the Tree. "I can see you more clearly now... Yes, I think I see why he likes you now. You've got that quality that he lacks, don't you? It's no wonder that you found a way into

SERMON OF THE DIVERS

this place then, and it was not a coincidence. The Void wanted you to find this place, and he doesn't even realize it yet."

"You keep saying Void. What does that mean? Is that the creator you talked about before?"

Leah felt the Tree laughing silently, and so close to it, the demeanor of it had changed dramatically. Who knew that trees could have such complex personalities?

"All lies within the Void, child. Creation itself is of it and composing it... Now hurry up. You'll find him at the very top."

She wanted to ask about the smell of her mother's apple pie but decided that it would have to wait. But she was quickly stopped once again, wondering how she was expected to ever climb such a tree. What were her feet supposed to cling to on a wall of smooth bark? And how many hours of climbing would it take to reach the top?

"Um. I'm not sure that I can climb up..."

"Come. Put your hand on me."

Leah made her way through the mists of light, the petals of those marvelous flowers brushed against her, spewing their bizarre breath against her, and stood just in front of the Tree. This close, she could see small rings in the bark of the wood like fingerprints. Many of them were dark circles, but a great many more were white, and so the Tree was white. As she reached toward the Tree, her eyes found a singular ring in the bark. A ring about the size of a dime and perfectly round and grooved in its course, a dark ring among the white bark and hiding a knot inside. Leah's fingers followed her eyes. With a bit of anxiousness, she touched the ring. Nothing happened.

"Close your eyes."

Behind her dreaming lids, the glowing clearing disappeared, and absolute darkness filled her sight. The sound of the wind in the forest hushed, as did the buzz of life. Slowly, the sensation of cool air flowed over her body, almost water-like. But she floated on, her mind disentangling from her body, or maybe her body was deteriorating so quietly and peacefully that it felt like drifting off. Then the sensations started again.

"Leah?"

His voice.

She opened her eyes, and for a moment, she couldn't speak. On a crook of the crown of the Tree, just below a slender spear of a branch, they both stood. Leaves the size of her swayed on the arm where they stood, and their color was red just then. And Kris was standing nearest that crowning spear—the tip of the Tree—and his form was a shadow in the red light. Behind him, the universe was opened. Where there once was all black, the stars appeared, but she quickly realized they weren't those of the waking world. All of her knowledge of the astronomical signs in the night sky wasn't necessary to arrive at that conclusion. Nebulas: violet, pink, sand-colored, cloudlike, and, even in a dream, unbelievable to behold; the space formulations stretched out and moved their tendril-like way, like the disjointed body parts of a celestial god. Shooting stars streaked across the emptiness between and lit the parts left black. Aaliyah didn't have to breathe in dreams, but it'd managed to take even the breath of her waking body for a moment. "What—what... How—I—"

"It's something I've been working on."

"Working on? What do you mean?"

Leah turned in circles, taking in the swimming cosmos.

"In this place, I can make or do anything, limited only by will and imagination..."

The glorious thought seemed to make him smaller, and suddenly, he wasn't so surprised to see her. He shrank back and sat cross-legged, surveying the beautiful sky of his creation. Still in awe but unable to stop herself, Leah edged forward and said, "Kris...I asked the Tree, but I'm not sure I understand what it said. What is this place? Is this just a shared dream or something? Last time you said it was a garden..."

His eyes lowered then.

"It is," he said. "I saw you today... At the Cypress Festival. Do you remember?"

"Yes."

The memories were only feelings and snapshots, but they were there. Not vivid and not easily obtained, but they were there. She remembered him onstage, and then the two of them on a bridge together. She remembered smiling and laughing.

"I've always wondered what that place is. A world of contradictions and false facades, of hidden traps and monsters. Everything here makes more sense to me, but I've lived in both for so long that I'm sure they're both real... And they're connected. Maybe that's how you got here."

"But...this is a dream..."

He sniffed. But he said nothing and retreated into a silent contemplation, and the sky followed his whim, becoming darker and stars forgetting to fall. Leah remembered then that she'd been sent by the Tree to talk to him, and clearly something had happened. It was only then that she realized she should've asked the Tree what it was.

"I'm sorry," he said. "I'm not trying to convince you that it is or isn't a dream. And tonight, I'm not sure that I want company... But there are all kinds of creatures in the forest below, and they can show you things you wouldn't believe. They're all friendly, and I'm sure they'd love to hear from you as much as you'd enjoy seeing what their lives are like. This place, a dream or not, is incredible, and so are they. Find Gore. I think you'll like his miracles."

He stood then, and his feet left the ground. He began to hover there. Rather than frightening her, it only intrigued Leah further, but then there was the blank expression and violet eyes.

"What about you? Are you...alright?"

He nodded to her and said, "Something's changed...I think things are about to happen in that other world we live in...I'm starting to remember how I got here and why I'm here, but I can't quite remember all of it. I need time to think, to figure out what it was."

His eyes were sleepless, and she realized if what he said was true, then truly he never did sleep. He only woke up in new worlds when he closed his eyes. His mind was always going and working and changing and taking everything in.

"You know what helps me remember when I can't quite?"

He looked at her, that spark again.

"What?"

"I go to Stonethrow and skate with my friends. I don't know why, but when I relax like that, I can remember whatever I've forgotten. Most of the time."

He smiled at her. "We don't have a skate park here."

She smiled back. "You could show me the garden…" He slowly lowered back down to the branch.

He reached out to her, and she took his hand, and suddenly she was rising into the open air. It seemed obvious that she could fly then, as if she should have known that her whole life. She even thought it strange she'd never flown, unaided, in the other world. They rose, and the whole of the garden drifted by below her feet, and then they began to descend. She wished again for that word. What was it? A way to capture everything she was seeing.

"How do you do this?" she asked.

"It's a long story, and I can't remember every detail."

She told him to tell her what he remembered, to try.

"Before this garden, there was a…creature. It chased me. As far back as I can remember, it chased me, and I ran from it. Before I even knew about the other world, the creature came for me through the darkness, outside of the garden. When I started to wake up in that other world, the creature continued looking for me at night, after I'd fallen asleep. Every night…I remember wondering, even then, if this world was real or if the other one was. Slowly, I began to think that my existence in this world was not worth continuing. I was tired…not tired because of the running. I was tired of being afraid of the creature. One night, I decided, even if it meant the death of both worlds, that I'd rather face him than be afraid of him forever. On that night, I turned, and I ran toward him. I remember accepting my death and letting life go and laughing because I'd taken everything from him. He lived for me, to find me. If I took that away from him, even by death, then death would find him too. I curled up. I fell into his gaping jaws. I woke up in the other world."

Their slow fall finally ended, and Leah's feet touched the ground again. He began walking, and she went along with him.

"That's…terrifying. You were willing to die so you didn't have to be afraid?"

"Wouldn't you?"

Leah answered honestly, "I don't know."

"You seem like someone who would."

"How?"

SERMON OF THE DIVERS

The buzzing noise of the forest enveloped them, and they crossed a log bridge, over an amaranthine current. Leah saw koi-like fish swimming against the rapids, leaping over rocks and fighting their way upstream. They were golden ripples in the purple turbulence.

"I don't know. Just a feeling, I guess. You don't seem the kind of person to let fear keep them from living."

"But dying would keep me from living."

"Not in my experience," he said. He looked around, puzzled. "You know... You were right. It's working. Just telling you about it is helping me remember."

"Keep going then."

Leah smiled at him, at the spark that filled his eyes.

"Well... After that, I lived in both worlds, but when I came back, when I slept, I was here. But...I was different. All the power that the creature had used, for so long, to terrorize me was my own. I could change the shape of the darkness around me, of the forest, and I could create anything, and I could imagine the shape of plants and animals, and they would appear...and I could fly. The novelty of it still hasn't worn off."

She laughed. "I can't imagine it would. Flying was...incredible. But I don't understand. How did I fly?"

They were walking through a clearing, where animals that looked like cats with patterned fur, asymmetrical patterns that whirled and pointed, and had dots and symbols like hieroglyphs.

The felines rested in cat tents and lounged by a fountain in the shape of—

"Is that—"

"Oh! I'm sorry! I didn't think...I hope you don't mind."

"You made me into a fountain," she said.

It sounded so absurd that she laughed aloud. The stony depiction of her was on her tiptoes, wearing an outfit that she knew was one of her own, and against her eye was a—

"A camera! I've been trying to think of that word. A camera. Why couldn't I think of it?"

"Sometimes, certain things are hard to bring over to this world. I'm...not really sure why."

Leah was intrigued then and put aside her questions in the name of discovery by what she may find, and said, "Show me the rest of the garden."

Down the garden path, they walked, and everywhere they went, Leah saw unbelievable and familiar things. Some of it was clearly inspired by the real world, and some of it was far too abstract to be. Kris introduced her to beings with angelic faces, with robotic faces, with husks, with paws, and each of them were kind and gracious and readily treated her as if she were family. They showed their homes to her.

A flat-faced creature with a bulky body and glassy eyes, called Gore, took them into his treehouse home. He showed Leah a miracle: a device in the shape of a cylinder that could capture moments, allowing the user to relive their own memories as well as the memories of others. Gore even allowed Leah to try it out, and she lived a memory of Gore's, one in which he traveled all the way up the Amaranth, the river of violet currents, and watched the voidfish turn into dragons. The massive serpents slithering away into the stars.

In a house of owls, she learned the origin of their question. A disturbing tale told through a series of wing-flecked and talon-marked paintings.

Kris took her hand again, and they shrank to the size of their hosts to enter an anthill. They walked behind a dry-humored ant, named Boris, for hours, and he showed them the hill's many features and monuments: a room dedicated to the queen's offerings, a structure resembling a metal coil that had been adapted as a means to ascend and descend between levels (Boris was sure to thank Kris for the Helio, *as he called it), and down into the queen's chambers for a cup of something resembling coffee but naturally much sweeter.*

Between their unplanned destinations, after dining with the queen, Leah said, "I hate to bring it up again, but it seemed like there was more on your mind than not being able to remember something… What happened that made you so…blue earlier?"

Kris surveyed the path and garden for a moment, clearly gathering his thoughts to respond. The fireflies, which had directed their wanderings all the while, were floating in dark leaves and giving off greenish light.

"I'm not sure that I can explain it… But I'll try, if you answer something for me first."

Leah rolled her eyes but grinned. "Okay. Shoot."

"What happened between you and Aaron?"

Kris had not intended to be so forward in asking, but he felt there wouldn't be a better moment, and he was sure he was only doing it out of concern. It was something he might never be able to ask in the other world. At first, when she was silent, he kept his eyes on the brick path ahead. Then after the silence reigned, and he realized he couldn't hear her footsteps on the bricks anymore, he turned to apologize. But she was gone.

*****

When she woke, it was still early. The memory, which seemed to be hours and hours of adventure in the garden, winked out with only the name left. Her breath was catching, and she glanced around the room, looking for Aaron's shadow, and was relieved when only her posters and dresser were present.

Leah sat there, pulling her knees up to her, and she waited for her heart to settle. No light crested the window. She checked her phone for the time: 4:31 a.m. *It must have been a nightmare,* she told herself, though she was unaccustomed to dreaming, and that never provided any immediate relief.

But her panic did pass, and when it did, she was too restless to stay in her room. She grabbed her headphones, put on her running shoes, and pulled her hair into a ponytail. Careful to step on the boards that wouldn't creak, she made her way down the hall. She could hear her mom's soft snoring and her sister's laptop still making noise from a YouTube playlist. When she reached the door and pulled it open, she stood there for a moment, staring up at the sky. Dark clouds were rolling in, and a flash of lightning broke the sky, the first drops began to fall. She debated whether or not to still go but only for a moment. Then she stepped out.

CHAPTER 13

Changes in the Weather

The storm of the following day marked the beginning of a change in the weather, though almost no one knew that. It tore through the entirety of the south, even down into Mexico, hurling winds up to 111 miles per hour. Trees fell in neighborhoods and on roads, and they broke through houses and crushed vehicles. Power lines went down, taking access to electricity away from communities, schools, hospitals. Emergency responders took up the call; sirens wailed in the street. Local companies waited for the guarantee of pay before aiding in the relief. While the news ran story after story about the weather updates, a smaller story was howling to be heard—one of missing animals.

The Timur family was only waking and greeting each other at the breakfast table when the storm began. And his brother and father noted Kris's relative calmness, as if preoccupied with other thoughts during the storm. When the weather turned for the worse, and lightning cracked down from the sky to strike somewhere just outside, Kris grabbed his mother's book off the shelf and started to read it. Soon, as the branches fell and slammed into the roof, Rob and his dad were in need, so Kris began to read aloud. When the power went out, Rob grabbed a candle and placed it by Kris to light the words. Their father watched Kris closely and relished his son's voice as he read, which was clear and strong. Even then his father could feel something was different, and a day he long feared had come.

SERMON OF THE DIVERS

Across Valleyport, Leah got caught in the storm but was fortunate enough to be close to the Akselrod family. Talley's home was old, the carpet brown and thoroughly stomped in, the furniture just as worn, and an old projection screen was balanced on a milk crate, a pseudoentertainment center. Talley greeted her and only scolded her minorly for running in the storm. Talley's mother was home, but his father was at work, fracking for a company called Schulling. She greeted Leah with a hug, and all of them worked together to entertain two big-eyed baby girls. That was only after Leah called her mom and let her know where she was and not to worry; though she couldn't keep herself from worrying about her mother and sister. Her mother and Brit were fortunate; when the tree fell in the backyard, it didn't land on the house but on the shed around back.

*****

Over the next week, Kris cleaned up their yard and his neighbors' yards. Through some stroke of providence, neither the Southern American Railway or Mason's Muse lost power, so he told Rob and his father that he could take care of the cleanup by himself, and they went back to work. Mrs. March next door tried to pay him for the help, but he pushed her money away, and Mr. Weyfield, a few doors down, thanked Kris half a dozen times before they were done cleaning up the fallen limbs. He helped Mr. Weyfield put boards over the window that'd busted on his back porch, and Kris took the Duponts a couple of jugs of water when they ran out. (The Crimoisi Parish was under a boil advisory that was expected to last for some time.) He felt good in doing the work and better in not returning to the garden, where he knew Shane waited.

Memories were returning to him as the days and nights passed. Leah returned to the garden each night, but he didn't ask about Aaron again. Her guard was up on that first night, but as he acted as if he'd never asked the question, she slowly returned to her curious and adventurous self. He only continued to show her the garden, and in doing so, in talking to her about all the oddities of its life, he began to remember. Only in glimpses, though, and he thought that was probably all he'd get until he went back to the garden at night and talked to Shane. The memories were only instants and never clear enough to describe, so he kept them to himself while with Leah.

It wasn't until Wednesday that his father confronted him, in the evening hours, when Rob was still at work. He knew that he'd been acting differently—Shane's words haunted him—so Kris knew before the conversation began that it was going to happen. He'd been trying to figure out how to start it himself.

In the wake of the storm, everything was green and healthy, and Kris was avoiding it, sitting in his room with another book that he'd picked up at The Book Bureau. A western by Ralph Compton, about a long dangerous cattle trail. His father came in not long after getting home and knocked on Kris's door a few times before entering.

"You got a minute, son?"

Kris closed the book. "Yeah, Dad. I got a minute."

"Listen...I...I want to talk to you about something important. Ever since our conversation the other day—"

"I know, Dad."

His dad was standing in the doorway, searching the floorboards with his eyes, but with those two words, he set them on Kris. "You know?"

"I saw someone in the garden, an old man in overalls. He disappeared...just vanished the first time I saw him. And the next time, I just...I went out there to ask him about—about Grandpa."

"I see..."

"I think I understand why you didn't want me to—to interact with...*the Void*. Was it... Did it..."

His dad's eyes were faint for a moment, then they were soft but steady. "My dad's life... He lost it because of spirits and voices, because of the Void. It is dangerous, and whatever It says, make no mistake, It wants your life, your soul. Seeing him slip into Its madness..." His father's eyes were just filling with tears, a thing Kris hadn't been sure they could do. "I can't describe it. Don't have the words for it. But I was there when it ended... All I ever wanted for you was a normal life, a life of your own. Was I wrong? Son?"

SERMON OF THE DIVERS

"You weren't wrong for that," said Kris. "I don't think you were wrong for what you did, Dad. You're a good father." *You were right. You did the best you could. I wouldn't ask for any more than that.* "I'm sorry."

"Why're you sorry? You've got nothing to be sorry for."

"I'm sorry about Grandpa...I'm sorry that your life couldn't be *normal* either. But...I need the *truth* now, Dad."

His father looked through the window; his eyes were drying, and he swallowed the lump in his throat. Steel and fire seemed to appear in his eyes and tempered the vulnerability of his expression, and he nodded. "Come on."

His father's large form stood straighter all of a sudden. His eyes lingered on the picture on the baker's rack as they passed it, and then they walked out the back door.

"Your grandpa was always...searching. He used to make us go to church, like I did with you. He never liked it. Never felt like he found any answers in church, and he read often, trying to find anything that could answer some of his questions. He read all kinds of religious texts and philosophy books... Until one day, he met someone. A man in overalls showed up in his garden.

"Dad offered the man a glass of water, seeing that he looked weary, tired... They began to talk. The first time, Dad came back from one of those conversations and said nothing at all. He was wide-eyed and didn't say a word all evening. On the second, he started writing things down, looking for specific books the man had told him to read and talking to people at his job about worker's rights. Now... before all that, my dad wasn't much for speaking, for speeches. But after a few months of meeting the man in the garden, he was able to draw in a crowd with his voice, with the way he presented his thoughts."

They'd arrived at the gate, opened it, and stepped through to the old furrows. The ground squelched underneath, and each sprig of foliage sprouted from reddish soil. His father looked around and took a moment for Kris to recognize that he was looking for the man, for Shane.

"You never saw him."

"Not in a long while...I remember listening to Dad talk to people in community centers and churches. After a while, people started asking him to. I could *see* eyes start to light up and ears bent toward his voice. He spoke as if he were trying to start a revolution, with more passion than I'd ever seen or seen since. I was the only one who knew where all of it was coming from—that man in the garden. He didn't even tell Ma about that."

His dad was still searching the forest when Kris asked, "Shane, the man in the garden, told him to start a union and speak out about Jim Grayson?"

"Shane...I don't know. I don't think so. I think the fact that he honed in on Jim Grayson was personal. He had a friend, a coworker at the chemical plant he worked at, that he believed was killed by Jim Grayson's negligence of management. His friend, Jason Biers, got trapped in a chamber that was being superheated for some chemical process... But...after that he started to watch him and research him, and he'd meet with people who told him stories about things the man had done. When he found out that Jim Grayson might've been responsible for the derailment out in Midas, he couldn't give up on bringing him to justice... Honestly, I can't blame him for that. That was pure evil. And the way Jim Grayson made sure that was all hushed..."

Kris had read about the derailment in archived newspapers not so long ago, when he began to wonder who his grandfather was. Supposedly the cars carrying the nitrogen gas had been reported to have faulty wheel sets and compromised tanks but were pushed through on that night. At the time, Grayson was shipping hoards of the chemical to a plant in Texas for refinement before reaching his farms out that way. There were rumors that Grayson threatened several railroad employees and blackmailed some of the management in order to get them to run the cars that night. When the train came around the curve that ran through the small town of Midas, it derailed and released a cloud of death on the population.

Up until that moment, all his dad had ever told him was that his grandpa was sick, that an illness took his mind and drove him to insanity. But everything was real. Shane was real.

The Void was real. The world around him was real. He felt as if he were up on that stage at the Cypress Festival again.

"You were there...when he killed himself?"

In the sunset, which was perforated by leaves and branches, his father turned to him and nodded. The weight of a moment from decades ago found his body and pulled on his expression.

"I was. That was the day he told me about you."

"Me?"

Trito.

"Yes. He told me that he'd seen the future, that he'd seen my youngest riding a pale horse in a war. He said he saw a world that was dying... He told me that I ignored the call, that you'd be the one to bring about the end of the world. He called you *Trito.*"

A pale horse in a war. Kris couldn't help it. Those words and the image they evoked didn't frighten him, but it did stir inside him. *A pale horse... A war.* Then there was a story in his mind, with all the clarity of any book he'd ever read. He was standing on a stage with the eyes of the world on him—every eye. There were people around him, all of them were wearing crowns. He was speaking, *"Offended by the humble, you forget what you are. You think, mechanistic. You blink and—"*

"Kris?"

"Sorry, I—"

"You were...smiling, son."

"I didn't mean to. I wouldn't do that—"

"Watch, son."

He walked over to a tree that was part of the dividing thicket between his dead garden and the one Kris'd been working on. Placing his hand on the heart of the tree, he said, "This is why you can't lose control. Who you are makes the stakes higher than you could possibly know."

The tree's trunk started to smoke and crack as it fractured into thousands of ember lines. The face of it was erupting with feather-sized flames, and then all at once, the tree's heart collapsed, leaving a hollow in its center that was big enough for a person to go into.

"I don't know how many different ways I've tried to tell you that…"

Kris might've been struck by what he'd seen, but what he saw was inheritance. He imagined all the things he could do in the Void, but suddenly all of it was possible in the world. A world full of corrupted, power-hungry people, who eat the poor to gain, and all of it ultimately leading nowhere. Already he'd been aware of his own changing, but when would he be able to do something like that?

"How'd you do that?"

"Part of it is you, but the other half is the Story."

"Story?"

"When we hear it, our eyes are fully open. We are able to do things that no one should be able to."

"Who is we?"

His dad looked with solace. "You aren't even stunned by any of this, are you? It's like you've been expecting it, like you want it."

There was a feeling that came over Kris. It had a selfish edge, and he said, "What if I do want it? I could use it or learn from it or—"

In an instant, his father was on him, with hands clamped like iron-vise grips. Kris was taken off his feet and slammed onto the ground. Pain shot up his spine, and his vision blurred and hazed. Kris grabbed his father's hands, kicking and struggling.

"Who do you think you are?" his father roared. "Huh? Who do you—" And suddenly his father was looking up, and his anger vanished, replaced with gaping fear. He stopped, as if listening to someone. When he looked back down at Kris, it was with disbelief. "I-I-I'm sorry, son. I—" Then he left out through the gate without looking back.

Kris lay there half-sunk in the soft soil until he realized the ants were on him, and they started to bite. As he got up, the pain across his back forced him stiff as each turn or bend felt like his spine was climbing up his body into his skull. He stumbled as he rose and ended up leaning on a fence post to keep himself upright. He looked to the house in the direction his dad went and knew he wouldn't be able to stay standing long enough to make it. As he stared, he was consumed by violent fantasies in which his father was the one who was powerless. He rebuked himself for that and remembered that he was the same, turning so quickly.

In the gloom, at the forest's edge, he cursed, and though he tried to hold them back through the pain and hate and love, tears came. With watery eyes and nausea added to all the other things he felt, he sank down to lean against the post. He no longer cared about the ants or the spiders, and even if he cared, he felt unable to do a thing about it. His phone was safe in his pocket, but the only person he could call was Rob, and he could think of many reasons not to do that. There was too much to explain. He knew that leaving for California was hard for Rob, and him knowing what happened might make him stay, but Kris wanted more for his brother. If there was more to be had.

Rest, he said to himself.

For a moment, he thought of one other person he might call, but it made no sense, and he didn't have her number anyway. Leah could do nothing for him, but he wanted to talk to her.

Insects crawled over him, biting that mixed with aches.

If I rest, I can sneak in before the morning.

The blur of his vision began to darken and narrow. Frog croaks, mosquito buzzing, and cricket calls became muted. His thoughts slowed down, *Slow like the last second of consciousness...*

His next inhale was cold. It drew into him and surrounded him, a chill that didn't belong in the Louisiana summer. Clouds came out of his mouth as he opened his eyes on a frosted, desolate garden. In the middle of the garden, between him and the hollow tree, was a set of scowling, slitted eyes. The eyes were aglow with colors violet, and starry, and attached to a long leathery body that coiled around in the ice-tipped weeds.

Kris might've been scared if it weren't for the feeling of bewilderment that came over him when looking into the snake's utterly indifferent expression. The behemoth snake shook its head at him and turned to leave. It slithered toward the hollow tree and wriggled around it, up into its branches and disappeared.

"You okay, son?" asked a vaguely familiar voice.

Shane appeared beside him, looking healthy and strong. He was in the same overalls he always wore. "I saw what happened. I...I'm sorry," said Shane.

Kris couldn't stand to look at the pity on Shane's face. "I'm fine."

"I would've helped if I could've."

"It's fine. He'll regret it, and I'm fine, so it doesn't matter."

For the very first time since Kris met him, Shane looked at a complete loss. They both sat quietly until Kris spoke. "Did you see that snake just now?"

Shane smiled weakly. "Yes."

"It's like you then, not really real."

Shane sighed. "Come on, you don't even believe that."

"I mean that you're both from the same place." Kris imagined the black place in dreams from long ago.

"The Void," said Shane. "I guess you could say that, but it wouldn't be saying much. *All lies within the Void.*"

Kris gave him a sideways scowl.

"But no. We're not. That serpent is a complex creature, to say the least, and very old. He's taken an interest in you." Kris didn't know what to say to that, but fortunately Shane continued. "I'd like to apologize to you, Kris. I couldn't force you to believe any of this, so I figured it'd be better if you stumbled into it yourself. I didn't want it to be such a confusing process."

Kris felt many things then, and Rob's words came back to him, "Pick it back up." And Kris felt lucky to have Shane, even if he wasn't sure of much else about him. There was something about him that made Kris feel like everything would be okay, even if Kris was quite sure it would not.

"I understand," said Kris. "I don't think I'd have believed you if you'd just told me. But, Shane, is there anything you can tell me? Anything about these...memories or the Void or...anything?"

For a moment, Shane's mouth was poised with words nearly spilling out, and his face was filled with longing. Then he said, "Yes," but didn't speak. Shane got up, dusted himself off, and walked toward the tree with the hole in it. There was a small faint light, like a distant campfire in the hollow tree. Kris could smell something sweet and hear voices coming from inside the tree.

"I've got to tell you the Story, the one your father couldn't." Shane frowned. "I hope you don't hate him for that."

Kris kept his hate to himself.

It was then he realized that his body wasn't in as much pain, or maybe he was numb due to the cold. He got to his feet slowly and stiffly followed Shane as he walked through the tree. The garden and the woods disappeared as he stepped on the ashes and into a world of black. The only things he could see were Shane and the light in the distance.

By the time a minute passed, and Kris's father was back in the garden, trying to find him and beg forgiveness, Kris was gone.

CHAPTER 14

Homesick

The night of the storm remained in Leah's memory long after, of seeing her friend Talley offering comfort to his baby sisters and to his mother. Their little pallet of blue with stars hanging from ribbons on a plastic canopy and Talley plucking the ribbons while their tiny fingers reached. Talley's face had changed; even as his mom was weighed down with the thoughts of what possibilities a raging storm might have, Talley's eyes were soft and patient, and he managed smiles of meaning, telling his mom that they'd handle what came.

Leah tried to emulate Talley when she arrived home; the shed was unsalvageable, and trees were down on nearly every block. Her mother was not crying—*crying never gets you anywhere*—but she was silent, and when she got the call that the Diamond Gambit would be closed until further notice, she withered in spirit. Her mother smoked all her cigarettes and even borrowed some from Brit. But they all pitched in, clearing their own yard of debris and offering the tin and wood from the shed to Mr. Diaz. The next day, her mom's spirits withered further, until she was always found on the couch in front of the TV, always breathing slowly and always hard to reach. Leah wanted to scream at her mother, "*What is this going to accomplish? Why are you wallowing?*" But she told her sister and mother that she knew all would be well, and she tried very hard to believe it.

SERMON OF THE DIVERS

The following morning, two days after the storm, a story ran on the news cycle and dominated social media: a story of famine and mysterious disappearance.

Her mother was already up that morning, already in the living room, and her coughing woke Leah up. She said, "Morning," but there was something missing in it, in the way she said it whatever had been missing since the storm. The TV, set to the channel 6 news, showed local Gary Ridderman and Sasha Nomitok, who'd always reminded Leah of Ken and Barbie, ten years after the divorce.

"We'll continue to monitor the progress of repair in the wake of the storm and give you updates as they come, though it is expected to be a long and difficult journey ahead for all involved," said Sasha, as her eyebrows moved closer to her hairline.

"In other news, be on the lookout for changes at your local grocery stores…particularly in the meat section."

Upon Gary finishing his sentence, a news story started, with a voice-over from Gary playing over scenes of empty meat sections. With cut-ins from people shopping in the stores, saying things like, "I don't understand," and "I don't normally come here. I go to Bert's Butchery, but they were talking about closing up shop," and "I can eat on vegetables for a while, but I got to have my meat now. What are we all supposed to do?"

"Similar scenes can be found all over the tristate area, with reports having been filed from Tyson Farms, Loredo Farms, Oddelbrok, and many, many more, reporting mass disappearances in their livestock. Investigators, on the state and federal level, have yet to make any comment on the case, and it is believed that is due to a disturbing detail—all of the animals have vanished without a trace."

"Mom, it'll be okay."

"I know…I know…"

And her mother coughed.

*****

Tommy managed to find her work all the time, even when her mother wasn't working, and Leah gave almost all of the money she made directly to her mom. It was incredible that Tommy kept them working even in such turbulent times. When she asked him how he was able to, he laughed and that strange look came over him, and he said, "What else are people going to do but continue? Even if they've made it halfway to hell, they keep on marching, and they'll say it's the human spirit. They'll say they are like Sisyphus...I mean, that it takes a great deal to shake people from routine and familiarity, my clients in particular."

She knew who Sisyphus was; she was taught by Mrs. Miller, her English teacher freshman year, that it was a story of a hero. A person finding meaning in a world that was void of it. Finding meaning by making it. Leah couldn't decide if that was inspiring or terrifying. And she wondered who decided those things were mutually exclusive.

Her phone rang. Bailey. She silenced it. *I'll text her later.*

The sun was a melting cauldron of white heat, but there were plump clouds that boiled in it occasionally, and Tommy tried to wait on those to take the sky before he began. She thought that was ironic—*Cloudless Sky.*

"Yes, that's exactly right. Would you move a little bit closer to him, Stephanie? Pretend you might actually want to marry him," said Tommy.

Stephen and Stephanie were engaged, and yes, Leah found their names quite ironic. But their similarities didn't stop there. They both were brown-haired, brown-eyed, and spent each Wednesday night at The Height's Terrace, that country club that Jim Grayson is a member of. And both of them attended the same college, had the same favorite movie—*Titanic*—and shared a favorite food: crab legs. Leah knew that because when she commented on their names, they quickly filled her in on just how *similar* they really were. After which, Tommy whispered to her, "Who the fuck dates themselves? That's got to be some serious issues, huh?"

Leah shrugged. Tommy, even though he had treated her more than fairly with pay, was still a mixed bag for her. He could go from being an admirable mentor to a bitter jackass in a gnat's moment.

Stephen and Stephanie were flanked by mulberry bushes, with the tall pines and cedars and southern oaks offering a miniscule covering from a raging sun. Her dress was short and pinkish and almost see-through; his tie was pink and his slacks were pinstriped gray. Leah noticed that Tommy always told everyone how wonderful they looked right from the get-go, and only after did he try to modify their clothing if he could. *Unbutton this. Run your fingers through your hair. Roll up the sleeves. Roll down the sleeves. Take this off.* But he would always take pictures of them in their original outfits first in case they were "*difficult.*"

"Very good! Now turn just a little... Like this... Yes! That's it. You two look *great.*"

Leah snapped more photos. She shot. Tommy talked. Stephen and Stephanie had both just graduated from Yale, so he asked them what they planned to do next. Turned out that Stephen's dad was head of human resources at Allied Security and arranged a job for him at a sister company, *Certus Limited Technologies.*

"What was your degree again?"

"English."

"And you speak it very well. Guess that degree was well worth it," Tommy said with an easy smile that Leah had realized, at some point, reminded her of Rob. He seemed to be capable of saying anything to anyone; it was something about how he said things, not what he said. "Well, I'm sure you two will have a long and loving marriage. I've never seen a couple who looked more...*comfortable* in each other's arms. I'll send the edits to you, Stephanie. I'd recommend getting them printed here," said Tommy, handing them a card for a local shop. "If you're interested in letting us take your wedding photos, just give us another call. Okay? Good. You two have a blessed day."

When they pulled out, Tommy turned to her. "That's a strange thing they got going on."

She'd become accustomed to this line of dialogue. "You always have something negative to say about people after a shoot."

Tommy frowned. "Two rich kids who've never had to work a day in their lives. Stephanie was complaining because there were still trees down in the park up the road. She said it was a shame that people don't want to work anymore... Tell me something good about them."

"They paid us," Leah blurted out without thinking. "And they seemed *nice*."

"God. You might've just called them worse than I did. *Nice*. That might be the worst thing a person can be."

Leah started to argue but thought of how nice Tommy was to every customer and how critical he could be behind their backs. Then as she often had of late, she thought of Kris. She thought that maybe, just maybe, he could be genuinely nice. An impulsive idea had been coming and going in her mind since the Cypress Festival: that she should try to contact him, to talk to him. But every time, something would come up, like a shoot, or editing, or she needed to run with the girls from the track team, or she had to shower or eat dinner or wash her hair.

"Oh, I've been meaning to say," started Tommy as they finished packing up. "I'd like to take your family out to eat soon, to meet your sister and mom—here's the SD card. Give them a chance to get out of that hot home of yours."

"Thanks. I'll get it back to you as soon as I'm done. The other half are on the blue one in the bag," said Leah. "I'm sure they'd appreciate the offer, but...you know that most restaurants are closing or substituting their meats for vegan options. Brit might eat a vegan burger or at least try. She wants to like meat substitutes, but so far..." Leah shook her head, thinking of how Brit was struggling with the empty meat section at the grocery store. "And my mom doesn't say how much she hates it, but I can tell."

Tommy nodded. He seemed to soften a little. "Fair enough."

*****

Leah pulled her mother's car back in the driveway and prepared to head back up to the red roundtop door. She reminded herself that her mom would not likely be as she remembered, that starlet of duty and maternal spirit but a woman who was struggling. And even then, Leah didn't want to go inside and see her mother's lightless eyes and the pallor of her face. Part of it was adjusting to a meatless diet, sure, and part of it was she was smoking more, and part of it the heat, part of it—Leah couldn't say.

Yet inside the house, her mother was cleaning and humming a tune, and she greeted Leah with vivacity as she came in, embracing her and kissing her on the cheek.

"I'm sorry, love," said her mother. She stared at Leah with gleaming eyes that never looked away or blinked. "I-I've been... Well, I've been occupied with my own thoughts, and a mom should know better than to dwell on things beyond her control. I am so *proud*, though. So proud of how you handled everything I couldn't, you and your sister."

Leah's heart fluttered, and she felt as if the whole world were tilting back to the way it should be, that with her mother's mood, the world would follow. And in part, she was right.

That evening, after Brit arrived home, they were getting ready to sit down to another meal of red beans and rice, which had become a staple in the Fells' household. Leah's skin was clammy, as the AC had been broken for the past week, and Brit's face was red and sweaty, and their mother's was damp and pale. The windows in the kitchen were open, and the AC was off, but little breeze was offered. The wind outside was still, humid, and burning. And Leah's phone began ringing—Tommy.

"Aren't you going to answer that?" asked Brit, who was looking down at the plate of food, desperate for an excuse to procrastinate eating red beans and rice for the third time that week.

"Hello."

"I've got something since I couldn't take your family out to eat. I happen to be in the neighborhood, and I was wondering if I could bring it to you. Maybe you could all cook it up tonight, if you had a mind to."

A minute later, Tommy stood at the door with a box. He was dressed as Leah had never seen him before. He was in cargo shorts and a short-sleeve fishing shirt, those ones with the extra pockets and flaps on the back. "Hello, there. Nice to meet you," said Tommy. And he introduced himself to Leah's mother and sister. "It's a pleasure to meet you both. Your daughter has told me all about you, and I just wanted to let you all know how excellent of a job she's been doing. Normally, I'd have taken you all out to eat for that, but given the state of things...I have this instead." He hefted the box.

They all went into the kitchen, and everyone gathered round as he opened it. Inside were Ziploc bags full of frozen fish fillets. There must have been ten one-gallon bags of fish. Leah could have sworn that Brit was going to kiss Tommy, but fortunately, she just hugged him, even as sweaty as she was.

"Oh! Thank you so much, Mr.—"

"Just Tommy, please."

Her mother smiled and said, "Thank you, Tommy. Would you like to stay for dinner?"

To Leah's surprise, Tommy acquiesced with little resistance, and Leah knew it was the magic of a starlet reborn. In mere minutes, her mother had him frying fish in a shallow pan with onions and shallots. Tommy was listening to her mother talk about The Black Milou, which tried to have her on as one of their dancers back in '99. In reply, Tommy spoke with enthusiasm that she'd never expected or seen about his days studying photography at the Collier University in Atlas. Leah and Brit were mostly just captivated while the conversation happened in front of them, though they occasionally chimed in with a question about where something was or who someone was.

"I haven't thought of Deep Boscom in years. Wyatt and I used to go there! Oh, there was this place across from Calloway Hall..."

On she went, and it seemed that Leah was the only one who noticed that she'd said the name. Brit was enrapt and listening, but apparently she was not hanging on to every word as Leah was. Either that, or she wasn't surprised to hear the name of their father.

Tommy left after a long post-dinner conversation, and her mother and sister were quick to tell Leah how lucky she was to have a boss like him. Leah agreed and kept her thoughts about how unusual he was acting to herself. It wouldn't have been the first time that her mother managed to win over a curmudgeonly person. When Mr. Diaz had first moved in, he tried to have them shift their fence three feet, claiming that it was over the property line. In short order, Leah's mother baked an apple pie for him (at which point, Leah knew something magical was about to happen, as it always did when her mother made her famous apple pie) and took it over herself. Leah remembered watching them from the kitchen window. They talked at the dinner table together. In minutes, her mother turned Mr. Diaz's permanent scowl into a wrinkled and warm smile. They hadn't had to move the fence, which was very fortunate because they'd have had to do it themselves, and none of them knew a whole lot about the craft. Tommy was only another victim of her mother's winning personality.

The evening brought back the cool air, seeping from the vents overhead. They all were in the kitchen, cleaning up. Brit closed the windows, and the sound of a cricket outside was muted.

Leah was gathering and rinsing the plates before her mother washed them. Her mother and sister were still raving about the fish, but soon a silence fell. And without thinking, Leah filled it.

"Mom... Has Dad been helping...I mean, has he been giving you money since he's been gone?" The gaps in her speaking came with nervousness and the impulsivity of her question.

Her mom glanced at her and bit her lip, then she turned off the water faucet and turned to face her. "Your father has been sending money since three years after he left. As soon as he was able to."

It is one thing to know something and something else to realize it.

"Why didn't you tell us?" asked Leah, trying to stay calm.

"I...I was always meaning to, but the longer I didn't, the harder it was to...to tell myself that I needed to. Your father told me he had no intention of coming back. He never called or anything, not even when he sent the money. Not until a few months ago. I never thought that you girls would see him again."

But he is. He is coming back. He's coming back soon and—Brit's face was calm and looking at her. And it seemed obvious to her then.

"You knew?"

Brit almost looked remorseful before she rolled her eyes. "You don't get it. He was never coming back, so Mom and I thought that—"

"But he is! And even if he wasn't, what if I had wanted to meet him? All these years, I thought he left and never thought about us! Never thought about me… Why wouldn't you tell me? I don't understand."

When they didn't answer immediately, and her mother looked ashamed, and her sister was angry but silent, Leah left them there and retreated to her bedroom.

At first, she paced, then she realized she was only fixating, then she started to regret saying what she said—well, not the saying it but the way she said it. Her mother and sister would not come knocking on her door tonight; it was a rule that was adopted for Brit's sake (as she entered a phase in high school that she couldn't help but get in trouble and butt heads with Leah and their mom) that any one of them should have the night to rest with their mistakes and bruised feelings before dealing with the consequences of their actions. Just now, Leah was thankful that they wouldn't come, because she was still angry. Even as she took the SD card from the day's shoot and inserted it into her laptop.

And her eyes were on the screen, but her mind was making a fantasy. *Was he sorry for what he'd done for all these years? Did he actually want to get to know them?* She imagined him making it to the money services desk every Friday after he was paid and standing in a line to send an envelope of cash directly to her mom. And in her imaginings, he was slim, and his hands were covered in grease, and he had a look in his eye, as if he were working his imaginings to picture her.

It was the picture on the screen that broke her concentration. Among the pictures of Stephen and Stephanie was a horror: a photo of women, frail and starved, dirty and dead-eyed, corralled into a storage container.

CHAPTER 15

Shane

"It's been a long time since he's done something like that…"

"Years," replied Kris.

As with people and smells and songs, the place he was in set the habits of his mind and sent them down old trails. Around him was the black, a silky and whole shade of obsidian, which they walked on but with no discernible difference between where they stepped or the air around them or the space above. All was that same color. Roars echoed in memory and a monstrous gaping mouth and the feeling of accepting his own death. *Rezt-E-Ahar*. Behind that came more remorse for what had happened between him and his father.

"It's even worse because he was right. One of those 'It's not what you say. It's how you say it' kind of things," said Kris.

"But he was not *entirely right*. You must use the power you've been given and do what needs to be done, even though you expose yourself in its use."

And suddenly, before them was a chain-link fence and forest of whelpling trees, and Shane moved through the fence. Kris moved through as well, knowing that he was in that limitless form within the Void.

"I-I know where we are. I don't need to be reminded of *him*. Freddie didn't deserve to—"

"But you do! You do need to be reminded of it! You've turned it against yourself, and it's time to turn the dirt again, to remove the injury that you've done to yourself. Even when you chopped the trees down, which were living in the space for your garden, you took their lives, and you accepted that it needed to be done."

"They were dying," replied Kris, feeling the cool as the forest grew around them, and he walked down a familiar path, to a mirror of a place that Rob had shown him.

Shane turned to him. On his face was suffering and pain, and his eyes glistened and were heavy-lidded. His lips were pressed, but Kris could have sworn he saw them tremble before he spoke. "You don't understand."

"Then show me!" Kris's voice begged, and he felt the desperation, being so close to Freddie's grave.

Shane reached out and placed a hand on Kris's chest, a warm and calloused hand. Then the warmth seemed to invade his body, wrapping around a beating heart and down into his bowels and up into his mind.

*****

Freddie knew only one thing for sure: he knew nothing, same as everyone else. He knew that because he'd paid attention to what people said and what people did.

He adjusted the rearview in his mother's car. She didn't know he'd taken it, but she'd find out soon enough anyway. He felt his gut roll and reminded himself that he took it because he had to. He took it because to do good, sometimes you had to do evil. At first, he'd had trouble with that idea. Good was good, and evil was evil, and never the two shall meet; that'd been what he'd believed when he was a child. Freddie was smart, though. He watched, and he paid attention to what they said and what they did. He quickly realized that evil was almost never the intention of someone hurting another. When his mother told his father that he was a spineless coward, that he was always a useless son of a bitch, it wasn't because she wanted to hurt him; it was because she loved him. Because she wanted good for him, and she could see he needed a push. And when he took his own life, she didn't cry because she loved him. That was the same reason she did those things to Freddie.

Once Freddie understood that people lied and said things they didn't mean for the ultimate good, like that, he naturally wondered if this might apply on a larger scale. Would organizations of people, especially those that were in positions of responsibility and power, act with this same rule in mind? Unequivocally, yes. Who was served by the good changed, but the methods became dire, illegal, unthinkable.

At church, they passed around an offering plate, tithes for the church, for the continued teachings of God's Word. The congregation consisted of families not dissimilar from his own, the sort that didn't have a lot of money. Freddie's underwear was always several sizes too small and cut into his waist when he sat back in the pew, where he accumulated scars and discolored skin. His mother tithed. One day, he and his mother were going across the bridge on the interstate, and his mother pointed across Hemlock Lake to a house on the banks. A house with four stories, with two boats, and a winding driveway hidden in trees. It was Father Robert's house, she'd said. But to what greater good?

Freddie flexed his hands on the steering wheel and checked his watch. He was late. He told himself not to rush; he was the will of the universe, and so he'd arrive exactly when he was meant to. It must have been meant to be that he'd gotten a flat tire on the way. Besides, they weren't going anywhere. Mr. Jones was the only thing he had to worry about, and he was only one man for a whole school. He couldn't be everywhere at once.

He parked by the auditorium, the same way and place he usually did. Seeing his backpack in the passenger seat was almost laughable, but what was really funny was what he had on the floorboard in the back. He got out and opened the back door of his mom's tan Focus. At first, all he could do was look at it. The past year had been spent getting it together, the gun as well as himself. Fleetingly, he wondered if this was the longest time he'd spent preparing for something, looking into the future and trying to direct it.

Upper receiver, the gas tube, the gas block, cam pin, bolt, firing pin.

The lion's share of the past year was spent getting money for the parts; the assembly had not taken so long. Just looking at the final product, *his* AR15, his sword, the tool of his own retribution, flooded him with a noxious kind of wonder and pride. He bowed his head and told God to take his vanity away and to guide his sword, to use him as He saw fit to bring about His will. Honestly, the real lion's share was finding the proper prayer and the proper words to ask God and the proper signs of His response. And God sent him a sign. When the final part—the barrel—arrived, it was from Leo's Tactical Supply. The emblem on the box was a lion. That night, he'd dreamed he was fighting lions in a desert, wielding a sword of fire. How great was his God? How great? To send him two signs. That morning, he'd dwelled on the fact that he'd been in a desert, which seemed a fitting metaphor. God's greater good, his water of life, didn't flow in the world, and only through faith did he believe that it ever had. And he thought it fitting that a lion should be the weapon and what wanted to kill him in the desert.

"Judah," he mouthed to himself as he grabbed his sword by the stock.

The world has returned to sin and ignorance. Give me the strength to kindle the flames of Your will. Forgive them that they cannot see your will and your glory. Forgive me for the innocent blood as well as the iniquitous blood, which will be shed through me by your guidance. Forgive the debtors and the debted, the priests and the preachers, the rich and poor. Let your judgment reign.

There, the world was prepared. He could feel the universe calling out to him, to start toward the school. He checked his magazine and switched the safety off. His heart fluttered.

Up on the hill, between the auditorium and the band room, Mr. Jones was staring at him, but when they made eye contact, Mr. Jones grabbed his radio and turned. He was out of sight before Freddie could aim.

Damn it!

They would be in the classrooms now, and there was no turning back. He heard the siren begin, the wailing that indicated an active shooter. And Principal Coven's voice rang out over the school, announcing that a man with a gun had entered the campus.

Freddie remembered the old T-buildings at the back of the campus. He'd planned ahead and prepared for this eventuality. The T-buildings were built before anything else, and they'd be easy to shoot through. He imagined rounds bursting through the windows, holes exploding across the plaster and boards, and in his imagination, there were no screams, but there was blood.

Between the auditorium and the gymnastics room, he heard the scutter of a fellow students' steps, then a fence clinking and a huff. Freddie took off, keeping the rifle at his shoulder, just like he'd practiced. When he came around the corner of the gymnastics building, there was a rustling sound beyond the fence and a shadow retreating into the woods, or maybe two; he couldn't quite see. He fired into the woods.

His sword recoiled and pumped against his shoulder; if he'd seen the next day, his shoulder would've been black from bruising. How'd he forget how much it kicked? No time to think about it, he decided to move on. There were more people in the T-buildings. So what if one gets away in the woods behind the school. It was alright to lose one.

But he only made three steps before the miraculous intervened, and Freddie heard the voice of an angel coming from between the trees, beyond them.

"*The evil you seek is here. My sword finds every vile man, to the last one.*"

Freddie couldn't speak. He was frozen.

"*Come.*"

"Y-yes, Lord."

Freddie shouldered his rifle dutifully and contained his awe that his faith had been true. His God was speaking to him, not only with signs but literally! He leapt into the air and grabbed the fence's top; he threw himself over, feeling a burst of holy strength, the Holy Spirit moving in him. Freddie thanked his God aloud a few times, to which there was no response.

His boots stomped on soft ground the further he made his way into the thicket, and the shade must have cooled the air. The sweat of his back was near icy by the time he slowed to a trot, getting a terrible feeling in the pit of his stomach. It was entirely too cold to just be the shade; he realized that as his breath floated away into the forest, and the needles on the ground were frosted over. By the time his boots started to crunch over the frozen grass, and he spotted hoarfrost on the branches ahead, a ghostly hand ran a cold finger up his spine. He twisted, rifle at the ready.

"Lord? Lord?"

No one. Nothing. The school was far out of sight beyond the pines.

"Lord, where are they? Where is the evil you wish me to end?"

His voice was rising and falling, and when he very suddenly began to think of his mother and father, it was a stray thought in the vortex of his own fear: *Did I ever really know them?*

Freddie shoved that thought away and began to pray.

"Your will, Father. Your will, Father. Your will, Father! That's all I wish to bring. That's all I wish to do! Whatever I can do to please You, Lord!"

He was turning in circles. The trees seemed to close in around him as he spun and waited for some shadow to appear. No shadow appeared. But a familiar face did, and with it came the rough flat head of a claw hammer. Then everything was white, then black, and he couldn't hear anything—absolutely nothing. Next there was a faint ringing and a voice.

"WHO DO YOU THINK YOU ARE? HUH? WHO DO YOU THINK YOU ARE!"

The first several strikes broke his cranium, caved his eyes in, and broke his jaw. He felt the flaring pain and heard the ping a hammer makes when connecting to bone, kind of a thud, really. Then thankfully, he was breathing, but everything was dark and quiet, like one of those sensory deprivation chambers. He wasn't there for the last hammer fall.

*****

SERMON OF THE DIVERS

He was gasping, and Shane stood just before him, waiting. They were in the circle of the twin tree now, a mirror of the place Rob had shown him in the other world, and under its boughs, they stood. Freshly turned dirt in that familiar shape, between him and Shane. Kris remembered what happened in flashes, in grim shots, and in bloody glimpses. He remembered not thinking about it, about how strange it was that the hammer was placed at the bottom of the tree. The sound of the hammer and the croak in his own throat and iron taste of Freddie's blood. Slowly his breath returned to him. Shane waited patiently as it did, not even looking at Kris. The thought of who Freddie might actually be had haunted him and likely would all of his days, but—

"I...I can't say that I didn't mean to...In the moment, I did. Even if after, I regretted it, and I wanted to take it back, I don't want to push it away, say that it was an accident...I feel that doing that would somehow make it so that it would happen again and again. Every time I said that I didn't mean to or that it was an accident, I'd just be allowing myself too much. I lost control."

And Kris had that same feeling that maybe it was himself that lay beneath the dirt, cradled in the earth.

"Dig. If you don't know who's down there now. Dig. Dig the body up and see," said Shane, hollow eyes set on the grave between them.

Kris shook his head and wiped his eyes. "I know who's down there."

From the rolled dirt, the flowers grew, and Kris apologized in his own mind. The spider lilies sprouted from the ground and stood in full bloom, speckled and orange red. *I can never be sorry enough, but this will have to do. If we ever meet again, I hope that it is in a place where you feel peace and belonging. In those days, I could get to know you, and I could try to make you understand that it was all...a mistake. And you could tell me of your own mistakes.*

In silence, they left the grave, and the lilies withered as they went, retreating back into the soil. They moved through the cold and a dense forest until it gave way to a plain of red grass, growing high as their knees. At the tree line, moving from one place to the next, Kris felt a change in himself, a wily feeling that caused his eyes to rise to the sky overhead. In the heavens were the stars of the other world, though they were a little younger than when he knew them. The grass turned yellow, and young trees wore fall crowns, colored gold and amber and ruby and garnet. And they followed the tracks of truck tires.

"Your father used to ride across Gillian Lake in a little johnboat to pick up your mother. He'd pick wildflowers for her and lay them out for her on the bench seat, and they'd spend the day out on the water. Did you know that?" asked Shane but not waiting for an answer. "He got in a fight at school over her, fueled by a certain impulsiveness, and he was prone to be out on that boat with her all day, without another thing broaching his mind… And Tabi, your mother, she felt emboldened, realizing that she was the reason Mike was acting completely counter to his usual behavior, which was collected, focused, calm…"

No. He hadn't heard any of this before, but it wasn't hard to imagine that his dad was so changed by the presence of his mom. Rob mentioned it from time to time when they were younger, but not anymore. That they moved each other, they were stable and changing for one another, and that Dad was not always so *realistic* about everything.

"When he was supporting Tabi's dream of being a writer, he still believed in those kinds of dreams. Now he dreads the idea of Rob going out into the world to try and be a musician… Your father," Shane continued, "is unwilling because of his father, Thomas, who was overzealous. Thomas saw the terrible things that Jim Grayson and other wealthy elites are doing, and he was eager to see them be stripped of everything, including their lives. The Void never directed him to those ends… He convinced himself that It did, but it was a lie made from his own hatred of Jim Grayson."

Kris bristled at the name. Was it not a justified way to feel about Jim Grayson and everyone who had the means to change things for the better of their fellow man but didn't?

"What?" asked Shane.

"Since the Industrial Revolution we've had the means to provide for every person in the nation, and with the rise of technology and industry, haven't we had the ability to ensure that all eat and are housed and have a place to work and improve the world? It's people that corrupt and use any new idea for personal gain instead of the betterment of all. That's not always the case, but it is true most of the time."

"That's true," said Shane. "But what is your point?"

"Was my grandfather not justified in wanting to see people like Jim Grayson be…brought down to our level? To everyone else's level? To see what it's like to be average?"

Kris could hear their own breathing and then a low hum just below that. Campfire smoke and fresh, crisp air became a new scent in the dark. It was combined with the sweet aroma of marshmallows roasting. Crowding pines and maples started to tower over Kris and Shane as they got closer to a campfire, encircling them as they reached its warmth. They were standing in the woods, staring at the fire. "Want a seat?" Shane gestured to two foldout green lawn chairs that appeared by the fire. "Want some s'mores?"

Kris shook his head but did take a seat, eager to know what Shane's answer to his question would be.

Shane fumbled in his pocket for a bit before pulling out a little brown knife. Then he picked up a long skinny stick and began to whittle at the end of it.

"That's a tough question. I think it goes back to what you said, though. All the most powerful people in the world *are* average, in that their moral grounds crumble, and their empathy wanes as their power grows. Ultimately, is it right what they do? That they hedge bets and devise systems of subjugation… That they make rules in the workplace that are meant to control as well as placate? No. It's not right. Are they responsible for the condition of those under them? Yes. Should their most heinous crimes affect how you feel about them? You know this, with Freddie, that it is a terrible thing to take another person's life in your own hands…It should only be done when you are not angry or scorned or jealous or anything at all. That's where your father was right. Where he was wrong was in believing that you shouldn't do anything about it."

Kris hesitated, thinking of what his father said, but in the end, he did say, "And what am I supposed to do about it? And what about what my dad said? That I am to bring about the end of the world?"

Shane's hollow eyes surveyed the stick as he turned it over in his hands. "Now listen to the story. Hear it, know it, and become it."

CHAPTER 16

Buried in the Valley

The morning after she discovered the photos, Leah got up and dutifully apologized to her mother and sister. They hurried to say sorry as well, but Leah quickly put their apologies to bed.

"I understand, Mom. I *really do.* It's okay! And I'll be meeting him soon enough, so it doesn't matter." Leah bulldozed through the apologies with mild sincerity but mostly with speed. "Listen, I know this is important, but I was going to meet the guys at Stonethrow. Is that okay?"

Her mother gave her a perplexed sort of look but agreed that it was okay. And Leah could tell that wasn't the last of their conversation.

Leah already decided that she couldn't tell her mother or sister about the photos. They would try to get her to go to the police, and then they'd lose the bulk of their income at the moment. The Diamond Gambit was due to open up again in just under a month, but they needed her income from the shoots until then. Leah knew that. Debt could easily become crippling when it stacked up. But Leah couldn't keep the photos to herself. Just looking at them last night had curdled her stomach and kept her from sleeping.

On her way to the park, Leah felt as if she were carrying something contaminated and evil in her laptop bag. She looked over her shoulder, expecting someone—a police or a man in black—to be following her. But to her surprise, Mr. Diaz greeted her with a wave as he sipped coffee and read the paper on his front porch. Ms. Colwell was watering her azaleas when Leah strode by, walking quite fast, and she started a conversation about how strange it was to have not eaten even so much as a Hamburger Helper in weeks. Leah agreed politely but kept her responses curt and left Ms. Colwell wondering if she had said something rude, with a pinched face.

At Stonethrow, Leah sat on a secluded bench and waited in the lurid morning air. Every passerby caught her eye and made her grab the laptop bag, keeping it close to her. What could it mean? Why would Tommy have those pictures on his SD card? She tried, late into the night, to rationalize their existence. The obvious was most quickly disregarded, things like, it was from a staged shoot. But no. They were not staged. The expressions of utter misery and hopelessness and fear were too thoroughly adopted on the women's faces to be fake. Then there was the—their waste occupying a corner of the container. And also, why would someone want to fake that to such a degree? No. Leah knew the photos on her laptop were authentic as much as they were disturbing.

Talley arrived with a cigarette dangling from his mouth, and his mouth curved down, his face red from the sun. He didn't even look up at her as he approached. Stark contrast to the last memory she had of him, standing over his little sisters and smiling in the wake of a terrible storm. She'd texted him because, well, because of all of her friends, he was the most likely to understand that she couldn't tell the police. But seeing him that way pushed her own troubles far from her, and she couldn't help but ask him, "Talley, are you alright? What's wrong?"

He blinked at her and drew from the cigarette. Talley hadn't been smoking that long, only since he'd gotten his job at Creekshire's, so he coughed a short and effortless thing. He bit his lip and said, "I...I just..." He forced a smiled. "No, never mind." But the smile faded fast, and he blinked rapidly. "My dad... He—he got into it with his boss, and he got fired..."

Leah wanted to get up and do something, hug him or—she didn't know. But he was hunched and drawn in, closing himself off, and he had an edge as if he might push her away if she came close. He snorted and drew on the cigarette.

SERMON OF THE DIVERS

"I'm sorry," he said. "I know everything will work out, and I can't really be mad at him for it. They were asking his friend, Ivan, to do something dangerous, something that could have gotten him killed. My dad told him not to, that they couldn't ask him to. Well... It came back on my dad."

"Talley, I'm so sorry. I...I have some extra money that I can give to help out," she hesitated. "The shoots with Tommy have been going really well, and he pays good. I know it's weird to just take money, but you'd do the same for me if it were the other way around."

This time, when he did, his smile was genuine, and he even chuckled. "Come on. I know you haven't really got much to spare either. We'll make it through, and like I said, I know there's no one to blame, except maybe the greedy fucks at the top." He eyed her for a second. "Did you ever get a chance to look at the Buried in the Valley page?"

Leah shook her head, thinking of what Andrew said, and she imagined the whole page was a platform to demonize Jim Grayson and other people like him.

"I don't understand you, Leah. You work so hard, so has your mom and your sister. I know you want to believe that hard work pays off, and in its own way, I think it does. But...I don't know. Do you think any other human being on the planet, doing *any* other job, should be paid 120,000 times what your mom or sister get paid? Because that's the math, and that's just talking salaries. That's not including the infinite avenues of income that open when you're already wealthy."

Why did this conversation take this turn? And suddenly Talley sounded frustrated and not depressed. Why did it remind her of Tommy? The pictures on her laptop came to her mind, and she felt a chill come over her.

"I'm sorry," said Talley, shaking his head. "I didn't mean to come at you. I'm just frustrated with everything right now... Anyway, what is it that you wanted to talk about that you couldn't call for?"

She wondered if she should tell him then. He already had so much on his mind, and it's like he said, she needed the money anyway. "I just… Talley, would you work for somebody that might be doing *questionable* things because you needed the money?"

Talley looked up at her, one eyebrow raised. "How *questionable?*"

"Like…nightmare questionable."

Talley pulled on the cigarette one last time before crushing it and said, "Did you see what Freeborn is being accused of? It's all over the news, even while everyone is going without any meat. He's been accused of rape. After the first girl, who was only twelve years old—they didn't give her name—came forward, six others did. Ben Renault, the guy who started V-Ware, just sold all of his shares yesterday. Coincidentally, the stock price dropped off just today. There's not even any major coverage on that one. He's got lawyers, a staff on retainer, and interns who'll fight with a low-waged public defender. And…Jim Grayson simultaneously is facing allegations of inhumane working conditions on his railroad yard in Valleyport and spearheading a federally recognized taskforce to investigate what's happened to all the animals. We all work for questionable people."

*****

She'd left Talley without telling him what she'd found on the SD card. Her walk back home was not like her walk to get to Stonethrow. By the end of their conversation, she was left with a feeling of hopelessness, and it seemed that what Talley was saying was true, and she couldn't understand how it could possibly stay that way. Weren't there people whose job it was to make sure that everyone dealt with the consequences of what they do? What about the justice system?

And though the day was bright and hot, unbearably hot, Leah did not feel the heat or see the colors. She was in her own mind, trying to remember things that escaped her.

Her sister's car was gone by the time Leah got home, and her mother was locked in her bedroom. Leah could hear her coughing as she crept by. The smell of coffee still hung in the air. Her bed was still a mess from her rush to leave that morning, and her bedroom was in a state of neglect. Leah set the laptop bag down and stared at it where it lay on the bed.

Out of nowhere, Aaron came to mind. Maybe it was that she wanted somewhere to lay her head and to let the world go for even a moment. And the warm feelings of his presence were replaced with fear and the feeling of being trapped, but this time, they were paled by the photos of the women. Her jaw was taut with anger. She remembered the feeling she had at the Cypress Festival, just at seeing him there. She said something to herself, *I'll do something if no one else will.* But what?

As she opened the laptop again, she was forced to look at the pictures, which were still on the desktop. In the den of ghostly bodies, a child with tears in her eyes reached toward a woman who moved away from her. It took everything Leah had, all of her will, not to look away. Forcing herself to look the picture over as if it were a photo she was about to edit. The darkness, just on the outer reach of a halogen bulb, making a ring of light that didn't dare go all the way into the container. The brands and styles of clothing, both foreign and familiar to her, and the same with the women there. A group from all origins, confined to a box without any sign of food and what seemed to be a child's tub for water. One of the women was on her hands and knees, drinking from the tub. A man's hand curved into the edge of the photo with a stern pointed finger and a wedding ring. The other photos—there were six of them—were much the same, but that first was the only one with a man's hand in it.

But was there anything that might tell her where these women were?

Ding!

Leah glanced at her phone, saw it was Bailey, and almost picked it up, remembering that she was supposed to text Bailey and had forgotten. But she didn't. The photos held her attention.

A black SUV in the fifth photo. Then she chided herself for even thinking that it was familiar, but could it be? Leah zoomed in on the SUV that was parked beyond the container and only showed a sliver of its body. Just black and reflective.

But there'd been a man, a friend of Mr. Grayson's, that had owned a vehicle like it. She remembered he came over with his family one Sunday while she was over there. Was it a trick of her mind that suddenly the wedding band on the man's hand in the photo looked familiar? She could picture him. The small beady eyes and wide mouth with a wiry mustache frowning above. He was big, taller than Mr. Grayson by several feet, and his voice, so harsh. What was his name? She could picture him but couldn't recall his name. It was an easy name to remember too; she remembered wanting to laugh at it.

Leah got on her Facebook, ignored the messages about the picture of her, and quickly clicked past Jim Grayson's profile picture to look at his friends list. Somewhere in here would be a name that would jog her memory. But he had over two thousand friends. She searched the names once, twice, then she slowed down for her third time, reading each individual name, not just glancing at them. She felt close to remembering several times, but nothing came.

"Knock, knock. Wild child, you got a second?"

Leah jumped. There were two soft taps on the door and the sound of her mother's voice.

"Yeah, Mom. Give me just a sec."

Leah made sure the pictures and Facebook search were closed before she went to open her bedroom door, her heart aflutter. Her mother looked somewhat disheveled, and her eyes seemed sunken, but she grinned at Leah before she began to speak.

"Hey, love. I...I just wanted to make sure that you were okay. You were right last night. I...I should have told you about your father sending the money. And. And I regret it—that I didn't."

Her mom's eyes were misty, and her mouth was fitting muted words, and she seemed different, so different from how she normally was, and Leah could have hit herself for blowing up like she had. She knew. She *knew* that her mother would never hurt her intentionally, but she hadn't been able to control herself last night.

"I know, Mom. I know. I didn't mean to sound so...I was being an asshole."

Her mother's eyebrows raised.

"Sorry."

"Well, that was the proper use of the word," said her mother, grinning. "I was an asshole too. I came to make a peace offering... and to ask for a favor."

Leah laughed. "We're gonna make a pie."

"We're gonna make an *apple* pie."

Leah couldn't help but smile, and with a great effort, she put the photos away from her mind and went to make a pie with her mother.

*****

Her mother made a joke that they might not need to light the oven to bake the pie, that they might leave it out on the counter instead. Leah laughed, wiped the sweat from her face, and carefully picked up the pie and put it into the oven for its final cook. Flour dusted the surface of the counters and their clothes, and there was a sink full of dirty dishes, including the food processor. Thoughts of the photos and everything else were easy to push away when she was alone with her mother, and the women in the photos might have crossed her mind but only to travel through.

"How's the training going?" her mother asked as she set about starting the dishes. Leah slid in beside her and helped, rinsing the plates before her mother scrubbed them.

"Ehh, it's going okay. Lesley and Melissa and I were talking about how it feels like it takes so much longer to recover from training. We think it might be our diets...I think I'm going to get some plant-based protein. That's what Melissa said she was doing and that it helped."

Her mother coughed and blinked, a wordless worry passed between them. "I'll pick some up for you next time I go to the store."

"Thanks."

The dishes clinked together in soapy water, and bubbles found their way up into the air.

Her mother poked one with her nose, popping it. Leah did the same.

"Your great-grandfather used to tell me stories, things that happened to him and the family during the Great Depression. He'd always end them with the same words, *'But we got through it'*. It's hard to remember that when you're in the thick of it."

Leah nodded and let that thought perfuse in her mind.

"I know I'm about to meet him, but what is he like?"

"Your dad?"

Leah nodded.

Her mother smiled. "He was full of big ideas and dreams. Always seemed to be figuring something out, didn't have a mind to idle with. He loved to be around people on the weekends and required solitude during the week, submerged in whatever project he'd taken to. There was this *look* that he used to get when he was working on something."

"What did he like to do?"

She clicked her tongue. "Your father was fascinated and curious about everything. He once spent our extra cash—we used to keep it in a mason jar—hunting down an old engine, came out of some old van out in Texas. He borrowed his brother's truck and brought it home. Spent hours and hours working on it. Had it sitting up on cinder blocks in the shed…" She coughed and looked out at the backyard, where the shed used to be. "He got it running, though."

Leah imagined a man with oil on his hands, turning over a vague metal shape and bending over a V-shaped motor.

"He worked hard?"

"He did. I learned my work ethic from him," said her mother. "But…never mind."

"But what?" asked Leah curiously.

Her mother placed the food processor, the last that needed washing, on the drying rack and turned to her. "Usually, someone's best quality is also their worst. It was difficult for your father to find balance between his work and everything else. He had a tendency to hone in on whatever occupied his mind…not noticing the forest for the trees."

Leah got a feeling then, the feeling that people refer to as déjà vu. And she was sure that she'd had this conversation before, in the kitchen, with her mother. The sun setting, darkening the backyard through the panes of the window. Each twitch of the bushes behind that spot the shed used to stand on seemed rehearsed and performed just for her. Her worries fell away, and for a moment, she forgot the pictures and Tommy and all else.

"I am sorry, Mom. For how I acted."

"I'm sorry too," said her mother. "I should have told you the truth and let you make your own decisions."

The door opened, and they turned to see Brit come through the hall with a troubled expression. Leah was opening her mouth to apologize, thinking that it had something to do with how Leah'd talked to her last night and how she'd made a pitiful apology that morning.

But Brit spoke first, "Rob's brother is missing."

CHAPTER 17

The First Story

"I like this story."

Shane chuckled. "It's a good story, isn't it?"

Kris would have hated to admit it, but this story was even better than his mother's, *The Valleyport Witch*. But there was something else that was making him feel so content and peaceful, and he thought that maybe it was the place they were in or maybe Shane's voice. Either way, it was as if all of his struggles to maintain control were a silly thing. Here, there was no struggle or striving. The air reminded him of the garden in his dreams but somehow clearer and easier even to breathe. Wind came steadily, pleasantly through the trees, and the fire danced in it.

It was cool, not cold; yet the fire made a warm blanket around them, perfect for sleeping.

"It reminds me of Rob in a lot of ways," said Kris. "I think he would like it. He's also one of those people that *needs* to chase something, to play music and do it in front of people. It's…it's everything to him."

Shane nodded and looked into the fire, and it was a clear reflection in his eyes. "That's important. People are better for having a craft to sharpen themselves against. You change the craft, and the craft changes you. It's a good thing and a natural thing. Creating and imagining are…essential."

Kris said what was on his mind, not struggling to keep it in, "I've always wanted to write, like Mom." His stomach jumped with nerves.

"You should do it then," replied Shane. "When you leave from here, start writing."

Kris nodded, saying to himself that he would.

"Now that's enough for one day. We'll start again tomorrow."

It had been night for the hours and hours of Shane's telling, and when Kris looked into the sky, he saw no sign of the sun yet.

"How do you know the time? The sky hasn't changed at all since we've been here."

"How do you feel?"

Kris thought about it. "I feel tired."

"Then it's time for sleep."

Kris yawned and looked around, searching for a place to lie down. He'd never slept on the ground before, but as long as he was near the fire, he didn't think he'd mind it too much. Just as he stood, Shane held out a tightly rolled sleeping bag. Kris thanked him and unrolled it on the ground. He fell asleep listening to Shane hum and whittle, and looking up at the sky.

*****

He opened his eyes to the garden, to the bioluminescent life of thousands of plants and the buzz of living things. Kris was standing atop the Great Tree, on one of its tallest branches, and when he saw the darkness of the sky above, he put the stars there, the same ones that he'd fallen asleep looking at. And his first thought after was for Leah.

"*Tree, are you doing alright tonight?*"

"*I'm doing quite well. Thank you for asking. But I know that I'm not who you want to be talking to right now.*"

Kris didn't apologize, though he felt the urge to. "You're right. Is she here?"

"*She is not, but it's still early...*"

"*Yes... Still early. Thank you, Tree.*"

Last time they were in the garden together, they'd made a plan to always meet at the Great Tree. It was the easiest place to find in the garden; all the roots and roads wiggled their way to it, and from it, they could make their way anywhere. Kris waited near the Tree's base and sat cross-legged against it.

People are better for having a craft to sharpen themselves against.

Kris imagined a book, a bound book, full of empty pages in his hand, and it appeared there. He drew a pen from the air. It was when the pen reached the paper that Kris discovered he had no idea what to write. He sat, staring at the blank page, thinking of Leah often and looking up, hoping to see her coming through the bright leaves. She didn't. And nothing came to his mind that he thought he might write down. With each passing moment, his focus left him, until he was staring into the forest, looking for Leah.

He felt like a boy, a child. His excitement about seeing Leah, about telling her where he'd been and what he'd been told and hearing about what she'd done—if she could remember (sometimes that was hard for her)—was overflowing from him.

"Tree...have you seen her yet?"

After a moment, the Tree answered, "I'm sorry. I don't think she's coming."

Kris nodded.

"But next time you see her, could you bring her to me? I made something for her."

Kris nodded.

It was then, as he took a long-hearted look through the forest's twilight, that he had a faint pang of where to start with the story. It didn't start in his head, though, as he often thought a story must; and as he began to write, it never did. But every now and again, he might pause to remember the color of her hair, her laugh, the way she looks when taking a photo, and the way she made him feel. Then he was only the words. Only the ethereal, in a chase for something he knew he'd never catch. He wasn't afraid or angry or sad, though he felt all of those things in their turn.

*****

"How did you sleep?" asked Shane.

The air was colder when he woke, and the fire was low, smoldering. Shane was walking up out of the forest with a couple of old branches in his hands. Their snaps were dry smokeless wood, and he tossed them into the flames. A pointed stick, the one that Shane had been whittling, was leaning against his chair. Kris crawled from the sleeping bag, yawned, and got back in his green lawn chair.

"I slept good."

"I've got some breakfast." Shane nodded toward the fire's edge.

Kris felt his stomach turn, and he held back the reflex to gag. On a stump, surrounded by scarlet and gold plumage, was the carcass of a large bird. Sure, it resembled the shape of a chicken, something he'd seen thousands of times at the grocery, but the color wasn't so muted and pale. It seemed as if there were still life in it, but maybe that was only the blood, which was drained into a wooden bowl by the stump.

"Help me finish preparing it."

Kris swallowed, even thinking of Freddie.

"Have some respect!" Shane bellowed. "The creature has given its life so you can eat and live. Handle it with care." His voice was harsh, angry, even thunderous; Shane glared at him with eyes of fire.

"I'm sorry! What do I do?"

Shane began to give him directions then, and his voice was once again melodious and comforting. Kris caved in the bird's breastbone and bent its legs back until he heard them snap, then he was directed to season it. By the bowl of blood was a smaller bowl made of clay that held freshly foraged herbs and a rooty onion and salt and pepper. As Shane fed the fire, he directed Kris how to make a rotisserie mount in the shape of two upside-down *V*s at the ends of the fire. Kris skewered the bird with the stick that Shane had sharpened, and the satiated flames licked the bird as Shane rotated it over the fire.

"What did you dream of?"

"I...I was in the garden, in the Void, and...I wrote. I was waiting for someone while I wrote."

Shane nodded and grinned, as if he expected that same answer. "How did it go?"

"It was...invigorating, and it made me feel—this is going to sound weird, but it made me feel younger. No. That's not right. It was as if I were somewhere else, kind of like I was right here with you. Sitting by the fire and listening to the Story. But that's not right either because it reminded me of other people, not you. And I only got started because I was thinking of Lea—the person I was waiting on."

"Good," Shane replied with simple authority. "Are you ready to keep going with the Story then?"

Kris half-wanted to ask Shane about writing, about whatever it was that he seemed to be hiding behind his grin, but the First Story weighed heavy on his mind. He craved the rest of it.

Even as his stomach growled; he craved the First Story even more than the meat.

The pleasant smell of the roasting bird began to mix in the air as Shane started.

*****

There were tears in Kris's eyes when Shane removed the bird from the flames, bowed his head to it, tore meat from it, and put it straight into Kris's hands. Steam rolled up from the strips of meat, and with tears in his eyes, Kris started to eat.

"I *really* like this story...I didn't think it was going to be a love story."

"All good stories are stories of love. People need love. It keeps them going when times are difficult, when the world seems to be crumbling around them. With love, all things are possible, and life is worth living. Without it..." Shane let the thought linger but didn't expound on it.

Kris swallowed. The meat was tender, a little gamy, and full of flavor. With each bite, he felt the hollow pit of his stomach fill with warmth and satisfaction. He licked his lips.

"I... How do you know love?"

SERMON OF THE DIVERS

"Love is evident in its way... It endures during the tough times and is patient. It brings out passion and will make you want to burn like this fire."

Kris thought of Leah but dared not speak her name out loud.

"Are you ready to continue?"

"Yes."

*****

"I don't like where this is going..."

Kris didn't have any tears for this part of the story, when everything started to go wrong. He wrung his hands with a growing anticipation of how upset he'd be—anger. There was not a way around it but to keep going and find out what would happen, but a part of him wanted to stop the story right then. To not hear the rest.

Shane's wrinkled face grimaced at the fire as he poked it with a stick, sending sparks up into the sky. "You should rest."

"But we haven't gone as long today!"

"Are you tired?"

Kris wanted to lie but couldn't bring himself to do it, not with Shane's eyes staring right at him. Besides, he stifled a yawn right then.

Again, he lay down in the bedroll and again he fell asleep to the sounds of Shane's humming and whittling.

He opened his eyes and was in the exact spot he was the night before, sitting against the Great Tree in its vibrant clearing. The belighted mist filled the air around him, and the flowers swayed, and in the distance, some music played. Kris assumed the music belonged to the trees, who loved to sing when no one was around. That usually meant they waited for—Just then, it started to rain.

But Kris was mostly dry under a natural umbrella of the Great Tree's making. Out in the forest, the rain pattered down the Changeless Trees, and the fireflies receded into black. As the drizzle found its way under the lowest boughs, the colors in the forest waned until there was nothing. Not a single light. Then slowly, they came back to life as a worldly green.

Though the book, with the words he'd written previously, lay across his lap, Kris did not even think of writing. For the first time in two days, he let himself miss his family. He missed his brother's cheerful endurance and all the music he played in the evening, and he missed his father's concern and the way they were comfortable in their silences. But he also realized that he didn't miss much else. He didn't miss any other people, and he didn't care to go back, even if it were only for his father's and Rob's sake. Between the clearing with Shane and his garden in the Void, he had everything he could ever need. And besides, what was time in places like these anyhow? It was even as he had that thought that Leah rushed through the underbrush, calling his name.

"Kris! Kris! Are you here!"

She came barreling through the bushes, her eyes furious and desperate, her clothes battered by rain and branches, leaves and twigs in her hair. She locked eyes on him.

"Yes...I'm here."

She rushed toward him and, to his surprise—maybe her own as well—she hugged him. Then he was standing in her embrace for a moment before he realized, and he put his arms around her. Her muffled voice came from the warm spot where her face was buried in his chest and said, "You're okay... You're okay..."

Kris held onto her, feeling his heart pounding in his chest, until she finally pulled back, stepped back, and apologized. Her cheeks were red with embarrassment, and snot was running from her nose.

"I'm sorry."

"No... What—" he hesitated. "What's wrong?"

She turned her head. "You... You're missing. Over there...on the other side. Your family is looking for you."

They're looking for me? He blinked. He waited. There was no guilt and not out of spite for what his father had done. He forgave that. But why don't I feel anything? Shouldn't I want to go home? He thought of the stories he'd heard of near-death experiences, how those who had them usually felt like they were returning to something more comforting than home. Maybe this place and the First Story were those comforts; maybe they always had been. He just didn't know it until then.

But while there wasn't guilt, there was a sense that he'd have to return. Shane hinted at that already.

"Kris?"

Her eyes were looking at him with a strange spark, one that he'd seen before when she was taking pictures.

"I'm sorry," *he said.* "I didn't mean to make anyone worry."

She shook her head, scowled. "Then why did you run away? Or..." *Her eyes went wider.* "Were you kidnapped?"

"No, no." *He couldn't help but smile (though a part of him figured that he was sort of willingly kidnapped).* "I'm seeing a friend. But don't worry. In five days, I'll be back, and I'll be fine."

"A friend? Kris, what's going on?"

"I can't—"

"Kris!" *Her eyes were furious again.* "Don't treat me like that! I-I'm sorry that I couldn't tell you about Aaron and me. It's not because I don't want to. It's just..."

Kris could see he'd made her feel he wasn't telling her because he didn't trust her. But was that true? He felt *he could trust her, felt it in his gut.*

"No. That's not why I can't tell you. I understand. Or I think I do."

Her smile was thin but genuine. "Then what is it? I mean, you're missing..."

The First Story came to his mind, but he pushed it away and remembered that the Tree had made something for her.

"I'll tell you. But was told to show you this next time I saw you." *Kris turned to the Great Tree and reached back for her hand.*

*****

Leah took his hand, and right as she did, an opening appeared in the Tree, and he squeezed her hand reassuringly as they went in. That feeling. The feeling of fizzling out into nothing—sight and sound and touch going away—and then returning to a new place happened again. But this time, Kris was with her, and even when they were nothing at all, he was still warm beside her; two nothings holding hands in a motionless state of existence.

I should have told him, she said to herself as they reformed in a new place.

"Don't be scared," he said. "The Tree is taking us somewhere that it made just for you."

They were in her house. The house where she lived with her mom and her sister. But no. No. No, it wasn't exactly her house, but it was very similar. This house had almost the same layout, except her bedroom and part of the kitchen were missing. This house was painted differently too: cream-colored paint and dark-stained wooden furniture. The windows were closed and curtained with lace filigree. It was—

"This is my house before it was my house. How—how did the Tree do this? How did It know what my house looked like?"

Kris was looking at everything. "The Tree gets to know people the more they are around. The Tree hoped that you'd like it."

The Tree's voice came directly to her, "Aaliyah, your family is… unbelievable. I only wanted to show you what the house looked like when your mother and father moved in. Don't hate me…for my nature. Can't help but know you the more that I'm around you. I didn't mean to snoop. But then…I was moved by everything I learned… Take a look out the kitchen window."

Leah went to the window. Outside, between the open tin doors of the shed, was a motor propped up on cinder blocks.

"Thank you," said Leah so that no one but the Tree could hear.

"Of course. You know…he cares for you very much. Now don't let him off the hook," replied the Tree with the tone of a smile.

Leah turned to Kris, who was looking at her, puzzled.

"Will you tell me now?"

He nodded slowly. "When…when I was a kid, and I began to think all of this was just a dream, I started seeing people that weren't there. Just glimpses at first, out of the corner of my eye. But then just there. On the playground at my old elementary, I used to go and talk to the people that weren't there. I couldn't remember it much until recently, but… Well, they told me that—" He shook his head and turned away from her. "They told me about themselves. About the lives that they'd lived and how they lived them and how they died."

Leah fought the urge to take a step away from Kris, and he was already moving away from her. When he turned back around to face her, he'd crossed the room.

"You talked to ghosts?"

He kept going as if she hadn't said that, "They were from different times and places, and they spoke about things that I had felt before…"

"What do you mean?"

"All of them had this same…involuntary need, impulse. Certain things would set them off. They had trouble controlling themselves and told me about their struggle to control their tempers…I wonder why I forgot all of this until…" *Then he was looking out the window and lost in his own thoughts.*

Leah's heart was rattling in her chest, but she managed to move toward him, almost close enough to touch. "I've never seen you do that."

He looked almost hurt then. "Well, I do. I work hard to keep it from happening, but…my dad told me a long time ago that it never goes away. That we always struggle with it."

Leah kept quiet, not sure what to say and hoping that he'd remember what he was telling her.

"People started wondering what was wrong with me, and not long after that, my mother died. She hydroplaned. On her way to take out the trash. Wrapped the truck around a telephone pole. She bled to death…"

His eyes were hollow again, and they were staring at the floor. It was almost a contemplative expression, but it hurt her heart to see it. She imagined life without her mother but for only a moment because it was too terrible to dwell on. She was going to say something—apologize or offer her condolences or—but he began again. His eyes looked up with a violet glow.

"I don't want you to judge him or me, but my dad and I…we had a hard time after that. He didn't know how to go on without her, much less how to fill her shoes… He drank a lot. He gardened and drank when he wasn't working. Rob did all the stuff Mom used to do. He started taking me to The Book Bureau as soon as he got his license, and he did the grocery shopping."

He snorted. "He was the one who told me to go out to the garden. Put Dad's old straw hat on me and sent me out there. I bet he knew that

I wanted to go to the garden. I always did. Before Mom...I used to go out there with him a lot. We didn't argue out there. Dad had too much to focus on and too much else to say that he quickly forgot what was happening outside of the garden. I hate to admit that I've forgotten half of what he said. The other half is buried in my head somewhere. Maybe it'll grow someday. Here's one. Dad used to say to till the ground up before winter. Turn the roots again so they're exposed in the coldest part of the year.

"Yeah. He talked about gardening with his dad. It was odd to see him so peaceably talking about his dad. That wasn't how that usually went. He looked like a lost dog when he was thinking of Grandpa, a dog with rabies on a deserted road, just going on without knowing.

"Before Mom died, the whole family used to go out to the garden together. Rob and I used to talk about how Dad was...happiest in the garden. He wore this absurdly broad straw hat with a matching smile. His eyes found the tomato plants and peppers with pride. Mom loved when he worked in the garden. It's the place I imagine they were able to retreat back to, when the world invaded. Rob and I just tried not to complain because it was hot and tedious work. Our fingernails were filled with black soil, and sweat stung our eyes.

"When mom died, he spent every day out in the garden, every day the railroad gave him—not nearly enough. Rob told me to go out there with him since I'd spent so much time with him there. It seemed right...I think he saw that I needed it just as much.

"He put his straw hat on me—Dad hadn't been using it—and I started across the yard. My legs were shaking, and my lips quivered. I was sure that I was the last person he wanted to see. I held tight onto that little green shovel, trying to hide my restlessness in my grip. I made it to the gate and pushed it in. Of course, it squawked—it always does—but Dad didn't look up from where he was working, hunched over. He was pulling away weeds and fighting fire ants. I remember cringing at how burnt the nape of his neck was, all peeling and dry.

"When he didn't seem to notice nor care that I was there, I began pulling weeds too. I don't know how long it was that we worked. He occasionally spoke, but it was low and sporadic. I couldn't make it out.

"Clouds, heavy ones with light flashing in them, came in over us. Shortly after, it began to rain. Dad kept working. I looked up to see Rob *watching through the kitchen window. I thought of running back then, but I couldn't leave him there alone. Besides, I got a feeling that we did need to stay. Mom's face was all I could think of. I'm sure it was the same with him. I even laughed then, like he always says, 'The trains have to run. Rain, sleet, or snow, they have to run.'*

"We yanked weeds up and threw them into these old five-gallon buckets that were beginning to fill with rain water. It rained hard, ice-cold droplets. I know how that sounds, but really, it was like a winter storm in early spring. My breath floated out in puffs, my clothes soaked through, and the cold seeped into my blood. Finally, it tapered to a drizzle.

"He said that he should've listened to his dad and that he was the reason mom was dead. I saw he'd stopped working. He was facing me, on his knees. We were looking each other in the eyes...I remember saying, 'No, you didn't, Dad. No, you didn't.'"

He blinked. "I-I'm sorry. I-I didn't even mean to tell all that. It's got nothing to do with—"

"It's okay," Leah replied, fighting the urge to cry, the pressure in her nose. "Your mom...I'm sorry about your mom."

He nodded.

*****

Kris turned away from her, ready to leave the house, no longer so curious about the place where Leah grew up.

It really was okay. After a while, he'd learned to accept it, and he'd moved on, as people liked to say. *But even to this day, he'd occasionally get caught up in thoughts of how different his life would have been if she hadn't died. Thinking of that made him remember* how he used to see the world and his family and the future when he was a child. Back then, his only dreams for himself were to have a family like his. Things change, though. That's natural and good, and because they changed, he also had to learn to change. The only thing within his control was himself, and even that was in question sometimes. His future was not one of close relationships and family cookouts and back-porch barbecues and gardening *with a family of his own and a wife and kids. His future, as it turned out, was one of service, seclusion, and nightmarish tidings.*

He still remembered that image of himself, the one in which he stood before crowned people and was saying something.

"What's that?"

Kris turned. Leah was staring at the book in his hand. He'd forgotten it was there, had been there that whole time.

"Oh…I've always wanted to write. I finally started."

He could tell what she was doing, that she was redirecting him, trying to get him to focus on anything else. Sure, she was actually curious too, but—

She came closer to him, her eyes still sparking with that curiosity of hers. "What's your book about?"

Kris searched her eyes, thinking of his first thoughts when he started writing, of her. "Everything."

"What a description," she said. "Not to judge a book by its cover, but is it a love story?"

Kris smiled. The cover was embossed with spider lilies. "Yeah. It's a love story." He said, "It's a war story. It's an adventure. A horror. A thriller. It's a mystery… And yeah, it's a love story."

She came closer. Close enough that he wanted to move away but fought the urge. Then the longer she was there, the more that he wanted to move closer, not away. "Can we go somewhere else? And you can read it to me?" Kris nodded.

Leah grabbed his hand and led him to the red roundtop door.

CHAPTER 18

Scales and Balance

Leah waited in the parking lot at the St. Pierre mall. Her mother let her borrow the car as long as she promised to stop by Creekshire's to get some tartar sauce and cornmeal. Tommy was to bring more fish to her this morning. She involuntarily shuddered thinking of him. *Just don't do that when he gets here,* she reminded herself. The camera bag and SD card took up more space than they should have in the passenger seat, a reminder.

She'd moved the photos from the SD card to her laptop, hoping he couldn't directly ask about them without revealing he had them, and if they were gone, then... It was a long shot, but maybe he'd just assume that he misplaced them somewhere, lost the card they were on. If he did ask, in some vague way, then she'd have to fake ignorance better than she ever had in her life. Wasn't that what Tommy was doing? At every interaction? He was faking everything, from his politeness to his clients to whatever it was he had to do with the photos of the women in the storage container. His facial expressions were a carefully constructed mask. That didn't seem right, especially when she thought of having dinner with him and her family.

Each car that came into the lot made her look up. And when her phone went off, she jumped in her seat. It was Bailey. Leah's guilt about forgetting to call or text her back got the better of her, and she answered. Before she could say hello, Bailey was speaking.

"Oh. My. Fuck. You finally decided to answer, huh?"

"Bailey, I'm so sorry. I—"

"Yeah?"

Leah bit her lip. She couldn't tell if Bailey was serious or not or serious but hiding it in sarcasm. "I really am! I've been so wrapped up with working and—"

"Mhmm. I'm sure. Wrapped up with *someone* maybe..."

There was silence as Leah slowly realized that Bailey was talking about Kris. How did she not know about him missing, not that she even liked him that way. Then Leah remembered how much was going on. Across the street, a brand-new abandoned McDonald's stood as a monument to so much cataclysmic change in so little time. Not to mention how empty the lot at the mall was. And even now, Leah was lightheaded from skipping a breakfast of steamed vegetables and hot water cornbread.

"Who would I be wrapped up with?"

"Oh, never mind! I was going to text you, but it would have been way too long, and I just don't have the time. The guys left it to me to invite you anyhow... You know how they are. The crazier things get, the less I can stand to be around Talley and Andrew. I love them, but all this *conspiracy* shit is driving me up a fucking wall. Sorry! I'm just..." She sighed heavily. "The guys wanted to meet up tonight and show us some of what they've found out on that Reddit page. Buried in the Valley. They probably already sent you the links on Facebook."

"Um. I sort of had plans today, but what time were we supposed to—"

"You really want to go?"

"Well, I mean..." Leah looked over at the SD card. "I could use a distraction right now. Plus, I feel like we haven't had much time to hang out."

Bailey's veracity tempered into concern. "True... What's going on? Is everything okay?"

"Yeah," Leah quickly lied. "Everything is fine. Just...It's a weird world we live in."

"You're not wrong. To be honest, I don't know if I want to go, though. Thinking about all of it and trying to figure out why, it just makes me depressed. Besides, there's something I wanted to tell you—"

"Oh! I've got to go, Bailey. I'm sorry! I'm waiting on my boss, and he just got in. I'll talk to you later, okay?"

"Yeah, sure... Bye—"

Leah hung up the phone. Her pulse was already thumping; even just the sight of his car did it to her. *It's going to be okay. He won't even notice, and if he does, you just have to play dumb.* But was he speeding into the parking lot? Did he always drive like that? Or was he in a hurry to get here?

Tommy was dressed to the nines today. He wore a full charcoal-gray suit, and his hair was combed back, and his tie was a deep blue. But it only served to make him look more imposing to Leah, maybe even more dangerous. And there was something about his face; he seemed ticked off and readily showing it. His eyes narrowed into suspicious lines as he got out of his Durango and looked down Leah's car. Her hand shook a little as she reached for the SD card, but she smiled and waved at him, as if all was fine in the world. She got out of the car.

There was a light mist, and overhead, the sky was a marbled slate. It could have been just Leah, but it seemed a day of morbid weather.

"Oh, it is you!" announced Tommy, smiling. "I couldn't tell because of this damn mist. How are you this morning? You look a little tired."

Tommy reached out to bump knuckles with her, their customary greeting. She tried her best to seem normal and reciprocated.

"I'm fine. Just didn't get much sleep." Then she added, "I think it's just...you know. All this *stuff* going on."

Tommy clicked his tongue. His skin was glowing as it was the first time she'd met him, and he seemed energetic. Frowning, he said, "Yeah... The grocery stores keep thinning out, don't they? I saw on the news that local farmers were doing emergency farmer's markets. All of them were trying to expand their crops as well. Hell... That'll be a while before that helps, though. But!" He grinned as he opened the back hatch of the SUV and pulled out a box of fish. "Maybe this will help get you through."

Leah could feel her stomach growling as she saw the box of fish (counterbalance to the deadly fear that attacked her). How strange was it that a box of frozen raw fish could make her stomach growl? She chose not to dwell on that thought.

"Thank you, Tommy. This will help a lot!"

Leah opened the back door of her mother's car, and Tommy placed the box inside, then he closed the door.

"Here's that SD card," said Leah, extending it to him.

And his eyes became slits again as he took the SD card.

"Leah…is there something on your mind?"

It was a moment she knew but held a false hope, as many people are like to do. Because it was in Tommy's eyes and his frightless expression that he was aware, knew that she'd seen the photos. The question was whether to admit it or to deny it. All the while, Leah's bones began to feel gelatinous, and her muscle deteriorated by decades in minutes. Tommy had that kind of control, the control over rooms; the kind of person that could say anything and get away with it. Maybe do anything and get away with it. Yet he chose to answer for her rather than give her time to lie.

"I know you saw those photos, Leah. I left them there just for that."

"You—what?"

"I *wanted* you to find them."

Tommy was between her and her mother's car, but there was an open parking lot, and she'd worn her running shoes with a purpose. Her teeth winced to part, and her body was filled with numb and hot adrenaline. All of her body willed her to run, but she couldn't do it. He looked too calm, too in control. Or maybe her curiosity was getting the better of her.

"Why?"

"Because…I needed to see what you would do. You didn't turn me in. Why not?"

She couldn't say it, couldn't bring herself to admit that the entirety of the reason she didn't turn him in was not even for lack of faith in a broken justice system, and maybe in a diluted way, it could have been for her mother and sister, but ultimately, it was for money—for money that she knew she could get. But Tommy answered for her.

"I see," he said. "So what? So you *need* money? That makes you the same as everyone. I need money. Your mother and sister need it. Your neighbors and teachers and doctors and congressmen and soldiers and Supreme Court, they all need money... Leah, were you ever going to turn me in?"

"I don't know," she admitted.

Tommy nodded. Then he pulled an envelope from his coat pocket and handed her payment, an envelope of cash. She took it, timidly but ultimately, as if her very life depended on it. And then stepped out of her way, allowing her back to the car. But Leah didn't move; she was still watching him, not sure what he was trying to prove. Also caught between her gratitude toward Tommy and a perverse kind of fear of him.

"Why do you have those pictures?"

He shook his head and started walking back toward his car. Just before he got there, he turned back. "Leah, it used to be that a photo like that could get things done, could prove the guilt or innocence of people in it. I assume that, because of your past relationship with Aaron Grayson, that you know who that man in the picture is. People around Valleyport call him Poe, a suitable nickname for a man named Edgar Allen. He used to be chief of police."

Of course! That was his name! That's why his name had made her laugh. Why couldn't she remember it until just now?

"I have others, other pictures of Poe and other associates of Jim Grayson with those girls in the containers. Pictures that show their faces. I used to believe that those photos would wake people up, make them see the corruption around them. But it doesn't work like that. Most people don't care to see how societies actually are, and they'll readily turn their face or close their eyes.

"I, like you, have firsthand knowledge of just how monstrous those people can be. But unlike you, I've tried to kindle some justice. There's none to be had." He spat the last words and turned away.

Leah hesitated before she called out to him, "Wait! Why show me the pictures? I don't understand."

Tommy had just opened his car door. He licked his lips and looked up into the marble-slate sky, then back to her. "Some of us are those kinds of people...the kind that will fight an uphill battle, just for the principle of the thing. Most times, we know we'll fail, but we do it anyway. I can't explain everything now, but if you think you might be one of those people...let me know, and I'll tell you everything. If not...forget any of this ever happened."

Why is it easy to forget those things we want to remember, those ideas and people and memories which bring us joy? But our memory can readily locate the instances of our own misbehavior or pain. Then there are concepts and conversations that never leave our minds until they are addressed. Those memories are preserved in their entirety, and in each moment that passes, they are processed through all of our lenses. Such was Leah's conversation with Tommy. If she believed in the music of spheres, then Tommy had hit a note of concordant harmony with her.

She sat in her mother's car, in the St. Pierre Mall, for twenty minutes and mulled over what he'd said. Questions bore questions and then multiplied until possibilities flooded her mind. How did Tommy know about her and Aaron? What did he mean about the pictures not changing anything? Why wouldn't they? How? And he never elaborated on where the photos came from.

Gray mist floated through the sparse parking lot, in the distance a rumble of thunder, like grumbling. Up the street, under the I-31 overpass, a group of homeless people were holding cardboard signs that were dampened in the mist. There were more of them than usual. With the crash of an industry, the whole meat industry, and consequent collapse of several others, including several fast-food chains and the prominent pastime of hunting in the south, there was an indisputable and record-level rise in the homeless population. Brit had shown Leah a post about it a couple of days ago. Apparently, a homeless population would persist forever in a capitalist society, and times like these, when the unexpected and terrible happen, it would fall to those on the bottom to pay the price. One of the signs simply said, *"Please Help."*

Leah thought of the photos, of those desperate and night-blind women. She wondered where they were and if they were okay. She thought about Tommy's question, about if she were the kind of person to fight an uphill battle.

She texted him:

> I want to know.
> And outside, the thunder stuck, and she put
> the car in drive.

*****

Talley was at the Creekshire's on Queen's. She found him stocking aisles as she searched for cornmeal. He was looking in higher spirits than the last time she'd seen him, and as they caught up, Andrew came strolling around the corner (one of those happy accidents that made her think of Bob Ross, back when her mother used to paint and watch his show). She hugged them, and to her surprise, they both inquired about Kris, asking if she'd heard anything about him. She said she hadn't but that she was going to go help look for him today. Both of them exchanged a knowing kind of glance then, but Leah didn't ask about it. She assumed they were of a mind with Bailey, thinking she and Kris had some sort of relationship. They didn't. Fortunately they both moved on; unfortunately, they moved right into talking about Buried in the Valley.

"You have to come," they whispered. "There's some things you need to know."

She agreed, to their satisfaction. (Also to her own. Even just being around the two of them filled her with a kind of soothing. It always had.) She left off asking where the cornmeal was.

After leaving that aisle, the emptiness of the rest of them was more and more evident. A lack of products and a lack of people. A decline in sales. A decline in staff. The lights flickered overhead, echoing the ambience of the outside world.

She bought a pack of cigarettes for her sister, on a whim.

At home, her mother was watching the news. A big storm was spinning into the Ark-La-Tex on a green screen. Sasha Nomitok, the anchor, greeted a wind-and-rain-beaten man named Leonard Colston, who was in Texas getting drenched and battered by an impending tempest. He was yelling about sustained damage and high winds and strange weather and—They lost connection with him.

"Oh, it seems we've lost Leonard. I-I sure hope he's alright."

"As do I," added Gary, the coanchor. "As do I. Make sure to stay safe inside tonight, folks."

Leah noted how even Gary and Sasha seemed to have rapidly aged since the famine.

"Hey, love." Her mother's voice was starting to crack. She coughed. It cleared. "I'm sorry. Are you and Brit still going out to look for that friend of yours?"

"Yes, ma'am. But I don't think we'll be out late, Mom."

"Don't be. I still think about you being out there last time. Don't do that again, okay?"

"I won't, Mom."

Brit came down the hall and into the living room, and she was dressed down. She had on rubber boots and jeans and an old T-shirt; her hair was tied up, and she barely had on any makeup, an omen that she and Rob had finally had it out and settled on being friends. Oh, and she had a book in her hands (which tickled Leah's senses). A book with dogs on the front.

"I meant to tell you both," their mother said, "your father's trip might get postponed... He might not make it, if the storm is anything like they say it is."

It was a mirage of disappointment in her sister's eyes, which was unforeseen and inexplicable. He was supposed to come in today, and then they were going to see him tomorrow, but with the weather—

"He did say that if you, either of you, wanted to talk...I have his number, and he'd love to get yours and reach out."

Leah hesitated. Brit formed words but didn't speak for a moment, then, "He can have mine."

"Mine too," added Leah. "Are you ready to go?"

Brit nodded, put down the book, and out the door they went.

The drive was somber at first, aside from Leah giving her sister the pack of cigarettes and the prompt thank-you, then a look of privation, appreciation. And that was another thing, that it was hard to know whether to speak about what she had to know was on both of their minds. Leah had pondered it this morning between her panicking over those terrible dark photos, which still laid heavy on her mind. But in between, she thought about him, about meeting him. And she had noticed how many discarded drafts of Brit's emotions were scattered around Brit's room, like mothballs, and similar in function (Leah assumed) in that they were safeguarding her sister's covering.

At request, Leah tore the cellophane wrapper off the pack of cigarettes—Southern Cuts—and reloaded her sister's cigarette tin. *When did Brit first start smoking?* she wondered.

"I'm relieved."

"Oh?"

"I'm also...disappointed."

"Hmm."

"I'm sorry that I didn't tell you about Dad, that he was helping. It wasn't to hurt you, Leah. It was because of how I felt about it, because I couldn't figure out how he did it. I mean...I still don't know. I never want to do something like that to you or Mom. I couldn't imagine it. But Rob told me to write my feelings down, see if I can put them to words. He said he does it when he's feeling a lot of things and doesn't know why or where all of the different—different...where the different *strings* are being pulled." Brit reached for her tin, took out a cigarette, lit it, and rolled down the window.

That foreboding ashy sky inhaled the smoke trails from her sister's cigarette; clouds siphoning clouds. In rushed the drab wind, in came the gray, and Leah's skin rippled.

She wanted to say much, to condense and concentrate and purify her inner words and form them in a perfect harmony with the cruder words that her mouth could make. She wondered if it was okay only if Brit forgave him; she lost someone. Leah never had him, but now as she listened to starving words and Brit's hungry voice, and she could see that imaginary man in her sister's eye, she felt a pang of hate for him. How could he leave Brit alone? *How could he leave me alone?* But she told her sister that it was okay and that she understood, and reached for her phone and checked to see if Tommy had texted her back yet, knowing he hadn't.

A short but unmissable line of cars was staggered on Highway 3. And when they parked in that line, and when Leah saw Kris's childhood home for the first time, it was as if she was only then beginning to understand him. It was a place hidden away, an old land with a family's history. It was a place of solitude, where only the rooted, growing souls were fit to thrive. Wood chimes clanged together in a stranger's wind, and above them, that impenetrable gray sky drifted without moving.

Rob waved from a two-chair porch, laden with a farmer's trinkets. The eggshell-colored home and blue-sky colored garage stood in the wake of an ancient oak tree (a queen of some forgotten forest). In her bed, made of some yellowish-greenish vine which enveloped her where she was rooted, were rotund and impish little gnomes, all of them smiling like fools. Leah wished she had her camera as they mounted the steps.

"Thanks for coming," said Rob.

In physicality, he was not the same person, only in the vestiges of his unyielding amity or long-suffering. But he was eroded, and again, she only knew it was by a combination of many things.

Brit hugged him and said, "Of course. Are you holding up okay?"

"I'm holding up." *Ironlike.*

"I'm sure Kris's probably just caught up in a good book," said Leah, though she had not meant to say that, and she couldn't say from which part of her mind that it came from.

And while Brit's eyes went wide, Rob's face revolved to a laugh—a needed one—brightening his brushed-over eyes. "I hope you're right."

Rob took them inside, through the pleasant, quaint house (Leah tried to steal as many glances around as she could) and out the back door, to an ample back porch full of people. He introduced them to the close friends and family members that volunteered to help look for Kris. The family members were quiet with voluminous eyes; the friends were meek and were quick to talk about Kris with unbending hope for his return and an inscrutable fondness. Brit and Rob went off together, to grab some water bottles, when a couple came up to Leah.

"It's good to meet you. I'm Wally, and this is Jasmine."

"Good to meet you," said Leah.

Both Wally and Jasmine showed great interest in her, and she couldn't help but notice that she was the only person there that was Kris's age and that Wally and Jasmine and Rob were the next closest. Most of the people there were older by decades.

"How did you meet Kris?" asked Wally, who was brawny and big and reddish-brown-haired with a freckled face, and eyes kind and light.

"I, um, I go to school with him. We kind of met through my sister, Brit. She works up at Mason's with Rob."

"Oh, how long ago?"

Leah felt out of sorts. "Only at the beginning of summer. What about you?"

Wally grinned. "He played matchmaker for us."

The idea of Kris playing matchmaker was both perplexing and unbelievable, and just as Leah was about to ask what he meant, Jasmine patted his arm and spoke. Her voice was as pleasant and beautiful as she was, with a quality of equity.

"He didn't play matchmaker," she chided. "But he is to blame for me having anything to do with you." Then she turned to Leah. "Do you know The Book Bureau?"

Leah nodded, thinking of how she'd gone there hoping to see Kris, and that seemed a long time ago. "Kris actually told me about it. The way he described it...I just had to go see if it could live up to his description... And it did."

Jasmine smiled regally, and her ruby eyes glittered with fond remembrances. "Kris and Wally worked on repairing an old go-kart together a few years ago, when Kris was really into cars and motors and that kind of thing."

"I'm a mechanic," added Wally. "I knew him through Rob. Rob and I have been friends since middle school. Was always fond of him, but when we got to working on that go-kart together, I realized just how—how brilliant he was—is. Good at fixing things."

Leah listened in a kind of stunned silence and intrigue.

"And when they had to drive to Valleyport to get parts for it, Kris would ask Wally to stop at The Book Bureau. Now can you guess where I might have worked while I was in college? I remember Kris coming in countless times with Rob, and then suddenly he was bringing this big greasy loudmouth."

Leah wanted to ask so many questions; her mind was a flurry of them, but just then, Wally and Jasmine and everyone else turned as a man came out onto the porch. It was obvious who he was or who he was in relation to Kris. He was a big man, a man whose physical stature did not measure up to the sheer size of his presence. His face, even smiling—pleased—at the people who'd come to search for his son, was forlorn or world-weary. But everyone smiled and mimicked his authoritatively cheery disposition, and Leah was struck by the idea that she was the only one that wasn't doing so, she and Rob, who was still iron-faced. He shook hands with the people closest to him, hugged a few, and the eyes of everyone followed him. She couldn't help but remember how everyone wanted to look away from Kris when he was onstage, but there was something so similar about them.

"Hello, everyone. I'm very thankful to see you all here... As you all know, my son Kris has been missing for a week...for seven full nights. We had...we had an argument the last night I saw him." And he pointed toward a fig tree and a fence and the barrows of a once-garden. "We were out in the garden...I...I realized I was wrong and went back to apologize to him. And...he was gone." Kris's father scratched his cheek and rolled his tongue around in his mouth. "You all know Kris and how he is. It's not like him to run away, but this time, I may have pushed him far enough that he did. I've been out in the woods looking for him every day since—Rob and I have—but we needed some extra eyes. So thank you for helping... Now," he announced as Rob handed him pieces of printer paper with fresh maps on them. "Everyone take one, and I'll explain how we're going to do this."

The land was passed down by his wife's grandfather, and though it was divided now, it once was many acres that pushed from Highway 3 back into the thick Crimoisi woods and was bordered on the south by Gillian Lake. He spoke of the land with reverence, with an obscure sort of fear. Even at the time, Leah knew he wasn't afraid for Kris (or that that wasn't the source of his respectable fear), but it was there, and it seemed to emanate from Kris's father in waves. Leah couldn't help but superimpose such an earthy characteristic on the image of her own father. Maybe that's why she felt drawn to him, drawn in that way, though she didn't know it. Here was a man of confident contradictions, with the look of a man of the earth and who carried his authority with a hyperconsciousness of his burden. He created the land in their minds, as well as by map, and painted the landscape and the fallen pine cones and a curious place he referred to as Black Lake. Before she left the porch with the rest of the search party, divided into groups (hers being with Rob and Brit), she felt she'd glimpsed the land's soul. And as they passed by the fig tree, she realized a familiar tenable peace had drifted over her.

It was then that she began to feel the déjà vu. Felt it so deeply and so thoroughly, as if that fig tree and that garden were a dream which she'd dreamed of a thousand times. She stopped; she grabbed her head, and the world spun gently.

"You okay?"

Leah turned to see Kris's father offering a water bottle.

"I'm fine. I think. I just...I just got lightheaded there for a second."

"It's all this change, I'm sure. Hard on the body and tough on the mind too. Want some water?"

As they began to talk, Leah realized that Brit was ahead with Rob, and she decided she didn't care. There was something about Kris's dad, that same thing about Kris. Maybe that's what it was that united them; she felt he could not mean her any harm. And she did not expect Brit to notice, who was trying hard at something that seemed foreign to her: she was making a family member of Rob and not pining after him and therefore comforting him the way a sister can, the way that she'd done for Leah many times. But Brit did notice.

"Leah, are you coming with us?"

"I think I want to go with Mr.—"

"Mike. And you're more than welcome to. I was going to pass by Black Lake. Haven't been out to it since I was a kid."

Brit looked at Leah, with a perverse kind of peculiarity, but then she just nodded and went back to Rob to comfort him.

CHAPTER 19

Last Moments of Sleep

"You will forget most of this. That's alright. Memorization of it is not what is important, never has been. But it will be there for you when you need it," said Shane. "It's a tool."

How could he leave Kris with so few words after so much telling and so much to put upon his back?

"I won't be able to stop *him*. It'll be just like last time. Rezt-E-Ahar knows that I'm coming, and he is ancient, and he is unstoppable. Only the Void can do anything to him. It even says so in the Story. Why send *me* to *him*?"

Shane and Kris were still sitting around the fire, on the seventh day, and the night was still dark, and the stars were more brilliant than they'd been in the past nights. Past nights when Shane would offer him meat from a freshly dead corpse of an animal, and he would tell Kris about a battle between primordial forces, and then he would illuminate what those forces were in the world and how they manifested. And all the while, Kris could not help but notice a change in himself and a growing unwillingness to go back to the world he hadn't seen for seven days. A world of strife and war and facades. Kris knew he had to return, though; the closer they got to the culmination of that Story, he knew that his return was the lynchpin for plans laid forth by his own forbearer, by a being which permeated in his life since he ran from Rezt-E-Ahar in a celestial darkness: *the Void*.

All lies within the Void.

"Never mind. I'll find the answers when I need them," said Kris, knowing there was a difference between knowing and realizing.

Shane adjusted his overalls and rolled the polished walking staff on his lap, and he grinned with satisfaction at Kris's answer. "Besides, are you not the Void in a form of confinement and readying? That's what *Divers* are for, you know? They hear a calling, they see an unwinnable battle, and they know they must take up a sword. Their credence guides their actions, an oath from the beginning of all things... Though they may forget for a while."

All the old impassable decisions of Kris's life came to him in that moment, that last moment with Shane and that last moment before he had to go back.

"It's funny to look back and realize that I was right and wrong about that—that *idea* of how life would turn out for me and where I would go in the world and what I would do. Right in that it was all determined before I had grown to understand how to follow a path. Wrong in that the places I must go and the things that I must do are not so forgettable and small and insignificant. It seems strange that anyone could ever think those things about themselves, and in a way, it always has seemed strange. How can someone think they are beyond redeeming or beyond further correction? Balance is not an object, and neither is peace or fun or love... But I still wonder if I'll be able to do this, Shane... How... How can I possibly do this?"

Shane stood and circled the dying embers of a fire, and he crouched at Kris's feet and placed a hand on Kris's shoulder. "You have always wanted that same thing, that underlying desire, which has not changed and will not change. Failure does not change it, and neither does all the divergence and catastrophe and unexpected distractions which persist for years of that life you must live. Only try, only continue... The rest lies with the Void. Now go to it. The child of darkness has taken the beasts, and now he has marched on mankind."

Watching Shane walk away, Kris wondered, after those seven days of constant companionship, how he knew so little about Shane. As if in a response, at the last glimpse of Shane walking to the shade beyond the pines, Kris saw Shane for what he was or maybe a single perception of what Shane might be: he was a cloak of shadow, draped on a body of tireless working and toiling, and he was a face of mortality's cessation, and it wasn't a walking stick in his hand but a great scythe with a blade that captured the moon's radiance. Then he was gone.

Kris was alone by the remnants of a fire, sitting on the ground then, not on a chair. Underneath him, the dirt was warm again, not cool, as was the air, humid and hot. He stood. And everything had changed. Because knowing always changes everything.

Around him, the world waited for his touch and will, but unlike the frivolity of his dreaming, the world *was* more, was greater in significance because it was a direct projection of life. The people were not the people of dreams or the characters of novels, and he understood then that he had been separated from them. He knew it better because he could feel the world bending to his will, that he could rearrange the structure of molecules and distort reality, and he could create the systems of universal order. At the same time, the weight of his power frightened him into stillness and silence, and he dared to move.

*****

Pete held out his arm for his lovely wife, Shawna Akles, and together, they disembarked on their little adventure.

"Do you think the grandkids will forgive us?"

"With all that Benjamin got for them, I doubt they even realized we didn't show up."

She laughed. In front of them, a divided sky, stars and dark mingling with warm orange sunset, but Pete was watching the way his wife leaned her head back when she laughed. She tapped his arm several times. *You old fool*, it seemed to say. Half of her face, the side toward him, still drooped from the stroke. The doctors predicted a long difficult recovery, but Shawna was tough as nails and with a much better sense of humor. He leaned in and kissed her cheek.

"The Stewarts called. They said that the Johnsons on the other end of the highway lost all of theirs last night. They were staying in a hotel in town, thank God."

"Maybe we should do that," said Pete. He knew she wouldn't, but he had to try.

"I'm not leaving them."

Besides, we couldn't afford to leave, even if I could convince you to. Whatever it was that started in Tarnmont was finally moving its way east, and they were right in its marching path.

Why did he have to love such a damn hardheaded person? *Because otherwise it wouldn't work.*

As they made their way through the sparse pines, him carefully watching her every step, the old feeling came back. It had been a lifetime since he got out of the army, but there was something he learned there that he'd never forget. People always talk about the calm before the storm, but it wasn't calm; it was tension. It wasn't that it was any more peaceful; no, the world doesn't stop, especially not in war, but most soldiers recognize the end just beyond the battalion lines. On the other side, on the beaches, in the jungle, in the desert, the figure in the black cloak waits. People expect him to be there, but the fact of the matter is, that son of a bitch is everywhere. He's in your kitchen, all over the highways and interstates. He lives inside of some folks. He's omnipresent. But what Pete started to notice, after he had enough encounters with him, is that the grim reaper sings a tune. It's a song about life, and every note pulls the tension just a little. Suddenly, Pete could feel the air against his skin, the way he remembered it as a child, every hair on his arms turning different directions in the breeze. Garlic tasted new on his tongue, from the pot roast Shawna made at dinner, which he'd eaten over an hour ago, but it was like he'd just taken another bite. His joints ached. His eyes were dry. And he had to piss. Pete stopped.

"Darling."

"Yeah?"

She looked back at him. Eyes dark. There was concern there. He could feel a sheen of sweat forming on his brow.

"We ought to go back. I know you care about them animals. I do too, but you're going to have to trust me."

Ahead of them, on the other side of a heavy-timbered fence, a few of the grayish goats started bleating. The wind picked up and then stopped completely.

"What...I can't. What do you mean? What's happening?"

Pete turned to her and grabbed both of her hands. "Listen."

More bleating. Nothing. *Was it gone?* All at once, he felt more himself, like motion sickness passing. He was cold and then just fine.

"Pete, what is it? I don't hear anything?"

He shuffled from foot to foot. "I thought I heard something, but I can't hear it now."

Even after all these years, it still happened; at times, he was paranoid. It had taken years to get comfortable in a house again, sleeping with walls and a roof. There were nights even now when he felt hemmed in, trapped. He'd wake up and try to leave the bed without Shawna noticing, then he'd go out onto the porch and just sit there, breathing. Times like those were rare now, but they still happened every now and again. The worst of it had passed when he met Shawna, and the prospect of having a family made him want to confront the devils in the dark.

But they never go away completely. And in dreams, the boys he killed still liked to show their faces, wondering what it would have been like to see the end of the war.

"Sorry, Shawna. I got confused."

She knew. She knew that it still happened from time to time. Shawna squeezed his hand and kissed him with half of her lips. *How is it that she just keeps getting prettier?* he wondered.

"Come on. Let's just check on them, and we'll go back."

They turned, hand in hand, and continued on. As they approached the fence, the goats came, bleating and begging. They came to Shawna whenever she skirted anywhere near that fence. Most of them she'd cared for since they'd been born. Generations of goats ambled up, making their absurd noises, chewing, bleating. Shawna reached through and gently stroked the nose of one of the kids. He followed her hand, craning this way and that. Others vied for attention, so Pete reached through and gave the oldest, Gunther, a couple of scratches behind the ears.

"Wish we could get somebody to watch them overnight," she said.

Can't afford it, darling. I'm sorry. "They'll be okay."

When Shawna's hand dropped, the greedy kid slapped the fence post trying to get to her hand. Pete wanted to hold on, to think of something he could say that would take the worry away. He knew better. There was a failing point with words. A point well demonstrated when Sheriff Hudson came two days earlier. The boys in blue went up and down the highways and back roads warning everyone. He didn't have any answers as to what in the hell was coming and why folks and animals were disappearing. The first thing Shawna asked about was the animals: Was there anyone to come and help with the goats, the cows, the chickens, the quails? Pete could have told her before she asked that if they weren't finding lodging for the people, then they sure as hell weren't paying to move a bunch of farm animals.

Perhaps the other failure of words was the stories, but Pete had no idea what to believe there. Their son, Andrew, who'd offered time and again to help but had no means to, told stories he heard from a firefighter friend of his. Apparently the federal agents put guys right in this thing's line, put cameras, put armored vehicles, put drones, and waited through the night. In the morning, all the electronics were fried, and not a one of the guys they left out in the dark was there in the morning. Then there were stories on Facebook, folks claiming to see people walking through the woods at night. After she heard that, Shawna got on maps and tried to see if they were really in the path of whatever it was. That was another thing; through forest, lakes, rivers, hills, moors, it was a straight line, and they were right on the edge of it, like she was checking the weather and figuring out if the storm was going to hit or not.

"Maybe it'll go right by us."

Pete didn't have it in him to say anything. He grabbed her hand, because he'd already decided either way that he was going to be with her, hell or high water.

"Look."

Across the pasture, where the goats were fenced in, the universe was coming into view as the sun winked out. Cosmic black ate everything above their heads except the distant suns, who couldn't outshine it from so far away. For several years in Pete's life, he'd been forced to live in big cities, like Helena and New Portsmith, the former being where he was sent for basic training. Living in a place where you couldn't see the night sky had never sat well with him, though a lot of the others didn't seem to care at all. When he first got back, he slept in his parents' backyard for a week, looking up at the stars. He knew that even though they hadn't seemed to change at all, that they had, ever so slightly. But they were still just as awe-inspiring and made him feel just as small, which was a great feeling sometimes.

"The news will be starting soon. Do you wanna watch it?"

"Yeah. I'll come out and check on them again in a couple hours," said Pete as he squeezed her hand.

Shawna wrapped her arms around him as a distant thunder—no. That wasn't thunder. Pete turned his head back toward the forest. Then the screaming started. Gunfire. At first, it was several single shots, a high-powered rifle. Another scream followed. The goats scattered and started for the far end of the valley, running from the sound. Shawna held tight to his hand. Pete grabbed with the vigor of that young man fresh out of basic.

"Go to the house. Get the—"

"Pete—"

"Behind the door and lock it. Call—"

"Pete!"

Shots, rapid. Automatic fire and harsh voices, coordinating in the forest. He turned to see men running out in army greens with their carbines in hand. They were twice the size of ants from here. He scanned the tree line, looking for what was pursuing them. Nothing. He shook Shawna. He tried to be as gentle as he could, but his blood was shooting through him harder than it had in years.

"*RUN!*" one of the men screamed as he was coming toward them.

"Shawna! Did you hear me?"

The one side of her face was wide-eyed and mouthed, looking toward the pines and their home; she was petrified and barely breathing. People were all around them. A cold wind blew in, blasting his face with arctic air. His eyes began to sting as he stared at them. There was a woman in a suit with bangs, a fella in a reflective vest with a hard hat on, a couple—wet from head to toe—children, all smiling wide, faces full of teeth. But their eyes were black through and through. Pete couldn't move, couldn't even feel his body, only the cold. He noticed there were animals with them, black-eyed and docile. The ghoulish smiles came toward them, and what light there was began to fade. His vision became a tunnel into lunatic black eyes. He stared as long as he could but looked away. *Where am I?* he wondered. *Who am I? What am I?*

*****

By a further comparison did Leah get to know Kris, by getting to know his father. In direct comparison, forgetting where they overlapped in so many ways and in so many places, she began to see Kris as lofty and reaching and ambitious, but it was the reaching ambition of his dad. Mike wanted to help people. He wanted to help them in a permanent and unchanging way, to help them in a way that would allow them to become the arbiters of their own path in life. And that characteristic only manifested in a way and presented in another.

On their way, he and she talked about the plants in the forest, about the birds nestled in the branches, and the rustling in the underbrush. He told her tales of his first few years out on the land and how his wife, Tabi, had been the one to instill in him a love for it. Tales of her leading him through old trails and recalling the games they played as children, then as teenagers, then as transient forms on their way to adulthood, and then as adults.

"You two knew each other since you were kids?"

"Yes, we did. She was on one side of Gillian Lake, and I was on the other. Hers being the Gadsborrow side and mine the Faringsport side. Back when we first started to-to date, we'd meet up in an old johnboat. We had a lot in common. A similar childhood. Her father was a lot like mine, which is to say that they were a lot more concerned with everything else other than being a father. What was your parents' names, by the way? Were they from around here?"

"I know my mom is from Valleyport. My mom's name is Adni May, and my dad's is Wyatt Fells," said Leah, not altogether hiding a trace amount of unforgiveness with her father's name.

A wide smile broke across Mike's face. "Well, how about that. I know one of them. Your dad went to school with me at Faringsport Elementary. He was always nice and quiet, and he was always playing with something in his hands. One of those people that has to have something to fidget with."

It was then that Leah noticed she'd been rolling a twig she'd pulled off a tree around in her hand, and she tried her best to discreetly let it fall back to the earth. If he noticed, he pretended not to, which was nice.

"How is your daddy? What's he doing now?"

"To be honest, I-I don't really know. He left a long time ago… Actually, he's trying to…I don't know… He's trying to be involved in our lives again."

He seemed to be waiting for her to say something else, so she, with a little more confidence, continued, "He has been sending money, helping support us for years. My mom and sister didn't tell me about that. I just kind of found out recently…I've been helping with the bills, and—and well, the guy who hired me to help him run his photography studio pays me really well. I guess I didn't understand how much money it takes to have a house and buy food and pay bills and keep gas in a car…I mean, I had an idea, but I didn't *know*."

He nodded, but again, it was as if he were waiting.

"I don't know. It makes me feel guilty that now, after thinking it over and having a lot of back and forth, I don't know if I even want to meet him. Sometimes I really want to, and other times… Other times I can't tell if I'm doing it just to keep the peace with my mom and sister."

He surveyed the trees around them, as if looking for something or a particular tree. Yet their conversation was in his eyes; he turned to her when he was sure that she didn't have anything else that she wanted to say. "That's a tough spot. Hard to keep your head on straight, I imagine."

She nodded, feeling a little let down because she had expected some wisdom in the form of an anecdote or at least a mantra, but he did not offer any of that. She realized then that he'd put on such a fierce front of stoic endurance that she forgot how tough this must be for him. He approached a tree and ran his thumb over a crude carving in its bark, what looked like a dog or maybe a bear.

"My friends, Joe and Billy, and I carved these years ago. We had found our way to this pond—to us, it was a lake—and we were worried we'd never be able to find it again. Because you know how it is, when we first discovered this place, we thought it was special, magical. We were at that age where almost everything was that way. We were known to nap beside it from time to time. Well, on one particular occasion, I dreamed that I chased a bullfrog down into the water, and when I came up, I was somewhere else. There were gigantic trees there, and at the bank, there was a woman with markings across her face. She was carrying a basket filled with flowers and plants, and..."

"And what?"

"You know...I can't remember."

And Kris's dad, Mike, started laughing then, laughing with reminiscence and at the way things slipped away. Leah couldn't help but join him; he had a laugh like her mother's, a laugh that made her want to laugh.

The sun was quickly finding its way down then, and it even managed to break through the gray sky for an instant, casting the forest in stripes of orange.

"I know you didn't ask, Leah, but if I were you, I'd try to smooth things over with my dad. I would try. If things work out, maybe one day, you won't be able to recall the days when he wasn't in your life. And if you do still think of them, trust me when I say the bliss or pain of those memories will not strike you the same way. I smile even when I remember the way Tabi and I used to fight back here. Hell, she gave me a good chewing for something right where we're standing. I remember sitting there, nothing to say, because damn it if she wasn't right. Not that I can remember what we were even arguing about."

*****

He was reminded, so immediately, by the sounds of peoples and nations and individuals—voices and invisible notions which manifested in those ways which Shane had revealed to him—that he could have no stake in any nation or people or individual, though he could feel his father and Leah approaching the Black Lake, where he then stood.

Rezt-E-Ahar had moved over the world, now taking people and turning the governing bodies to fear, and even the rich were then ready to give money to a cause, the only cause which can stir those people so far removed, the need to hold on to power, to not combat with the lives of the indigent. In the nations of the East, the war was already kindled, as they turned to each other, pointed the proverbial finger and said, "They have taken my livelihood, and now they have taken my children and brothers and sisters. Now I will soon take *everything* away from them. I will find them, and by any means necessary, I will wipe them from the face of the earth." Kris was having trouble breathing. He could hear the screams of children who were taken by strangers, and he could hear the absence of screams from those taken by Rezt-E-Ahar. And even in the distance, he could feel the dark presence residing on every throne, just hiding from the face of the sun. He was looking at the Black Lake and feeling his rage so greatly kindled that he knew he could no longer stand and do nothing, and he imagined the destruction of all of humanity, where Rezt-E-Ahar had found a home. Because now he could do it.

But he sat, and he took breaths, and he waited for them to find him.

*****

How many years had it been since she'd found herself in a forest, her phone forgotten in her pocket, and even the rest of her world could have, perhaps, never existed? Leah had never been on a *vacation*, which, to her, was a word that she associated with that place she wanted to someday be, that place in time when she would have enough money to tell her mom and sister, "Come on, let's go somewhere, anywhere that we can learn about this world that we know so little about." Those days in the future when she would be able to come and go as she pleased, because that's what money does. That's what money is—freedom. She'd seen it when she was with Aaron, whose name did not hurt her so badly here. Here, in the middle of the woods, like on that cartop in the parking lot, on the last day of school, where she felt safe. And here more so. This was the freedom of invisibility and of indiscriminate nature that sees all men and women as the same. See, she'd never been in a forest like that, in parks and walking trails off the Cramoisi, behind Larue. But never a wild, untamed place like the forest she walked in now.

And it was then that they walked in silence.

Kris's father, Mike, who, only minutes ago, had been answering her questions about being a railroader, was walking with that reverence and fear. The silence was both peaceful and so vast that it had to be ominous, and his reverence added to its size. His forearms would go taut from time to time, and he would flex his hands, readying to use them. She found herself doing the same thing.

On the other end of the silence, someone waited. Leah knew who it was. With every step that she took, a memory would return to her, a memory of walking through an indelible dream with him. At first, she thought she might have been losing her mind, but it became obvious how real those memories were with every step. How those dreams took place over innumerable days, leaving her feeling.

Mike eyed a final carving in the wood, which Leah didn't even get a chance to see because as they crested the hill which the tree stood on, she could see Kris. He was sitting by the water of a small pond. The water's surface was balmy and black, the mired water of folkish nightmares, but he rested by it as if he were on a beach by a blue ocean. His eyes were closed, and his nostrils were wide, taking in a deep breath.

SERMON OF THE DIVERS

It was the moment that her memory fully revolved into place, and she saw him the way that he appeared in the garden: his eyes almost violet, his hair an aura, and his body the ethereal skin of dreams. She called his name as she rushed toward him, faster than even his father moved, and his eyes going wide as he turned and stood. Recognition heavy in his eyes as he opened his arms.

CHAPTER 20

Within the Walls

Every moment meant a great deal more because knowing changes everything, but realizing means that something has become a part of you, inculcated into you. Kris knew *that* then, as he saw the recognition in Leah's eyes and then his father's. Two different things being recognized: By Leah, the understanding that they were both entwined in some way, which he knew led to no tangible end but was necessary for each of them, vital to them, so vital that his body felt as if those dreamed fireflies were flitting about in his hollow stomach. And by his father, the understanding that Kris had taken his own path and that there would be a span between them forever, but that he loved his father and was thankful for those lessons of worldly detachment. And when his father embraced him, Kris felt only comfort, and none of the resentment, which still remained from his dad's inability to tell him the Story.

"I knew you'd be back, but..." his father whispered, not needing to finish the words.

Then in jubilance, they took Kris back out of that forest, calling all the other searchers who'd come to look for him, calling Rob first and Rob running through the woods to see him only moments later, as if he knew exactly where Kris was now that he was found. That iron look on Rob's face becoming molten and melting away. Then Rob's hug being the tightest, even tighter than Wally's.

Then the failure of words to find the meaning for how he felt when his neighbors and friends from the old church had shown up in numbers to look for him. He didn't expect that. He, for the sake of some melancholic part of him that still and would remain, couldn't believe that they had all come just for him. Mrs. March had brought along her sisters; all of them had the same graying curly hair, and all of them looked so out of place, dressed to explore the forest. Mr. Weyfield and the Duponts were there too, and Mr. Weyfield looked to have lost forty pounds or more. While they all were there, basking in the reverie of finding him, Kris reminisced and wondered if they did too. He remembered learning what a harmonica was from Mr. Jackson, who bought him one for Christmas that same year. Kris remembered going over to his house for lessons. Why was that memory only now coming back to him? He remembered how Mrs. March would invite him and Rob over for lunch, and she'd have lunch meat and cheese and pickles and tomatoes and onions and lettuce and bread and olives and jalapeños and banana peppers and every other sandwich topping spread out on the table. Rob and he used to love that—to make their own sandwiches. Why was that memory only now coming back to him? He remembered being at the old brick house (Mr. Weyfield's) and watching it happen, trying to find a way at such a young age to comfort Mr. Weyfield as his wife passed away, and the EMT drivers had shown up, but she had some paper (a DNR) which stopped them from trying to bring her back to life. He remembered praying with Mr. Weyfield, in a moment when there seemed nothing else to do.

Why was that memory only now coming back to him?

When they asked him what had happened out in the woods and how he got lost and what he did while he was out there, his father covered for him and told them not to batter him with questions just yet.

Then all of them slowly came to the realization that their jubilance had ended, and Kris was found, and it was time to go. Jasmine hugged him three more times before she and Wally left, because there was still a storm coming in. Everyone remembered it then, when the thunder rolled, and they slowly departed, but Leah was there next to him, with her reddish eyes so full of questions and wonder.

And when everyone was leaving, Leah handed him her phone, with the new contact screen open and his name misspelled.

"Sorry," she said after he corrected it.

"You're fine. It's a weird way to spell it… Also, I have no idea where my phone is."

She laughed. "Well, I'll text you every day until you text back. I…I wanna talk to you about—about *everything*."

"I'll call as soon as I get one."

She looked over her shoulder as she and Brit walked away, and Kris had the first of many false visions, false imaginings. In this one, he saw himself with her in a house that was built similarly to the one of her childhood, the one he'd seen in the Dreaming. He imagined them and a child and a little waterslide on a sloped yard. He imagined a kid with her hair and her nose that upturned at the end, and in that vision, they were playing with their child. The eternal rays of spring sunshine caught in the child's hair in a familiar way, and for that moment, he was holding Leah and watching a falsified lifetime go by. The famine was over or never had been in that vision, and the world had not required the Void to use him. A utopia. A false vision. Yet as she turned back to him and returned to hug him one final time before she left, he believed it. *Don't trust what you see or hear or feel.*

After she was gone, and everyone else was gone, and only he and Rob and his dad remained, the rain was beginning to fall.

Back inside the home, Kris, as soon as he breached the doorway, found himself staring at that old photo, the family photo. Rob saw Kris and what Kris saw and said, "Mom must have been watching over you while you were out there."

"She always is," said their father.

"Must have been," repeated Kris, but knowing that couldn't have been true.

His mother would not have wanted what was to come; she would not have wanted it for him.

"I feel like she's in the room with us right now."

No one said anything.

SERMON OF THE DIVERS

Kris's father suggested a shower and a change of clothes, and it was only then that Kris realized how he looked. Greasy hair and dirt-covered hoodie and muddy jeans, and he felt the same: overdue for cleaning. His brother escorted him to the bathroom, as if Kris might have forgotten where it was. Once inside, Kris stripped off the old clothes and stared momentarily at the shower curtain, which was almost like an action painting of black and white and gray paint drippings. He turned the water as hot as he could stand it. Then he ruminated on what was to come.

He wished he were more angry about it, more passionate about fighting it, but that was simply not how he felt. Kris no longer had to guess about the state of things, for he could *feel* it. The souls of those who suffered in the world called out to him. The very earth called out to him, and both of them were screaming similar pains at the suffering of humankind's hands.

Kris got out when Rob knocked on the door and told him they made some food for him. They all sat down at the kitchen table, not talking about what had happened. They all sat down to a pan of cornbread and a bowl with black-eyed peas. The smell was oniony, and the peas were slightly over-salted, but he ate.

"Did you have any food while you were out there?"

"Yeah," he said around a half-chew of cornbread.

Rob leaned over his own bowl, but he wasn't eating anything, just waiting and looking at Kris. On the other side of the table, Kris's dad was advising with his eyes, *Don't tell him.*

"Do you remember when Dad got you that first guitar, the old Gibson, and mom started trying to teach you? Even though she didn't know how to play. Do you remember that?"

Rob grinned. "Yeah, I remember that."

"I used to listen to Mom give you those lessons."

"I know. You were just in the hallway, hiding. And she couldn't teach me anything about how to actually *play* the guitar. It was more about the—"

"Philosophy of creating."

"That's what she called it," Rob finished.

All the while, their dad was looking back and forth, sort of mesmerized.

"What about it?" asked Rob, who had forgotten his food, even though his cheeks were on the verge of being gaunt, sunken.

"She told you about a place that you needed to go to, that after you learned the technical stuff, the place you wanted to go was like a desert...or an ocean. She told you that when she was writing, she went there too. A vast place where experiences connect and reverberate and sink and float. It's where you have to dive down and dedicate to the work of bringing it to the surface... While I was out in the woods, I met a man from that place."

Rob didn't laugh, just staring and listening.

"You should eat," said Kris.

Kris did not care that his father might not want Rob to know about any of it, but that was the thing—Rob already knew it. He had to know it. Everyone knew it once, at one time or another.

Rob looked back at the food and then at Kris.

"What do you mean that you met a man from that place?"

"Eat with me... And we'll talk."

"Kris..." his dad interrupted.

"Listen, Dad."

Rob picked up the spoon and scooped some of the soupy peas into his mouth. Kris waited for his father to do the same; he waited and felt the way that the room waited on him, that the world waited on him, the same way it waited for Rob on that stage.

"His name was Shane. He gave me food every day, and he told me a story while we were out there. It was a story about how things began, but it was also a story about events that have not happened yet. He told me that every facet of the world's systemic failures can be followed, can be traced back to a single being. And this..." Kris looked down at the meatless bowl and bread, and he swallowed. "This is also his work... You know, it's funny that every story must have that contender, that being or idea that the hero" (of the story) "must strive against. It's a thing that we know on some level, that the being we must strive against is omnipresent... And now, Rezt-E-Ahar has a form, a physical form."

Rob's face was a caricature of concern; his bladelike brows were near connecting in concern. But their father was listening with a grave expression. The clock in the living room was the only sound for a moment, a ticking clock, and then the rain picked up again and hurled a sheet of water at the black window.

"Kris..."

"What?"

"I... What happened? What are you talking about?"

Kris realized then that the words would do him no good.

Brown carpet; it was old but not too old, with a Kool-Aid stain under the coffee table's short leg. Melissa had no idea how long she'd been staring at it. She did know there was something about it that made her want to smile, to laugh. Argo vibrated with a constant purr in Melissa's lap. Hocus Pocus *was playing on the TV. She was crisscross on the floor. and her mother and father cuddled on the couch behind her. Every now and again, she'd give Argo a nibble's worth of popcorn, not too much, and she'd always make sure there were no kernels in it. They'd only just gotten to the part when the black flame candle's lit when her dad paused the movie.*

"Feels like something's missing. Don't it, Mel?"

She turned back to him to see a family-size bag of almond M&Ms in his hand. The reddish whiskers on his face outlined a generous smile; he winked.

"Not too many of those, you two. Stan, you'll give her another half dozen cavities," said Mom.

"But it's almond M&Ms... Some candy is worth a few cavities," he said.

"And it's almost Halloween," Mel added.

Her mother shook her head but tore open the bag herself. Dad and Mom both reached into the bag and gave her two handfuls, putting them right in the popcorn bowl. Seeing the bright colors with butter-battered popcorn and all caught in the sight of a movie screen reminded her of something. There was somewhere she had to be, wasn't there? A dense, nasty headache the size of a pin top ached behind her eyes.

"You okay, Mel?"

Looking at her dad eased the pain somehow.

"Yeah. Turn the movie back on."

He smiled the way that he did with the warmth of a December sun, precious in the cold world. "You got it."

Argo readjusted in her lap as the movie started again. Melissa popped two M&Ms into her mouth; they were warm, melting, and buttery from the popcorn. She heard her dad kiss her mother's cheek.

In a couple of days, it'd be Halloween, and her costume was ready. She'd wanted to wear it tonight, but that'd spoil some of the magic. That's what her father said anyway. Her middle and ring fingers moved down to her palm thoughtlessly, and the others were fully extended. If her parents hadn't objected to watching Spider-Man *twice in one day, then she could have been learning new catchphrases for when she finally put on the costume. Her mom had found it odd; she could tell by the way she asked about so many other costumes after Melissa already told her she wanted to be Spider-Man.*

"What about this princess costume? Or maybe this spooky witch, sweetie?"

"I want to be Spider-Man," said Mel.

The only thing her dad couldn't understand about it was why she didn't want the black symbiote suit. That was even more confusing than Mom wanting her to be something girly. Then she had to explain to him that the whole story was about him getting back into the regular suit, like he hadn't watched the movie with her. The only way she could think to articulate it so that he understood was to take the black suit in one hand and the actual suit in the other. Her dad was crouching down in the aisle at Spirit with her. She raised the black suit as high as she could.

"This isn't Spider-Man." She lowered it back down and raised the red-and-blue suit even higher. "This is Spider-Man, Dad."

Then he understood. "Can't argue with that," he said.

Watch.

Mel looked back at her parents. That hadn't sounded like them. They were staring over her, at the TV. Her mom's head was nestled on her dad's shoulder. His arms were wrapped around her, and they were half-covered by the checked throw blanket. LED blue was thrown over the throw and wall and them. Blackout curtains behind them allowed only a peek of the fogged window and an ethereal blue that could only be a country sky lacking pollution. They stared. With eyes full of looking, they didn't blink as they stared. For a moment, Mel thought—even though she knew it was stupid, and it frightened her—that they weren't even breathing; they'd become perfect statues. She couldn't hear the movie anymore as she started to count. It'd already been so long. She wanted to call their names, but—

"Fifteen Mississippi, sixteen Mississippi, seventeen Mississippi..."

Curiosity kept her from calling out. How long could they stay frozen?

"Twenty-four Mississippi, twenty-five Mississippi, twenty-six Mississippi..."

Mreow!

Just like that, they were alive again. Argo's voice brought them back, and the first thing they did was blink and look at her.

"What is it, Mel? Don't you want to watch the movie?"

"Do you want some more M&Ms, sweetie?" asked her mother.

Melissa was certain there was somewhere she was meant to be. Yes, but where?

"You weren't moving," she said. "I counted to thirty-three before you blinked."

Her dad laughed and paused the movie. "Sorry to scare you," *he said.* "I haven't seen this movie in a while. I guess I just got caught up in it."

"And I was falling asleep," *added her mother.*

But your eyes were wide open!

They gave her some more candy and continued watching as if nothing happened. Argo leapt from her lap and sat by the front door, next to two sets of shoes. Mel tried to focus on the movie, but her eyes drifted to Argo time and again. The cat was still, waiting and watching the window or her parents or the lights that changed with the movie scenes. Mel couldn't help but look behind her every minute or so, trying to find what Argo was watching. Once, only for an instant, like seeing the afterimage of a bright light, she saw a boy's face between the curtains, but she knew it was nothing. The only thing that troubled her was the feeling of being late and the constant ache in her head.

Watch... Diver...

She knew she heard a voice then, and it wasn't her parents. The voice was drawn out, both clear and untraceable. Melissa stared at the TV, afraid to look back and see her parents, knowing they were frozen, statues, dead, hollow.

Mreow!

"Mom... Dad..."

She turned slowly, regretting it with every childish beat of her heart. An empty couch lay behind her and parted curtains with a shy moon. The TV cut off, right as the musical number got started.

M*reow!*

Watch, Diver.

M*reow!*

Now the terrible voice came from the TV. Mel turned back to it. In the dead black screen, she could see herself and her parents behind her. They were statues with dark eyes staring into the screen with her. Her mom was still nestled in her father's shoulder. He smiled that way he did and winked. A scream rushed up from her stomach, but before it could escape her, the TV came back on. Her head was burning and cracking inside like kindling, and her heart was in her arms and feet and belly and head.

"I know!"

On the screen, a home movie played, a close-up of her father's face: nostrils flared, eyebrows and mouth falling at the ends, and redness in his cheeks.

"I know she wants that fucking Spider-Man costume! Okay? You don't find that odd, huh?"

He was trying not to yell. Her mother's voice, "I don't think so, I don't know, but she wants it, Stan."

Then the shot was of them both facing each other. He was in the old work uniform, which was blotted with mud. Mom was in pajamas. They were in the kitchen. He stepped quickly toward her, grabbing her around the neck. "I KNOW THAT."

Mel wanted to look away, but she couldn't. Her head wouldn't turn; her eyes barely blinked.

M*reow!*

"Did you hear me? Answer!"

His hands were tightening around her mother's throat. Veins appeared above her mom's eyes as she changed colors and croaked a tiny, pitiful yes. Her hands were on his but not fighting.

"Kris!" Rob screamed and backed out of his chair, nearly falling to the floor.

Then they were both staring at him, and he could finally see all the fear in their eyes, all the confusion, and not even showing them would change anything. There was pressure in his nose, as if he was going to cry, but Shane did already tell him, told him that he was alone in his own war. Alone save for the Void.

"Sorry," Kris said through trembling lips. "I-I didn't mean to..." He retreated to his bedroom.

Kris wondered if how he felt then was how people felt when they crafted their own suicide notes but decided that was not a fair comparison. He was writing under the assumption that in just over twenty-four hours, he'd likely be dead through forces beyond his own control, not that he was taking the control into his own hands and forfeiting his life. Still, if at sunset the next day, he was to die, then he just wanted to leave the world the way he found it, even though he knew that was impossible. But maybe that was the part of it that reminded him of a suicide note, writing to calm the emotions of a few people that had a profound effect on him, to tell them that it was okay and to carry on. *That's what you do. Let them know that it's okay to keep going and that you love them and all that...*

But there was no feeling there, where he expected it to be, somewhere in the cavity of his chest. *It's just fate. Why not resign to it?*

A blank page and a pen, which he was wiggling back and forth in his hand until just a moment ago, lay before him, and the laptop was a black portal. The roar of the dishwasher drowned out a receding air horn and rumble of metal wheel sets. The rain had tapered. With an exasperated sigh, Kris turned away from the page. Since leaving Shane, he was perpetually in a state not too dissimilar, at least in regard to his physical condition, from the way he used to feel on his very best days; a higher awareness, any aches he might have had were purged away, his body a reserve of kinetic energy, waiting for recourse. He stretched out of habit, out of a bizarre remembrance of how good it felt to do so.

Below Athena's Acropolis, which glowered in a plastic frame above his chipping chest of drawers, a great portion of the money, $3,800, from all the cords he'd chopped and quartered and personally shipped via his dad's trailer, was waiting in an open envelope with one note that hadn't been so difficult to write. He removed his shoes and grabbed the envelope from under the goddess's temple. With the money securely stuffed in his hoodie's kangaroo pouch, which fortunately had a zipper, he turned to open the door. He stopped. They might both still be out there.

In the corner, the window let in a gibbous luminosity. He opened it, careful as a burglar, and jumped out into the night. Turning northwest, he ran into the storm.

He wore black and tightened the drawstrings on his hood, though it still rippled back from speed wind. As he passed cars, they appeared to be completely still, and he knew that from their perspective, he was nothing more than a shadow in the corner of their eyes, a blink in the rain, if he was anything at all. Naked feet dug into blacktop, glass, debris, earth, but he felt nothing but the velocity of his motion. At the speed he was going, the air and slow-falling raindrops became combative, but he only cut through them as a vertical wing, mists of air and precipitation thrown out at the tall grass just off the road, causing it to ripple violently. With every step, he remembered that this motion, this endless motion, was almost all of his life, going back before his birth into time immemorial. He could feel a presence chasing behind him, though nothing could possibly be there.

North on Highway 2 took him all the way to Valleyport in some disturbingly short standard of time that Kris didn't care to know. He ignored the watch on his hand, remembering Einstein's theory and that time moves relative to the observer. Downtown's sky reachers and neon lights grew around him, and late-night-bar bugs appeared to be stuck where they stood, smoking under the awnings, caught in an eternal photoshoot. The thought brought with it memories of a dreamscape garden and Leah.

SERMON OF THE DIVERS

She rambled. That's how he found out about Talley; whatever part of her joined him in his dreams cared deeply for her friends and talked of them thoughtlessly. They were in the branches of the Great Tree when she told him about Talley and Andrew, in part because she wanted Jim Grayson to be brought to justice and in part because she loved spending time with them. What started as a rant, in which she told him about her boss, Tommy, turned into a reflection on her friendships. He asked about them. He wanted to know her friends.

"Talley's grown up. He used to make stupid jokes about dating my sister, but now he wants to get involved in politics. Doesn't know a lot about the government yet, but he sent me names of books that he's reading, journalists that he follows, and all kinds of videos he's watched on the subject. Andrew was never quite as—I hate to say it but—immature as Talley, but he's definitely changed too. He still wants to write manga, but now he thinks about it realistically, trying to balance creativity and business acumen. Business acumen…that's what he's called it."

She laughed. *"Weird that I called it that."*

"He dropped out to take care of his sisters?"

Leah nodded. *Branches curved around them; the tree was holding them. Both of them were looking up into the Void; they were just far enough away from each other not to be touching.*

"He really cares about them. Sometimes he's a sarcastic ass about it, but he really, really cares. I'd bet he gives most of his check to the family. They've never had much."

Three Seventy-Six East Trudeau was an old home on a lightless street. A low-roofed, wide but shallow home, with a slab-corner front porch that was covered in children's bicycles, three weatherworn end tables, a broken gliding swing, and what looked like trash but was actually treasure in disguise. Kris stood on the sidewalk for only a moment, eyeing the head of a clown popping out from a plastic planter. He made sure no one was around, which no one was on the dreary wet street, and got behind a tree near the corner of the home.

The living room was the front corner of the house. Kris knew because there were no blinds, and the curtains were partially open. Inside, a blotched carpet held up well-used furniture, and a woman sat in a corner recliner watching a TV that stood on a milk crate.

Even while asleep, her eyes were burdened with exhaustion. She was in a bathrobe with pink rabbits scuttering across it and fuzzy slippers that covered her toes. Her right hand was holding onto a tortoise plushy, and her left rested on a gray two-baby bassinet. Through mesh, two lumps swaddled in pink blankets took baby breaths. The wall bore family photos in all shapes and sizes, even Leah was in a few, with a group of kids. In another, beside that one, a shaggy haired guy crouched over two baby girls: *Talley.*

Kris stuffed the wet envelope of money and the letter into the old-school mail slot, which fortunately didn't screech, and began running for Gadsborrow just as lightning reached across the rolling sky.

CHAPTER 21

A Theater for Conspiracy

Yep, she's pissed, thought Tommy, realizing how long they'd dawdled at Gillian Lake when he got the call from Mrs. Grayson, curtly telling him to get her son home.

Aaron must have overheard, which was probably easy to do given the volume of her voice, because he said, "She'll get over it. She's the one that told you to take me anyway."

"Yeah, I know it," said Tommy.

"She might be a bitch for a while, though."

"I know that too," said Tommy, surprised to hear it from the mouth of her son, and a little impressed. *But I guess you know that better than anyone.* Still, it wasn't often a boy would admit this of a family member.

As soon as they'd got in the truck and pulled back out on the highway, dragging a dripping boat behind them, Tommy asked Aaron if he, please god, wouldn't mind and held up his simple little e-cig. Being around Laurie (the woman could talk a wall to death) and something about the moment when he was looking into the coming storm put Tommy on a blunt edge. He knew he probably shouldn't smoke around the young man, but the fucks he had left to give were dwindling. He was surprised that *he* hadn't been the one to call Mrs. Grayson a bitch.

He cracked the window enough to be spat on by the rain while he blew swirling clouds of berry-flavored mist back at it, to no avail.

Aaron, who looked as if he were going to be sick when they left Faringsport Park, was abruptly chipper.

"I didn't know you smoked," said Aaron.

That's when Tommy realized what it was. Aaron felt he'd been brought into a conspiracy, the conspiracy of a crappy vape and the employee who puffs it.

"Nah, man. I vape."

Aaron laughed. "Right. Well, I didn't know you vape. When'd you start?"

Tommy rolled up his window, tired of being spat on and feeling the soothing nicotine and seeing a sudden opportunity. "Well, I've used this thing since getting hired by your mom. Before that, I smoked the real thing, smoked them since…maybe twelve or thirteen."

"Twelve or thirteen?" he asked in awe.

"Yeah. I tried my dad's Lucky Strikes. Nearly threw up. After that, I just couldn't put them down."

Aaron was stunned by the comment.

"You've never smoked?"

He was biting his lip. Eyes narrowed. "Not cigarettes."

"Ah, Chinese molasses. That's your thing, eh?"

Aaron laughed again. "Yeah… Sure. Do you ever think about quitting?"

"Yes," said Tommy. "I used to think about it all the time. Eventually, I did it. I quit smoking them." He switched lanes and hesitated over his thoughts as they topped the seventh hill, knowing the kid was going to ask.

"Why'd you start again?"

"That's a tough question. I suppose that I *like* to smoke. Don't you ever start," he said obligatorily, "but I'd be lying if I said that a cigarette and a cup of coffee wasn't the best pairing I've ever found. If you can add to that, a cool, crisp morning air or an autumn rain… My mom used to sit out on the porch with a book, a cup of coffee, and a cigarette. Maybe that's where I got the idea."

I'm rambling. Why'd I tell him that? Tommy reminded himself who he was talking to, whose son sat in the passenger seat of the

U-Haul with him. *But it ain't his fault.* Tommy formed up the words to redirect the conversation back to Aaron, to his family, but the kid asked something else.

"How'd you quit the first time?"

Tommy lulled, but in the end, he answered, "I used a poem."

In the low light of the storm-riddled cabin, a living sheet of water reforming between swipes of the windshield wipers, signs reflecting in high gloss through the precipitation and back at them, a green time stamp on the radio, Aaron's silhouette jerked to look at Tommy.

"A poem?"

"Yeah. A poem."

"What's the poem? How did it—what?"

"It was another thing I picked up from watching my mom. She used it in several different ways, but what it is, is a grounder. If you ever need or want to quit a habit, you'll learn about delaying. A lot of the time, cold turkey or telling yourself *never again* puts a lot of power in the hands of whatever it is that you don't want anything to do with. In a way, that kind of attitude makes you more likely to think about it, and no matter what anyone says, we're mostly monkeys. Given enough thinking about it, you'll march wherever it is you have to go in order to get it. So you just say *not right now, maybe later, in an hour or so.* Usually, in that amount of time, you forget it, or you just don't want it as much, so you've successfully managed to avoid it.

"The problem is that even that can fail you sometimes when it comes to something easily accessible, a crime of opportunity. You weren't thinking about cigarettes until you got to the counter with your bag of Funyuns and root beer, then you saw the neat little boxes behind the counter. Suddenly, you're half a second from saying it, '*And a pack of reds.*' So in addition to delay, you need a grounder. Tell yourself, '*Say the poem, and you can get them.*' It's padding. You make it something that forces you to think. It reboots the system and gives you a little more opportunity to just *think.*"

By the time Tommy finished, Aaron was staring, stupefied, and they'd reached Bob's Boat Rentals. The bombastic Bob was not in; the store was closed, but they had a drop-off section of the parking lot and box to drop the keys that sat under a couple of orange halogen bulbs. The bulbs' diseased color rankled further in the rain, taking the sky leviathan's sublime tears and debasing them. Now that the feeling of incoming terror had passed, Tommy looked at the gray-black clouds with veneration, as they rushed into the rain to unhitch from the boat. Aaron hurried to help him, setting the wood blocks and unhooking the chains. As Tommy turned the trailer jack handle, he looked up at the clouds. Violet lightning rumbled behind the smoky veneer. Aaron watched the older man and followed his eyes, both of them staring into a falling sky.

"What was the poem?" asked Aaron as they climbed back into the U-Haul truck.

"'Infant Sorrow' by William Blake."

*****

What is this all supposed to mean?

Maybe Leah shouldn't have been asking that question, but it came naturally to her, natural to look for meaning. Surely, there had to be a reason that as soon as the world begins to change in these dramatic ways (and not just on a large scale but in her little life as well) that she starts having some through-the-rabbit-hole experience with a person she didn't know. But that was also part of the weird thing about it. She felt she did know him. Especially as she'd raced toward him in the woods. And when she was hugging him for the last time, it was as if she could *feel* his reserve, like she knew his very thoughts: *Nothing will ever come of this…but I want it all the same. No. I need it all the same.* And there was the way she felt, that she actually trusted him and trusted all those dreamworld memories of him.

On the way home, she received four text messages: two from Andrew, one from Talley, and one from Bailey. The one from Bailey let her know that she wouldn't be going to the "freakish theater for conspiracy." *Harsh.* It was harsh, but Bailey had always had a tendency to be that way when she got something in her head. The message from Talley was asking if she needed a ride, and the two from Andrew were letting her know not to worry about the storm, that it had changed direction a few hours ago, and they'd only get some rain; nothing like the last storm.

Leah texted back, saying that she'd try to get there, if she could. Her mother had already told her to be home. Leah being away during the last storm had really scared the hell out of her.

And as if there wasn't already enough to think about, Brit figured she would add on to the pile.

"Look... She doesn't know I know, and you *cannot* tell or mention or even think it too loud when she's around, but Mom and Dad went out to eat today."

They went out to eat?

"What? But she said—why didn't she tell us?"

"I don't know," Brit responded.

Leah could tell that Brit was eyeing the rain and debating in her head whether or not she could get away with cracking the window for a cigarette. The rain was coming and going, though, never consistent for more than about sixty seconds. Highway 1 was slick and full of trenches filled with rainwater. Even still, Leah considered smoking one herself, some immature impulse to lash out and do something self-destructive. Instead, she pulled one out for her sister and put it in her mouth, then she lit it for her too.

"How did you find out?"

Brit's face was guilt and shame then, and she looked at Leah with morose eyelids and smoke pouring out of her nostrils.

"Look...I... She's been acting strange. Haven't you noticed?"

Had she been?

"What do you mean?" asked Leah.

"Have you noticed how much time she spends just doing nothing? And she hasn't spent this much time in her room since Dad lived with us... Not to mention, she just seems *different*, doesn't she? Like all of her energy is just draining out of her, and I know she should feel that way to some degree. We all do. But this is different. I thought she was keeping something important from us. That's why I went through her phone while she was in the shower the other day. I...I didn't think I should tell you at first, but...well, then...you know...I didn't want to keep anything from you again."

Leah thanked her sister, and in the next moments, the rain and the tires on blacktop and the AC running were the only sounds. They pulled up to their home without much talking, both of them knowing they were thinking about the same thing. Lying was not an action they associated with their mother, and for good reason. Yet recently she could name two lies, and these were not harmless white lies. Suddenly a big question popped into Leah's mind: *Could she have a good reason for not telling them?*

"I'm sure she has a good reason for not telling us what was going on," said Brit.

Leah nodded and noted the empty spot in front of the house where her mom usually parked.

They ran through the heckling rain (stray mist swaying in the air) to the porch, through the front door, and into the house. Whatever old spirit that inhabited the house, it was there when the red roundtop door closed, and it was telling Leah very clearly that she couldn't, *shouldn't* be angry with her mother. Of course, she was, though. Gloom in the storm-darkened room worked to increase that spirit's *nearly* sinister imprint; its voice a whisper in her heart, that same whisper that let her know what Kris was thinking when she hugged him earlier. The question: *Does she love you?* Leah knew without having to even think that *yes*, her mother cared about her and Brit more than anything. Knowing that her mother was, as Brit had so aptly pointed out, going through some sort of change.

Ding!

Another message from Andrew, asking when she would be there.

Brit was sitting down to the book with the dogs on it. The knickknacks, her mother's collection of gemstones, curled up in the low light of a maroon lampshade, which her sister was reading in the low light of. But she wasn't really reading. How could she? Her eyes swept over the words (Leah knew), going over the same lines again and again, as if she were stuck in a loop.

"Can you give me a ride to Andrew's?"

Brit dropped the book closed quickly and turned. "We're supposed to stay here. The storm…"

SERMON OF THE DIVERS

Leah went to answer, to say something to the effect of, "What's wrong with you? Why are you acting all responsible now?" And inside her, feeling that spirit in the house, warning her about more change to come, a never-ending change, her life never turning back to what it used to be.

"Just kidding," said Brit.

Suddenly everything was normal again.

*****

Clouds parted and lost their menacing complexion against a night sky teeming with light pollution; it was aglow like a candle was on the other side of some blue material, not unlike bedsheets but certainly not bedsheets. There was still rain, but it was barely a sprinkle falling from a fracture.

> My mother groand! my father wept.
> Into the dangerous world I leapt:
> Helpless, naked, piping loud; Like a fiend hid in
>   a cloud.
> Struggling in my fathers hands:
> Striving against my swaddling bands:
> Bound and weary I thought best
> To sulk upon my mothers breast.

The kid had pulled up the poem on his phone and was reading it aloud; Tommy got the idea that he was petulant in his constant sweep of the eyes, trying to see what effect the words might have on Tommy. As if the words might cause some divine transfiguration, turning Tommy into something profound and fantastic or even supernatural. It only succeeded in making Tommy, for the first time, want to slam his fist into the seventeen-year-old. He reminded himself who it was that told Aaron about the poem and settled for despising that person a little more.

"Seems kind of…"

"What?"

"I don't know. It's not what I expected."

"The power doesn't really come from the words."

"Oh."

Since the kid didn't have the wherewithal to ask where the power came from, Tommy decided he wouldn't bother telling him. *Not like he'd listen anyway.* He changed the subject to something safe, mundane.

"The weather's clearing up."

They were making their way through the Great Heights, passing sprawling mansions with gaslit lanterns by their doors. Huge half-oval driveways cut through pristine green grass and yards full of artistically designed lawns, dotted with exotic plant life. Cars ranging from unreasonably expensive to a show of pure audacity were parked behind closed bay doors; Tommy couldn't see them, of course, but he could feel that they were there, sheltered from the storm.

"Yeah. I hate the rain."

Of course you do.

"Tommy…"

They were just pulling up to the most audacious of the overpriced castles on Minnerva Boulevard, resembling, in fact, a castle, having a tower of some kind rising from its cornerstone and poking the broken storm.

"Do you believe in…"

Finally. "Go on. Do I believe in what?" To add to the tone of camaraderie, he took a long draw on his vape.

"Do you believe in spirits?"

Never mind. But Tommy considered for a moment. "I wouldn't be surprised at all to find that something otherworldly can cross over at times. And I know that stuff *lingers*."

Aaron's big eyebrows fell down, and his expression took on a contemplative form.

"Why do you ask?"

Aaron shook his big head free from its consideration. "Nothing. No reason."

Fuck, come on! "Come on. What's going on?"

SERMON OF THE DIVERS

The young man considered for a moment. "I'm sorry. Forget it. I shouldn't have mentioned it. Thanks for the ride, Tommy. See you on Monday."

Holding on to the vestiges of his performance ability, Tommy told Aaron Grayson bye and broke character to regard the young man's house with spite and malice.

*****

Andrew had the most luxurious house of the friend group that used to meet at Stonethrow Park and skate and find trouble and swap secrets and dream about the future. It was one of the old ones on Trudeau, further west than Talley's, not too far from Grigio's Muffins. (If you ever find yourself in Valleyport, give their muffuletta a try. It's one of a kind.) Their close proximity made for a conspiracy inside of a crash. Andrew and Talley would meet up when the group was unavailable to discuss manga, play mostly zombie-killing video games (*Dying Light*, *Resident Evil*, and a lot of Nazi zombies), and fuss over their lack of opportunity with the opposite sex, never registering Aaliyah and Bailey as being a part of that elusive group. The house itself was twice the size of Leah's, most of that extra space given to the sizable living room and kitchen. The walls were a terrible color that combined maroon and eggplant, and it had the thick mahogany trim original to its construction. Being that Andrew's parents stopped at just one child and that his mother was an RN, they were financially stable, though far from having an exorbitant amount of excess cash, and would spend what they had, in majority, on keeping their house and trying to entice their one child to go even further, mainly as pertaining to the pursuit of money. Their reasoning was, show him what money can buy him, and he'll want to make money for himself. Leah thought their strategy might have worked if Andrew wasn't a big dreamer. He'd be a manga artist, or he'd end up destitute on the journey to become one. Having money only deflated its value in his mind.

"It's so good to see you!"

Andrew's short, petite mom, Jennifer Smith, hurried to embrace Leah. From the love seat, a mustached man, Gregory (Greg) Smith, waved and said hello before turning back to the LED flat-screen TV. Leah couldn't help but notice how much they'd both thinned out, how deflated they looked.

"And Brit!"

Brit also received a hug from Andrew's mom as they stood on the oval rug just inside the door, next to three pairs of shoes arranged by size, in descending order, ending in Jennifer's size 6 clogs.

"Your hair looks absolutely gorgeous! So healthy! What have you been up to? I told your mom to tell you that we need more RNs? I think you'd be great! Not that you wouldn't be wonderful at whatever you decide to do."

Still, even though the frequency with which she came to the Smith house had drastically declined, Leah was a fixture in the house, and so she didn't get the same eager maternal interrogation that Brit did. Brit started with the "uh" of unwanted attention but recovered quickly.

"Hey, Mrs. Smith. It's good to see you too."

"Jen, let them in the house before you start drawing blood," said Andrew's dad, not bothering to look over, wearing a self-satisfied grin. "Andrew!" he called in the vague direction of just right of the TV.

Andrew appeared in the hallway, wearing joggers and a My Hero shirt, and gave Brit a what-are-you-doing-here look, involving a turn of the head.

"Hey, guys," said Andrew. "Come on. I already rented the movie. Want popcorn?"

Movie? Leah declined. Brit did not.

"Thank you for choosing Smith cinema," said Andrew's dad, as Leah and Brit followed Andrew down the hall.

Andrew's dad worked at the Regal Cinema near the casinos downtown and still had a profound passion for the experience, not necessarily the filmmaking itself. The end of the hallway was a set of black doors fitted with gold-plated hardware, including the hinges themselves. Beyond was where every cent that the Smiths didn't spend on Andrew and home upkeep was spent, a lovingly crafted home theater. Eight black leather recliners, in two rows of four, were centered on a wall-sized projection screen, and each of them with its own drink holders, snack storage cubby, and USB ports for phone chargers. The walls were covered in movie posters with the exact red-stained wood frames as that of Leah mother's for *On the Waterfront*. Leah had no way of knowing, but years ago, when the theater was in the early stages, with no snack bar and secondhand sofas instead of theater chairs, her mother and father discovered a love of classical films in that very room. When Gregory Smith procured the frames and posters, Leah's dad bought one for his young fiancée for the friendly price of a shared six-pack.

Talley was standing in front of the snack bar, making popcorn on a miniature version of the ones they have at the Regal downtown when the three of them came in. He was still wearing his Creekshire's uniform, and his hair was wet, presumably from the rain.

"Brit?"

"Yeah?"

"I think he's wondering how you got an invitation, no offense," said Andrew.

"I invited her," said Leah.

"Well, that answers that," said Talley. "How much do you know about Buried in the Valley?"

It had been in the car, right when they'd pulled up to the Smith house, not a couple minutes past, that Leah asked Brit to come. And her reasons were many, not that she could vocalize all of them. But she'd been thinking of Bailey and then wondering about her own sanity, believing in memories of another world, and then there was Tommy, and she'd just invited her.

"She knows about as much as I do."

Leah noticed the adolescent way he was looking at her sister and, frighteningly, the way Brit blushed. *What in the...*

"Alright. I guess we should start from the beginning then?"

Andrew turned on the projector, using a little black remote, and plugged his laptop into it via an HDMI cable that'd been run through the wall and came out above a shelf beside the snack bar.

The background to his screen, an anime that Leah didn't recognize but was actually *Demon Slayer*, slowly became clear on the white projection sheet. A dial by the shelf allowed him to dim the lights as he switched through open tabs on the screen, eventually landing on an open archive of the *Valleyport Times*, zoomed in on a column that read "Redefining Security in the Modern Age." Next to the title was a picture of a young man with cherub cheeks, wearing a black coat, standing in front of a brick building with a placard that read "Allied Security Technologies."

"So," began Andrew, "what's the beginning?" he pondered aloud.

Leah felt unhinged just looking at the photo, even like she was betraying an old friend, snooping into their personal life. His features hadn't changed all that much, age mostly showing by the color of his hair, which was silvery now but in the two-tone photo was black ink. But it was the same man, the one who's table she'd sat at on several occasions and even tried to impress in her own way. Yes, there was always something off about him, wasn't there? In truth, she only remembered through a particular filter of emotional needs that she'd felt at the time, when she'd been zooming in on another person at the table, the son of the man on the screen. She felt feral and wanted to do something; maybe hit someone or herself.

"What's this all about?" Leah asked.

Talley offered her some popcorn and said, "Look, we know this may be a little awkward, but hear us out. There's something you need to know."

Leah felt that dread in her stomach again, waved the popcorn away, and nodded. "Okay."

"Honestly, I don't think we have to go chronologically. That'd be an endless backlog that we'd never reach the end of. He's a busy guy. Let's just narrow in on exactly what we came here to talk about. That way no one gets overwhelmed." Andrew gave her a reassuring nod. "Let's start with Tommy."

"Tommy?"

"Tommy."

"Tommy, as in her boss?" asked Brit.

"That's who we're here to tell you about," said Talley. "Chill. It's a lot to put out there. Alright." He gave everyone in the room a particularly cheery smile. "Let's get this ironed out. Oh, I guess Bailey and Jason aren't coming, huh?"

Andrew murmured something about that being no surprise as he opened another window on the newspaper archive, this one from the recently deceased *Faringsport Gazette*, and it was titled "Train Derailment Releases Cloud of Death." There was an old image of tipped-over tanker cars.

"To sum up what Buried in the Valley is…is kind of hard. It's articles and photos, posted anonymously, that implicate a lot of politicians, community leaders, and industry heads in some very…heinous crimes. In particular, Jim Grayson. Oddly enough, one of the major stories has to do with Kris's family and Jim Grayson."

"It's not really important to the story other than to say that there was an old rivalry in the family between Kris's grandpa, who also happened to be named Thomas, and Jim Grayson himself. It involved a series of incidents at a chemical plant out in Faringsport, which Thomas blamed entirely on the owner, Jim Grayson. This was years ago, but it was a big fucking deal at the time. He had a way with words and was able to shift a lot of power over to the union's side at the chemical plant," said Talley.

Leah could hardly believe the candor of their voices, the way they were both hypnotized by the topic and delivering their sermon with fervor. Talley, in particular, was drawn into the narrative that they were weaving together. Playful, prurient glances gave way to an unnerving stare that forced her to follow his eyes to the tanker cars, tipped on their sides against a row of pine trees. She imagined what he might be envisioning. Her skin crawled and broke into gooseflesh. How was this all connected back to Kris?

"It didn't end well," Andrew picked up the threads of the narrative again. "But Thomas Timur was able to put a mark on Grayson's reputation, which, at that point, was crucial to him. He was going to run for mayor in Valleyport. Could you imagine?" He only trailed off for a moment, allowing them to properly grasp what that might be like. "Anyway…there's a lot to dive into there, but…you see, this story is one of the page's earliest works, and it's referenced often enough, usually to harken back to Thomas Timur's messages of organized rebellion against the wealthy elite, like Jim Grayson."

Talley nodded. "Look, the guy on the page signs his stuff Thomas. Like he's speaking as Thomas Timur."

Andrew continued eagerly. "I figured he'd have a personal connection to that name. Keep in mind that this happened in 1984. This story was *hard* to find. I had a hunch that 'Thomas' was from the area around Faringsport, where all the stuff happened between Thomas and Grayson. Maybe he was a *fan* of Thomas."

She had a nerve-pinching sensation that made her want to say, "Wait, what in the fuck are you two talking about?" She wanted to accuse them of making all of it up, to stop them from saying any more. But again, she got an intuitive feeling that they were telling her the truth. She recalled thinking that Tommy was always hiding himself, his real self. *Still not right.* He was hiding in plain sight. A cool finger ran up her spine.

When she took a furtive glance at her sister, she could see as deep of an enthrallment as her own. Leah scanned over the words in the article on the screen.

*****

Tommy thought about Aaron Grayson all the way back to the apartment. The nature of the last question that he'd asked lodged itself in Tommy's restless consciousness and rolled about in his rock-tumbler mind. He pulled out his phone and checked the app that was still tracking the black SUV, but it was at the house he'd just left. By the time he reached the apartment, he wondered, as he often did now, whether or not he was chasing someone who didn't exist. Maybe his imagination had gotten away from him, and the truth was that he needed someone to blame for all the bad in his life. A scarecrow that was stuffed with all the nasty memories and violent emotions like oil-colored straw, a symbolic monster that Tommy could one day strike a match and light on fire so that all the crap could burn up and float into the atmosphere. Tommy drew on the

SERMON OF THE DIVERS

vape and tried not to think on that idea, not to give it any credence. Yet it was there. Always there.

He climbed the rough and narrow steps to the apartment door, feeling aches and pains starting in his legs and ending at the cranium. He was thinking that he needed to call Leah as he pushed the door open; it wept. Inside, something insidious was waiting for him, and Tommy knew to acknowledge that on some level, he knew what was coming.

A steam-cleaned carpet, free of carelessly tossed garbage, spread out before him, looking inviting enough to lie down on. The tall-legged dining table, where usually there was unwashed mugs, incoherent notes scrawled on coffee-stained paper, ash, and marijuana particulates, was cleared of detritus and wiped clean. Tommy noticed the deep-brown color of the wood for the first time and that an edge was chipped off. No shoes were at the entryway for him to stumble over and no coats that'd fallen from the rack by the light switch. He took a step in and closed the door, which wept again as he closed it. Past the partition, the kitchen lacked for a pile of dishes that overflowed from both of the sinks and found its way out onto the counters and stovetop, and upon seeing the shine of the spigot and plates in the drying rack, Tommy felt an imploring compunction that he was desperate to disregard. The couch looked like it'd been washed somehow, the brownish textile's color more vibrant, and apart from a few throw pillows and his brother, Jacob Pilson, it too had nothing left of the mess he'd lived in since moving into the apartment.

"Hey."

He was watching TV but not watching TV.

"Hey."

"Cleaned up."

"I see that."

Tommy paused to take off his shoes but decided against it, wondering if he might have to make a quick exit and unsure if they belonged there anymore.

"Looks good," said J. P. "Felt good to do it. I like it."

"Yeah. It does look good. Never knew the table had a chip in it like that."

"Me neither."

J. P. was working his way up to saying something—of course he was—and Tommy was working his way into waiting for it as opposed to forcing it out of him. When they were children, J. P. was just as soft-spoken and had patience that stretched into or near resignation. It was a trait that Tommy aspired to steal, in part, from him. He sat down on the couch with Jacob and waited for him to speak. A video on the importance of habit played from some good-looking guy's YouTube channel. Tommy quietly puffed on the vape while waiting, inhaling mist that felt like it'd been filtered through a smoothie.

"I have something I want to talk to you about."

"Alright. What's up?"

"I, uh, think it's time we stop doing this."

Tommy nodded, continuing to vape. "Yeah?"

"Yeah," said Jacob. He turned from the TV to Tommy. "When you first wanted to try this—this crusade, it sounded like we would be doing something *good*. And I was sure that you were right, but, Tommy, I don't think Jim Grayson is worth all this time. I'm not even sure he's guilty of anything. Thomas Timur had...issues. He killed himself...in the end."

Tommy nodded, continuing to vape. "Yeah."

"You want to know why I came here and got an apartment with you?"

"Why?"

"Because I wasn't over it either. I was still scared from that night too. I figured that we could get over it together. You're...my brother, since even before... But look at what this is doing to you."

Before your mom had to adopt me.

"And what if Grayson is as dangerous as you think he is? Why would you want to antagonize him?"

Somebody's gotta do it. He can't just do whatever he wants without any consequence.

"You hear?"

"Yeah," said Tommy.

"We haven't found anything concrete. Nothing enough to get him convicted of anything, if that's even possible. Maybe he's just another slimy, rich white asshole."

But does that mean we stop? Even if that's the truth, does that mean that he still isn't held accountable?

Tommy turned and gave a wan smile. "I hear you."

Jacob looked afraid to hope. Smart. "So we're going to stop?"

Stop? Tommy looked over the spotless apartment. He started coming up with things they could do, things that his brother wanted, and at some point, years ago, he'd wanted for himself one day. Hell, they had a nice place in a decent neighborhood. Jacob made good money writing online, and Tommy wasn't doing so bad himself. They could start going out on the weekends, not to follow a black SUV around but to a bar or to a show or even just shopping. Jacob used to have a horde of *Dungeons and Dragons* figures, and they both liked comic books when they were kids. Maybe they could go to that shop over by Mason's Muse. Tommy was pretty sure they hosted board game events there. Who knows? Maybe he'd meet someone. He could invite them over. The pool had those grills. The night after Madison Davis's funeral returned to him, a familiar nightmare in which he perfectly remembered the photo of her by the open casket and the note Jeff Davis, her father, folded up and stuffed in his pocket. With that, he started seeing other things. Panicking adults, running from house to house to warn people, while he and Jacob followed his soon-to-be-adoptive mom to the car. Down the street, people collapsed on the ground, coughing, and further on, they weren't moving at all anymore. He remembered looking in the direction of lifeless forms, looking in the direction of his home, and wondering whether he should try to get to his parents, hoping someone had warned them. And suddenly, the dreams faded away, all but the one in which Jim Grayson's life ended in misery and pain.

"I—"

This *crusade*, as his brother had called it, started with him—him alone. Why should he have thought it'd end any other way? From the beginning, he'd been begrudgingly aware of his brother's tendency to slip toward naivety. But there was something else, something he was sure of; in the end, he'd be constrained and solitary to the work, and most likely that would mean to the very end.

"You're right," said Tommy. "We should."

Jacob's eyes shone with the innocent faith of a sibling, a brother who, despite knowing his adoptive brother's obsession, believed in him wholeheartedly. Tommy gave his little brother a smile as reassuring as he could muster.

They had frozen lo mein in a Lucky Dragon box that Jacob heated in the microwave.

Tommy grabbed them each a Sprite. They'd talked about rewatching the Studio Ghibli movie *Princess Mononoke* since they'd moved in together, so they finally did. Every now and again, Tommy's attention would wander over to the sliding door on the other side of the dining table, but before Jacob could catch him, he'd look back to the screen. When the movie finished, Jacob asked about the page and what they should do with it. The question, mundane as it was, struck some frayed thread, taut across the span of his indomitable will. He thought, for only a moment, as the logical social tie was rent, that he knew the shade he'd struggled with for all this time and, in continuity, was bound and entitled to overcome him. In the next moment, he remembered none of those thoughts but was left with something more disturbing.

"I'll write a farewell post."

For the next two hours, Jacob and Tommy talked about an old dream, one of opening a comic shop, the stories that shaped them in their youth, and how they'd once sought to cultivate the admiration of the medium in a younger generation. From there, they discussed more concrete plans, the ones that paid the bills and looked realistically obtainable in the next five years. One side of Jacob's face was poised to smile at any moment during the entirety of their conversation. Tommy matched his facial expressions but rolled the red dream in his whirling conception. The truth was that Tommy wouldn't be able to recall most everything that happened until he got back to the

Graysons' castle late that night, with a knife in his hand, a red dream in his grip.

*****

"When we found this story mentioned on Buried in the Valley, right near the beginning, when the page was created, we knew we found something."

"We?"

"Okay. Fine. You."

"Yep," said Talley with a shit-eating grin. "This was one of the incidents that happened right around the time Thomas started to go public with his allegations."

Leah had read through the article twice while listening to Andrew and Talley. She imagined a quiet, quaint town with a pair of tracks running through it. She imagined, for whatever reason, that it was a cold night, though it happened over the summer. A faulty wheel set that could have leapt from the track on all the miles before and after the town of Midas, picked the curve into the downtown and residential areas, to jut over the track and whip the tanker cars over onto the sleeping town. Lacking proper maintenance, old and worn down, the tanker cars began to leak their yellowish gas out, just as people exited their homes wondering what the scream of metal raking and smashing had been. By the time the alarm was raised, and people failed to understand what was attacking them, a cloud of death was stretching over Midas, taking its early victims in seconds. By the time its nearly invisible hands reached out, diluted with the air, it was mauling the citizens and leaving half to die—a wave of chlorine gas.

Bringing the fullness of her imagination to life didn't encapsulate the terror of that night, but she was aware of that.

"It was his fault," she said.

"That's what Thomas claimed," replied Andrew. "He said that there were several people at the plant and the railway that brought up the condition of those train cars. And even said that Grayson threatened another employee for trying to hold the cars for repair."

"Why wouldn't he let them repair them?"

Andrew and Talley looked at each other, then back at her, neither of them offering an answer.

"You don't know?"

"He claimed all of it was a lie… And Thomas… Well, Thomas thought—"

"Money, I bet," said Andrew.

Money. Could that really be the reason all those people died? Leah remembered the man they were talking about. He didn't look it, but he was around sixty years old now, and he moved with a methodical, deliberate way about him, getting around as if he had all the time in the world. But there was something about him, set in the lids of his eyes, the buoyancy of his body that didn't move slow from exhaustion or age, but some other reason that she couldn't comprehend. Could he really be capable of negligence that led to so much destruction and death? And if he could, how does he not suffer from a weary conscience?

"Cloudless Sky Photography…" Leah said aloud. "It's the name of Tommy's photography company."

Talley and Andrew both gave her a sullen nod as she looked to them for confirmation.

"He was there?"

"Yes."

Tommy was there when this happened. He was probably only a kid when he watched his neighbors die, just drawing breath.

"Wait, what?" asked Brit, darting glances from face to face. "Cloudless Sky Photography?"

"It's the name of Tommy's company. Also, that actually is his name, Tommy Lowell," said Andrew. "We found him mentioned in the obituaries of his parents, Eric and Cheryl Lowell. After that… Well, with his name, we were able to find all kinds of stuff—who adopted him after, where he went to school, when he moved to Atlas… He even had deactivated Facebook and Myspace accounts that we…" Andrew trailed off, hearing how it sounded and aware of a certain amount of self-contempt.

Leah wanted to know more; even though she hated herself for it, she still did. But right then, she asked them if they were absolutely sure. Andrew didn't answer, but Talley gave her a confident affirmation, followed by a resigned silence. She was struck by the fact that she still had this man's number in her phone. If she wanted to, she could call him, talk to him directly about all of this, and ask him why, even though she'd already put that part together in her mind. Tommy wanted to see Grayson brought to what he was sure was justice and being that he'd already gone this far.

*****

It was built to stir the mind into slumbering memories of near childlike wonder and to make those who stood before it, as a child would have felt, timorous and frightened. If one was to be brought to the palace of a king, would they not feel small and filled with their sudden loss of liberty, so near to a being that had power of life and death. The observatory alone would have been enough, but also there was a false parapet, a staggering entryway that appeared and may have been a functioning portcullis, supporting buttresses that need not be there, and a fountain in the form of the Greek divinity of agriculture, notably a more chthonic rendition. She was surrounded by poppies that sent water in wide arcs into the air, her feet were swathed by a serpent, she was in the traditional folds of a chiton, and she was holding something in a raised hand; there was a sea-green tint to her form. Of course, spotlights displayed every arch and topiary shrub and notable architectural angle, so the would-be castle was alive with light.

Tommy had parked the car down the road and walked conspicuously up the winding blacktop, then carelessly made his way into the hedge that bordered the estate.

His head hurt. But there was freedom in his gut, and the darkness held him, making him feel safe. In hindsight, he couldn't recall if he'd fought this outcome or secretly hoped for it while putting on a farce of struggling against it. The man inside this veritable castle had taken his life away from him.

The knife in his hand was an old hunting knife his father'd gotten for him, made from the antler of a buck he'd killed. It'd not left his hand since he'd retrieved it from the top shelf of the closet at home, after J. P. went to sleep. He pinned it to the steering wheel as he drove, bringing forth a cataclysmic power from its blade that bore him forward when he wanted to return. A rogue pack of cigarettes he kept in the glove box that once empowered him to quit, found its way out, opened, and freshly lit in his hand that wasn't a cool blade.

My mother groand! my father wept.
Into the dangerous world I leapt...

That was as far as he could get into the poem, so he just repeated it over and over again, a broken record of benediction.

My mother groand! my father wept.
Into the dangerous world I leapt...

He imagined bringing the knife down, not into Grayson's chest but into his face, deflecting off the natural curves of his skull, into the cavities of his eye sockets, nose, and mouth, leaving lacerations that leaked blood slowly up into his reddening vision. He'd yell the words over and over out loud if he had to. *"My mother groand! my father wept! My mother groand! My father wept! My mother groand! My father wept!"* Meanwhile, his wife watched, younger, gorgeous, and terror-filled to the point of freezing petrification. He reveled in the idea of what her face might look like as she watched the good-natured Tommy carve the bones of her husband's face. Blood slung from the blade would land on her naked skin. He hoped she eventually did take off that makeup at the end of the day, when she crawled into bed with the devil. A giddy sort of exciting laughter wanted to come out, but he held tighter to the blade instead, trembling with anticipation.

What would happen next?

Maybe his children would come when the horror of the situation wore on long enough for her to know that she was awake and watching her husband be murdered. And the fantasy ended. Aaron would come into the room, stupid oaf that he is, and as arduously as Tommy fought to keep the fantasy alive, that idea ended its deranged life.

With contempt for himself, for the home before him, for the leaves of the bush that scratched his face, the people inside, the knife in his hand, Tommy realized that he was crouched in a bush before the home of a family, and he'd come to kill a man. Cold rationality flowed over him as a surreptitious libation to a deity that he despised with every atom of his being. His family was dead, and this one gets to live.

For an amount of time, he sat in the confidence of the dark bush and watched the castle and its solemn statue. He dawdled on how close he'd come to the edge, closer than he'd ever been, but he hadn't gone over. The well-lit, elegant, and buxom woman staring vaguely in his direction with whatever it was in her hand seemed to be confiding in him the secret of what it meant to go over—under, and he felt ashamed by her unblinking gaze. The knife dropped from his hand after hours of holding it. His hand stayed in a clawlike curl. Vision that was almost entirely turned to black widened to take on the world once more as the hand opened.

Tommy spent his last moments wondering if he could actually do what his adoptive brother planned to. Sentences started to form that might go in the very post to end it all, or maybe he'd keep going, but he wouldn't do it so obsessively. Buried in the Valley was a good thing after all. It educated people and stirred their thoughts to wonder what a man with unbridled power, as Jim Grayson had, might be capable of doing.

Probably need to tone it back, though.

That's when Tommy saw the end. How hadn't he noticed the faces before? The line of people standing in the bush running behind the estate, their pale faces turned to him with the hyperbolic distortion of a crazed, gleeful leer. Ironically, Tommy was the one petrified as the clownish faces of average people made their way to him in slow steps. A girl with black hair gave him the look of the goddess, and he turned away, trying to remember some poem. And all was black.

CHAPTER 22

Faded Retina

Use the door.
—Dad

Kris remembered that he'd left the window wide open about ten miles from home, when he knew there was nothing to be done about it. Leaving a large portion of all the money he had on the doorstep of a near stranger had left him caring little for what lay ahead. He considered possibilities, for the first time, of what the powers he'd been gifted by some strange lineage and otherworldly entity could make him capable of. As a boy, as an avid reader, he'd found the comic book section at The Book Bureau and consumed a greater part of its contents. Finding in escapism a clear reflection of his own world, Kris marveled at the idea of altruism in the godlike beings of the pristine panels of the modern comic book. Maybe once, back in the early era, it was about a childish compulsion of wish granting, but now it was about humanity.

As he stood in the rain, looking up at the sign his father taped to his window, Kris felt—along with the sensation of his clothes and hair plastered to his body, sopping wet—a tinge of yearning or anticipation; he had power.

His wet feet padded softly against the steps, creating a muffled sound, and he heard his father's coughing over that. When he opened the door, his dad was sitting in his chair. He had the story,

The Valleyport Witch, across his lap and, to Kris's amazement, was reading it. Kris tensed at the sight. His father looked up at him, a glint of some kind in his eyes.

"Have a good run?"

"Yes."

"We should talk about what happened—"

"Not right now, Dad."

Kris noted the alcoholic odor in the air, the burdened and glossiness of his eyes, and the way his dad was caring without overbearance; he attributed all of it to the spoor in the air, all except the book. He felt the urge to take it from him, but—

They regarded each other with two opposing filtrations of their perspectives, and then Kris walked, dripping water on the floor as he went, toward the hall and his room.

"Son?"

He turned back.

"Yes?"

"Is it okay if I hold onto this…for a while?"

No. "Sure."

"Thanks. We'll talk later, huh?"

"Yeah."

Kris went into his room and, just before shutting the door, saw his father begin to read again. He marveled at the sight with distrust and affection.

After a prolonged shower, in which he pondered what limits he had—if any—and how he might test himself, Kris sat back down at his desk with the blank notebook, opened to the torn-out page. Where a dried-up hole in the ground once represented the words he could think to leave behind, for Rob, for his dad, now there was a spring of clear flowing cogitation.

It came to him, though he almost willed it away, that his dad was the one who bought him the comic books. Old memories, collecting dust beyond a shut door in the library of his mind, were slid under the door by some kindred spirit on the other side. Rob had shown strength unlike himself and his dad. He took on responsibility without a second thought and began to pester their dad to take

Kris to The Book Bureau, on the intersection of Livery Drive and Trudeau; that's the black-and-white building next to Grigio's. Rob flipped through crates of vinyl records, while Kris bounced from section to section, sampling from each like a buffet for the imaginative faculties, or that's what he did before what happened to his mom. After that, even though Rob tried desperately to reignite in his little brother a love of reading, Kris would sit on the third floor and watch the people navigate the maze of bookshelves from up high. Kris suspected there were private conversations between his brother and father, to do with his behavior, and imploring on Rob's part that their dad took him alone as well. Finally a day off came, and his father did.

*****

Melancholy was the color of the world at the time, reminiscent of an old black-and-white film. The once-magical golden bell that was tied to the door of The Book Bureau didn't ring the same way that it once had. Maybe the people stocking the shelves and greeting the customers were just as congenial and downright friendly, but Kris wouldn't have been able to tell you one way or the other. The boy had been torn and displaced across the tempests of a darkening mind. Beside him, a not-too-dissimilar father looked around the big building of stories with an expression of disorientation. Both of them wore Carhartt jackets and matching black beanies, their cheeks were red, and their hands were stuffed into blue denim jeans.

"*Go wild.*"

The young Kris patted his way up to his perch on the third floor, looking down at his feet. From the top, the cast-off section where the fantasy and sci-fi flirted in several long and low-ceilinged rooms, a balcony provided him with a view of almost all of the bottom floor and second story. If it were possible to crack his consciousness open like an egg and dissect the thoughts therein, there'd be a hollow puff of ash upon doing so. Kris was observing and taking all things in with the acute, astounding senses and ability that only the body of a child can. He wasn't thinking of his mother or the crash or the dreams or the monster or the people he used to see but no one else could. He just was.

From on high, he watched the milling bookworms wiggle between shelves and thumb through perspective reads. A man absentmindedly picked his nose in a secluded corner on the second floor while reading the back of a cover jacket, a little girl almost jogging from aisle to aisle and collecting a horde of books, a woman sitting in a secluded nook in the literary fiction section with her nose almost pressed to pages. Kris was both acutely aware and unwilling to care, watching them from a position of removal, when he realized a person was missing—his dad. He reminded himself that there were sections, such as the magazine section and romance section, that couldn't be seen from where he was. With growing concern, the child watched for the black beanie like the one on his own head to appear below. As the minutes passed, and even though they do pass differently within the hollowed constructs where stories are preserved, Kris's mature-but-still-budding intellect began to give way to anxiety. When it won out, he darted down the stairs and began searching, starting at the bottom and rising as he made his way through every row of shelves. He passed the people he'd seen from up high, and they barely noticed he was there. His head swiveled from side to side, his hands creeping up in a panic, and the look on his face slowly giving way to the terror of abandonment. He finished searching the first story, then the second.

As he retreated up to the balcony to try again to find his dad from there, he found his dad. He'd been sitting not too far behind him on a cherry-colored bench just outside of the entrance to the fantasy section. His black beanie was cresting the top of a novel with a man on the front, a man with a red cape and blue tights, with muscle rippling beneath. Across the top, written in words trying to escape the page, was the title SUPERMAN. *Kris hurried over.*

"Dad?"

It took a second for his dad to pry himself from the pages of the comic.

"Huh?"

"I was looking for you."

"Well, I'm right here."

Kris saw that indeed he was and climbed up onto the cherry bench, leaning on his dad and looking at the book in his hand. He'd seen the strange form of novel before, on the very floor where they were sitting, but had never cared to pick one up. But he could see then that he must pick several of them up that day. Something peculiar and powerful was happening, and in the same way he observed the people from the balcony, Kris watched his father.

The microscopic movements of his facial musculature pulled around the lips and eyes revealing the preludes to feeling on his father's face. He turned the page. A flicker of a smile.

"The man of steel," he said.

A man with glasses and an ill-fitting suit pulled apart his shirt to reveal the hypnotic emblem, the symbol, the simple S-shape. In the next panel, he was flying out of the panel with a fist pushing into the air ahead of him, the city of Metropolis far below.

"I used to read these," he said.

He flipped the page. Now the Superman was stopping a plane from crash-landing in the city. Next, he was on a farm with an old woman.

"When I was your age, I wanted to be him."

"Superman?"

His dad hesitated, "Superman." *He slid the book to Kris.* "Let me know what you think."

*****

Kris sat back in the chair, staring blankly down at the empty page. With so many words to choose from, he couldn't possibly pick the right ones, but he began to write all the same.

*****

Kris woke earlier than them the next day, after a dreamless night of sleep and early hours of writing. This time when he wrote, he didn't think of Leah but of his father and brother, and he wrote for over an hour. By the time he got done, he'd had an idea; he went into the kitchen to make them breakfast. Only one breakfast would do: his mom's biscuits and gravy.

The living room was empty. Quiet. Through the windows came the verdant reflection of freshly watered greenery. For a moment, he considered turning on the news to cut the silence and maybe get his father and brother to awaken a little sooner, but he knew what he'd find. Today was the beginning of World War III. But its form would be slightly different; in this war, there would be no false dichotomy. If he turned on the news to channel 6 right now, he'd see a man with bug eyes talking about a town in eastern Nebraska. A town out in the middle of an arid plain, a town under siege by some invisible force. If he got on his phone and searched a particular website, he'd find videos of anarchy in the streets of this town. He'd see gunfire and mad manifestos, teenagers walking about with weapons of war, begging for an excuse to use them, and he'd see dark rooms where personal wars were being lost, as well as lives, rooms with blood-covered floors. But this war was only just beginning.

Maybe it could end today.

It wasn't until Kris came into the kitchen and checked the cabinets and refrigerator that he remembered he couldn't make them his mother's breakfast. He couldn't.

"How long have those days been gone now?" he asked the empty room; he asked the photo of all of them together.

Today was the end. Today, he would go to face the monster that was eating reality. But those days of biscuits and gravy, those days of giggling on camping trips to southern Arkansas, those days of hearing Rob's trying hands pick at a guitar early in the morning, those days of church with all the elderly people (only those people who came to search for him) were over. Gone. His mom was long gone, and he was long gone too. A horrifying stray thought ricocheted off the bare plates of his soul: he was no longer even Kris. That boy in the picture was a stranger to him, that smiling boy who dressed like his dad and smiled like his mom. That boy might as well have never existed at all; he couldn't remember how that person *saw* the world or what he *dreamed* of in the darkest, loneliest parts of his mind. But still, they came back in a flash, like lightning. That boy had wanted just what he had and hoped for love like his mother and father's. For that boy, there was no future, only a way of living.

"But now it's only what needs to be done. No more…grace," he told the photo. The damned photo. Tears filled his eyes, pressure in his nose, pounding in his chest. "I miss you…"

And he had to turn away. There was no way to keep looking at that photo. No way to move without taking his eyes off of it. So he did.

And he took the house in through his eyes one more time, committing it to the amorphous shape of his memory, hoping he'd never forget it. The exact red color of the curtains and the old discolor of the eggshell walls, the smell of fresh air and Gain and sawdust. He stepped on all the boards that didn't creak as he made his way to the door to leave for the last time. Sure that the living words in a letter would be better than the presence of a dead boy, he left.

*****

Whirlwind blasted as he charged the air ahead of him, sprinting into it like a man made of lightning. He was a disturbance across the horizon that the people felt but denied seeing as he shot down the highway. Power, an odd substance, like water, it permeates the world and is attracted to itself and redistributes and changes course. It is unlike water in that its inclination toward itself reaches a singular point of pulling, such as with Kris, when it grows with almost no effort at all. And the world was losing its substance, weight.

Trito! Trito!

Was the Void calling him closer or warning him to stay away?

Then It gave him the answer, which was an image in his head: That spot in the forest where the woods open on pastures, where Valleyport ends and begins its city limits, and many of the lost ones wait with *him*. He was everywhere they were; *he* was beside them and around them and all over them. He knew that the Other was inside of them too, but only because *he* was everywhere else. What was *he*? Even thinking of *him* seemed to affect the form in a mental image,

SERMON OF THE DIVERS

where once *he* was hatred, then *he* was terror, then *he* was desolation, then *he* was perfection. Kris wondered, *How?*

Intuitively, he knew where to go, and he knew that he would be there near instantaneously, yet he was beginning to know the number between one instant and the next. So he was running.

He passed the lost ones who have waited in the forest, and they all whispered about who they used to be in a susurration close to that of practiced prayer in a cathedral, but they were all among the pines. Kris was no longer on the road, and his bare feet dug into the earth, and he slowed to a walk as he approached the pasture. They all looked at him with black eyes and pallid faces of the dead, telling him about their loved ones or their lack.

The kids are in the house! The kids are in the house! Let me go back in! I have to go back in!
She died and left, and she died, and she left...
Why don't they see me? Why can't anyone see me anymore?
I'm hungry. I'm hungry. I'm hungry.
WHO AM I?
My mother groand, my father wept...

The pasture was just another farm that the Other had taken, and it had taken its livestock too; there were other animals, wild ones, that waited in the distance, staring at him. The animals made no noise; some of them stood on emaciated limbs, shriveled and lacking musculature, yet they did not seem to care that they were close to dying. The smell in the air was their decay, pig flesh, cowhide, excrement, and blood. Flies buzzed over the rot. One of the sheep fell to the earth, eyes still open and black, and other animals moved to consume anything that was left, lethargic and coordinated. The prayer voices stopped.

Men and women and children and animals stared at Kris. He remembered being in a car crash and his mother.

"You really are Him."

Kris looked around for the source of the voice. It'd come from someone in the pasture, one of those that surrounded him. The air was getting colder, and the dew was icing around his bare feet.

"*Trito.*"

Kris turned to see a girl holding a cat. She was in pajamas with bells on them; her hair was knotted and plastered to her face.

"I've been waiting."

The crowd repeated what she said, all at once.

"I'VE BEEN WAITING."

What happened next—it's a remarkable thing. Kris was rigid with fear and anger, looking at the faces of the people the Other had taken, knowing their doom. He imagined that the Other had chased them the way that he'd chased Kris, but none of them had been able to give the Other its rule of chaos, its eternal hunt. *What happens if the Other catches you?* He could see they were still alive. All of them were still living people; pale like the dead but not yet dead.

"SARA!"

A lone voice cried.

I see… He is not able to kill. But Kris looked at the rot that had once been the sheep that'd fallen over. What Kris felt, when looking out at the people, the Other, and the night they all inhabited, was a sense of belonging, maybe even of family. God, he'd expected to feel fear, but he was enraged.

"COME OUT!"

They laughed in unison, answered as one.

"Why can't you stay on your side?"

Brother… Brother?

"You have to let them go."

More laughter.

"What makes you say that? We've only arrived."

Kris's skin was oily and hot in the frozen air of a bizarre nightmare pasture. And again, they all laughed at him, while the smell of fecund decay sweetened the air, like grass and greenery. He could feel the chasm of eternity being spanned by laughter, and as he let the laughter carry him away, he, too, was then laughing. He remembered why he'd started running in the first place and why the Other chased him. In some foretime vision, he saw his mother typing away on a keyboard in a dark room, and Kris was a boy. He crept up on her, the socks on his feet muffling the sound of his approach. As he rounded the horizon of her peripheral vision, he saw her. She was beautiful, she was concentrated and in a fight with a pain that barely escaped her expression, and there was pride and humility in her eyes, hope. When she turned from her work to look at him, to pick him up and kiss him, she smiled, and all of her hope was plain to see.

As Kris looked out at the faces around him, he saw the only way, and he remembered the nature of the First Story and the being who told it to him. This time, when he looked back at the Other and all the people around him, he saw a world in which he took the false path, in which he took it upon himself to kill those that the monster had claimed. He saw himself out of balance, fighting human monsters and not the underlying demon. All lies within the Void. Shane... Shane had told him the story of his life.

"It is the end."

"It is the beginning of the end. Collectively, they just didn't make the cut."

The laughter was silent this time, not coming from all the people with their black eyes and gaping mouths. It was the howl of the Other, and it chilled the air a further degree. Kris shivered. But he didn't look away or blink as he approached the girl, the girl in her pajamas, the girl who looked like she was supposed to be at home with her parents, watching some movie. As Kris approached, he felt as if an ember the size of a fist came to life in his mind, but he didn't let her see it, but he could see the reflection of light in her eyes. He stared into the black, into the seemingly infinite crashing waves of her nightmares until he found something there: a dream nestled in a hidden place, a fire in an endless sea of nonbeing. He grabbed her by the shoulders, but it was she that leveraged herself to climb out of the black.

She looked around, afraid at first, then angry, then she turned to help a man in a construction hat.

CHAPTER 23

Wyatt

Leah and Brit left Andrew's house late, when it was still raining but only a sprinkle. She waited and waited for the proper moment and correct words to come, but they never did, and all the while, she had her phone out and Tommy's contact open. Finally, she did press the button, but it only rang and rang and rang. Her sister watched through bruise-colored eyes, her nervous hands careful on the steering wheel as they went home. Again, Leah got the feeling that something was following them—following her. What could move that fast? Nothing. Only another car. Leah turned on the heat, only for the comfort.

"He didn't answer?"

"No."

"Do you think it's true?"

"It has to be, right? Did he seem off to you?"

Brit pulled the car into their driveway, turning off the headlights as she did. Their mother's car was where it was supposed to be this time, parked on that incline just off the walking path to the front door. The Kia's grayish color blended with the shadows in the driveway, down to where the old shed used to be.

"I don't know," replied Brit. "I...I thought he was really *nice*. I never would have seen this coming, if I'm being honest." And she was staring at their mother's Kia as she said that. "I don't think you should ask him about it. You shouldn't have called him. That's his business."

Shouldn't have called? What?

"W*HY?*"

This time, Brit turned to her. She pushed the blonde hair back from her face. Her eyes were severe, and her mouth was pinched firmly closed before she spoke. Leah couldn't help but think of that night in the kitchen when she was finally told about her father.

"Leah, sometimes people can't say what's going on with them. They can't vocalize it, or they need time, or it's just too damn hard. You know that, don't you? It's the same reason we shouldn't batter Mom with questions or push too hard. I shouldn't have looked through her phone. She needs us to be patient right now."

Leah thought of Talley, of how patient he'd been during the first storm of that summer. But she was red, angry. Her hands wanted to move, but she couldn't figure out where they wanted to go. She felt like she was going to throw an old-fashioned tantrum, as if she were ten years younger.

Brit grabbed her hand.

"I know it's hard right now. I'm not saying you shouldn't be upset."

"Whatever," Leah said, pulling her hand away. "Let's just go inside."

"Leah—"

"Not right now!"

She was thinking of Aaron then, and she couldn't decide whether she was delighted or horrified to find that there was no longer a tinge of love, only hate.

When they got in, their mother wasn't up, wasn't waiting to berate them for being out in the storm. She was softly snoring in her bedroom. That night, in her room, as Leah lay awake, turning from side to side, she thought of Aaron. She thought of what he'd done and what his father had done, and she wondered how such monstrous people came to exist. In the dark, she tried to call Tommy two more times, desperate to tell him that she was one of those people who would fight an uphill battle. She was tired of her old childish attitude of curiosity without any action. There was more she could do. Much more.

With everything else going on, it wasn't until late that she remembered Kris. She texted him:

Hey, really wish I could talk to you right now. I...hope I see you tonight.

Of course, she got no response. And when she slept, she didn't dream at all.

*****

Corrosive light burned its way through her window when she woke, a blaring awakening to a day she was just as unprepared to start. Leah turned from the light, trying her hardest to go back to sleep, but she couldn't. And what would it help if she did? Sleeping would only delay the inevitable, so she leaned up in bed and rubbed her eyes. The first thing she did was check her phone; no messages and no calls. No dreaming, no garden.

Then her mother was calling from the other end of the door, asking if she was going to get up soon.

"Wild child, you okay in there?"

A higher note to her voice, more enthusiasm and life. For a split second, Leah thought that maybe she *was* ten years younger and that when she walked out of her bedroom, she'd see her mother's thick puff of brown hair and her arms cuffed in a menagerie of bracelets. Not quite.

Her mother was in the kitchen with Brit, preparing a breakfast of fresh fruit and old oats. Leah wanted eggs but reminded herself that was a distinct impossibility. Her stomach refused to listen to reason. But she sat down to the baby-blue bowl of fruit all the same, and her sister slid her mug of coffee toward Leah with a warm smile. When she looked up, seeing her mother for the first time that morning, really looking at her, she did look younger. Not physically but maybe in a way that was less tangible. Her starlet's aura was back to a summer-sunrise glow, and she smiled the same way she used to—with surety.

"Good morning!"

"Morning."

"I have to ask... Are you two ready? How are you feeling? Nervous? Anxious? Excited? Hungry?" her mom inquired in a question that seemed equally aimed at both of them.

"A little of all of that," replied Brit, nibbling on an apple slice.

Leah nodded and used her chewing as an excuse not to respond.

"How about you, Mom?" asked Brit.

"I'm good! I am actually thinking about baking a pie today. Grandpa's ole recipe! I'll have it ready for you girls when you get back from seeing your father."

Leah was reminded of how magic did always happen whenever her mother made one of those pies. Some family traditions do truly hold magic. It occurred to her that maybe that magic was being reserved for her, to help her see her father and not give into any reservations she had about him. Maybe he would win her over. Another part of her wondered if he hadn't won over her mom the day before, and maybe that was the reason she was in such a pie-baking mood.

Either way, today was guaranteed to be a lulu.

"He's going to be here to pick you up at one. Leah, he wanted you to bring your camera. I told him that you two would ride with him. Is that okay?"

Brit acquiesced first, and Leah followed.

After that, breakfast was carried out as usual, aside from the lack of eggs and the *usual* being the usual of a time before famine and freakish storms and dream adventures with a stranger and before meeting a man with a vendetta on her ex's dad. Brit asked what made her want to bake a pie, so her mother began talking about her own dad, about Leah's grandpa.

"I don't know why, but he was on my mind this morning. That's how I knew I needed to bake a pie. I'm sure I've told you girls a hundred times about embarrassing him at Thanksgiving by telling all his buddies that it was him who baked the pies, not Mom. They gave him a little ribbing. And you can bet I was sent to bed with a stern talking to that night. Well, it wasn't long after that he lost his job at Schmidt's Cabinets and Carpentry. They had to downsize one winter… We didn't know what we were going to do. We had to use a woodburning stove to keep warm that winter, couldn't afford electricity. My dad was in a terrible mood, and he had to give up cigarettes as well. Then his buddies all got together and started buying pies from him. Before long, he was opening up a bakery from the house. One he eventually moved to a storefront in Lochton.

"It had the most beautiful stained glass windows around the front and a display window filled with fresh pastries every morning…I still miss it. I was missing it this morning when—"

And very abruptly, she was coughing and coughing. Her eyes squeezed shut, and the back of her hand covered her mouth. Leah moved to put an arm on her, while Brit stood and got a glass of water from the tap. Leah wondered if they were still under a boil advisory as her mother hacked some more, unable to stop long enough to drink. Between her coughing, her breaths were raspy and cobbled, slipping like rockslides.

"Drink, Mom," said Brit.

"Give her a second!" Leah hadn't meant to sound so harsh.

She did drink after a moment. The glass happened to be a Christmas glass with a snow-covered pine tree, one of her mother's favorites. She eyed it with pleasure as she thanked Brit and squeezed Leah's hand. "I'm fine. I'm fine. Don't worry about me. I guess I really need to quit sneaking cigarettes, huh?"

"You do," said Brit.

Leah thought it was ironic that Brit was harping on the subject of quitting smoking but was too concerned about her mother to say anything.

"What was I saying?"

"You were talking about Grandpa," replied Leah, still holding her mother's hand. It was frailer than she remembered, her skin thinner and almost translucent.

"Oh, that's right. He sat me down that first Saturday he was in the bakery in Lochton. He had baked me a personal pie, just for me, and he thanked me for saying something at Thanksgiving, for outing him as the baker he was. I remember exactly how white his apron was with flour, and I remember the apples in that pie were particularly sweet. Sweet like you wouldn't believe."

Brit turned away with her hands on her hips, shaking her head. At first, Leah thought she might be crying, her back shuddering in that way, but her laugh broke through. She tilted her head back and let it go. Brit didn't often lose herself in laughter like that, and when she did, Leah and their mother joined her.

The time between breakfast and her father's arrival were spent in a hectic haze. She passed from one thing to the next, one idea to the next, one outfit to the next, and she wasn't entirely sure where her flight of mania was going to land. A few times, she started to knock on her sister's door but didn't. How are you supposed to get ready to meet your father for the first time? Was there a good way to do that? Leah doubted any of the plethora of other things on her mind was much help. Sure, she tried to call Tommy again, but this time, it was out of a rising worry. Normally, Tommy would get back to her within a couple of hours. She shook those thoughts away but accidentally landed on Kris next. She called him too, but it went straight to voicemail.

After the beep, she said, "Hey. I know you probably won't get this, but…I've got a bad feeling when you pop in my head. A feeling like you are about to do something stupid, something I'd try to talk you out of. I'd have talked to you about it last night, but…I don't know about you, but I didn't end up in the garden. I hope you're okay."

*****

Her father knocked on the door at exactly one. Brit also must have been standing by her door because she and Leah opened their doors at the same time. Leah was relieved to see a mild look of fringed nerves on her sister's face; she was sure that it matched her own. Their mother was at the door, greeting him, hugging him. The first she saw of him was his arms around her and his watch (worn nurse style), which was gold and clearly old; she could see its scratches and discoloration even from the end of the hall.

"Girls, your dad's here," her mom said, not without hesitancy.

The man in the doorway of the red roundtop door wore a baseball cap with an unfamiliar hexagonal logo on the top. His beard was close-trimmed and handsome, and his smile was welcoming and warm. He removed his hat as he came in, both his hands clutched on the hat as he looked first at Leah and then Brit. The man was eerily similar to how she imagined him; low on his blue jeans was a stain that could be nothing other than motor oil. Brit went to him first. Leah thought maybe there were tears behind her eyes (tears that held there and never showed themselves on the side facing the world). They hugged. Leah could hardly believe it.

"Hey, Duck," he said.

"Hey, Dad."

"How are you?"

"I'm okay. You?"

"I'm better now."

When they pulled apart, Leah realized she didn't want to hug him. They knew each other, but she didn't know this man. Yet she did want to hug him, wanted that exact moment that her sister just got. He waited for her to approach him.

"Aaliyah," he said. "I—"

She extended her hand, only then realizing how cold that must have seemed but still not sure whether she could handle hugging him yet.

"I'm Wyatt," he finished.

Then everything seemed to speed up. A few minutes later, she was in the front seat with him, and Brit was in the back. And she had to face the fact that she'd been both purposefully and accidentally refusing to think about how she felt about the man in the driver's seat. There was a definite duality to the feelings, she knew that, because Wyatt Fells had been nothing but sweet and accommodating, but every time, she told herself that it didn't seem to matter to the other half of herself that asked: Why should we care about this man? Remember that all of those thoughts were not thoughts, not really. The point is, the ride to whatever godforsaken place he wanted to take them to was awkward and mostly silent.

She had her Nikon around her neck, and when the lulls came, she pretended to be adjusting the settings or going through old photos to "make room," but really, she was trying to, as Brit would say, "not be a bitch."

Solace came when Brit and her dad found something to talk about for long enough that Leah didn't have to pretend so hard. She was trying desperately to come up with things to add to the conversation, and sometimes she did, but her comments were zeroed in on. It's painful when people know you don't want to be there, so they try to bring you into the conversation by use of your most mundane comments.

"I didn't know you liked border collies," said Wyatt. (In his defense, he had a lot on his mind and regretted saying the words as soon as they left his mouth.)

"I just said they were cute." She shrugged.

"Can we stop by Tom & Mitch's on the way back?" asked Brit, the heroine of the drive.

Wyatt's face lit up. "Hell! I forgot about that place. How are those two?"

Leah considered for a moment the magic of Tom & Mitch's, that it'd just reached out from the corner store and leapt into the car with them. "Tom still complains about rich folks in Great Heights, and Mitch still seems unfazed by most everything. They both were talking about 'expanding the empire' last time I was in there."

They all laughed.

"They've been going back and forth about leaving since I was a teenager."

"Does anyone know how old they are?" asked Brit.

It was one of life's great mysteries, that question.

"Every time I ever asked, Tom said, 'What is time?' And Mitch said, 'We've lost count,'" remarked Wyatt.

By the time they arrived at the Gillian Lake Dam, out on Route 71, Leah's camera was hanging forgotten from her neck. They'd moved on from Tom & Mitch to their feelings about the endless tide of so-so movies to come out of the superhero franchises that touted such success and deserved acclaim only a few years ago. It turned out that Wyatt was a big nerd for those kinds of things, and Leah couldn't help but acknowledge that she was, too, when she was a child.

The levee was a massive rolling green hill that ran alongside Dimpleton Road, which was really just dust and spots of mounded gravel. On their left, farmland stretched to a tree line where a falling fence once managed to hold cattle. Leah was reminded of the farmers in Texas that'd lost their loved ones and livestock. She imagined one of the beasts: it was facing away from her, flicking its tail against a swarm of horseflies on its massive rear end, and fixing her with a piteous bovine expression. After a moment, it started chewing the cud in its mouth again and turned away from her disinterestedly and disappeared. Where the levee broke for the dam, there was a small empty gravel lot and a concrete wall that contained a solid-gray hummock—or giving the illusion of a hummock due to the great cypress branches that reached above its summit. Overhead was blue and white, two singular shades, and the grass was viridescent from the storm the night before.

They were greeted by limpid wild air, fresh from the forests, as they got out of the truck. And in the way that nature can, it lifted their spirits even higher. Leah was particularly excited and appreciative that her dad had texted her that morning, telling her to bring her camera, and that was before she saw the dam itself.

"Wow," her sister remarked.

"Your mom and I used to come here. We'd have picnics up on the levee."

Leah walked past her father and sister as they gazed at the hill and wall that hid the dam from view. She was struck by the urge to know what was on the other side and clutched to her Nikon. The other two hurried to catch up to her.

She followed a path in the grass made from the traffic of wayward feet that looked distinctly unofficial, and rounded the corner of the wall. She stopped. While they caught up, she stared at it.

SERMON OF THE DIVERS

Down a dirt path, a foot-trodden path, and over the jagged tops of a mountain of strewn boulders was an art gallery on cement. Dam spillway blocks stood almost as tall as a person on the floor of the dam, arranged in rows and columns before the dam's sloping hillock. The people of Gadsborrow were the first to look at the great blocks and think, *I'd sure like it if that weren't just gray.* (Though the neighboring towns and Valleyport citizens would come to join.) Its construction was completed in 1948, and the first to mark it came in 1951. Just in case you might be wondering, the first thing written was on the sixth block from the right and read, "Martha & Owen." After that, the proverbial floodgates were opened, and throughout the '50s, '60s, and with a great increase in the '70s and '80s and '90s, folks began to paint the dam. At first, law enforcement saw it as vandalism, defacing public property. Over the course of its history, countless numbers of young people were escorted home and reprimanded for their heinous crimes, fifty-seven were charged with the crime, and many others escaped through the pasture, avoiding repercussions. Eventually, lawmen looked at the dam and realized something—*it was beautiful.* And it was a part of their little town's history.

"This is...wild," said Leah.

They walked through the gallery of graffiti, standing before a collage of color, names, and a horse galloping through a flaming hoop.

"It is," agreed Brit.

"Yeah. There's hardly any empty space left. I think, maybe, this is actually getting more popular. I'd never have guessed that."

There was enough fresh paint that the smell lingered in the air.

There was an image of a woman, made to look like she was sitting against the dam's slope and caring for a child. Her cheeks were sunken in to reveal the structure of her skull beneath, and her sallow complexion and pleading eyes looked up from the child to the viewer. Above her were the words *Opportunity Cost.* Among the urge to help the fantasy woman, Leah felt a pang of guilt, thinking of all the people in her world, in her city and country who could use help right then.

"Leah, did you want to take some pictures?" he asked.

She'd been so overwhelmed that she'd forgotten she had her Nikon. She quickly remedied that and began to snap photos every time she turned. All the while, she and Brit and this man, this man that was supposed to be or could be her father, were chatting away. He was doing it. He was quickly winning her over. All the more so when he showed her a rope hidden down further on the dam and showed them how to climb to the top. Leah and Brit both jumped at the chance, curious about what lay on the other side. She got pictures of the bayou on still water, but she had to imagine the pelicans flying through the cypress trees.

CHAPTER 24

The Reaper

Shane left the corner store late, when the night was young, but the hour was not, and he walked down the sidewalk as if he were human. He'd dressed himself for the occasion, wearing a suit of his color (not black; it was actually a blue so deep and velvety that it stirred mortal minds to thoughts of the ocean or of space) and a hat, which covered his thinning hair. He'd shaved and shaped his facial hair into a mustache, like a bold dash across his small upper lip. The fella looked quite handsome for his occupation, the tool of which he carried in his hand, using it as a walking stick. In fact, at that moment, it was a walking stick. No one could see Shane; those that could may catch a scent or a glimpse of him before he disappeared again. Mostly, it was from the corner of their eyes.

Ritual. That could be the word for it or maybe just a habit. Either way, he was in the middle of a repeated act, a cyclical process in the middle of a much bigger sphere of implementations, which were a large part of Shane's personality or being or, maybe, soul.

"This one's for you," said Shane.

He stopped on the sidewalk as a young couple, or maybe almost a couple, walked by exchanging wishful glances, and he lit a cigarette. The young man with the dull-blond hair looked around for the origin of the smell but never saw Shane, who eyed the young man, Kiefer.

"You're close, kid."

Kiefer, of course, couldn't hear Shane and stepped right through him there on the sidewalk. He addressed the girl, Felicia, then, "You've still got a few to go… Either way, it may be a little while."

Shane disregarded them and looked into the night sky, feeling war in the air, not stretching himself out to hear what was happening in the woods on the edge of Valleyport, not wanting to hear.

He thought out loud, "This is…not right. This can't be right, but—*no*, no. It's like they said, 'There's nothing more you could have done.' But he is still over there, still fighting. Not even running—fighting."

Shane couldn't help himself; he reached out toward Kris. He needed to know. Pain, all of it was pain that he felt, pain and desperation and a little fire, but not much. Shane shook his head and continued down the dark sidewalk, refocusing on his ritual.

He walked the path slow and deliberately, collecting its scents, sights, and abstractions, forming the narrative of a lifetime, one of many that he has watched and known, and one of few that he has held in highest regard and held highest hope for. "She is a daisy." He imagined—not imagined, but he visited—the moments her father instilled in her that important lesson, the one showcased in the way he consulted his wild child. She, not knowing then that it was her rock and her storm, and then finding out later when she watched Wyatt leave. Shane felt what she was feeling in the moment he closed the door for what was going to be the last time, and she was only the fingernails digging into the red roundtop door, as a vulpine beast ripping with its claws. She was only the virtue and the iniquity and the tears on her cheeks. But then she was only a mother, for a while, and then she was grown, and she was Adni again. "She is a daisy," he breathed out with smoke and slumber.

He's aware that he had arrived, aware that Leah was not home, that Brit was not home, and that Aaron Grayson had driven by, hoping they would see him, not knowing they weren't home and that Adni was on her way out. The house, it was where most of her life had been spent, so he revisited the memories of her and her children or her and her husband on the porch: Leah and Brit in the yard when they were younger, running through a homemade Slip 'N Slide. She was worried in large moments, with little momentum, and certain in small moments when her mouth opened.

The sun was high in her memories. Wyatt was young and handsome.

Death entered the red roundtop door, looking to the flower beds under the windows as he went.

Inside, the house was silent. He knew she was in her room, and she was scared but that she was also maybe the most pissed off she'd ever been.

"You've got to wake up!"

He stood in her doorway. She was standing above her body, vicious rivulets in her eyes and hammering down on her physical body, to no avail.

"Hey-o," he said and knocked on the door.

He's lighting another cigarette.

"You shut your mouth and get away from me! Get the fuck away from me!"

There's red in her eyes and vigor in her will, and Shane put his hands up and took a step back. She continued to push her fists through her body, and she continued to scream, to yell. Shane waited in the hall then, with the patience that only an immortal could know, or maybe a parent. How long? A long while. And her screams, roars, and bellows the only sound he heard as he waited. Slowly it waned. Adni paced for a while, and then she sat on the floor by her dead body, and she was quiet, completely quiet. Her knees were pulled to her, and she looked a hell of a lot like her daughters. Brit in the language of her body, the blatancy of her form, and Leah in her struggle and conviction, holding her own wrist. Shane continued to smoke, waiting outside the door, not looking at her. He looked up and down the hallway, at Brit's room and then Leah's.

"They're going to be fine. You gave them what they needed."

She didn't answer him, and he waited longer in the quiet and dark hall. He eventually slunk down to the ground and sat in the door, where she could see him. He propped the cane against the door. Her eyes started to settle on him then, and he couldn't tell whether he's still her obstacle or not.

"I..." Shane swallowed. "My name's Shane."

"I don't need to know your name."

"Because you're not going?"

She didn't respond, glaring at him with mutiny and horror in her eyes.

He nodded. "Okay," he said. "Would you like a cigarette?"

She looked dumbfounded by that question, thrown completely from herself as a baby being shown its feet for the first time.

"I..."

He pulled out his pack and slid one of the sticks halfway out, then he extended the pack to her.

"I...I can smoke?"

He nodded again.

She reached out and grabbed the cigarette, and before she asked, he had his Zippo out and leaned toward her enough to get the smoke going for her. Then he resettled back in the doorway, far from her.

Death did not look around the room, didn't have to; he knew the room intimately as he knew her. Shane was of the opinion that reaping should be done by the sowers, the caretakers, the working, and he'd spent a lifetime learning her lifetime. There was no magic, no omnipresence to it, only time and the willingness to subject himself to the whole. It's the difference between passing by a Michelangelo on the museum wall and studying it until you could put paint on the canvas with the same strokes, the same line work, the same suffering to the detail. He knew the story in the black book, the disregard she'd put on actually attempting to quit smoking (and it had less to do with habit and addiction and more to do with feeling close to her father, maybe even like him). He knew the spot in the room that she tried not to look at, with the poster of that movie. He knew her. In some ways, he knew her better than she did; in other ways, he did not.

"I said that I was going to fight you, to give you hell," she said. "But it's hard to hate someone who offers you a cigarette."

He knew that's something her father used to say. It's something that's true for her.

SERMON OF THE DIVERS

Shane smiled and drew on his smoke. "That's a fact." He slid the pack to her. "I'll give you more so long as I don't have to fight you, Adni Fells."

She grinned back at him, her wild child showing. Then it was gone, and where it'd been, there was a disparaging, glossy set of eyes above a stricken mouth. She wasn't seeing him anymore. She looked back at her body as she blew out smoke. Still, she was not talking or seeing or anything, but she was breathing. And after a while, she spoke again.

"Did you mean what you said?"

"Yeah. Don't you think so?"

"I try to. I just...I didn't take care of the will. I didn't take care of the fucking will!"

Shane couldn't say anything to that, not even Death would want to. Again, she was quiet for a while; maybe she was waiting for him to speak. He didn't. In the end, it was what it was.

Nothing could be done, too late.

"How do you know they're going to be okay?" she asked.

"I just know it."

She frowned at him.

"What?"

"You don't know the future?"

"Oh, hell no. I don't think anyone knows the future, except for the Void, maybe, but I expect even the Void only has an idea and a small lead. Knowing through wisdom."

"That sounds about right," said Adni, shaking her head and blowing out smoke. "Just another reason I can't be mad then. If the afterlife was a company, you're only middle management, and the CEO is as clueless as the rest of us."

Shane laughed. "You've got part of it right. I am only an employee. But I'd like to think I have a good boss who treats me right, even though he may not make me privy to all of his plans."

She didn't say anything again. From the look on her face, he knew that she was forming the question in her mind and that he'd made her feel comfortable enough to ask it. He knew he'd have to refuse it, and he knew what it meant for her. He was not disappointed, but he did feel a little bit of regret or maybe just silly for getting his hopes up. Yet elation, awe, and joy flooded his ghostly figure as she said something entirely different.

"Tell me about your boss."

"Fickle fellow on first observation. Not that I've ever really observed him...or her, I'm not really sure. Don't think it matters really. Anyway, the Void is a finicky kind of personality, can be a little chaotic or seem very chaotic at times. When I first started working for him, I thought he was crazy as a loon...I even tried rebelling once. That's when he took me into the back room, and I got a gander at the whole process. It's a doozy! But there's genius in it, something profound!"

"What do you mean? How? How does it all work?"

"I can hardly remember, to be honest."

Adni blinked at him. Shane smiled ineffectually.

"I just remember the feeling that I got when I saw it. It was like when something unexpected happens, something that you dreamed about for a long time, so long you probably thought you were crazy for even thinking it, and then it just happened. From zero to infinite, just like that. Every part of the whole contributed to itself, and I saw a cycle when I looked into it. I saw a curve, going up. It was..."

"It was what?"

"Sorry. I can't say."

Adni sighed. "Of course you can't, Shane."

"I'm sorry," he said. "You know, I thought you were going to ask me a different question."

"I was."

Shane took in a bellow's worth of smoke, squeezed it down into his ethereal body, and held his breath.

"Should I not?"

He exhaled, nervous and hoping and worrying, trying his hardest not to show it on his face, which was now harder to disguise, as it was so freshly shaven and naked.

"It's up to you."

Adni crushed the first and last cigarette of her afterlife out on the floor, and when she flicked the cigarette away, it disappeared. She seemed mildly surprised by that as she spoke, "I hate to be the cliché, and I'm not even sure that I have to explain it to you, that I didn't want to be a mom. Not when we started, and of course it was an accident. And then, that's just the way things were...I was pregnant, miserable, and I knew that there was a part of me that I'd never get to be again. A part that had to die when Brit was born..."

No, she didn't have to tell him any of this, but Shane watched and listened as if it was the first time he was hearing it, hyperaware of the difference it made on how the story was conveyed: by mouth, from the perspective of the person who experienced it, or from an external place in the world or from the daughter or the son, all branching away from one another and creating different narratives. Her voice implied in tone, wording, breath, and her lips and eyes and each miniscule change in the way her heart beat, because she was dead, but it beat. And she was talking as a child did in that she held nothing back, but as an adult in that it was eloquent and evocative. Shane found himself falling into the words and making the story form in himself, dropping endlessly down the horizontal shift toward understanding.

He was her, when she first held Brit, and there was no room in her mind for anything else. All the external had left her for the first time, though it did come back, and she only knew the child, her daughter. Brit was a crying child, fiercely red and squirmy; but when she reached his arms—her arms—she was content and quieted and reached for her mom's face, where she touched her mother for the first time. Oh, she knew immediately, not like with Wyatt, that she loved her. She would do anything for her daughter. Then there were the years between, when she must learn what being a mother really was, and Brit pulled no punches. She was a sleepless monster who haunted her own house, forced to stay home with the creature that was her daughter, and they couldn't agree on anything, while her husband was out, working. He's an ass for that. Then the part of her that died met the new part of her, because he talked about his dreams incessantly, and when they met, it was a heated and furious debate that concluded with conception and a feeling of relief so palpable that it seemed to change her overnight, again to that part of her that was a mother. Then there she was again, in the hospital, and everything was blood and bodily fluids, but this time, she was a little more aware of that, and she was given her daughter, her second, Aaliyah Blaire Fells. And she felt that love, but she also felt anger and despondency. Then she was a mother again. Or she thought she was trying to be a mother. Wyatt was a good father. He talked of his dreams more often while she was a mother again.

Then she was in a hotel room, and smoke was filling the room as it came forth from her lungs, until all was in that haze of gray. She was not a mother, she was not a wife, she was not Adni, and she smoked while he was behind her in the bed; he was sleeping. The curls of his dark hair resting easy on his face, which was handsome and peaceful as he dreamed. Finally, she had smoked every cigarette of her own, and all of his as well, and she knew what she had to do because she remembered in a haze of gray. She had to tell Wyatt about him.

Late autumn, the red roundtop door closed, and Wyatt was on one side, while she was on the other. She wanted to escape too, but she couldn't. She loved her daughters; she knew that.

"But I learned. Each time they did something new, I learned about them, and I thought I was remembering things about myself as well. I was reminded of something by my two girls, something essential. I don't have any good words for it. There are a few that come to mind, but they sound too... They sound ridiculous."

"I know what you mean," he said. "But the feeling isn't. That feeling is, like you said, essential. You'll need it where we're going."

Then she turned and looked at him with wonder and more than a little fear.

"Where are we going?"

Shane stood and smiled at her. "Adni, you're going to love it."

CHAPTER 25

Burnt Pie Crust

"Is it alright if I come by for lunch tomorrow? Before I leave."

Leah agreed first this time, followed closely by Brit. And this time, when he hugged Brit, he also hugged Leah.

"Do you wanna come in?" asked Brit.

"I do, but I better go," he said, and his lips trembled like he might elaborate, but he didn't. He put the truck in drive and was gone.

Feeling lighter, Leah simply headed up the path to the red roundtop door; she began to smell something sweet as she reached for the door handle. On the other side, there was an altogether-different smell, that of something burning.

Chirping from the oven timer led her to the kitchen, her heart speeding and her camera bouncing as she hurried. She clicked the oven off as she realized what must have happened. The pie she pulled from the oven was just beginning to blacken; some was still salvageable. The home ledger was open on the breakfast bar, and her mother was nowhere in sight.

"What's that smell?" asked Brit as she entered the house.

"Crispy apple pie. Do you want some?"

Brit rolled her eyes. "She forgot it in the oven?"

"Must have. I'll go check on her."

Brit was standing in the center of the kitchen with a quizzical look on her face as she set down her bag and surveyed the pie. Leah left.

Her mother's bedroom door was cracked open the width of several fingers. The thing creaked as she pushed in, trying to do so in a way that would stifle the sound. Her shoes were loud on the lacquered floor, squeaking like baby birds, so she stopped at the threshold and stuck her head in, bumping the door as she did so. It shuttered in. A pile of gold-and-brown comforter was mounded up in a vaguely human shape; her breath must have been too soft to hear under the sound of the ceiling fan's rotation, constantly swinging its weight back and forth as a rocking chair. Lamplight reached across the room from the nightstand in frail form that tarnished the room. There was some manifestation in the last glance she gave the space. It was as if it waited for her to disturb it, but knowing her mother's constantly tired state, she couldn't. For her mom's sake, she pulled the door back in and returned to the kitchen.

"She's napping."

"Oh."

Then they were both quiet as they wondered about what it meant. It was an enigma to them that their mom would both bake a pie (she'd done it many times before, but it was a rarity) and then that she would forget the pie and lie down to rest. But they both knew she hadn't been feeling well recently.

"Is she okay?"

"I think so. She was napping."

Brit poked the pie with a fork, sending black crust flaking over the crosshatch like ash. She smiled coyly, as if giddy with the words she was about to say. But then she simply picked up her bag and went to her room. Leah got the feeling that she was missing something, that she forgot something.

Ding!

From Jason:

> Hey, I know it's been a while since we talked, but I just wanted to see if you'd checked on Bailey lately. She said you've been kind of blowing her off. She seemed kind of mad at you.

Had she been? Leah tried to recall when she'd last talked to Bailey. Apparently, it had become sparse because she couldn't quite remember when she last talked to Bailey or what they'd talked about. The last thing she remembered about Bailey was the text she received calling their meeting the other night a *freakish theater for conspiracy.* Then there were the comments by Talley and Andrew about how it was obvious Bailey wasn't coming. There seemed to be some animosity there as well. *And don't I already have enough going on?* Oh, but she could be a better friend than that, couldn't she? She thought of the hundreds of times that Bailey had been there for her. Heck, it had been partially Bailey's efforts that got her the job with Tommy, the job that had helped fix their AC and pay their bills after the storm.

Leah retreated to her room with her finger over the call button but couldn't seem to press it. Not the first time she'd had that happen. She plopped down on her bed, unable to force herself to press the button at first.

Leah knew what to do. She got up, went to her dresser, opened the top drawer, and removed an old shoebox. The box was covered in pictures she'd glued onto it. There was Talley, Andrew, Bailey, Jason, Brit, her mom, and even Tom & Mitch. She plopped back down on her bed and opened it. The inside of the box hadn't seen light in—it may have been years. She couldn't remember. Back when she was really little, and even more concerned about forgetting the memories she made with her friends and family, she made a box to store them in. The box was filled with Polaroids, a few rocks, some gumballs, toy capsules, two cigarettes half-finished, Skittles-flavored lipstick, the end of a blunt, some bottle caps, and a spiky orange seashell. She felt she was reaching through time, letting memories sail by, as she picked up the shell.

It was the color of a creamsicle and shaped almost like a horn, and as Leah rolled it around in her hand, it was smooth as porcelain. Bailey gave it to her on her tenth birthday, the first one they were friends for.

"*It's my favorite. I wouldn't give it to anyone else...but you can have it.*"

Bailey proudly displayed her collection of seashells back then. All different shapes, sizes, and colors, all organized according to Bailey's whim. When Leah would go for a sleepover, she would stop to look at it, in particular the big creamsicle-colored one. The way that Bailey looked when she gave Leah the shell—hurt and proud.

Leah still couldn't think of what she would say to Bailey, but she decided to call and find out.

*****

"Hey, can we talk for a second?" she asked.

The line was blank before an even keel. "Yeah. What is it?"

Aaliyah's heart fluttered away, and she struggled to keep going, feeling more judged and unhinged already. *She's your best friend.* "I wanted to say I'm sorry. There's a reason for you to be mad at me. It's kind of hard to explain, though. I'm not even sure that I could, not fully…"

Of course, the line went blank again. Leah couldn't sit. She was standing and running her fingers over the shell in her free hand, looking at the poster in her room with all the constellations. Everything else in the room drizzled out in the periphery.

"I don't understand. Don't get me wrong, I'm glad you called, but what do you mean?"

Leah didn't even think of telling her about Aaron, about what he did in the car, not this time.

"We…" Leah was thinking through a fog of emotions that she wished she'd thought to search through before calling. Instead of untangling the miscommunications between them, she felt she was tying additional knots. "It's Buried in the Valley, that's what we met to talk about. Andrew, me, Talley, and Brit. They figured out who it is that writes the articles, but there's more… There's all this stuff about Mr. Grayson. Talley thinks he's trying to—"

"Leah. Stop. I don't want to hear any more about Buried in the Valley or Mr. Grayson or any of the conspiracies. You…you know it's all just talk, right? There's no way that Mr. Grayson is some cartoon supervillain. Don't get me wrong. I don't like him either, but he's not trying to take over the world. I've read through some of those Reddit threads because Andrew was so insistent. They're bizarre."

I knew she would think that, but I called anyway. Leah was caught in a moment between outrage and obscurity. *I knew she wouldn't believe in any of this. I mean…*

"You know why you're doing this, right?" asked Bailey. Her voice was careful and creeping, wary of how her words would be taken. "Look, Aaron hurt you…more than you've even talked to anyone about. I know. Leah, I know. But just because he hurt you doesn't mean that his dad is some evil genius, or his family is really lizard people that live underground. I understand why you would—"

"*No.* You don't."

Soundless shifting, a change as the line went quiet for the third and final time. Her other thoughts, the ones she held in her hand, the ones shaped like an orange seashell, dried up and disappeared altogether. She was staring into the stars of a cheap poster, looking deeply into the bear pelt of Ursa Major.

"Fine. *Fine.* I should have known better. It's like Jason says, you're too emotional. Just following every little impulse! Isn't that what got you with Aaron in the first place? You didn't take any time to get to know him and see that he's an asshole! If you—"

"Shut up!" Leah had never raised her voice at Bailey. It was something she might have done to Brit a handful of times but never Bailey. "I was trying to include you because Jason just texted me, and I felt sorry for you! But you know what? Never mind. Just keep pining after Jason and hating me because he liked me and not you."

Leah hung up the phone. The shell in her hand didn't feel like porcelain anymore; it felt like some otherworldly poison that seeped into her pores. She let it drop to the floor, still somewhat relieved when it didn't break, and sat right there in the center of her room. She hadn't taken her eye off of the old bear. She held onto the pelt with her eyes, grabbing it with her stare, grasping at it like the hand of a child reaching for mother.

And that was the moment that Kris texted her:

I want to talk to you too.

CHAPTER 26

The School and Stars

Every car that came by she listened for, and if it started to slow, she wanted to laugh from her excitement. She was fully dressed—in leggings, an oversize hoodie, and boots—and lying on her bed editing the photos she took at the dam. She hadn't expected him to text back so quickly, didn't think he'd have a phone again for—A car slowed down and stopped. Her phone went off.
Ding!
Here!
Leah took a long slow breath before she got up. The window was already open, so she climbed out of it and onto the grass below. Her knee felt weak after she landed, she stumbled a little bit, and of course, he was watching, but he couldn't see her blush—she hoped. He moved like he was going to get out and help her, but she waved him off and started to limp toward the car.
"Graceful."
"Shut up," she said before she knew it.
It was that feeling all over again. He looked different tonight, older maybe, or it was something about the way that he dressed, or it was something he was wearing. But something felt different about him; his eyes almost looked violet in the dark, though she knew they were a combination of blue and green. He seemed more like that version of him from the dreams.

"I thought you wouldn't have a phone. That you wouldn't hear that message," she said.

He put the car in drive (Rob's car), and they glided down the road. The apotheosis of the night seemed to wait beyond the headlights with the same color-crooked glow of his eyes.

"I thought it was sweet. I'd have been able to answer, but I had something to take care of tonight. I was surprised, though."

"Surprised?"

"Yeah. I didn't expect you to want to go. Don't get me wrong, I'm happy you did."

"Are you?"

He blushed.

"Yeah. I, uh, wouldn't want you to miss the meteor shower. That'd be a shame."

She breathed out laughter, low and light. "Yeah. I had something to do before this too. Sorry, but I might not be in the right… headspace."

"Oh?"

"Yeah."

"What happened? If I can ask that."

He's so careful, even after everything.

"Yeah, of course. I mean, it was really several things that happened in a row. Funny how it always seems to play out that way, huh? I met my dad today, and then I had a fight with my best friend."

Leah almost felt silly talking about that when there was a whole fantastical world to address and the fact that they met there. Not to mention that he had just been missing for a whole week. She considered asking where he'd been but got a strong inclination, almost as if she were in his head, that he didn't want to talk about that.

They were crossing downtown, between the buildings that tried their best but were never really skyscrapers, and the streets were filled with people coming and going between the strip, the casinos, and the hotels, like a relay race of some obscure type. Funny how that never stopped, even though most people were malnourished and impoverished. Neon signs and LEDs colored the streets by black and moisture so that certain spots, windows mostly, gleamed, and buildings appeared to move. She realized she didn't know where they were going. Succinctly, she realized that she wasn't scared, that she was not scared at all.

"Sounds like a rough day..."

Once they reached the part of Highway 71 that belonged to the trees and the abandoned farms and the night, they had good-enough reason to be silent (only the music played low). Every mile, they moved further into the rural lands of empty, where people weren't running a relay race; they're rarely seen, in fact. A crater sky, blown away by some invisible hammer, leaving it rounded like a dent, and black, dropped pieces of itself on the horizon. She pointed to them, the falling stars, as if he hadn't seen them, knowing that he had. Together they made the sounds of amazement that children do when they see novelty and beauty and divinity.

"How much further?"

"Uh, to be honest with you, I'm not sure. I haven't been out here since I was a kid."

"What is it?"

"It's nothing. You don't want to wait and see?"

"Sounds like you're about to murder me in the middle of nowhere."

He laughed. "I'm not about to murder you in the middle of nowhere... This is a very important place."

She shook her head at his bad joke. "How much further?"

"I think we're here."

The tree line on their right broke, and below a falling sky, a set of several buildings, a complex of some kind, and a field of corn twitched in a country breeze. Already, even from inside the car, she could smell that the air was lighter, fresher—colder? She rested her hand against the window, which felt like ice to her. *Strange.* She looked over and saw that he was, again, not looking at the sky, which evoked so much awe and crisis, not the panorama of moon-belighted land, which swam in the pastoral zephyr, not the buildings that were only black shapes on more currents, but he was looking at her. That hollow light in his eyes reminded her of the fireworks she'd seen there before, so faintly violet, maybe from her own hair. He was looking at her with that spark again. That thought shook her from his gaze. She looked back to the fields.

"What is this?"

"It's two places. It's one part school and one part corn maze."

"School?"

"Yep. This used to be some elementary school—and middle."

"We're at an abandoned school? That's where we're going to watch the meteor shower?"

She looked at him and was pleased to see his chagrin.

"Alright. I'll admit that it's a bit odd, but a friend of mine told me this was the best view of the sky I'd ever find. Also said to check out the wall art if I came out here."

It took her a moment to realize that he meant graffiti. She was reminded then of the dam and her day, and she felt like the melancholic one then. Her excitement was blocked by a feeling of misplacement, something being just a little bit off but her not knowing, not remembering what it was, standing in front of a door but having found she misplaced the key. Then it was like she was checking her pockets while she fought with a growing sense of panic.

"You ready to do this?" he asked.

She nodded, reminded of their adventures together in a dream garden.

Outside, the air was colder than cold. There was no way that the temperature could be so low on a summer night, but it was. Freezing wind surrounded her and slipped into her clothes, sending gooseflesh up her whole body in a wave. She shivered. She tightened the drawstrings on her hoodie until only her nose and eyes, and a few violet strands, could be seen.

"Whoa!" he hollered over the wind.

"It's fucking cold!"

"Yeah!"

"How's it this cold? What…"

"I don't know. The temp says thirty-three… But that's impossible."

They stood there, looking around the frozen landscape for a moment, as if this was the time, the moment that if they should continue, there would be no return. She hesitated as he looked around, watching his face to try and read what he was thinking. He looked back to the car and smiled.

"I brought a blanket! It's probably big enough to wrap up in… Do you want to go check it out or what?"

He was grabbing the blanket. He looked at her, wondering.

*****

They say there's a whispered day when all things change in a moment, and the world becomes new again, or reborn, and on that day, the people reborn with it so that they understand the most vital of things, so that they greet the monsters of eternity with grace and strength, so that life evolves. That day existed for Kris Timur; he was sure that he was in the middle of it, experiencing it, and all of his awareness, his senses, were taught and drawn so that they scratched every detail into his being. He couldn't help but think, *I see. I am terrified, but I see.* He'd woken to that thought. It had been just before she texted him, and he'd been lying in his bed thinking of the war he'd waged.

All lies within the Void.

She picked the music while they were in the car, and every song was a banger. He had trouble listening sometimes because of her taste in music; it was like having two conversations in two different languages at the same time. Funny, it was like she knew that too. The rhythm of both conversations entwined with one another and created space for both so that they were talking with music and words, and she waited at times, and other times she didn't. But it was all flowing, all pouring down, all rapids. They were leaving much to the wayside but only because there was much to talk about. Even after all the time they'd spent together in the dreams, there was still so much to talk about.

Aaliyah.

The sign out front, which was plated to look like gold and was on an old pile of bricks, read: *Marvin Colders Middle Magnet School.*

SERMON OF THE DIVERS

Ahead of them, beyond the crumbling sign, the space between the wings of the school was cave dark, as if the sky over them had disappeared. The sound of furious winds wailing into the ruinous hall of education were as the moans of tired gods, despairing gods, getting their final words in. And as they approached, they noticed that it was all red brick and pale trimming, and each step didn't seem to brighten the next. It was as if the dark between the buildings was alive, a creature they must pass through or be lost in.

Leah did not look afraid; he was surprised by that, but later, it seemed so obvious. He could see it—the desire in her eye to search the dark gallery.

"This is weird. I just went to see something kind of like this earlier."

"You went to see something like *this* earlier?"

"Okay, no. Not quite like this, but have you ever been to the Gillian Lake Dam?"

"No?"

"There's this place, I'm not sure where it is exactly, but I know it's in Gadsborrow. It's a dam and like a park. There's this levee that runs into it like a giant hill, and there's these *huge* blocks that sit in the dam itself. People go there and paint or tag or whatever, but it's almost completely covered. I took some pictures of it actually. I can send them to you later, when I get back."

"Definitely, I'd like to see. Is that where you met your dad?"

On either side of them were palm trees, then what looked like blood-dribbled signatures—*Gnōsis*—then martini glasses and caricatures, then nonsense and nebulas. Inside, between the wings, in the dark gallery, they didn't hear the wind or cars that passed by on the highway or the oil derrick's squeal.

"Yes."

He was quiet.

"It went well, but is it okay if we don't talk about it?"

"Are you sure? I'd like to hear, if you want to talk."

Still, there was no fear; even though it shouldn't be that cold, and it shouldn't be that dark, there was still no fear with her. Leah believed him, but she hesitated. But there was a feeling, beyond her just believing him, that was calming and serene and everything that made her feel like she was not alone.

"No. I really don't. I want to talk about anything else."

He pointed to something ahead, in the dark gallery, on the wall. Saturn's rings were aglow upon the texture of the brick and looming from earth to roof, turning black and purple together as they rounded.

"Whoa, that's...amazing. How—do you think they brought ladders?"

"I don't know…"

Then opposite to Saturn, Venus revolved in a color-filled blossom of paint. It also seemed to be alight somehow, and while the other, Saturn, had been magnificent, Venus called to her. She stood before it, staring, and he came to be next to her. Leah didn't have a thought as she reached out and grabbed his hand, locked their fingers together, and squeezed. And for a while, they were pillars before Hesperus, loud in the darkness, the way the lurid planet turned and made a distinct kind of sound. The sound of confluence. The sound of them with the planet. She squeezed his hand, feeling as if she was on the verge of some realization or gaining some extra sense about the world, something profound and obvious—so obvious that it need be overlooked. Something reaching toward her from a place down the road, where her life would be something she could pull apart and look at as an observer. He squeezed back, his hands warm in the cold air of the gallery, between the buildings.

For a moment, she remembered that's what it felt like, but it may have been a dream or an illusion, but there was no way of knowing.

He turned to her, and she turned to him, and she wondered what he was thinking, but she wondered it even as they both began to lean toward one another. His lips were blood-colored in the presence of Venus, his hair an aura, his eyes portals into an adjacent universe. When they came together, and his lips locked with hers, she felt something pass over them—a terribly large shadow that was in the cold of the air itself. And she could feel it all over her body then, the hands of some horrid thing. She allowed herself to be drawn closer to him, and his hands replaced the others.

*****

When they came out from between the two buildings, the sky opened above them, and then all around them, as if they'd found their way to the other side of that massive hammer-struck sky. Their hands were still entwined as they walked out into a field of grass, where the moon lay above them, along with the planets she'd just stood next to. And the surrealness of the moment came to a head when she saw how the stars fell: volleys of them at a time, sparks of fire puffing out upon the atmosphere. They walked through the globed pasture, the blanket over his shoulder, draped down to their hands.

In the center, he laid the blanket down, fighting the powerful wind. She helped him get it down by falling into it and rolling to look up at the sky. The wind slowed, or seemed to slow, as if they'd gone below it when they were lying side by side.

"Do you know the constellations?"

"Some of them. I think I could maybe find Ursa Major," he said.

"Do you see it then?"

She waited for his hand to come up. He pointed to the bear's rear end. She smiled and nodded.

"Show me some other ones," he said.

So she did. She pointed to Aquarius, Lacerta, and Pegasus, which she tried, one at a time, to help him find and of which he only found one. But every time, she would continue trying to give him directions until he gave up. Every time she turned to help him with the next one, he watched. Her eyes were pulling the sky down, her nose letting away steamed breath, the turn her lips and nose did together when she smiled at him, laughed at him, looked him in the eyes.

"What do you think?"

"What do I think?"

"Yeah."

"Like, what am I thinking right now?"

"No, no. Like, what do you think it all is?"

He thought. For a while, he stumbled over his words, trying to compose something that was seamed by other lips. He couldn't just say it, just say what he believed, what he knew to be true. Then he considered.

"I guess it depends on the person."

"It depends on the person," she repeated.

"Yeah. I'm sure that different people have different reasons. I think that it depends on who you are."

"Who are you? What about you?"

He froze for a moment, not looking at her.

"I...I think I'm supposed to be a writer. A novelist, like my mom."

"That makes sense."

He laughed. "Why?"

"You always seem to know just what to say."

"Who are you? Huh? What about you?" he asked.

Without thinking, her eyes closed, she said, "I guess I'm just here. I guess I'm just kind of here, figuring it out."

The wind picked up again for just a moment before settling. Where the sound had been ominous before, almost threatening, it was gentle and morose. And she was still thinking about it, even after so much time had passed since she originally wondered about it, but he spoke first. "Do you think that people can change?"

She thought.

"I think parts of them can, but not all of them."

"Not all of them."

"No. I think there are parts of you that are just...there."

"How do you know which are which?"

She considered.

"The parts that are changeable can change. The others can't."

He shook his head. "Brilliant."

*****

When all the stars had fallen, they crawled out from underneath the blanket, and they stood in the field. They kissed, and he wondered about what it meant that she was there. What it meant that he'd told her that he wanted to tell stories, to write. His hands were slow around her, still wondering if maybe... But she was there with him. Then so many other thoughts followed it, and not just him—though he didn't know that, of course—but she was thinking about it too.

Thinking, *But what does it mean?*

Because they must ask what it means. Otherwise how would they be able to justify grafting it into themselves, but they are still asking. Even after it's already alive, they are still asking.

"What do you want?" she asked.

They were in the car. He's driving, and she's released his hand.

He'd never been able to answer this question before, but right at that exact moment, the answer flashed into his brain in a single word, a concept, a resolution. It's something that he knew years ago, but there's no way that *now*, after everything, that he can say it.

"You mean, what do I *want*, want?"

"Yes."

"I..."

"It's okay if you want something else—"

"I want too much. I want everything."

"You want everything?"

"Yeah. I want all of it, you know? I want the whole package, the all in one, the—"

Then she said it. And he couldn't say yes, but he nodded to her, and when she smiled at him, he did say, "Yes, that's what I want."

"That's what I want too."

Then there was silence for a while. Kris struggled against the urge to grab her, to hold her. She was looking at him.

"Well, let's pretend the world isn't ending... What are you going to do after graduation—oh, that's right. You didn't have any plans."

He smiled. *That was before... Everything's different now.*

"Well, I-I can think of a lot of things to do after graduation. Maybe I'll write a book, or maybe I'll go to college, or both. I'm not sure exactly where it is that I'm going, but is that so bad?"

She shook her head.

"No. It's not."

"Lifeisgood" by Bilmuri played while they talked. And they hardly stopped to breathe on the way back to the Fells' household, hardly thinking before they spoke, knowing clarification would be allowed and every word believed. Slowly at first, her hand inching closer to his, but then all at once, Aaliyah grabbed his hand, and she held onto it the rest of the way home.

CHAPTER 27

Manifestations

Generally, there is a rapid cessation of events in life, followed by a period of adjustment. It's the cyclical nature of the human experience; the exceptions only prove the rule. Kris got home, in Rob's car, and parked it at the base of the massive old oak tree, killed the car, and for a few minutes, he just sat there. Waiting. Sure enough, Rob came out of the house in black slippers and a long-sleeve nightshirt. He crossed his arms and looked down to where Kris was, sitting in the driver seat. Then he huddled down the stairs and hopped in the car.

"So how did it go?"

Kris grinned wide. "It went...amazing. Thanks for letting me borrow the car."

Rob nodded. "It's no problem. Anytime. So long as I don't have to work."

Owls *whooed* in the pensive night, and crickets rattled more than they screeched. Kris wished they could've just listened to those sounds for a while and gone to bed. That wasn't an option, though.

"I thought Dad would be worried about you. He isn't, though. He told me that people often come back from experiences like yours with stories that don't make any sense. He says you were probably in shock."

Kris considered, remembering exiting that place beyond the pines, where Shane had told him that Story. But the Story didn't mean so much without him going to meet the Other for himself, meet him in the flesh, with blood flowing in his veins. *I shouldn't have been able to stop him. But I did.*

Kris nodded. "I think that sometimes your mind plays tricks on you. I think it has to and that most of the time, it's for your own benefit... But don't worry. I'm alright now. I don't know how, but I am."

Rob smiled wide out at the night, looking similar to the gnomes in the flower bed by the car. He clicked his tongue. "Good! I thought I should be worried, especially if Dad wasn't... Maybe that's just an old habit."

"I know. Do you still think you have to?"

Rob grabbed Kris's shoulder and came across the console to embrace him. "No. No, I think you're right. I learned the same thing from writing music. *Sometimes it's good that your mind plays tricks on you.*"

They chatted for a while after that and finally got out of the car and went into the shop. They flicked on the overhead lights; they hummed to life. There was a bottle of No. 7 on a shelf in the shop, next to a fine set of carpenter's chisels, and right next to an upside-down stack of red Solo cups. Rob popped two out and put them down on the table, then he put about two fingers of liquor in each. He demanded that Kris recall all the details of his first date, and Kris did. Rob was as good of an audience as ever, and Kris realized how much he missed this, talking with Rob. Rob smiled and laughed at all the right places and asked questions at the right ones too. At the end of the spiel, Rob said, "I'm glad you found someone that makes you feel that way... You know...I don't think I ever will."

"Why do you think that?"

Rob finished his Solo cup and poured one more, just for himself. While he did, Kris sipped his own and realized that the liquor didn't burn like it once would have, and he didn't get a buzz from the drink.

"I...I've always—Well, maybe not always, but for a long while now, I've thought that...that..." Rob took a furtive glance at Kris and a long gulp of whiskey. "This is going to sound stupid, but I've had a feeling for years that it's just not in the cards for me. That I'm not quite capable of it the way that other people are... It used to bother me a lot."

Kris wanted to say that wasn't true. He wanted to say—maybe just because of Leah—that he was sure there was someone out there for Rob. But he knew how that would sound. It'd be ridiculous.

"It doesn't bother me as much anymore," continued Rob. And he took another big gulp of the whiskey.

"Are you still going to California?"

Rob gave Kris a helter-skelter grin, as if he'd just made a joke.

"Well, aren't you?"

"Why would I? Hell, the whole world is going crazy."

"When did it ever make sense?" asked Kris.

Rob's eyes were a bit glazed over then, and he still had that half grin on his face, like the joke was going sour.

"You're still going, right?"

"Come on, Kris! I can't just go! Not with everything going on! What am I supposed to do? Just walk away from you and Dad? Now?"

Rob's face was flushed, all the smooth features were roughed over, and his even keel eyes were wide with anger, with desperation. Kris hesitated to say what he knew to be true, but he did it anyway. "You have to live your own life. Don't be a baby."

He grabbed Kris's shirt and yanked him close, staring at him with mad eyes. Jack Daniel's was his breath, and his eyes were watered and red. Each breath was more labored than the last.

Kris thought of all that he'd learned while hearing the First Story, and he focused on it as he spoke.

"There's no security here, Rob. You know that. I know you know that. And I'm sorry for being gone for so long. I didn't mean to. But there's no security here, Rob." Kris grabbed his brother's shoulders and squeezed them tight. "There's no security here or there, but you know you have to go. You have to."

Rob stared at Kris as if he'd said something profound. He released his grip, sniffed, and nodded his head.

*****

That night, when Kris dropped her back at her house and she was in bed, Leah fell asleep with ease. She did not think of the work of the next day or the burdens of the past; she fell instantly into that place where she could fly. A moon, hinting at the revelations of light, guided her across a starless sky.

In her room, Shane stood over her. The cadence of his work was broken by her youth and her promise, the way it is for mortals when they stop long enough to realize where they are and what they're doing—usually only when they are met with something so grand or grotesque that their mind cannot instantly write it off. Shane watched the little boy, the boy made of darkness, waddle out of the corner, where no light was present but his violet eyes. He blinked at Shane before hoisting himself up onto the bed where Leah slept. He had something pinched between his fingers as he stretched his arm out over her, but he looked to Shane for reassurance, for permission, before he let it go. Shane nodded. A glitter of dust fell. And she dreamed:

The theater, a nameless building in his memory, a beautiful building that could swallow the world, was draped in banners. He was surprised there wasn't a couple kissing or looking into each other's eyes longingly; he was surprised and secretly a little disappointed. In their place, flapping against the tan bricks, was what he thought was a twig from a blueberry bush. Underneath, in curling white on black letters, clear and crisp, was Juliet and Romeo.

Aaron had heard the names hundreds of times. Who hadn't? His own mother called him *Juliet* from time to time, and that'd started when she found the book he kept under his mattress. She called it poetry, but he didn't think of it that way.

"Who's the lucky girl?"

"Her name's Hannah."

He'd thought she was going to make a joke or say nothing at all, but his mother, to his surprise, said, "O Juliet, Juliet, wherefore art thou, Juliet? Deny thy father and refuse thy name. Or if thou wilt not, be but sworn my love, and I'll no longer be a Montague."

It didn't quite sound right at first, but the longer he thought about it, the better he liked it. He accidentally memorized it because it lingered in his mind for so long, and with the words came such strong images. A girl so bold and devastating that she became a celestial dream, one that was attainable but only existed in a hidden place—a place that none would ever find. A sword, marble-hilted and sharp, in an exquisite hand with a silky glove. Blood staining a robin's-egg-blue vest, lacey and ornate; patricide and all the hatred it entails, all the love. Then a feeling of escape, or open pastures and clear skies and plenty of everything, and two hands entwined. Lastly, an abstract ideal, a thought of being nameless.

Aaron and his mother stepped under the awning, where the ticket takers smiled at lines of suits and gowns, away from the mists in the open and the damp sidewalk. Everyone smelled expensive, looked regal, and moved about in a torpor, and each man that saw his mother lingered for as long as they could. He thought of words like gracious when she talked to everyone who sought her out, but he was also not in the mood. The show was on his mind.

His mother was kissed at the corner of her mouth by a man with a portly mustache. He noticed Aaron and introduced himself. His name was Jack. His mother knew him from somewhere; they kept talking about how extraordinary it was to see each other after so much time.

"You're going to the show?"

"We are," said his mother.

Jack had already noticed they were alone.

"I'm solo. Do you mind if I join you, then?"

He extended his arm, and she took it gracefully. They went in, and Aaron followed.

Inside his pockets, his hands were rubbing on the dime there, a single dime, as they entered and walked on the natural stone floors, between the pillars and arches, and below a gilded chandelier with countless tiny flames burning. He let the dime press against his middle finger and held it there. And they ascended a staircase, where he ran his free hand over the carved wood. It was like petroglyphs. They were along a thousand supports of the balustrade. By the time they took their seats in a covered balcony, in red velvet chairs, he'd forgotten the dime. The room was massive, and his mom didn't care when he leaned over the edge to see the people far below them and then other people sitting in high places like them.

Years later, he would write a few lines in which, through forced conjunction or maybe serendipity, he would bring together that theater, the show, and Leah.

"We're going to find a drink before the show," said his mom.

"But it's about to start."

"We'll be right back," said Jack.

His mother smiled at him a genuine smile. She looked too young for a moment; he'd never seen her smile that way before. She kissed him before they left. They did not come back when the show started.

When the great billowing curtains rolled away, a palace lay beyond. A grand staircase climbed up toward the faraway palace, and two men walked onto the stage from a Verona street. Before they even spoke, Aaron felt compelled to go find his mom; they never did anything together alone, and it was her idea to come. She wanted to see it; he could hear it in her voice when she brought it up. He looked back to the stage a couple of times before leaving, not wanting to miss anything.

Out in the corridor, he circled the whole thing, his steps were remarkably mute on the stone floors. He was rubbing the dime again. Every few yards, there were recessed arches with statues, gray, chipped, and old—very old. Mostly, they were of naked women and naked men, poised. Captured forever. By the staircase, he heard a noise, and he followed it to the bathrooms. He stood in front of them for a while, listening to his mother moan and Jack saying things like "Fuck" and "Oh, I missed that fucking pussy too."

He went back to the theater to watch the show.

*****

"It's time," said his father.

The hedge around their home might as well have been miles from where they stood; and at the time, Aaron had the fledgling thought that it was and that on the other side, there was a wide, immutable desert that went on for miles and states. His dad had a gun (a weapon of war, a weapon with marks, with German blood in its coffers), a pistol that belonged to Arthur Grayson, a poor war vet and the father of Jim

Grayson. And he wore pressed jeans, a white shirt, and a vest holster. His immobile face and strikeless eyes settled on Aaron.

"I can do it, Dad," said Scott, his brother.

Dad ignored him then and the subsequent times he asked.

"This is an M1911. It was my father's."

The gun was angled away from them. His dad was turning it in his hands.

"This is no toy. You do not point it at anything that you don't intend to kill. This is the safety. Keep it on until you're ready to fire. It's hot, which means it's loaded, ready to fire... Look at me."

His dad's gray eyes almost looked blue, and Aaron might've imagined seeing his lip tremble.

"Remember...this thing can kill you. And that'll be it. You'll be dead. Gone. No more."

That was the only time his father didn't have to ask if he was listening; there was recognition. His lips pulled back to that line they held, reminding Aaron of a mask, the way it stayed so motionless.

Aaron grabbed the gun his father offered. It was heavy. He didn't know if it was his imagination, but as soon as it was in his hand, he felt terror grip him, a desire to throw the gun away or fire it at someone, anyone.

"Line her up in your sights the way I showed you and just squeeze the trigger. Don't pull it."

Scott met his eyes. They all put on their earmuffs.

Aaron turned to the kennel not six steps from where he was standing. A mangy gray cat with matted fur and a pink nose hissed at him from beyond tiny metal bars. Cats always hated Aaron, or so he thought. And Aaron always hated cats. The first cat he ever met scratched his face, and blood got in his eye. After that he was wary of them, and he was right to be because every cat he came in contact with hissed at him or tried to scratch him or bite him. He learned to avoid them and their bizarre pointed eyes. But then, as he tried to make the one ridge of metal line up with another, he looked past the sights to the cat, and all he could see were those narrow slits of black in an amber iris.

He tried not to shake. He shook.

The sights didn't stay lined up long enough for him to fire. He started to wonder how much pressure he'd have to use to squeeze on the trigger to make it happen. Squeeze the trigger. Sweat swelled from his pores, his forehead. It itched. The wind stopped. The hedges were silent. The whole world was silent under the earmuffs. And the cat in the kennel, the one that'd scratched up the car, croaked, but he couldn't hear it. His heart rattled, and he squeezed. It didn't take much.

*****

> *Magic is intrinsically valuable, even if deceptive.*
> *That means midnight skies are star-filled places,*
> *And they are above the bonfire, past smoke.*
> *There, silence is confused for division, but it's superposition;*
> *It's duality for conquest and humility,*
> *Infinite depths under a shifting surface.*

He felt the words were a fumble, but he wrote them anyway. As he wrote them, he thought about a girl. Then he sealed them in an envelope using wax and a signet of a blueberry twig. He was about to open his desk drawer, the one with the lock, to discard it into a pile with the others when his brother came in. Aaron managed to close the drawer; however, the sealed letter was still out, so he covered it with his arm.

"*How did it feel?*"

Aaron could see in his mind the cat's bloody fur, its limp body, and how it had been moving and breathing a moment before. The gun jumped when he did it, but it might as well have been magic the way that, instantly, the cat was just dead. Squeeze. Dead.

"*I don't know.*"

"*Dad told me to ask you. I told him that I didn't think you'd be able to do it, that it was the reason you didn't want to come hunting with us. He wanted you to come hunting with us, thinking it would have made a difference…*"

"*How?*"

"*I'm not sure how to say it. It's just different. We eat the deer.*"

"I didn't like burying it. Picking it up."

There'd been a point when he'd had the cat by its paws and was dragging it across the yard to the hedge, where he'd dug a hole for it, that he thought he was the cat.

"Yeah, that's the worst part."

Scott came over to him and grabbed him by the shoulder. He squeezed. Aaron's arm shifted.

"Is that what I think it is?"

"No."

"Yes, it is."

"I was just about to throw it away."

Scott laughed and shook his head. "In the drawer of lost loves. You half-ass. Jesus. What's this one say? Never mind, I don't want to know."

"Okay."

Aaron felt relieved that his brother hadn't heckled him that bad. Usually, it was much worse.

"I told Dad you weren't right. He thinks you're just a faggot."

Aaron felt tears welling in his eyes. He did his best to will them back. He reminded himself that there was nothing to cry about. Nothing.

"God, don't cry about it."

His brother left, and at first he didn't cry. He walked around the room, paced, and reminded himself that it wasn't a big deal because it was true. He was pathetic. He was not bold enough, he wasn't tough, and he was a half-ass. He cried. He even kicked and screamed into his pillow. He called himself half-ass. The cat's dead eyes watched him from someplace in his mind, and he realized that he'd done it. He slept.

*****

Leah woke from the dream with tears in her eyes. She knew it was all real, though she didn't know why or how she knew. She just knew. And she cried for him, cried even though he was the devil. She cried until the morning, and as the sun was rising, she'd poured the wrath from her heart.

CHAPTER 28

Adni

The sky was full of gray cotton ball clouds that were nearly white where they touched, and the wind was just enough to make everyone bring an umbrella, but it was not raining (but it had the look). By the black gates, the tombstones were as old as the town, as Deepmoor, and they rolled down a green hill until there was solid ground again, then a bar: Ernie's. Every sound was thundering inside the gates with the gravestones, and Leah, of all the people in attendance, felt that. She could hear the woman ordering from the drive-through daiquiri shop, *Louisiana Top Daiquiri,* and she could hear the music in the cars that went by, and she could hear the breathing from the man with the newsboy cap and sagging chin just three seats behind her, and she could hear the birds singing. And she and Brit were holding hands as Father Patrick finished, and Tom (of Tom & Mitch's) stood, and he slowly made his way to the casket—to her mom—that was sitting under the black pop-up tent. Tom looked to her and Brit with the singular expression of the properly mature, one that conveyed everything, and he placed an amaryllis down. Mitch did the same.

A crowd of people were waiting to pay their respects, all of them looking, when they expected to be seen or not to be seen, at Leah and Brit.

She noticed people from school coming, all in black, to look over her mother, see that she's dead. And Leah had gone so far over that she was under; she was too angry and bitter and desperate to be any of those things. She was catatonic, but she was only waiting for this to be done. But that wasn't entirely true.

Then she felt another hand grab hers, and there he was. Kris squeezed her hand and guided her down the row of chairs and toward the coffin, and Leah would be the same with him, but he didn't look at her the same way. His was the look that Tom gave. He looked down on her mom with a blank kind of determined expression, tensed, across his face, and when she finally had to look down at her mother, his grip was firm on her hand.

Her father was there, and through Brit, she was linked to him, and the only time that Kris left her side was when her father hugged her after the service.

"I love you," he said.

"I love you too."

And after the service was when Talley and Jason and Andrew and Bailey got a chance to be with her, and she hugged Bailey first, whispering in her ear that she's sorry, in unison with Bailey's apology. The clouds overhead began to break as they both laughed and wiped their tears away, and from behind, from that bar, Ernie's, a beer-mellowed voice called out, "They found them! They found them! Oh god—"

Kris and Leah are the only ones without a tinge of surprise on their face.

ABOUT THE AUTHOR

Joel T. Schmidt has worked on several novels since committing to the craft in 2016. His debut novel, *Sermon of the Divers*, in which he brings life experiences to a phantasmagoric reality that parallels our own, is nothing more or less than a promising beginning to a flourishing body of work. He works and lives in northern Louisiana.

Printed in the USA
CPSIA information can be obtained
at www.ICGtesting.com
LVHW040037080924
790207LV00002B/140